PRETTY LITTLE ISLAND

Rhea Ryan

To my mom who said to me, I don't think there is a single woman who doesn't dream about that.

****TRIGGER WARNINGS****

Gore
Violence
Mental Health
Open door sex scenes
Bullying
Death
Cliffhanger

PROLOGUE

"London. London. Over here?"

I step out of the limo and onto the red carpet, running my hands down my sheen gown as camera flashes momentarily blind me. I'm surrounded by people yelling my name, and I don't know where to look.

The diamond embellishment sparkles in the early evening California sun as a gust of wind tickles the open section of my backless Jovani dress. I chose the black one as it shows just enough cleavage and hugs my curves like a second skin. It's the piece he picked out for me because black is the only color I wore for months, and he gets sentimental.

He waits in the limo, wanting me to have my moment in the spotlight. While it is our story, this is my night, and he gets plenty of airtime.

Paparazzi are everywhere, and my heart races when I realize I have to answer questions on television. The world wanted to hear from me, but for four years, I remained silent and refused. It was easier to hide behind my husband and avoid the inevitable questions, assumptions, and judgment of what really happened, especially when everyone else already recounted their side of the story. I can't talk about it without reliving everything. Every nerve vibrates, every emotion stirs, every single layer of my veins seems to thin out. After we were discovered, I numbed the pain for months until I finally opened the thick bounds of my beat-up journal. Then the floodgates were open, and the words poured out of me—the therapy I needed to heal. I shared my truth with the world, but I needed to tell the story my way.

Am I actually ready for this?

A man steps in front of me, shoving the microphone in my face. "London, how does it feel to see your story play out on the big screen?"

A smile hints at my lips and a wave of relief hits me.

That is a simple question.

"It's surreal," I answer, looking right at the camera, keeping my head high and voice steady. "Lots happened out there. I lost everything, yet found my strength in ways I never thought possible. In the end, I found everything I needed, and I'm just happy to be alive."

"Do other survivors agree with how they are portrayed?"

Depends on what survivors he's referring to.

I shrug. "Ask them."

Everyone told their version of the truth. They planted our faces in Time Magazine and the front page of newspapers across the globe for months. My version is the one the world believed.

And justice is a cruel bitch.

"*Pretty Little Island* is up for best picture at the Oscars. Did you ever think that would happen when you wrote and published your book, especially since some survivors are now in prison?"

I take a deep breath and clench my fists, facing him. I will not put their words in my mouth; they cannot expect me to atone for what they did or even make sense of it.

"I wrote my story and the truth of what happened out there. The decisions of others is what got them convicted, and it had nothing to do with my book."

Done with his questions, I turn away from him.

A surge of cheers erupts from the crowd as powerful arms wrap around my waist. I soften against him and run my fingers behind me, grazing his torso till I find his hand and slide my fingers into his, not realizing how tense I am.

I turn my head and peer up at his chestnut eyes as he runs his hands down the waves of my dark hair that matches my dress. Everyone is now staring at him, calling out his name, but his eyes are only on me. He still makes my heart race, yet he is also the only person who can bring it down.

A young girl screams from the crowd, "Matei, I love you!"

My husband is loved by the world, but our world holds hockey superstars on a pedestal.

He turns and leads me down the carpet along the row of palm trees and a sea of cameras and people. Tomorrow, he leaves for a six-game road trip. But tonight? Tonight, he's all mine.

CHAPTER ONE

FOUR YEARS EARLIER

This summer is the warmest on record, yet the chilliest I can remember. The scorching heat is making my skin melt as I lie in my bikini, resting under an umbrella by the beach near my house. I've spent a month utterly alone in a town that is unwelcoming and icy to newcomers.

Although, I'm not exactly new.

For the past hour, I've stretched my legs out of the protective shade, tanning my legs and enjoying the last weekend before I start my new school. Every so often, I dart my eyes from my book to the ocean and cloudless sky, enjoying the views of this small, rich seaside town.

The beaches are nice here, and there are landscaped parks with grassy areas and huge elm trees that scream old money. Very different from where I grew up in Portland.

The view of the sun indicates late afternoon. My dad and his wife, Maggie, will worry if I'm gone too long—and have been worrying ever since I arrived in New Ocean three weeks earlier. It didn't take me long to find my place of solace at this beach, away from their judgment.

I'm the disgraced daughter.

I heard the whispers of my arrival. I felt the lingering looks at the coffee shop, the stares of recognition that I am Charles King's daughter. I rarely see anyone my age, few people pay attention to me, and certainly no one makes any effort to welcome me. I doubt my father told anyone the real reason I moved here, as to not besmirch the name he's trying to rebuild, which is fine. I'd rather be invisible, anyway. I'm hoping I will be a faded memory for those who used to know me.

I spent my first few days wandering the shops and stores on Main Street until I found a used bookstore and took up residence at the park near the ocean. Time is stagnant here—nothing's changed since I left, but not all the memories here were horrible. We lived a good life before my mom and I moved, and sometimes I wonder what my life would be like if I stayed.

Would I have been happier?

All summer, it's been quiet and heavenly, with just waves and seagulls brushing my ears. Since I arrived, I've read over thirty novels, which has helped ease my anxiety about starting a new school at eighteen. I'm worried about fitting in since groups will have already been established, and the town and school are pretty small. Reading helped me forget about my home for the last eight years and exist in the in-between before enduring another year of high school. This place is peaceful, but I know it won't last much longer with summer ending.

What's kept me at the beach longer than normal today is a group, of what I'm assuming will be my new peers, hanging out thirty feet away.

Six of them—four guys and two girls, from what I can tell.

I'm trying to focus on my book with my sunglasses hanging down the brim of my nose and avoid making eye contact with any of them. They weren't here during the summer, so I assume they were vacationing, which I used to do. In fact, the whole beach is full of people today.

One girl shrieks, and I can't help but stare at the group who set up close to me. They have the best spot on the beach, and everyone else seems to give them a wide birth. However, I full-on stare at them, then lower my book when an attractive blonde girl hangs off one guy as he sits alone with his back toward everyone else. The way she is positioned, pressing her chest into his back and kissing the nape of his neck, tells me she is claiming him. His body language seems rigid, and he doesn't seem to respond to her.

The alpha.

The girl gives up and lies on a towel with her friend, both wearing swimsuits and tanning in the sun. She spans her attention to the two other males—wrestling and rough-housing nearby—vying for attention and leering at them. It's like an episode of *Animal Kingdom*, and they are akin to monkeys in some sort of mating competition. If pressed, I bet they'd all turn on each other on a dime. They appear attractive from a distance, but I can't see the details of their faces. A bigger guy, the size of a football player, walks and sits next to the alpha. They face the ocean, just as I have all summer long.

I lean back and take a sip of my water, forgetting to hide the fact I'm leering at them, too. I see a lot of myself in the blonde girl, or at least, the girl I used to be before my life shattered and all my friends stopped talking to me.

The blonde girl whips her head toward me. I pull my sunglasses over my nose and sit upright, trying to calm my climbing heart rate. I'm not that girl anymore, and I don't want my first conversation with my new classmates to be with her. She's the big fish in a small pond—probably a barracuda.

It's too late; she saw me looking. She stands and wipes sand off her bottom before she walks over to me, jerking her head to the other girl to follow. She looms in front of me, and I lower my sunglasses and smile at her—a courtesy she doesn't provide me back.

She tilts her head and peers at me through her designer glasses. The other brunette positions herself behind her as they stand over me.

"Who are you?" the blonde asks with genuine curiosity etched in her voice. "And why are you staring at us?"

I'm glad the sun has already reddened my face as I feel the heat rush right to it. I swallow but keep my voice steady, despite my shaking hands. "I wasn't staring at you. I'm just sitting here reading."

Her mouth tightens. "Umm, yeah, you were. I saw you."

My breath deepens, but I hold it in and shrug, seeming as disinterested as possible. "I didn't realize you owned the view," I say curtly.

A laugh escapes her friend, and the blonde tenses. I have to be careful with my sharp tongue, even though I'm right. I'm trying not to be that girl anymore—the one who seeks attention. Her face flushes, suggesting she's not accustomed to being spoken to like this.

She snorts and looks back at her friend, who turns her laugh into a scowl. I wasn't meaning to stare; well, not openly, anyway.

I apologize and ignore her dark expression, keeping my sunglasses off so she can see the sincerity in my face. "I didn't mean to upset you. I'm new in town, and I've been coming here to read. It's just a nice view."

It's an apology without actually apologizing. I mean, she doesn't own the beach.

She grins and nudges her friend behind her. "Hear that, Serena? Apparently, she was admiring the view." She gestures toward the guys, who are all packing up and drying themselves off with towels. All muscles, height, and pure testosterone glistening in the sunshine. "It is a nice view, isn't it?"

Even though I'm far away and can't see them clearly, it's a nice view, indeed.

The pretty brunette stands forward, the nicer of the two. "Can you tell us who you are? We've never seen you here before. We're not trying to be mean."

Yeah, right, I've seen these intimidation tactics before. She is sniffing out my weaknesses, finding out what I'm made of. With a girl like Serena and her blonde leader, I'd stand up for myself, but with my confidence rocked, the words I try to muster up don't come. It's easier to stay quiet and hope they go away.

The blonde alpha female speaks next. Her voice is sweet, but everything about her has an edge. "So, umm, can you tell us your name? Or are you going to sit and stare at us all afternoon?"

My attention shifts to the one I was staring at as he rises and turns to face us, noticing this interaction. Noticing me.

She kicks at my feet. "Did you hear me?"

A ripple of annoyance courses through me as sand kicks up in my face. I don't want to dignify her with a response, and my jaw clenches. "My name is London," I tell her through gritted teeth as I breathe in a face full of sand.

I'm not used to being spoken to like this, either. I have no desire to play along with these girls right now. Last spring's drama brought me here, but now I want to stay low key. Maybe if I give her what she wants, she'll realize I'm not a threat and will leave me alone.

The blonde leader takes off her sunglasses, a glint flashing in her almond-colored eyes as I get a good look at her. She is quite attractive—long blonde hair she pulls back in a ponytail, athletic build, slim. Slimmer than I am, since my hips thickened a few years ago and my body rounded out, but I have bigger boobs, for sure.

"I knew it," she says. "You're London King, aren't you?"

Shit. Somehow, she recognizes me, even though I haven't lived in this area for eight years. We were like, ten when I left. How does she remember me?

My forehead wrinkles and my memory of her hits me like a needle piercing my skin.

She crosses her arms. "I'm Naomi Wilson. Don't pretend like you don't know who I am."

My stomach drops as my past creeps up to me, and an image of a girl with braces and pigtails comes to mind.

Naomi Wilson, of course. We went to school together for years, and I remember her always being a complete bitch.

"Yeah, I remember you," I mutter.

But it is the thought of her mother that has me wincing. Speaking of alphas, my father never got over his primitive urge to mate. Her mother was one of the many married women my father fucked in this town, and she is the reason both our parents split up. Naomi's mom was the final straw for my parents' marriage, and then we moved away from New Ocean shortly after. Mom and I had moved to Portland, never to look back, and my father had married his new wife. I had hoped time made people forget that scandal.

Naomi tilts her head and gives me a look of utter disgust. "Why are you back here?"

I open my mouth to speak, but my throat goes dry. This is the one question I should be prepared for, but I'm not.

"Naomi, Serena, let's go," one of the guys yells from where they are standing, watching us.

I raise my eyebrows as Naomi examines me, as if seeing me for the first time. An array of emotions are visible in her eyes. I'm a living, breathing reminder of when her life got torn apart, and I'm far from the gangly girl with braces who only ever had her nose stuck in a book. I still read just as much, but I look different. Her eyes linger on my cleavage, then down my legs as she takes me in one last time, probably realizing I look just as good in my swimsuit as she does. A gleam hits her brown eyes before she places her sunglasses back on and clicks her tongue. "This school year will be fun, London. I'm *so* happy you came back."

She saunters off and I breathe a sigh of relief once she's gone. Her friend Serena gives me one last confused look before she follows Naomi back to the guys, who have now packed up their beach stuff and are impatiently waiting by a tree.

I pull my sunglasses up and pour myself back into my book, but doubt fires at every nerve. She doesn't blame me for what happened back then, does she? I didn't spare Naomi a single thought when we left—and I hadn't thought about her since, having blocked that part of my life out. Should I have cared more about her?

I have no clue how many women my father slept with, but I do know he slept with half the town when I was younger. I didn't want details. The town of New Ocean is nothing but a collection of meaningless memories I tried my hardest to forget, my father's indiscretions being one of them.

I spent months as a pre-teen helping my mom through her tears and depression after news broke of his cheating ways. She got her shit together and sucked a few million out of him.

I blow out a breath. I made a mistake by coming back, but it's the only way I can finish high school. I have always dreamed of attending the top journalism school, and returning is my only option to make that happen. Online school won't cut it when co-curricular are equally important as academics.

A wind gusts over me as a cloud pulls in front of the sun. Dark storm clouds now loom, blowing in over the ocean. I sit up and pause as I notice one guy lingering, staring at me. I pull down my glasses and squint, trying to get a better view of him, but a beam of sunlight shines right through the clouds and onto my face.

He's the one Naomi was all over, and his body looks like it belongs to a bloody Greek god—so it must be him. Naturally, Naomi would be with the hottest guy in the group.

Every muscle is cut and shimmering, and he stands a good two feet taller than me. I'm tempted to get up and say hi, but he makes no motion that he wants me to. He just stands and stares, making me feel as if I should pull my towel around my body instead. After a few seconds, he turns and walks away from me, his entire tanned body leaving little to the imagination.

Today was supposed to be ordinary and dull, but instead, all my anxieties come rushing in. Tomorrow is the start of school, and I need to stay invisible. I have a nagging feeling I am far from done with dealing with Naomi Wilson.

New Ocean is not my home anymore, but now neither is Portland. I'm running from one life I want to forget and toward the other I already ran away from once.

CHAPTER TWO

"London King, please come to the office," a loud nasal voice calls out from the intercom. I slam my locker shut, aware of all the eyes burning into me and a blush creeps my face.

My plan for a low-key first day is already not working out the way I expected.

With my head down, I adjust my uniform—that I purposely ordered one size too big—and walk down the hallway through the sea of people. I knew I had an appointment with Mr. Grandle at 8:30 AM sharp, but I still have ten minutes, so the intercom announcement was entirely unnecessary.

I had a tour of the school a couple of days ago, where they gave me their welcome packet and access to my locker. The whole time I was equally mesmerized and annoyed by the lush leather seating, the marble flooring and gold-plated trophy cases, and all the other over-the-top amenities this school holds, while I've spent the last eight years in a concrete jungle in the inner city of Portland—just something else my father ripped away from me.

I'm not bitter, but I wonder how my life would be different if I never left.. My mom gave me a good life—the best life she could, given she had to start over in her early thirties. Not New Ocean Prep good, but better than most. It seems like I've gone full circle, as I ended up here, anyway. She pushed a lot of her childhood dreams onto me, ballet mainly. I loved all of it, until I didn't.

Until it hurt—until he hurt me.

Never again.

I returned because a man stole a piece of my youth. And I've returned to a place I vowed never to step foot in again. It seems like fate, almost.

More like desperation.

I'm nearly at the office when a hip juts into me, nearly toppling me over. A group of girls in blue outfits pass by, and Naomi and I exchange looks. She has a smirk on her face and her blonde ponytail swings as she struts away. The others in uniforms cover their mouths and chuckle, giving me a once over as they trail behind her.

I ignore the pain in my hip, not wanting to show them fear. These girls are wolves, and I am a lamb to the slaughter. I resist the urge to pounce on them because I know that won't solve anything. I'm more hot-tempered than a fighter, as my mom would say. Maybe I'm just as primal as they are. Slithering through them, I head straight to the large oak doors of the office. I try not to look back as they whisper and laugh.

Naomi obviously has a bone to pick. This is not normal new girl hazing; it's personal for her.

Not a good start.

I step inside, and a middle-aged woman with a tight bun and glasses hanging off her long skinny nose peers up from behind a desk.

"Can I help you?" she asks, pulling her glasses up and looks at me cross-eyed. I recognize the nasal voice; she obviously knows who I am.

My eyebrows arch. "I'm London King," I respond with an equal amount of enthusiasm.

She nods but focuses on her computer. "Of course. Have a seat, Miss King. The Dean will be with you shortly."

The Dean.

I can't help but smirk at how elitist that sounds, given we are still in high school. I throw my backpack onto a plush-looking leather couch and sit next to it, huffing out a breath. The secretary taps her pencil, and I focus on her heavy breathing as I tamper my nerves.

This place has me on edge.

The office is as elegant as the rest of the school, with rich mahogany wood panels, fake plants, and expensive decor with dim chandeliers.

After about five minutes of keeping me waiting past eight-thirty, the receptionist stands. "Mr. Grandle will see you now, London."

I rise and throw my backpack over my shoulder, then follow her through two more large oak doors and into Mr. Grandle's office. He's sitting behind his oversized desk and stands as I walk in, reaching out his hand. He's a middle-aged, gray-haired man who fits the bill of exactly who I would think would hold the title *Dean* in a conservative town like this. The office smells like old books mixed with his heavy musk scent.

"Miss. King, welcome to New Ocean Prep. We are happy to have you."

I'm sure he is. He knows how wealthy my dad is, and the tuition for this school isn't cheap. I sit across from him with a tentative smile and notice a flicker of recognition in his eyes. Likely at my stark similarities to my father, whom I know he knows well.

My father claimed he pulled a lot of strings to get me in last minute, and he doesn't hesitate to remind me of it. But it's not like he had to move mountains when I asked him if it was possible. My dad has a hefty bank account, and he golfs with Mr. Grandle at the country club. Each student brings in thousands of dollars in tuition revenue per month. I think he was surprised I asked him, and I actually agreed to step foot in this town again, or speak to him, for that matter. Barely anyone is speaking to me back home, so it was nice to have some company.

He looks me right in the eye. "I check in with students on their first day for a smooth transition. Many of our students have been together for most of their lives, so it may be harder for you to adapt here than what your used to."

I pull my hair behind my ear and shift in my seat while he peers down at a black folder in front of him. "I'm up for the challenge, Mr. Grandle." I'll be more than happy to pretend to care for ten months.

I have some catching up to do, anyway.

The journalism program I have my heart set on is hard to get into, and after my mishap last year, my grades fell behind. Especially since I only recently decided writing is what I wanted to do. I was convinced last spring that I would eventually join the New York Ballet, but that is out of the question.

He raises his eyes to meet mine. "It looks like you've practiced dance, but I don't see you signed up for any of the tryouts. May I ask why?"

"I'm not interested, sir."

He arches a brow. "That's unfortunate. We have an excellent dance and cheer program here, Miss King. I think with your experience, you'd fit in well with that group of young ladies. Would you like to reconsider?"

Dressing up and prancing around for others makes my toes curl. I'll do nothing that has me objectified. I refuse to put myself in that position again. If I am ever famous for anything, it won't be based on my looks.

I shake my head. "No, thank you."

He leans back in his chair and presses his lips together, watching me. I'm not sure what my father told him, so I say nothing. But the look in his eye is like the busy body ladies I saw staring at me on Main Street. He knows something, but I'm not budging.

"I see, Miss King. Our other programs are almost full, I'm afraid, and this school requires each student to have an extra curricular. If it's not dance or cheer, then what are you suggesting?"

I straighten my back. "I want to join the newspaper."

"The newspaper?"

Annoyance tugs at my gut and a flush hits my cheek. I'm unsure why he finds this so shocking—it's like this place breeds conformity. "You have one, don't you?" I ask.

He nods. "We do. A good one, too. But I'm confused how the newspaper fits into your academic plans. You have no history or experience writing that I can see, and your father told me you are a remarkable dancer. We were hoping to have you try out for the competitive team."

I blink a few times. "That's not what I want, and it's my choice, yes? I turned eighteen last spring, so I don't think my father has any say in it."

He lifts his chin. "It is your choice. The newspaper demands a lot of work. The group of students are very dedicated, with an overbearing and highly qualified new student editor. I'm sure Nigel will have no problems pointing it out to everyone if you can't perform."

I grind my teeth. "I understand, sir, but if there's an opening, I'd like to join the newspaper club."

He snaps the folder closed and feigns a smile. "Very well then, the newspaper it is. What role do you see yourself having?"

"I want to be a writer."

He gives me a knowing nod. "They meet in the afternoons, so you can join their meeting today." He snaps his fingers, apparently done checking in with me. His secretary appears moments later, followed by a stout, pretty-faced girl with mousy brown hair.

"London, this is Jade. I've asked her to help you for the first couple of days. She will show you around and make sure you feel comfortable here." He turns to Jade. "London has also decided to join the paper so you two will see a lot of each other."

She peers at me through her bright brown eyes and the edges of her lips tip upward. She tilts her head slightly as she takes in my rugged appearance, and her hair bounces at every subtle movement. Everything about her is shiny and round, and she exudes innocence.

Mr. Grandle rises and extends his hand out to me, which I shake about as confidently as Jade's smile. "Enjoy your time here, London. Try to have a good year."

New Ocean Prep is worse than I thought.

I've avoided this school for my entire life, and probably for the better. The kids here seem dull, if not typical, and completely conformed to their lives of privilege and prosperity. They don't actually know how the world works beyond their dark walls and shiny cars. They stroll through the hallway in their preppy uniforms on marble floors, staring at their trophies in gold-plated display cases, as if they need a reminder about how amazing they are.

The bell rings and Jade walks up beside me as I head out of math class—a class she is in, too. "London, wait up," she says excitedly and pulls her backpack over her shoulder.

At least Jade seems nice and somewhat normal.

I pause as a stream of people walk past me and let her catch up. She will walk me everywhere today—Mr. Grandle instructed her to—but I don't want to pressure her to hang out with me.

I cast my gaze downward. "It's okay, Jade. You've already brought me to all my classes this morning. If you have things to do, I understand. You don't have to stay with me all day."

She frowns. "No, no. Don't be silly. It's a good opportunity for you to meet everyone. We have our first meeting this afternoon, and we usually eat with each other at lunch. I can introduce you to Nigel. I bet he'll be excited to have you."

Jade visibly tenses as a few guys from our class strut by.

"Hey, new girl," one of them coos. "Wanna come to my car and eat lunch with me?" Jade blushes and I ignore them, just like I did during the entire class as they were whispering profanities in my ear during the lecture. I don't engage, but they keep leering as they walk by, like I'm a shiny toy they can't touch but really want to play with.

"You can come, too, Jade," the other one taunts, and they both chuckle.

"Sorry about them," Jade says, frowning. "They are part of the hockey team, and, unfortunately, all the athletes in this school act like that. The hockey team is the worst, though. They're so cocky and arrogant."

"I'll happily ignore them," I say, smiling. She shouldn't be the one to apologize for their shitty behavior. I resist the urge to turn around and punch them. From Jade's reaction, I can tell this is a normal occurrence for her, and I'm immediately protective of her.

She squishes her face. "Unfortunately, they are not even the worst of them. But we aren't all like that here, I promise. I'm sure everyone at the paper will want to meet you. We don't get new faces in our group... like ever."

I force a smile, sick at the thought of having to meet and talk to new people. "So, where do we eat lunch?"

Her body relaxes, and she faces me. "We usually eat in the lunchroom, but don't worry, we have our own table. People usually stick to their own groups."

My chest tightens thinking about walking into the wild and navigating the ever-shifting landscape of human adolescence. Somehow, I think animals would have better manners, especially since Naomi will be there, and I've avoided her since our unfortunate interaction this morning.

Walking past a large window, I dream of sitting under one of the oak trees that line the property on the south side of the lawn. The weather is still warm, and all I want to do is curl up and read my book for an hour like I've been doing all summer.

It looks like a nice spot to hide.

Instead, I tighten my ponytail and follow Jade's lead and head through two large doors that lead into a buzz of students already in the lunchroom. The cafeteria is huge, lined with tables and arched windows with a beautiful ocean view.

She must sense my tension because she turns and looks at me, softening her brown eyes. I'm about to find out where Jade sits on the hierarchy, and I'm sure it's not high.

She pushes through a group of people, and everyone focuses on me, ignoring her. Sometimes I wished I was still a wallflower. Jade is pretty, with smooth skin and dimples on her left cheek. Her hair is shiny and falls just below her shoulders, and she looks amazing. But she's thicker, and unfortunately, it seems people gloss over her.

I spent most of my adolescence like that.

A nerdy girl who liked ballet, but not geeky or hot enough to attract much attention. My breasts grew two full sizes last year, my hips plumped out, and my waist tightened. People took notice as I filled out my tights differently than they were used to.

He started watching me.

Even though my beautiful dancer's body changed drastically, I liked the attention.

Jade points to an empty table in the corner. "We usually sit there, and it looks like we are the first ones here."

I sit across from her and observe the room. Directly across from me are Naomi and Serena. Serena sees me and nudges Naomi, who whips her ponytail around and our eyes meet. She sneers at me before turning her back, icing me out.

I turn away to avoid further eye contact, and relief washes over me when she seems to be busy talking to her friends to pay me anymore attention. My stomach rumbles, and I grab a sandwich from my backpack. Jade keeps talking, and I give her short, one-word answers, trying to remind myself to be nice.

It's not her fault I'm in this mess.

My eyes drift to the puffy clouds in the distance, thinking about all my horrible decisions that led me here.

"Uh oh," Jade says, pulling me from my train of thought. "It looks like Naomi Wilson has noticed you."

Shit. Naomi is definitely staring again.

Jade frowns. "Try to avoid her, London. Naomi can be really mean sometimes. I find if you don't pay her any attention, she will usually get bored with picking on you."

It seems like she knows this from experience, but I feel like I'm just getting started with Naomi.

I fidget and readjust my uniform as both Serena and Naomi keep luring my attention through their mean girl antics and stares. I think of the two guys she was toying with at the beach, and I wonder which one she's with.

Jade furrows her eyes at me and ignores the malevolence shooting in our direction. "Why do you dress like that?"

My eyes whip toward her, and I can't help the twinge of a smile that hints my lips. "Dress like what? We're dressed the same."

Apparently, even when I try my best to fit in, I still stand out.

She inspects me—stares at me—as if wanting to ask me a million questions but doesn't dare to.

Why does everyone have to stare?

She inspects the buttons I have fastened to my chin. "You dress like... I don't know. Like you don't care or something."

I scoff and ignore the look of pity she's giving me. At least she's being real with me for the first time. I'm sure she's nice, but she must have questions, especially since I took all of two minutes to get ready this morning, and it must show. Plus, I showed up in this town out of nowhere.

A shadow catches my attention, and someone pauses in front of our table. He is wearing a bow tie and stands with a puffed-out chest.

Nigel, I'm assuming.

It's hard to place Nigel. He's not as unattractive as I thought he'd be, which makes me vain for even thinking it. He's shorter in stature, which explains why he's not athletic in comparison to the giants in this school. He's well-groomed, with blonde hair that stands on end like a brick from how much hair gel he has in it.

Jade blushes as soon as he arrives, her nervous energy radiating off her.

"London, is it?" he asks me, taking a seat on the other side of Jade, closer to the window.

He exudes confidence, and I know I have to do my best to impress this guy. He will make or break me here. If he doesn't give me a reference, there is no way in hell I'll be getting into journalism school.

Jade introduces me, and I shake his hand from across the table. Luckily, a few others joined, and the conversation shifts to the upcoming school year and newspaper plans.

I only half listen.

The chatter in the room grows quiet when two guys walk in. By their swagger, I can immediately tell they were the guys from the beach. Even though I only saw their silhouettes, there is no mistaking their toned physiques. I didn't see them in any of my classes this morning, and I try not to stare as they walk by, but the one in front is incredibly attractive. Probably the most attractive guy I've ever seen.

At least six-foot-two, strong and lean, with olive skin and dark hair styled just right, that the hair falls to the side and accentuates his high cheekbones.

My face heats as he walks by and his hard eyes connect with mine. His lips are pressed together in a scowl. He looks closer to twenty-five, just based on his height and muscle mass alone. Too old to be in high school.

My heart takes off beneath my chest, and I instantly want to pinch myself to snap out of it.

No guys, London.

That was a promise I made to myself before coming here. My lusting is what got me into this position in the first place.

His gaze is intense, so I dart my eyes away as a tightness fills my chest. He and his larger friend I saw on the beach head directly to the table where Naomi and Serena are sitting, of course.

The alpha.

His friend is even harder to forget, with his sheer size and muscle mass.

Jade leans over the table. "That's Micah."

She knows exactly which one I was looking at as I glance back at him as he sits across from Naomi and pulls out his laptop, ignoring everyone around him. His face is completely void of emotion, with not even a hint of a smile.

"And the bigger guy is Thomas," Jade continues. "They are part of the hockey team."

I gathered athletes just by the way they carried themselves.

Jade looks over at Nigel to make sure he isn't listening. He's busy talking to someone else and not even facing us. However, her deference to him doesn't go unnoticed, like she doesn't want Nigel to catch her looking, but I catch a lingering stare at Thomas.

I pull my attention away just as two more guys walk in the doors, catching my attention immediately.

I do a double take. One of them looks exactly like Micah. The hair, the eyes, the build—identical twins.

My heart pitter-patters.

God. There's two of them.

"And that..." Jade says in a slight whisper, "is Maison, Micah's twin brother."

Unlike Micah, Maison looks friendly, and just as sexy as his brother, with the same swagger. Behind him is another taller guy, with a slimmer build, narrow nose, and angular face. The second guy looks as impressed to be here as Micah does.

"That's Ezra behind him. They are both part of the hockey team, too," Jade tells me.

I glance at Ezra, who glares at me with beady eyes. He's attractive too, with a thin nose and blonde curly hockey hair that frames his narrow face. His skin looks like he had a generous summer, golden from the sun.

But I can't rip my eyes from Maison as he smiles at nearly everyone who looks at him. He looks nice, approachable. His eyes are like deep chocolate and glow, and his body is generously tanned.

Maison's eyes find mine and his smile shifts to a cute little grin when he catches me staring. He pauses and tilts his head and starts toward me.

"Oh my god," Jade stammers. "He's coming over here."

My breath shallows as he approaches.

Fuck, London. Get it together.

He stops right in front of us, and I can't help but notice the entire table shuts down their conversation to watch—though the opposite happens with Naomi's table, and it seems we've caught the alphas' attention. Nigel doesn't seem too happy at Jade's jaw nearly hitting the floor. Playing it cool, I avoid looking at him, even though my heart is hammering out of my chest.

I meet his eyes, and I'm drawn into them. The gold in his eyes is accentuated by his black uniform.

"Who are you?" he asks, his voice sexy, raspy, and deep.

"This is London King," Jade answers as her cheeks fire red.

My mouth falls open, knowing I probably look exactly like her. I wasn't expecting to react this way to anyone on my first day, and I seem to have lost my ability to speak.

"She's new here, and joining our newspaper," Jade continues.

He glances at Jade, but spans his attention back to me, trailing his eyes to my over-sized crumpled shirt and mascara-less eyes. I wish I put more effort into getting ready by the way he seems to scrutinize me.

It's probably confusing to him, given the girls he hangs out with and how they present themselves—both of which are staring at us like a hawk.

I get my wits back and press my lips together, staring at his deep brown eyes for longer than I should, then arch a brow at his awkward silence. If I'm icy, hopefully he will leave me alone. I have enough to worry about with Naomi glaring at me all the time, and I certainly don't need her to think I'm trying to grab the attention from one of her guys. Ezra hangs back and says nothing—just a stone-cold glare.

Maison merely smirks, and my eyes are drawn to his plump lips. He seems oblivious to the weird energy that surrounds us. "Nice to meet you... London King," he says, annunciating the *L* and the *K,* then walks toward his hockey group.

God, his voice...

My head moves with him as he effortlessly jumps over the table and sits next to his brother, but he keeps his eyes on me the entire time.

Micah looks up from his laptop and his expression hardens as he follows his brother's gaze toward me. Their simultaneous attention is the only vibration in the room. I feel their stare all over my skin as my stomach quivers from the unwanted attention, even if it's for a moment.

Their eyes are penetrating—full of an emotion I can't quite capture.

Jesus.

They start in on conversations among themselves, as if I'm quickly forgotten. Their focus moves to their friends and the two girls in front, and the moment passes as if it didn't happen at all.

Jade's watching me closely. "Stay away from them, London," she warns. "They're not worth it."

Agreed. That interaction was intense. But I wonder why she is telling me this.

Nigel pokes his nose over Jade. "Causing a buzz in the school already, I see."

Jade swipes his hand away. "Take it easy, Nigel."

I remember my sandwich and take a small bite, forcing myself to eat and hoping it will distract me. Jade and Nigel obviously know something they're not telling me.

I shake my head and a gleam hints in Nigel's eyes. "I doubt they have any interest in me."

"I'm not so sure about that," Jade scoffs. "This is the first time Maison Matei has stepped foot at this table or interacted with us. Although they've been gone a year, so maybe he's changed."

Nigel and Jade are both watching me now, and I bite the inside of my cheek.

Matei. Of course, I remember them. Their father was a rich investor of some sort and, if I recall correctly, is some billionaire. Their family was the richest in the whole area. They were always so mysterious. I only knew of them and never interacted with them, so I remember little about them, but damn, they aged well.

They were one grade ahead of me and should have graduated by now.

"Why are they here?" I ask.

I'd get it if one of them flunked, but both to be held back? Jade loses color in her cheeks, and it's Nigel who responds, staring at me straight in the eye. "Well," he says flippantly, "if you really want the gossip... they killed someone, London."

My jaw drops.

Jade elbows him. "Nigel, you don't know that."

He shoots a subtle look at the twins, with something dark behind his eyes. "I'm pretty certain of it, Jade."

"Oh, always the astute journalist, Nigel. Not everything is a story." Jade leans into me. "They were in a car accident, London. That's all."

My stomach twists. "Both of them? Were they together?"

Jade shakes her head and Nigel just rolls his eyes. "No one knows what happened for sure. Micah briefly went to jail because of it, but his dad got him out pretty quickly. The charges were dropped, but their parents sent them away to some rehab facility for the past year."

"And their daddy got them back in school," Nigel quips, sounding hostile, even though this has nothing to do with him.

Jade parts her lips and gives Nigel a side glance. "They came back this summer, and their dad got them back in this school so they can graduate and play hockey," she says. "They basically run the school. Micah is the hockey team captain, but both of them are good, so I'm not surprised they were allowed back. Even after what happened."

I swallow a pit in my throat. "Who did they supposedly kill?"

Nigel and Jade exchange another look.

"A girl from Douglas Cove," Jade says. "Her name was Olivia, I think."

"A girl no one here gave a shit about, apparently, if we can't even remember her name," Nigel adds, his voice laced with malice.

Not surprising. From what I recall, kids from Douglas Cove and New Ocean Prep were not friends, with little interaction other than a fierce competition over sports. Douglas Cove kids held up on the hockey rink from what I remember.

Jade pauses and takes a bite of her apple. "All we have are rumors, but I hear she was pretty messed up when it happened, like high on drugs or drunk. Micah shouldn't have been with her; she was Maison's girlfriend."

"And Maison wasn't even there," Nigel interrupts in a singsong voice.

Jade just shakes her head. "People saw Maison with her in town earlier, so we don't know why she was with

Micah instead of Maison. The accident was Micah's fault, though, and she flew right out of the windshield and died in his arms a few minutes later."

Nigel stiffens. "I doubt Olivia even cared which one she fucked that night. Rumor has it they shared her."

A prickle twinges the back of my neck as I turn to watch them. A tinge of pink hits Jades cheeks at the erotic turn of the conversation. Of course they shared girls. The poor girl was probably in love with them, and they just used her. I know the feeling; I fell blindly for someone once, too.

Jade runs her hand over my arm. "Just keep your distance, London, and you'll be fine. They had a reputation with girls before this happened."

I narrow my brows. "What was their reputation?" I shouldn't care so much, but this story is beyond fascinating. It makes my shit look like child's play.

She presses her lips together. "Maison is really nice, but I'm pretty sure he has slept with half the school at one point or another. It's how he is with girls, though, and they just seem to flock to him. Micah is flat-out scary. He's always had a bad temper, and he gets in lots of fights."

From the sounds of it, Mr. No Emotion is quite emotional after all.

I lift a brow as I watch Micah's arm slide around Naomi—the first sign of affection he's given her. "What's the story with him and Naomi?" I ask. "Are they together?"

Jade clamps her lips, showing there is a whole other juicy story to unpack there.

"Naomi's always had a crush on Micah. Until this summer, she had an on-and-off relationship with Ezra for years. Naomi dumped Ezra before the school year because Micah was returning."

"And they are cuddling right in front of him?" I ask.

Jesus, everything about this group of friends is toxic. No wonder Ezra hasn't smiled at all. He's almost as broody as Micah.

The bell rings, signaling the end of lunch. I grab my bag and follow Jade and Nigel out of the lunchroom. I need to take Jade's warnings seriously and remain focused. As I walk away, I resist the overwhelming urge to look back at the twins.

CHAPTER THREE

Jade warned me about Nigel and how he takes his job as being editor of the paper seriously on the walk over to the newsroom. Everyone is whispering about the twins' return to New Ocean Prep, and the rumors are swirling. Nigel is a journalist at heart, so, of course, he wants the real story behind what happened between the three of them. And secretly, so do I—although it makes my stomach twinge.

The idea of talking to Maison again bothers me. Flirting with me and then Serena, he clearly knows how to charm girls. I am feeling quite annoyed with myself for the way I reacted to him, acting like I was a star-struck fan girl. I acted the same way with Chris when he started paying attention to me last year, the same flutter in my stomach and everything.

Maison's relationship status and how he can be in the same room with Micah after what happened is a mystery to me. Something else is going on, and Nigel has good reason to suspect something a lot more sinister happened.

Nigel walks a few feet ahead of us and turns to look at Jade before we enter the classroom. Arching a brow, she gives him an encouraging nod. He only became editor this year, now that he is a senior, and I sense perhaps a bit of insecurity—although I suspect he's just as ostentatious as everyone else at this school.

They seem close, and I wonder if there is more happening between them. She gave him sidelong glances and centered the surrounding conversation around him when we weren't gossiping about the twins. She probably tries to make him shine every chance she gets, and he clearly takes her for granted.

I'll flatter him just the same if I need to, since he seems to react positively to praise. His eyes glaze toward mine, and he adjusts his bow tie as we walk toward the wide-eyed newspaper team.

The U-shaped table in the classroom is already full, mostly with people we sat with at lunch. Everyone still stares, though. I take a seat beside Jade, who sits directly next to Nigel.

Unlike the rest of the bright school, this room is windowless and dark.

Their chatter continues, and no one pays him much notice as Nigel stands at the front and opens his computer. A big screen with a calendar is displayed behind him. Jade pulls out her notebook and a pencil and taps at it, staring down at a blank page, looking bright-eyed and hopeful.

For the first time since arriving, butterflies fill my stomach, enjoying the buzz of energy around me. Being a part of something bigger than myself is exciting, a dream I've suppressed. This newspaper is the silver lining of a very dark storm. Writing excites me more than dancing ever did over the last four years.

No one pays Nigel much notice as he tries to look all big and important. The table fills quickly, and Nigel clears his throat.

"Everyone, it's time to start," he says, rapping his knuckles on the table before him.

They ignore him.

He coughs, straightens his bow tie, and rubs the sweat off his neck as if his nerves are getting the better of him, despite his false, confident exterior. "Enough," he yells out loud enough that I bet neighboring classes can hear.

He swallows hard and regains his composure, grazing over the group and over to me like he's trying to prove something.

"We need to get started. We have a lot of planning and events to cover this year. Our first issue comes out in one month, people, so this isn't social hour."

The long-haired guy across from me speaks. "Hey Nigel, relax, man. We're all just catching up."

Nigel slams his pencil on the table harder than necessary. He's uptight, for sure, an edge hidden below the surface marring his polished aesthetic.

"I'm in charge this year," he spits. "And I'm sick of the lazy work this paper produces. I want exceptional stories on my watch, not mediocrity, so leave now if you're not here to do your best. Do you all hear me?"

Silence.

"Good."

He picks up his pencil and shoots me a look, and to my relief, his face softens. "We have a new member of our club. Everyone who hasn't met her yet, this is London."

He glances down at a sheet of paper, at what I am assuming is my student profile.

"London, what's your experience in journalism? It looks to me like you belong in a gym prancing around in spandex, not here doing real work."

I bite my lip and try to suppress the blushing in my face as the room gives out a collective chuckle and stares at me. He had all lunch hour to ask me this, yet he chooses now? Jade softly nudges me.

"I'm new, yes, but I bet I can write as well as anyone else here."

I'm not exactly sure if that's true, but I will pretend. I'll die pretending until I get what I want.

Nigel folds his arms. "Well, you need to catch up. I don't have time to teach you anything."

He gets a thick textbook from his desk, brings it to me, and drops it onto the table. I look down and see it's titled *The Art of Journalism* before he snarks, "Read this on your own. I expect a comprehensive paper summarizing your learnings in two weeks."

Christ. There goes my evenings.

I'm already sick of the hot and cold games, and the power moves by Nigel. Jade trusts him blindly, but something seems off about him. He fits right in with everyone else here, I suppose. It must be the conditioning of New

Ocean. Excessive fulfillment leads to hostility, and Nigel appears on the verge of attacking someone.

He doesn't give me a chance to respond as he strides to his spot in the front. "Okay, then. First order of business. The hockey tournament in Alaska is in less than a month. Who wants to cover it?"

The whole table shoots up their hands. He scans the room as if considering every single person before his eyes land on me. "London, are you up for the task?"

My eyebrows shoot up as everyone turns to look at me again, the heat I can't control rising to the surface of my skin. "You want me to write the story?"

He nods. "That's why you're here, isn't it?"

"Yes, but..."

"Yes, but... what?" He tilts his head, mocking me.

I shift in my seat, crossing my legs. *Is he messing with me?*

A blonde girl with glasses sitting to the left of me speaks up. "That's not fair, Nigel. She doesn't even know what the hell she's doing. You can't give her Alaska."

I will not let her tell me what I can do. This girl doesn't even know me, no one here does.

He snaps his eyes to her, a drop of sweat clinging to his forehead. "I can do whatever I want, Elle. And the story you submitted last year was utter crap. So regardless, you're not getting the assignment."

"Give her a chance," Jade speaks up. "We all have to start somewhere, and this is an exciting tournament."

I bite the inside of my cheek. "I'm up for it, I promise."

A smile forms on Nigel's thin lips. "Good. Well, it's settled then, but please, still submit your paper by the end of the week, and bring warm clothes, as it gets chilly in Alaska." His eyes zip to Jade, and the smile on his face doesn't quite reach his eyes. "You can come to shoot the photos, of course."

Jade nods and I look over at her, and she gives me an encouraging smile while beaming at his compliment. She told me she's one of the few photographers in this group, and I'm thrilled she's coming.

"And I might tag along, too," Nigel adds.

A knot fills my stomach. I don't know Nigel's intentions, but I'll find out while we travel, I guess. It also hits me it's the hockey tournament I'm covering, which means the twins will be there. And if they are as good as Jade says they are, I'll bet they will be the primary focus for my story.

"Alright, onto new business," Nigel says, drifting his attention to the calendar. We then spend the next hour planning, scheduling, and plotting for the first issue. The bell rings and I gather my book, hooking my backpack over my shoulder.

Nigel stands behind me just as I'm trying to leave. A bit too close.

"London, one moment, please. If you don't mind."

I flinch but put on a fake smile and sink back into my chair. He sits next to me and I face him, expecting to see his condescending smirk and him telling me how much of an honor it is to be the chosen one for Alaska.

"I'll meet you outside," Jade says, passing a look to Nigel, as if she knows exactly what he wants to talk to me about.

I shift my gaze to him, surprised to see the malice from earlier is gone. His mouth is tight, and for the first time, I notice circles under his eyes, like the past hour exhausted him.

I narrow my brows. "What is it?"

"I'll get straight to the point." He sighs. "I think you have a lot of potential, London. You seem smart, and this tournament will help build your portfolio for college. I don't care why you are here, although I'm sure you have a reason, but I'm bored with the same old stories we write every year. Take this trip as an opportunity to learn about sports journalism, but also how to dig deeper."

I press my lips together, taken aback by the surprise compliment and the simultaneous insult. "Thank you, Nigel. I really appreciate it. I'm up for it, I promise."

To me, this seems beyond the hockey tournament, and it makes me wonder what he knows about me. But nothing was posted online about what happened—the police made sure of that when they filed the investigation to protect me. Despite my willingness, I was considered a vulnerable youth because of my age and his role as my teacher. Even so, there might have been something. All it would take is one post.

He raps his knuckles against the table and sighs. "I assume you know what I'm talking about?"

The hair on the back of my neck stands on end.

"The twins," he says, and I blow out a breath. He doesn't know why I ended up in New Ocean. He's just smart enough to realize something must have happened.

"I'm sure you are aware there are many types of journalists. And on the surface, you can learn to cover a great feature about a national high school tournament for elite teams and athletes. And don't get me wrong, I still want you to write that story."

I sit back and wait for the other shoe to drop. I know why he chose me over more seasoned journalist.

I shake my head. "I'm not a spy, Nigel."

His voice is calm, calculated. "These stories are rare. Maison and Olivia were the golden couple of New Ocean, but she ended up dead in the arms of the other brother. Now both twins act like nothing happened and continue with their lives as if it's all completely normal."

A shiver runs down my spine. I think of Chris and the fact that he is still teaching somewhere, even though he pursued one of his students. He ruined my life, and he got to move on with zero consequences. The authorities considered it a gray area, because I was so close to being eighteen, which is why he got off without any charges.

This is the same type of scenario.

Privileged guys taking what pleases them, treating women like cattle. She was a girl, probably my age, with hopes and dreams. I was awarded a second chance to start over, and Micah took that from Olivia.

A dark gleam hits Nigel's eye. "We can expose a much deeper subject and write a story that addresses the judicial system's lack of accountability for the wealthy. Micah should not walk among us right now. What Jade neglected to tell you earlier, because she doesn't know, is that girl had lethal amounts of GHB in her system when she died. That was the real cause of her death, not a car accident, as everyone says. He killed her. He should be in prison, not the main focal point of a sports tournament."

I can't say I disagree, but how does he know this?

He squints as if he knows exactly what I'm thinking. "They changed the story. Their lawyers fabricated the truth that went out to the public. I guess that's what you can do when your father is a billionaire—control the media."

I frown, having to think for a second. "You mean…? You're saying she died of a drug overdose from a date rape drug?"

He leans his arms forward. "That's exactly what I'm saying. They drugged her, or one of them did, at least. Then they crashed the car to make it look like an accident. But that's not even the worst part of it."

I swallow hard and look at him, hoping he continues. He has my full attention now as he pulls out his phone and brings up pictures of her. Pictures of the crash scene, specifically of her dead body, before she was pulled away. I hitch a breath when I see how gorgeous she is, even in death. Her face is angelic, almost perfect. She had a heart-shaped face, blonde tresses down to her mid-back, eyelashes for days, even as her cold, blue-eyed stare bores into me. They hadn't even shut her eyelids yet in this photo, that's how freshly dead she was. My blood runs cold seeing this. Not at all what I was expecting on my first day at New Ocean Prep.

Nigel seems bored with my reaction, as if he's already spent so much time staring at this photo, he's unaffected by the atrocity of it. "When I did some digging," he says, ignoring my startled reaction, "I found pictures of her online. Those bruises on her neck and shoulder are old, you can tell by the color. One of them did that to her… I just know it."

Jesus.

I go completely still and my pulse ticks faster. I don't think I want to know how Nigel got access to this photo. I'm thinking his skills run deeper than being a mere high school journalist. He would have had to hack into something to access these.

"What makes you think they will let me in? They don't seem like the most accepting group." I don't miss the shift in his face as he scrutinizes my chest and my general ruffled appearance.

He pauses and blinks. "Try undoing your top button to start."

The weight of what he said hits me. How to gain their attention and trust is resting in the amount of cleavage that's hidden behind my XL shirt, and I feel that weight in the pit of my stomach. Do I want these guys to notice me?

Nigel sits back and watches me, giving me a moment with my inner turmoil.

"No one said this will be easy," he says after a few seconds and I've still yet to say anything, "but a story like this can put you on the map and get you into any school you want. This is bigger than anything I've ever seen or come across, and I don't think anyone else at this school can handle a story like this."

He eyes me curiously, and I'm not sure what sort of first impression I gave him to make him think that I can. "You won't be alone. I'll be here to help and guide you, but it will be up to you to do whatever it takes to get them to trust you."

I swallow and nod, suppressing the dread in my stomach. "Okay," I tell him, "I'll deliver you the story." I'll do it for a girl I'll never meet, but who symbolizes every young woman who didn't matter. I joined the paper for this reason, and Nigel is giving it to me on a silver platter. Maison will be my starting point. He seems the easier of the two, and given he's already flirted with me, hopefully, it won't be too hard to get him to open up.

Nigel stands and heads to his desk. He grabs a leather-bound book and hands it to me. "I don't know if you journal or not, but you should. Every good journalist should write daily. Start by observing them and jotting down everything you see, even if you think it's trivial. Watch and learn each of them, study them."

I grab the soft book from his hands and press it against my chest. Butterflies hit my stomach, those same butterflies I felt earlier when I looked in Maison's eyes. I don't want to relive what happened last year, but if my future and happiness rests on taking down two egotistical, spoiled rich kids who hurt and utterly destroyed a girl, then so be it.

CHAPTER FOUR

Ten Days till Alaska

Nigel knew from the second he saw my reaction to Maison that investigative journalism was what would draw me. To uncover the story that everyone in this town is ignoring. I don't know if I'm cut out for it, but while I'm searching for something nasty and dark, I'm hoping I'll find something bright and beautiful. At least when it's done, I can leave and never look back. These people are irrelevant to me. I have to remind myself of that.

I have had no contact with the twins since my interaction with Maison in the lunchroom on my first day. All week, at lunch, it was like I didn't exist. I avoided staring at them, and I don't know how to enter their world, especially with Naomi always present. She won't let me near them. Micah rarely speaks, and when he does, it's usually only to Thomas. Sometimes Naomi sits on his lap and his hands go right to her hips, but his eyes are distant, as if he doesn't see her. When he's not around, she's next to Ezra, which makes sense given what Jade told me. Maison is carefree and smiles constantly. His smile is nice, and he's flirty, especially with Serena. But I don't think Serena is too special, considering I've seen him hit on other cheerleaders, too—but she obviously likes him. The twins hardly interact, despite being together all the time. Maybe everything's not as good as it seems between them. Alaska is in ten days. I have to be ready.

I flick the sweat off my brow and lean over to untie my sneakers. My body is drenched from my run out on the track. My face is beet-red, and my skin is like an oven, but I eye the showers and how amazing one would feel right now as the steam drifts into the rest of the large locker room with its lemon scent.

I wait my turn, sitting on a leather chair in front of a gas fireplace, popping out my earbuds when the last of the girls exit the shower area wrapped in white spa towels. No one tries to talk to me, so when they all trickle out, taking their laughter with them, my chest lightens.

I slip off my shorts and tank top, then shove them into my bag and place them in my locker. I reach for a towel to cover myself, hiding from the few lingering girls in the locker room as I head to the showers. I fully intend on utilizing this luxury as often as I can.

Stepping in, I close the opaque glass door and turn the dial on hot. The steam hits my throat and I stand for a few seconds, letting the water flow over me. I run my hands through my dark hair that falls over my shoulders. My fingers trace down my collarbone, and I let them rest on the swells of my breasts, remembering how Chris's hand used to touch me there. Except for the beach, before anyone was back in town, I've hidden them since it came out that we were sleeping together. Which is odd, because my body was the focal point of my identity.

Chris was the first and only guy I've slept with, and I can't imagine getting to a place to do it again with anyone else. I haven't properly healed yet. If Nigel's idea was for me to sleep with either twin to get information for this story, then that is a full-stop for me.

The thought makes my breath grow heavy and a pulse of pleasure shoots between my legs, causing my hands to draw back. I shift those thoughts out of my head.

I move my hand down my stomach, then toward my thigh, which has grown weaker in the months since I've quit dance. Running today felt good; it gave me a burst of energy and dopamine my brain needed after weeks of feeling sorry for myself. I keep moving down between my legs to relieve that little pressure that's built up there, letting out a soft moan as I do so, feeling the curves of my body I was once so proud of.

My eyes grow heavy, and I sit on the bench in the shower, turning off the water and just let the steam engulf me. My hands move back between my legs and, for a few minutes, I work myself until I give myself full relief, trying not to picture certain athletes while I do it. It's quiet. A few minutes have passed since an echo of voices bounced through the locker rooms, so I'm completely alone and in no rush to leave in my post-orgasm haze. My dad and Maggie are out for dinner tonight, and I only have reading to do, and I'm feeling pretty confident in my facade "story" and features I have planned when covering the tournament. Two of which rely heavily on interviewing certain individuals, and I plan to make the most of those interviews when the time comes.

I finally get hot enough and turn off the steam, taking one more cleansing breath. Just as I walk out, the lights in the locker room shut off. My body freezes as I look around, letting my eyes adjust to the darkness. There is no one in here. The lights must be set on a timer, and all I can hear is the hissing of the steam from my shower.

I feel my way back to my locker, fully intending to grab my phone to use it as a flashlight. When I arrive there, I reach for my bag, only to find it… *empty.*

My heart quickens as I do a double-take to make sure I found my locker and not someone else's. It's mine, and someone stole my fucking clothes. My heart beats even harder as I wrap the towel tightly around myself and make my way to the exit. I peer out into the hallway, which is empty, and only amplified by the arched hollow ceilings in all the main areas of this school.

The towels small, but it's big enough to sneak to my car in. Who ever did this to me was gracious to leave my phone and keys, so I know this is some sort of prank.

I weigh my options, and the prospect of humiliation outweighs the thought of waiting in this locker room like a little lamb. These kids can't, and shouldn't, scare me, but being caught like this in my most primal state is utterly horrifying. Like, whoever did this to me knows my deepest, darkest secrets and is trying to expose me, just as I plan to do to the twins.

Grabbing my bag, I slide out the door, half expecting someone to jump out at me and laugh. Instead, the hallway remains silent and empty as my bare feet echo against the walls. I decide to go full tilt and get out quickly. When I turn the corner, I barely have time to stop as I almost run directly into Maison coming out of the boys' locker room. His hair is wet and ruffled, and he's dressed in a pair of loose sweats and a T-shirt, holding a duffel bag.

I know it's Maison—I can tell by his smile, which quickly fades when he takes in the situation in front of him. He takes a step back and arches his brows.

I freeze and press my hand over my mouth, completely exposed. My worst nightmare is playing out in real time. A thickness hits my throat as his eyes wander to my bare legs, my dark wet hair, and sparsely covered breasts.

He lets out a little chuckle and tilts his head. "Hey there."

I drop my backpack and pull the towel up, then shift it back into position.

I keep my head down but can't help watching him as he takes me in. "Please don't look at me."

This is beyond humiliating. I wanted his attention, but on my terms, and definitely not like this, and especially after I just touched myself thinking about him. The heat in my face is not entirely from the steam.

His eyes flash with amusement. "So that's what you've been hiding under all those baggy clothes," he jokes. "*Impressive.*"

My fists clench. "Turn your head now."

His grin returns as he covers his eyes with his hand. "Okay, calm down. I won't look."

I take a few steps back, trying to decide if I should run to my car or to the locker room. My panting is already out of control, my chest rising and falling through the slit of the towel covering it.

"Can I at least help you?" he offers. "I have some extra clothes in my bag I keep for situations exactly like this. It will get you home at least."

My eyebrows shoot up even though he can't see me. "Situations like this?"

"You know, helping damsels in distress who wander the halls of school alone, afraid and completely naked?"

I roll my eyes. "I'm not a damsel, and I'm certainly not in distress."

He shifts. "Okay, but you're still naked."

I press my lips together. He has a point. I pause for a moment, watching him to make sure he doesn't turn around, not that I could stop him if he did.

My voice comes out like that of a mouse. "Okay, I'll take your clothes."

He pulls down his hand and his eyes meet mine before briefly flicking down my body. *He couldn't help one more peek, could he?*

The muscles in his arms and back flex as he bends over, and I fight a new little pulse I can't seem to get rid of, while also fighting the urge to run away. I really don't like the physical reactions he gives me, and that's only in the two brief interactions I've had with him. No wonder girls swoon.

He turns toward me and hands me a large black sweater before turning around again. It has the number nine on it, with Matei written in gold letters.

His hockey sweater. This sweater must be meaningful to him.

I quickly slip into it and revel in his scent, a touch of cinnamon or cologne. The sweater is oversized and feels nice. It's big enough to cover me, stopping just at the top of my knees, much better than the spa towel.

"You can look now," I tell him once I take a couple of breaths to control my raging heartbeat.

When he turns around, his cocky grin fades and his eyes move to his sweater, then my legs, and back up to my face. His pupils flair as he opens his lips to say something, but is interrupted when the locker room door swings open and Thomas, Ezra, and the two other hockey players that ridiculed me in math class come rushing out. Nigel made me study their profiles, so I had to learn these idiot's names, but from now on, I'll just refer to them as two and four.

They all freeze when they see me, then immediately burst into laughter while Maison leans against the wall with a smirk on his face, and the color drains from mine.

Thomas even cracks a smile, which is surprising since he usually shows less emotion than Micah. Thomas is even bigger and scarier up close. He's at least a couple of inches taller than Micah, with more muscle mass than I've ever seen on a kid his age. I didn't even think high school students came this massive, and he clearly keeps himself in excellent shape—although they all do.

"Right on, buddy." Ezra laughs and swings Maison a high five. "Already nailed the new girl, I see."

Maison laughs and looks me up and down. "We were just getting acquainted."

Number four steps forward, undressing me with his eyes. "When will it be my turn to get *acquainted*?" he coos.

The blood drains from my face as Micah comes out and darts his gaze around the group of hockey players who have now circled me, laughing.

He stands next to his brother and crosses his arms across his chest, but he says nothing. He looks irritated, almost bored by the whole situation.

Micah's wearing the same sweater as I am—the only difference being the number ten. Apparently, it's the number I'll be watching the most in Alaska with how good he is. His face is expressionless as he looks me up and down.

This couldn't get any worse. And Maison does nothing to stop it or defend me.

I squeeze my eyes shut, grab my bag, and I turn and run. *Fuck these guys.*

I dart into the empty parking lot just as the evening sun settles behind a cloud. I pull open my car door as footsteps shuffle behind me.

"London, wait," Maison calls out, jogging toward me.

I bristle as I throw my backpack in and slam the door shut, heading toward the driver's side. He's already two feet away from me by the time I turn to face him. "What do you want, Maison? Can you just let me leave?"

He holds his hands up. "I want to apologize for that. They're idiots sometimes."

My eyebrows arch. "Sometimes?"

He chuckles. "A lot of the time, but they were just kidding."

I cross my arms. "I'm sure. Is this what you guys do for fun? You steal girls' clothes so you can *save* them, then torment and make fun of them?"

His eyes sparkle and a tug plays on his lips. "We don't usually have to trick girls into getting naked; they do that all on their own."

Or you just drug them...

My jaw sets, and I cast him a glare. I see through his smile and the manipulation that drips from it. Everything that happened to Olivia—whatever that really was—was her fault in their eyes, I bet. Maison uses his smile as a weapon, and Micah... well, I'm not sure what he's doing. These girls fall at their feet—idolize them because of their stature in the sports community and pretty faces. Well, I won't drool just because he casts a smile at me. I was stupid enough to do that once.

"Why don't you go talk to those girls then and forget all about me? I'm sure there are lots of them here."

He slides his hands into his pockets and arches a brow, akin to a puppy. "It wasn't us, London. I promise."

I narrow my brows. "What? It had to have been you; no one else is here."

"This has Naomi written all over it. She did the same prank to some poor girl last year, too. She likes to initiate people."

I blow out a breath. *Naomi.* It makes sense. I was wondering when she was going to pop up again.

"You just caught us off guard," he continues, looking genuinely sorry. "You caught *me* off guard."

Adorable—he looks adorable now as his eyes flash and he purses his lips together. My stiff body loosens, and while I believe him, I also hate how soft I'm already feeling. But still—

"It might have been Naomi who pulled the prank, but you were all laughing." I keep my voice steady. "Getting acquainted? Really?"

He pauses. Those chestnut eyes drift back to my torso, to his sweater and my bare legs peeking out from under it. The same look he gave me before we were interrupted. How many girls has he given that look to?

"Well, weren't we?" he asks, his face now serious. "Getting acquainted? I was just about to tell you how nice you look in my sweater before those idiots came out."

I drop my chin to my chest to hide the blush creeping toward my cheeks. We stand for a couple of seconds, letting the silence linger between us.

He grabs my hands and my body jolts. "So will you forgive me?" he asks. "I'll do anything."

An idea forms in my mind. "Well... there is something."

His eyes light up and he doesn't let go of my hands. "What? Tell me. I'm dying to know what I can do to make you smile."

I press my lips together. I can't let this opportunity slide past me now that I have his attention. "Let me interview you for the story I'm doing on the Alaska trip. Right before the game would be best, I want to get a sense of your head space before you play."

His lips cast upward. "You're coming on the Alaska trip?"

"Yes. Does that surprise you?"

His hands are so soft, and mine are sweaty as he maintains his hold on them. He should have let go by now; instead, he circles his thumb in the soft spot between my thumb and index finger.

"In a good way, yes," he says. "A bunch of nerds usually cover that trip."

I frown and pull my hands away, lest should he capture my heart with his strong fingers. "I am a nerd."

He snickers. "Sure, if that's what you think. Just so you know, I rarely do interviews."

"I only need ten minutes of your time, then we can forget about all this."

He pauses to consider, and I think about all the reporters who must have hovered around the twins when Maison's girlfriend died. "Okay, I'll do it, just for you."

I tilt my head. "What about Micah? Do you think he would agree?"

He shakes his head. "Micah doesn't do interviews. He will never agree, not in a million years."

Of course he doesn't.

"Okay, just you, then." I swallow and dare a glance up at him through my lashes.

He's all flirty smiles. "Just me and you, London King. I guess I'll be seeing you soon."

Ignoring the swirl in my stomach from the way he says my name, I motion toward my car and get in. "Thanks for the sweater. I'll get it back to you tomorrow."

His eyes gleam as he steps toward the door. "Nah, you keep it. It looks much better on you, anyway."

The twist in my stomach is too much. "It's your hockey sweater, Maison; of course I'm going to give it back to you."

"This way you won't forget about me." The way he chews on his bottom lip causes my fingernails to dig into my palms. His eyes linger on the sweater that's ridden up, barely covering my lady parts. I'm not sure if he's clued in that I'm not wearing any underwear.

I close the door and slide the keys into the ignition. He moves out of the way as I pull out of the space, leaving him in my dust.

Forget about him? I don't think that's possible. Somehow, in the short time I've been at this school, these twins have become the centre of my world.

A pit roils in my tummy as I see his tall silhouette still staring at my rearview as I drive down the tree-lined road toward my dad's house.

Nothing about this feels good—deep down, spying on Maison is wrong. Perhaps I should let sleeping giants lie and not do this. I can still write a good story about the tournament and the athletes and stick to the assignment.

But the thrill of it all keeps me wanting more—the swirl in my stomach is more than just my obvious physical attraction to him. It's about finding out the truth, which is the reason I wanted to be a journalist to begin with.

At least now I can report to Nigel that I've made progress with the twins. Plus, that interaction was interesting. Maison does not seem like someone who went through a tragedy a year and a half ago. He's either projecting his emotions or hiding his true torment.

Either way, I cannot let him touch me like that again. I have to be stronger than I used to be. I won't sleep with him just to find out information, even if he tries. Because if I do that, then it will make me more of a villain than they are.

CHAPTER FIVE

FOUR DAYS TILL ALASKA

I covered my first hockey game last night. Nigel still expects full coverage of the tournament from a sports aspect, so I've been studying how to craft player profiles, how to write a high-profile event, and elements I want to include in my feature story—an ideal disguise for my real motives. With how exceptional this team is, Micah can't hide from me for long. Nigel's been researching public and private information on the case. All we know is that Micah spent three days in the state jail, and his dad must have pulled some serious strings because the charges were quickly dropped. Especially since the coroner's report showed Micah's DNA fresh inside her, along with the dangerous levels of date rape drugs. He was eighteen, so he would have been charged as an adult. He was stone-cold sober when it happened, but it was reported he was driving erratically. None of these shines on him in the best light.

The exhibition game against Douglas Cove was a brutal bloodbath. Blood literally stained the ice from the hits and fights. Olivia was from there, and that team wanted Micah's head. Students had signs saying 'Murderer' before the referee told them to take it down. Despite this, New Ocean still rallied around Micah. Maison was always there protecting him, like it was just the two of them. Thomas also protected him fiercely; at one point, he took a couple of guys who had pinned Micah in the corner and shoved his skates on their neck. The wild card for me is Ezra. I know little *about him, but given his complicated history with Naomi, I wonder how much love is there? If Micah wasn't around, he'd be the best player. By coming back here, Micah stole many aspects of his life—namely, his position on the team and his girlfriend.*

It's Friday afternoon, the last period before we leave for Alaska on Monday. English—the only class I have with both twins.

I'm the first to walk in. I just had study hall, so I came early. I sit by the window in the back, put down my notebook, and exhale. One more day till I can say I've survived my first couple of weeks at New Ocean Prep. The door creaks open as the athletic build of a twin walks in, and our eyes meet.

His pupils flash, but his face is neutral, and I give him a hesitant smile that's not reciprocated. Instead, he hesitates and sits with his back to me, ignoring me like I'm vermin.

Micah, then.

I'm not as good at telling them apart as I thought. Maison's smile, Micah's scowl, that's easy, but when their face is resting, it's impossible. They wear their hair the same, as if purposely trying to fuck with everyone.

He sits and squares his shoulders while I glance at my notebook and pretend his icy demeanor didn't sting just a little. I only smiled at him—would it be so hard to smile back?

A few others trickle in, including Nigel, who notices me and rushes over. The three of us have been tight since I've started with the paper, and especially since I've offered to help Nigel with his story.

I have Nigel figured out—he likes to control what tiny influence he has in this school. If he perceives you as a threat, he will try to take you down. He's smart, and I can see why he made editor, and I'm relieved I found people I connect with in my short time here. Jade, however, is not in on our little secret. Nigel made me promise not to tell her about the exposé we want to write.

"I learned something new about the twins," Nigel whispers as he joins me. He still wears his bow tie every day, so he adjusts it, pulls out his notebook, and leans closer. "Well, more about their father, but it's interesting."

Nigel's been digging into what he can about them and their family, but I know he is counting on me to make progress with them next week.

Jade strolls in with her bouncing brown curls and sits next to Nigel, flashing me a smile as Nigel goes cold on her. She narrows her eyes in confusion.

"We'll chat later," Nigel murmurs. "Meet me after class."

Jade's eyes brighten. "Why, what's going on?"

"Nothing, Jade," Nigel quips. "Not everything has to do with you."

I wince at the harshness of his words and their obvious effect on her as she shrinks down in her seat—not unlike how I just reacted to Micah. Spending time with them, I am convinced Jade is in love with him. She hangs on his every word.

I'm completely distracted as Maison finally walks in, holding hands with... Naomi. In fact, it gives me pause because I could have sworn it was Micah who walked in earlier. Naomi has perfect posture, her blonde hair pulled back with bangs framing her face, beaming by Micah's side in her cheer uniform. Ezra's not in this class because she rarely acts so flirty with Micah when Ezra's around.

They sit on a chair, and Naomi straddles him, obviously wanting everyone to see her, and my skin goes clammy. If that's Micah with his hands resting on Naomi's ass, then that means it was Maison who iced me out earlier.

As the rest of the class buzzes around us, I watch Maison, not caring at all if he notices me looking. Eventually, I get a small side glance before his head turns away. As the teacher walks in and settles everyone down, I notice those side glances become more frequent until he rests his eyes on me. His eyes are contemplative, and a tiny smile hints at his lips.

I don't return it.

Instead, I cast him a look of ice, and he chuckles as he looks away.

He's toying with me, and I hate it. Either that or he is embarrassed to talk to me. He waved at me during the game the other day and gave me a flirty smile in the lunchroom; he told me he was excited to see me in Alaska, then elongated my name, which made me die a little inside. So why couldn't he acknowledge me when he saw me just now? Serena walked in after Naomi, and he had no problems smiling at her.

I still have his sweater, which I fully intend on returning to him in Alaska. Maybe I'll try to get it to him sooner? Either that, or maybe I will play my game and interview every single player on the team *but* them.

That will get their attention.

My skin prickles when Maison side glances me. This time, when our eyes meet, I keep my eyes planted on him. I swear, at this moment, I can't tell the two apart. Their similarities are uncanny, and if Naomi wasn't straddling Micah right now at his desk, I'd have guessed they were the other way around. Naomi sees him looking at me, and her eyes narrow as she sees me.

Micah notices her looking and gives me a sharp glare while tensing his jaw, pulling Naomi's hips deeper into his.

I smile despite myself. It's the most emotion Micah's shown me in the two weeks I've been here—maybe there is some humanity within him after all. It also helps me identify who's who.

Mrs. Johnson clears her throat. She has a tight bun like the secretary and is very different from my previous English teacher. I can focus on this class and get the grade I need for my college applications. She immediately takes notice of Naomi on Micah's lap. "Find your seat, Miss. Wilson," she snaps. Naomi slides off him and heads to the empty desk across the room, giving me another dirty look as she struts by, looking like she feels mighty proud of herself.

The teacher walks to her desk and grabs a box, then taking a few books out, she begins passing them out to the entire class.

She waves her hand in a motion of silence. "As a group, we are going to read and analyze *The Great Gatsby.*"

Groans erupt around me, but a small smile tugs at my lips. I read it last year and adored it. This book made me realize I could have a future outside of dance. Well, Chris helped with that, too, but he liked my dancing. If the students in this school actually read it and pay attention to its themes, it might do them some good.

The hollowness of the upper class.

Careless actions with unintended consequences and are immune to the rules of the rest of society.

Wealth does not *equal happiness.*

When the book hits Micah's desk, he refuses it and instead, passes a copy to Thomas, who is sitting at the desk behind him, taking up most of it due to his size. Micah then leans back in his chair with arrogance and places his arms around his head, his fingers lacing together and his biceps rippling in his shirt. Those same hands bloodied another kid's face last night and bruised the skin of an innocent girl he shouldn't have been touching.

The teacher raises her eyebrows. "You don't plan on completing the assignment, Mr. Matei?"

Thomas smirks from behind him.

Micah merely shrugs in a look of utter defiance. "I've already read it." She frowns at him as if she doesn't believe his clear lie. "Don't worry, Mrs. Johnson," he says with a deep voice, "I'll write your paper."

A ripple of laughter hints from the class and she taps her pencil, contemplating. "Well, that's a relief, Mr. Matei. That's why you came back, isn't it? To finish your education and not just play hockey? Do you mind telling the rest of the class one key theme or takeaway from the book?"

I wish I had my journal out so I can document his response. It ought to be good.

He slides his hands from his neck to his front and crosses his arms across his chest. This is the first time I've heard him speak, so I lean forward, intent on capturing every word.

"That women are weak. Daisy had an opportunity for love and happiness, but she rejected it for a more attractive purse. She had a man who worshiped her, and she turned her back on him the first chance she could. She deserved to live in misery for treating him like that. My takeaway is... girls should stick to the kitchen, or better yet, the *bedroom*."

Maison and Thomas crack up beside him, and the rest of the room chuckles.

"You've got to be kidding me," I mutter out.

The teacher shoots me a look. "You disagree, London?"

"Vehemently."

Heat creeps into my face as the entire class turns their attention to me. Micah narrows his eyes, and Maison's eyes glint with amusement.

"Have you read the book?" she asks me.

I fidget in my seat. "Daisy's statement about being a beautiful little fool responds to the inequalities of the time. She did what she must to survive. In fact, it doesn't make her weak at all. I think that's a sign of strength and intelligence. Tom only controls her through force; she uses her brain to make the most of her life, despite her choice in not choosing Gatsby." My eyes find Micah's, and I pause for dramatic effect. "And Gatsby didn't love her at all... he loved the *idea* of her. He was obsessed with what she embodied, and the status and life he thought she represented. So perhaps you should just stick to hockey."

The class erupts in laughter, and when I glance back at Micah, I'm surprised to find his eyebrows arched to his forehead.

I avoid eye contact and keep my head down for the rest of the period. The teacher continues her lecture and tells us about the assignment that is due at the end of next week.

The Alaska week.

I plan to nail this project and re-read the book as many times as necessary to write the paper during the trip, among other things.

The bell rings, and I gather my stuff, keeping my head down to avoid catching any sort of interaction with Micah.

His accusations, arrogance, and utter disdain for women are unbearable. He may be in charge at this school, but after today, I will have no problem exposing him and taking him down. But still, he surprised me. He had read the book, even if his interpretation of it was completely wrong.

I push through the crowd and head to the newsroom with Nigel, giving Jade a sympathetic look as we abandon her. Part of me wishes we could tell her our plan for the story, but Nigel insists she wouldn't understand what we are doing. He's probably right; Jade isn't cut from the same cloth as we are. She's a much better person, innocent and bright—and doesn't think like journalists like we do. I know what pushes me, but I often wonder what fuels Nigel. What dwells below his surface? This town seems full of skeletons, so I'm assuming he must have at least one.

Once inside the classroom, I set my backpack on the table and sit, resting my head on my elbows. "Did you get the paper I emailed you this morning?" I ask him, picking at my nails. The essay I stayed up till one AM writing last night.

He lounges in his usual spot, grabbing his laptop and firing it on, zeroing in on the screen. He seems too serious about this story, like it's the priority for him over everything else. "I did," he says nonchalantly, clicking away at the computer before casting me a glance. "It was good. I'm impressed by you, London. You're much more than just a pretty face."

My pretty face is the key to his story, lest he forget.

"You have skill and a lot of potential at this club. In fact, you could be the best writer I have here." I know what he's really referring to, but I can't help but beam all the same.

His eyes narrow. "Have you made any more progress with the twins, other than getting completely played by them in English class today?"

My lips purse, and I stare at him with my brows furrowed. I run my hand through my hair awkwardly as he waits for my response.

He shakes his head and snickers. "You had no idea, did you? They are really that good."

What the hell is he talking about?

I shift in my seat. "I'm supposed to interview Maison at the tournament, if that's what you're referring to. This group isn't as easy to infiltrate as you think, Nigel."

"That little debate you just had with Micah?" he continues. "That wasn't Micah... that was Maison."

The little squirm in my belly turns into a monstrous wave.

Impossible.... Why would they do that? But I remember that little inkling I had at the beginning of class. Micah walked in... I knew it was him. Then he flipped right when he saw me, and I didn't think to question it. He walked in assuming he'd be the first person in class, so I must have caught him off guard.

He snickers. "They're good, aren't they?"

It's incomprehensible.

I bite the inside of my cheek. "How did... How did you know?" I ask tightly.

He taps his forehead. "Because I pay attention, London. Just as you need to do. Watch what makes them unique. Patterns, connections, subtleties in the way they move and what they say, even if it's importance may not seem immediately apparent. That's the sign of a talented journalist, and what will separate you from mediocrity."

"They may switch personas, but it's impossible to change personalities," I finish the rest of his thought.

A smile dances in his eye. "Exactly. Don't feel too bad about it, though. No one else in that class knew except for me. I bet that dead girlfriend of theirs didn't even know who she was fucking before they offed her."

Jesus.

My eyes shoot up. "Don't blame a dead girl, Nigel. That makes you as bad as they are."

He reaches down and grabs a folder, shuffling papers in front of him, but he still chuckles. "I don't think Naomi had a clue, either."

He has a point. I've rarely seen Naomi speak to Maison because he's usually all over Serena. When I caught Maison's eye, his hands were on Naomi. As soon as he saw me looking, he pulled her closer. And Micah.... He was staring at me all class, not Maison like I originally thought. Did Maison know Micah was looking at me? Did they plan that?

Nigel's eyes penetrate me as he watches my internal meltdown. "I suspected because I remember Micah was always terrible in that class, and Micah needs to maintain a certain GPA to stay in this school. Switching identities makes sense so Maison can do his pop quizzes for him, while keeping his grades up through papers." He places his hand on my arm. "You'll be fine. Please quit pouting. Now that you know, you'll pay more attention. But these guys are good; their manipulation is diabolical."

Attention. Do I want their attention?

I think of Maison's flirting and my bare legs under his hockey sweater. The reaction I had to him in the few minutes we interacted and how I secretly craved more of it. Maison's the nice twin... but is he? Perhaps Maison isn't as innocent in all this as people make him out to be.

I quirk my head. "What information did you find? You said in English class you found something about their parents?"

He smiles, showing his teeth, and pushes a folder in front of me. "These are bank statements."

My eyes widen as I peer down at them. "Nigel... how did you get these?"

He waves me off with one dismissive gesture. "Don't worry about it. Just look at them."

It takes a minute to comprehend what I am seeing, or the fact it's not the last name Matei I'm staring at, but the last name Schwartz. *Ezra Schwartz.*

I shake my head. "I... I don't understand what I am looking at."

"Micah's parents have done business with the Schwartz family for years. They did a deal a few years back, and recently, it went sour. What you are seeing is a large sum of money being transferred from the Schwartz bank account to the Matei family. It's an obscene number, in the millions. It seems like our dear friend Ezra is broke."

It takes all my strength to pick up my jaw off the floor.

"Is this why Naomi broke up with him?"

He curls his lip. "I don't think Naomi has any idea. She ended things with Ezra because she's been secretly pining over Micah her entire life. That girl is a whole other level of messed up. She was around when it all happened, and I feel like she's hiding something, too. Her mom's also a habitual mistress in New Ocean, and Naomi's a slut, just like her momma."

My eyes shoot up to meet his, and heat flushes right to my face.

Impulsive. I'm too reactionary. I need to play it cool with these people—Nigel, especially. If he has any indication that he knows about my shared past with Naomi and our parents, he says nothing, and I'm certainly not bringing it up. He must know, though.... If he's as good as he says he is, how could he not? Like he didn't look me up, I looked him up. He transferred here three years ago, so he didn't grow up here.

I look down at the statements, hoping the moment passes and my eyes cross the date on the paper he hands me. December of last year.

"This makes no sense," I tell him, changing the subject. "This school is expensive. How could he afford the tuition?"

He pulls out one more piece of paper from that dark folder of dangerous secrets and pushes it in front of me.

"That's where it gets interesting," he says, pressing his index finger down on a specific transaction. "It looks like the twins' parents are covering it, and by these monthly payments back to the Schwartz family, they are giving Ezra's family an allowance. Ezra's only in this school because the Matei family is *allowing* him to be here, paying every cent of his tuition."

I lean forward and press my hand on my chin and shake my head, glimpsing Nigel in the shadows of the room. He can't even hide the gleam in his blue eyes.

"Welcome back to New Ocean, London."

CHAPTER SIX

Day one of the Alaska Trip

This entire town is laced with lies and deceit. My mom left because of it and begged me not to return. A game of power, politics, and sex, and everyone here is tainted with it. Before I fled Portland, she warned me. It's a place where people hide their ugly truths behind a veil of sparkling diamond rings and shiny cars, each with their own hidden agenda.

I seem to fit right in...

I'm about to leave for Alaska. The trip is five days, and I suspect the only real way to be alone with the twins in any meaningful way is through the interview with Maison. It will be stiff and awkward, and in the hallway in the arena by the locker room—he likely won't have time for anything else. It's a high-profile event in the national youth hockey community.

I doubt Naomi will let me anywhere near them otherwise, and Jade already gave me the rundown, like how we are not usually included in their parties. Although, I do plan on somehow finding an excuse to give Maison his sweater back. It's a natural reason for me to get him alone. I'm unsure how he'll react when I show up at his room or what I will say to him. Unfortunately, Nigel can't prep me for that.

My dad's about to drive me to the airport. A part of me fears I won't be the same if I board that plane, but these twins are a mystery too inciting to ignore. And the further I delve into their lives, the more I resonate with the girl they tormented and killed. I was only on the receiving end of their manipulation in English class; I couldn't imagine what they do behind closed doors. Nigel is fixated on Micah, but at this point, both are equally guilty to me. Watching Maison's hands slide around Naomi proves he is capable of more than he's letting on. The cute, nice guy act is almost as bad as Micah's brooding temper. At least with Micah, I know what to expect.

When I step forward and do this, there is no coming back., and I truly do not know how far I will go to get the truth.

Jade waves at me as I pull into the Seattle airport parking lot in my dad's silver Audi. It's an hour's drive from New Ocean, and my dad insisted on driving me, even though I could have easily driven with Jade and Nigel since they offered.

My father's been a stranger to me since I was a kid, and I've been quiet and distant with him after I arrived and found my solitude on the beach. The first two weeks of school hit hard, and I've spent most evenings alone and studying in my room, including this entire weekend. My dad gives me a tight smile and a hug goodbye, and I head to the trunk to grab the single small piece of luggage I brought with me.

Five days is not a long trip.

I trudge over to where Jade and Nigel are patiently waiting for me. Jade looks shiny, as usual. Her hair has an extra bounce today, layered over top of her spaghetti strap yellow summer dress that's a bit too tight on her. She's fussing with her camera bag with her luggage placed in front of her.

Jade looks much better than I do. Her skin is sun-kissed, and she very much fits in with New Ocean. So does Nigel, who has on a blue argyle collared shirt and khaki shorts, and his token bowtie, of course.

Nigel frowns when he sees me in my basic jeans and tank top as I drag my suitcase over to him. He wanted me to dress sexier, but I don't know how. I've never really cared much for clothes, and I spent most of my life in ballet tights, anyway. Plus, I need comfort. It's a long flight north. I brought Maison's hockey sweater with me, to wear on the plane cause it's warm and I get cold easily.

I give them a curt smile, squinting as the late evening sun shines right into my eyes. We go to the charter flight terminal, check in, pass security, and reach the tarmac. The heat hangs in the surrounding air.

The hockey players are already here. Both teams, junior and senior, attend this tournament, along with the cheer team, us three from the newspaper, and two coaches. The athletes are in full suits and ties that cut right to their muscled bodies, and the cheerleaders are in branded New Ocean athletic wear, with Naomi at the helm with her signature ponytail.

My eyes draw straight to the airplane, which seems much bigger than expected. We aren't that big of a group, and this plane looks like it could carry our entire school, rather than just an elite part of it.

"We sit in the very back," Jade informs me as she notices my eyes widen at the size of the plane. The front rows are reserved for seniors, followed by juniors, and then the cheer team sits in the middle.

Of course they do.

"Why is the plane so big?" I ask them, "There are only like what... forty of us, total?"

Nigel slides up next to me. "Cargo. They bring crates of supplies up to Alaska since we don't fit the entire plane, and they cargo load at the bottom. It usually heads off to a remote community after they drop us off."

Makes sense.

I notice approximately ten crates lined up near the luggage.

The group moves toward the plane, and we fall in line behind them. My eyes draw to the twins as they stand together in the front. I can't tell who is who, but they look amazing in their pressed dark blue suits, and it makes it hard not to stare. It's criminal how good they look.

One of them turns to face me, as if sensing me. He looks me up and down, chewing on his bottom lip, and I feel on display as he doesn't hide the fact he's staring back.

It's Maison, I'm sure of it. He gave me that look in the hallway and parking lot. After he turns his head and smiles as if knowing he made me uncomfortable, and gets off on it. I don't know why he's looking at me like that—it's not like the cheer-team isn't doing everything they can to capture their attention.

Right next to him, and just as tall and lean, Micah stands more assertive in his motions, with his harder edges, and pays me no attention.

Subtle differences, patterns, and personality in movement.

I'll keep watching them.

The group finally boards, and we are the last to step inside. The supply crates seem to have more status on this airplane than we do as we wait and sweat it out till everyone else is seated, and the crates get loaded beneath. Jade and Nigel slip in ahead, and I walk on the plane, enjoying the blast of air conditioning as it hits my bare shoulders. Keeping my head down, the cabin is filled with shouting and laughter, and I slam into what feels like a steel wall. I look up as a broody face and deep brown eyes stare at me intensely.

I flinch at the hostility seeping out of them, as if my true intentions on this trip are branded on my forehead.

Micah lifts his arm and presses his hand up in the overhead compartment, further blocking any way to get past him. He makes me feel like a bug he's waiting to step on. "Maison tells me you want an interview," he says.

His voice is deep and raspy, like Maison's was in the hallway, and he smells amazing. Only his voice has a razor-sharp edge, and I realize this is the first time I've heard Micah speak.

I keep my eyes locked on him, despite my knees buckling beneath me at being so close, and hints of his aftershave tickle my nose. "That's right. I just need ten minutes of your time."

He shifts his body, his messy dark brown hair falls just above his hard eyes. Gold specs flicker as his pupils flare. "It's not fucking happening." The first row is quiet now, watching us. He's close to me, and his body language is nothing but that of pure intimidation as the fingers of his free hand curl into a loose fist. "I don't want any more stories written about me."

I instantly regret thinking how hot he is while he's in the middle of humiliating me. I choke on my words, glancing at his fingers only inches from my hips, wondering what it would feel like should he reach out and grab me. What Olivia felt in her final breaths while with him.

"Micah, man." Maison's voice breaks the tension between us. "Calm down, dude. Let her on."

Micah relaxes and my body composes itself. He steps back and lets me through, but his jaw tenses and eyes follow me as I walk by. The whole interaction was maybe ten seconds, but...

Jesus.

The heat in my face sears as I walk through the aisle and pass where Maison is sitting in the second row with his arm around Serena. Naomi is in the row behind them, and her smirk tells me she saw and heard the whole thing. I refuse to look at him, or her, or number two and four as they heckle me. Nigel and Jade are waiting for me at the back of the plane, and Jade's eyes are like saucers while Nigel merely shakes his head.

I grab my headphones and a few other items and tuck them under my seat in the aisle across from where Jade and Nigel are sitting, then toss the blanket on myself that's neatly folded on an empty seat next to mine and lean my head against the window.

My gaze shifts to Nigel and Jade, who opens her mouth to say something.

"Just don't," I snap at her, popping in my headphones. Music comes blaring into my ears and I close my eyes, blocking out every single one of them.

My eyes shoot open to the soft hum of the airplane and muffled voices and whispers from the front of the plane. The cabin is dark, save for a few overhead lights illuminating the aisle. I don't know how long I was asleep for, but I passed out and I'm nearing the end of the playlist I put on.

A flash streaks through a line of wispy pink clouds on the horizon.

Lightning. That's what must have woken me; heat lightning from the looks of it, as the sky is otherwise clear. The last trickles of evening light flows over a series of islands that hover in the distance. Massive mountains loom upon them, so we must be getting close to Alaska.

I shift the blanket around my legs and peek over the seat to check out the rest of the plane. Most people are settled and quiet now, either sleeping or mindlessly watching their devices. Naomi is leaning over the aisle, talking to who I think is Ezra, twirling her hair in a soft, flirty gesture. Micah is beside her, although his head is rested and he looks still. Her time is spent equally between the two of them, it seems. An interesting dynamic that, from what Nigel tells me, stems from the Olivia days. I'm not sure how she fits into everything, but I plan to explore it further if the opportunity arises. Especially with the new information Nigel uncovered about Ezra and his family's deep and twisted connection to the Matei family.

Naomi is a constant through all of it. *What involvement did you have in Olivia's death, Naomi Wilson?* She seems all too comfortable throwing herself at a guy who was once accused of murder.

Jade and Nigel seem cozy in the aisle beside me, and I'm grateful to have my row to myself. A sense of warmth flows through me as Jade rests her head on Nigel's shoulder while he is head down on his computer. A softness I've not seen in Nigel and confirms my suspicions of the closeness between the two of them. Although, I'm still not one hundred percent certain it's reciprocated on his side. I hope he pulls it together and sees the brunette beauty beside him for what she is.

I rest my head back on the window and peer outside to the increasing lightning streaks blasting across the sky and the cloud cover now below us. The plane shifts suddenly and the seatbelt sign lights up. I swallow a lump in my throat, dragging my seatbelt across my lap and clipping it in, thinking back to my first interaction with Micah, and how he could shift so easily from giving me side glances and smiles in the classroom to the angry person he portrayed this evening.

Diabolical, as Nigel had said.

The same way Chris was with me, sliding his hand up my shirt after my rehearsals, telling me how pretty and talented I was while his wife was at home, making his dinner. I knew he was married; I just didn't care. But I was a fucking child, and he took advantage of me, taking away any ability for me to fully trust anyone again.

I lean forward and grab a copy of *The Great Gatsby*, popping my overhead light on. I will not sleep anymore, so I might as well get a good start on my homework. As soon as I land, I plan to lock myself in my hotel room and dig into writing it.

After a few minutes, someone slides in beside me. Maison is sitting on the far seat. At least I think it's Maison. My judgment is clouded, and I've witnessed the games they play firsthand. It's also dark in the cabin, so the shadows dance off his face. And he looks ridiculously hot in his navy suit, that seems to cut around every muscle in his body. His brown hair is perfectly swept to the side and just a hint of facial hair teases his face.

I lower my book and arch my brows at the sight of his playful grin as he slides over one more seat. I guess Maison got bored with Serena.

He's grinning and checking out my cleavage in this tight tank top, while trying to not be obvious about it. The wisps of his hair lie just above his eyes, the same as Micah. But unlike Micah, his eyes are kind, expressive, like they actually have life in them. He shifts his gaze to my mouth, then eventually meets my thick stare.

How many girls have fallen madly in love with the look he just gave me?

I can't fall for it.

"Are you okay?" he asks me, and I suppress the twinge in my stomach.

"Why wouldn't I be?" I respond curtly, keeping my body angled away from him, returning to the book on the open tray in front of me.

A pause, then he says. "Micah can be a dick sometimes. He doesn't mean anything by it."

I shoot my head toward him and purse my lips. "I hadn't noticed."

He shifts beside me, only a hint of hesitation from his normal confident demeanor. "We're having a party in our room when we land."

"That's nice," I say dryly, keeping my voice sounding bored. Somehow, in the last thirty seconds, he's inched even closer to me and my heart spikes a tiny beat.

He rests his head on the seat, angled entirely in my direction, and ignores my brief responses as if he's unbothered by them. "You should come."

A scoff escapes me. "I don't think your brother wants me anywhere near his rooms."

Nigel is now side-eying us, giving me a look, telling me I'd be stupid to say no to this offer. Nigel will have to let me do this my way and stay out of it. I can't seem too eager.

The plane jolts from a hint of turbulence, enough where my body presses into Maison from the force.

"What if I want you there?" he responds, and I shiver from the small graze of his fingers as they rest mere inches from my leg. The hint of spice wafting off him makes my mouth water.

I move over an inch, keeping my eyes off him, trying to ice him out, and I shrug. "What if I don't want to go? I have reading to do."

"But you've already read this," he says, brushing his arm against mine, and he plucks the book in my hand and places it face-down on my lap. "Apparently, you can recite every word."

My body is acutely aware of his hands resting on my thigh, dangerously close to parts he shouldn't be touching.

My eyes find his. "And so, apparently, can you."

He smirks, and I wonder if he knows what I am hinting at. He leans over, and my stomach fills with heat as his hot breath tickles my ear.

"Come on, London King," he whispers in a lascivious voice. "I want to see what you're made of."

I force myself to keep his eye contact and his attention is directed at my mouth, at the lip I'm biting. It's intense and my pulse surges, and I hope he doesn't notice the effect he's having on me.

I keep my eyes on his full lips, scared to move in case he presses them into mine. He might, that's how close he is, and then I'd kiss him back, and he'd win.

I gesture to his friends, trying to control my heart rate. "Be careful, Maison," I murmur, "your girlfriend might not be too happy that you're talking to me right now."

I'm flirting now—or, at least, I'm attempting to, even though I'm terrible at it—but Maison makes it so easy. Nigel's presence is heavy in the corner—no doubt watching this entire interaction. Maison seems disinterested in him as he hasn't even so much as acknowledged my friends.

He angles his head and keeps his hand firmly planted on my leg. "Who, Serena? Nah, she's just a friend. I don't have a girlfriend, London."

I let out a quiet exhale and run my hands through my hair, guilt-ridden for how happy him saying that makes me. He's single and available.

It will make what I'm trying to do easier.

My head quirks and brow arches. "I meant Naomi. I'm pretty sure I saw her legs wrapped around you in English class. From the way your hands were positioned on her, it looked like you two are close... or did she not realize it was not her boyfriend's lap she was sitting on?"

Ha. Let him chew on that for a second.

I can't help but smile as he pulls his hands off my thigh and frowns.

Guilty as sin.

"Naomi isn't his girlfriend, either, London." My ears prickle. Not from the words, but from the way he says it...

Naomi was around during the Olivia era. Her involvement with Micah has something to do with all this; I can feel it in my gut.

"Does she know that?" I ask him, keeping my voice tight.

He shrugs. "He's into her at the moment, but Naomi is the type of girl who will flock to whoever she thinks is on top. Right now, that's Micah, but he will tire of her eventually, like he does with all girls."

My eyebrows arch. "What do you mean, tire of girls?" His eyes flash, and I press my lips together, instantly regretting my words.

It's enough, and he reacts, quirking his head. "What's your story, London King?"

I fold my arms on my lap and stare at him. "My story?"

"Yeah, your story. Where did you come from?" A slow smile spreads on his face as I fidget in my seat. "What? Am I not allowed to ask questions about you?"

He's avoiding my question now. This isn't getting anywhere.

I dip my chin and turn away from him. "My story is none of your business, so please leave me alone, Maison. Unlike you, I don't have any prospects for athletic scholarships. I have to get into school the old-fashioned way. So right now, I have to read this book and write this paper."

That wasn't nice... especially since I'm sure he's not used to girls *not* drooling over him.

He leans in closer, every movement so composed and confident. "So you are allowed to write an article about me in your little newsletter, but I don't have the permission to know anything about you? That hardly seems fair."

I press my lips together. "That's the benefit of being me. Nobody cares about the person behind the words, so I get to stay invisible. You're the one that matters, the one people want to see and talk about."

All those stories I read about them—the social posts, the gossip I found online, the speculation and intrigue, the whole town centers on these brothers.

"Is that what you're doing, London King?" My face heats as he studies me with his pretty dark eyes. "Hiding yourself?"

I dart my gaze downward. "Maybe."

He reaches for my chin and pulls my face toward him, but not hard or aggressive. His hands are soft and warm, and my entire body heats.

"Well, I want to see you," he breathes and blinks at me through his thick, dark lashes. "I bet, deep down, there is something beautiful behind this angry girl facade. And I don't mean under your clothes... I've already seen that. If you come tonight, I'll make it worth your while."

I cringe at the thought of the hallway in my most vulnerable state, but the cute smirk on his face makes my heart melt.

Nigel's voice slices across the aisle. "She'll go to the party."

Maison whips toward him, and I press my lips together and shake my head at Nigel behind Maison's back. By the time Maison turns back to me, I'm normal, and a smile is planted on his face. Nigel needs to butt out and let me do this my way.

He presses his hand on my thigh and my stomach twists. "Great. I'll come grab you so you can't run away from me when we land. Maybe we can even find some time to sneak off so you can interview me." He turns to leave, but pauses, turning into me, knowing Nigel is in earshot. He leans in, his lips close to my ear, shooting a chill down my spine. "But I absolutely refuse to talk about Micah, pretty girl. You're only allowed to talk about *me*."

I pull back from him, thinking he must be joking—

A fleeting flash hits his eyes, and just as quickly, he returns to his usual flirtatious self.

I didn't miss it, that dark flash, and I hitch out a small breath.

He means he doesn't want to talk about what his brother did to him. Betrayal? He knows, deep down, what I'm dying to ask.

The plane jolts again, and the captain's voice echoes from above, telling us we are hitting an electric storm and to stay in our seats.

The lightning I saw, the clouds in the distance, we are headed straight through it. The plane bounces around, and Jade snaps up from lying on Nigel's shoulder.

She looks around in confusion. "What's happening?

"I don't know," Nigel says, peering outside. "It's strange to have this type of weather so high."

I tighten my belt and look over at Maison. "You better go back to your seat."

Suddenly, we drop—at least ten feet straight down—so fast and hard, Maison nearly hits his head on the ceiling, and I whip my head back on my seat, giving me whiplash. Cries and yells reverberate throughout the plane as others jolt right out of their seats. Maison slides his seatbelt on. "Yeah, no fucking way I'm leaving you." He rubs the back of his head from where it slammed into the seat. "Are you okay?"

My heart is beating so fast, my body shakes. "Yeah." I muster out a breath, arching my head to get a better view of the outside, hardly believing what had just happened. "That was scary."

Something fucked-up just happened.

Outside, the lightning is all around. The plane dropped enough, putting us square in the middle of the storm. Maison rests his hand on my shaking thigh. "I'm not going anywhere, okay?" His normal confidence is rocked.

"I don't get it," I say, gripping his hand over my thigh so hard my fingernails almost draw blood. "Why wouldn't the pilot avoid flying into this?" He squeezes my hand as the plane shakes around us, and I'm happy to have some-one to hold on to as heavy precipitation blasts against the window and pure terror rolls through me.

The plane veers hard and nearly tips on its side, causing me to crash into Maison as luggage and bags fall into the unfortunate people sitting on the right aisle. Maison turns and wraps his arms around me as I close my eyes, hoping the worst of it's over, but it feels as if I'm on a rollercoaster with a really shitty seatbelt. The plane finally rights itself, and after the initial sounds of cries and crashes, it's quiet, eerily so, as everyone on this plane is stunned. The one flight attendant has vanished. She must have jumped into the cockpit with the pilots.

"Micah," Maison calls out, "you guys okay up there?"

Micah was sitting on the right side, so he would have had luggage fall on him. The darkness in the cabin stops me from seeing how many people are hurt, but I hear the muffled cries and utter shock.

"Yeah, man," Micah yells back. "Everyone, get back in your seats and get your fucking seatbelts on. Maison, get the fuck back here."

Anyone who didn't put their seatbelt on are now strewn about the plane, at least half of the students. The pilot's voice cackles over the intercom, but I don't understand a damn word he's saying. The coaches get up and try to settle the players, which is a hopeless endeavor given everyone is panicking.

My heart lurches at the thought of Maison leaving me right now. He calls out to Micah, "No way, man. I'm not leaving London right now. I'll be fine back here. Watch over everyone up there."

Me... He's not leaving me, even though he doesn't know me.

The plane jolts, vibrations hum from the bottom, causing instability in the cabin before a deafening boom blows from the bottom.

Oxygen masks fall as smoke quickly fills the cabin around us causing me to choke on the acidic air that fills my lungs. I slump forward and press my hands over my ears as my body ripples with fear as everyone on board screams and cries out.

The engine exploded—right in the centre of the plane.

"Holy shit," I cry out, and my chest curls and I cough as I inhale. Maison pulls the oxygen mask over my mouth, pinning it behind my ears. I finally open my eyes and through the lightning flashes, I see Jade and Nigel's bodies just three feet away, each leaning forward, trying not to breathe in this toxic air, either. Both scrambling to put their oxygen masks on as the dark smoke thickens, completely obstructing my view of anything.

They are on their own. I can't do anything to help them right now.

I dare to pull myself away from the dark safety of Maison's body. "Are you guys okay?" I yell out to them. Jade's hands are covering her face and Nigel shakes his head, letting me know they are absolutely not okay.

Maison grabs my head and pulls me back into him. "Don't look." His voice is eerily calm, given the circumstances. "Just hold on to me, London King. I think this plane is going to go down."

The acid fills my stomach, and a wave of nausea rolls through me. Maison grabs my head, his thumb a soft caress on my cheek. His hands are the only reason I haven't spilled my entire guts all over this plane yet. I breathe into him, trying to inhale him instead of the poison in the air, and focus on his spicy scent.

The plane tilts and overhead, there is another cackling sound as the pilot yells over the intercom. Then the plane seems to cease as gravity takes over and we veer downward toward whatever awaits us. This plane is landing, no question about that... except, I can't see what is actually below us, and I can only hope these pilots are skilled enough to land us safely.

Screams and utter panic ensues—horrifying cries of my peers while Maison shells himself around me. My body is small and tight, and I fit inside him.

He leans his head into mine. "Don't open your eyes for anything, pretty girl. Okay?"

My breaths become heavy as I hyperventilate, my pulse ticking harder than humanly possible. There is a strong possibility we won't survive this emergency landing, and I don't want to die—not like this. Five minutes ago, we were talking about a party, and I was flirting with him. How quickly circumstances can change.

I try to pull off him, to see what's going on, but he won't let me move.

The plane stops shaking, just wind, rain, hissing, and ringing in my ears as painful, precious seconds tick by.

"Maison...." I choke out a whisper, and he releases me enough to let me look at him in the darkness.

"It's going to be over soon, I promise," he whispers. "I will not let you go."

I completely surrender to him. He's a stranger, and an enigma I'm trying to figure out, but right now, he's my saviour as this life-changing moment passes between us. The last moments before sure death, and all I can think about is how I wish he would kiss me. How that would be a nice way to go.

I close my eyes, rest my head on him, and focus on my heartbeat while I still have one. His hands rub and relax me, and I imagine we are on a date at the beach. The sun is hot, and I'm in a bikini and he's rubbing sun lotion on my back. He leans down and nibbles on my ear and tickles my neck with his tongue. It's a nice fantasy.

"The pilot has control of the plane," someone yells from the front. "He's going to land it. Maison, are you still okay back there?"

Maison yells back, "Yeah, we're hanging on."

He's hanging on to me. I panic, my body shutters beneath him.

The screams echo now as the plane heads with alarming speed toward the ground or water, or wherever the pilot manages to land us.

The impact of the plane hitting the ground jolts me like a ragdoll. Maison keeps his hold on me as we screech and skid against uneven terrain. The smoke is so thick, I choke on my last breaths, as trees snag the nose of the plane and sparks fly all around us. Maison's fingers slide between mine and he squeezes firmly, so firm I might have told him to stop, but that firm grip is a reminder that I'm not dead yet.

Glass shatters, seats break loose, and the plane's wings shred. Bit by bit, tiny parts of the airplane rip off, ripping holes into its side. Windows break open as a heavy wind tunnel whips through the body of the plane. I hear the cries of the injured as liquid sprays onto my face, and I can only assume its blood from my classmates as the impact of the crash hits the inside of the plane.

Something slams into us, and Maison loses his grip on me, and the icy chill lingers from where he was just protecting me. I feel around for him frantically, but he's gone. Then more screams, more crying, and then...... nothing.

"London, London, wake up. Please wake up." Rough hands shake me, and I can barely make out voices from the constant ringing in my ears. The hands holding me now are not as soft as Maison's. My eyes are heavy, and it's easier to keep them closed than deal with the sight of the wreckage as my memories rush in on me. I must have gotten knocked out during the impact.

It's the smell of smoke and burning flesh that brings me closer to opening my eyes.

"I think she's dead," Jade's sweet voice pushes me back into consciousness, but it's Nigel who is looming overtop of me as I peel my eyes open amidst the chaos surrounding me.

Every muscle in my body pulses and my throat is on fire from the acidic smoke I inhaled during our descent.

I'm not dead, I realize, even though I might wish I were. We all might wish we were from the impact of that crash. I may have lost consciousness right after Maison lost his grip on me, but he sheltered me from the worst of it.

Where is Maison?

Jade's hands rub my forehead, and it's her lap my head rests on while she looks down on me in concern, although it was Nigel who jolted me awake. Instant relief hits me, knowing that she and Nigel seem unscathed from the crash. Based on the moans of despair around us, we are the lucky ones.

The fire flickering through the window is my only source of light. Outside—outside is nothing but trees and darkness. We landed somewhere... some distant, far-off place between New Ocean and Alaska. Unchartered islands, vast oceans, and the northern wilderness surround us.

My mouth is dry as I open it. "Where's Maison?" I choke out the words. Saying his name and the thought of him dying after sheltering me—

"He's alive, London," Jade says, her voice trembling. "He's helping Micah and Thomas get the others off this plane. Micah thinks it might either blow up or crumble, so we have to move. Can you walk?"

Micah's alive, too. Maison, Thomas, Nigel, Jade—who else?

I rub the severe bump on my head. "How... how long was I out?"

"Only a few minutes. Maison had to leave to help others with more severe injuries. Nigel and I told him we would stay with you."

I feel sick thinking about the screams, blood, and panic in the dark. A moment of pure terror my body is still recovering from.

"Come on, get up and walk now," Nigel says, grabbing me by the arms.

Gathering my strength, I push myself up, but my knees are weak and my mind is muddy as I fall back again. Nigel and Jade catch me.

"London, we can't carry you. Push yourself," Nigel says, his voice anything but soft.

Hints of orange and red glow outside, on what's left of the wing.

Burning... The plane is burning.

I reach over and grab my bag, still lying under my seat, and I lean into both of them to prop myself up. We step toward the emergency exit that's already propped open. I try not to look at the cause of the agonizing moans around me as we step over loose luggage and debris.

"Wait." I push off them as a hand grabs at my ankle from the floor in front of me. It's number two, I realize, and through the flames burning outside, I can make out a piece of glass sticking out of his leg. His bloodshot eyes are a stark contrast to the chirping boy he was in class. As his body convulses, the metallic smell of blood fills the air, staining his once pristine Armani suit. My heart breaks for him, but I have no strength to do anything.

"We have to help him, too," I beg Nigel and Jade.

Nigel nudges me forward. "You two need to leave the plane first," he says, staring down at the fallen hockey player. "I'll come back for him." By the way Nigel's looking at him, I don't believe him.

When we stumble off the plane, I fall to my knees, my muscles still in shock. My body sinks into the wet ground, but I welcome the feeling of damp earth after being on that plane. The fresh air and hard elements are a welcome change to the toxic poison and stench of burning flesh, metal, and chemicals. I wrap my arms around my knees and try to compose myself, try to calm my beating heart while I wipe the splattered blood off my bare skin.

A small group is already gathered outside. Two girls in their bright blue outfits are huddled together in an embrace, watching as the twins haul a few bodies off the plane, lying them on the ground as they whither in pain. Those are classmates who are worth saving I guess, and didn't die in the crash. Tormented screams still reverberate from inside, clawing through the air.

Nigel places Jade next to me. I've been too absorbed with my own injuries, so I hadn't realized how shaken up she is, too. "I have to go help," Nigel says, his brows narrowing as he watches her. "I want to go back and get my stuff. Are you two going to be okay for a minute?"

Jade closes her eyes and leans into me.

My eyes find Nigel's, and I shake my head, marveling at the fact he's standing before me, unscathed. "How did we survive this?" I ask him in a broken voice.

A shadow flickers within his eyes, and to my surprise, he laughs. "It's because we were shoved in the back. It seems everyone that's walking right now was either in the very back or the very front. When the engine exploded, it killed the ones in the middle instantly. It seems our social standing saved our lives."

He gives me no chance to respond before he rushes over to the other survivors and disappears inside the plane. I hope he's helping others who are hanging on for their lives, instead of grabbing... his stuff.

Micah, Naomi, Serena, Ezra, Thomas.

They took the front row—the plush seats and nearby exit probably saved their lives.

Maison stayed with me, so he missed the worst of the impact. I scan the carnage to find him, but don't see him anywhere.

Smoke trickles in the air as brush burns somewhere nearby. Rain patters down around us, making the ground wet and slippery. I'm glad I opted for pants, and I immediately grab my sweater I had tucked away in my pack as Jade stands shivering in her sundress. I give her my sweater, and grab Maison's, the one I had intended on giving back to him.

I kept it with me, and I didn't pack it. A split decision I made earlier and now these items are potentially my last possessions I'll ever own. I slip on his sweater just as two other survivors come and sit next to us.

Naomi and Serena—their pretty faces are tear-stained over thick layers of ash. Rain drips off their eyelashes and soaks their skintight outfits. Despite the heat radiating from the plane, they shiver down to the bone. Broken, battered, and only wanting encouraging arms around them. I recall their bullying and threats at the beach and hallway, and quickly decide I can't be that for them right now.

As the boys run in and out of the plane, the girls huddle quietly. They cry, moan, and sob, and I sit silent, watching the body count increase a few feet away from me; an eerie half light glows from the forest illuminating them. The boys, the ones still breathing, line up the bodies one by one, some still alive, most lay half strewn with limbs and flesh missing from their bodies. Thomas carries one girl over his shoulder and lays her down like a feather.

She doesn't move because she's already dead.

The fumes inside the plane become too toxic for them to get in and out of safely. Micah called it when Thomas came out puking and wouldn't let anyone else inside. A part of the plane looks like it might collapse any second, and Micah didn't want anyone alive trapped on board.

Whoever is still left in there is hopefully dead, or at least, they will be by the end of the night.

I can't think about that.

Maison is helping those he can, but he's not come to see me since we crashed. There are over forty of us on board who all need help, and he doesn't owe me anything.

I finally notice the tall frame of one twin hovering over a boy who is lying, grasping his side a couple of feet away from where I sit with my head between my knees. From here, I can't tell if it's Maison or not.

But the boy is still alive.

Move. I have to move. I can't just sit here while people are dying.

My muscles are locked in place, and I try to dispel a thickness in my throat, but I manage to crawl over to them, sliding myself against the slimy rock.

It's Micah—he's pressing his hand onto the boy's wound. I place my hand on Micah's back, and he flinches. He is so adsorbed into helping this boy he didn't see me coming.

"Let me help," I whisper as the whites of the boy's eyes find mine.

Micah shifts over to let me in. "Press down on the wound like this. Keep the blood from spilling out of him. That's the only way he will survive. Find an extra shirt if you can and wrap it around him."

I blow out a breath and mirror his movements, pressing my hand on the boy's shirt where something had clearly impaled him. Micah doesn't look at me as he rises to his feet, strong, unscathed, and pretty as always. He was at the very front.

"What do I do with him after?"

He swallows and purses his lips. "There is nothing we can do after. He'll either live or he'll die. He's in the same fucking boat we are."

I watch him in horror—the way he says it, so matter of fact and completely void of emotion. *Although, I guess he's used to being around dead bodies.* Nevertheless, he had laser-like focus trying to save this boy. He wants him to live as much as I do.

"What about the pilots and the flight attendant? Or the coaches?" I ask him.

A responsible adult who can help us.

He cocks his head as he finally looks at me. "They're fucking dead."

I balk in horror as he stalks to the next body, skipping those already deceased and focusing only on the ones convulsing. Conversation is over, I guess.

I focus my attention on the boy in front of me. I'm solely focused on preventing this boy from dying in my arms.

"What's your name?" I ask him, trying to place if he's on the junior or senior team. He has two cute dimples on his cheek, sandy blond hair, and eyes that seem to have maturity about them way beyond his years.

He lets out a heavy breath and smiles, his teeth flashing super white. "James," he says in a pained voice.

James Carey, the captain of the junior team. I hadn't given them much notice, honestly. All my attention has been on the two tall, mysterious hockey players on the older team. But I remember his name from the roster as technically, I was supposed to write about them, too.

I assess his injury the best I can. He's bleeding, but the cut on his side doesn't seem too deep, and the spilling blood is already subsiding.

"Tell me about yourself, James. Do you have any siblings?" Keep him talking. At least that's what they do in movies. His heavy eyes start to close, and I nudge him till he opens them again. "Keep your eyes on me, James, please. I'm not going anywhere, so you need to stay awake and talk to me."

A pause and then he swallows. "I have one brother."

"Does he play hockey, too?" I ask in a soft voice.

He manages a smile. "He's terrible at it. I was going to help him this winter."

I squeeze his hand. "Well, you still can. Someone will come help us soon. I bet you'll be skating around with him in no time."

A twinge hits my stomach. I'm surprised I haven't seen a helicopter swoop in yet. My estimation is it's been at least twenty minutes since the crash happened.

A missing airplane full of elite teens won't go unnoticed. Someone should be here by now.

James keeps his eyes open and locked in on me as a shadow looms over us.

Maison crouches down. "James, you okay, man?"

James winces but keeps his expression neutral. "I'm fine, Maison. It's just a small cut." A grin forms on Maison's face, probably because it's a bit more than a small cut.

"You always were a tough little motherfucker," he heckles him.

James manages a smile, even though the pressure of my hands must hurt him. They know each other. I had to ask his name, but Maison and Micah know him because they grew up with him. I'm a stranger to this kid and everyone else here.

Maison's hand rests on the small of my back. If he notices I'm wearing his sweater, he doesn't comment on it. "Are you doing alright, London? I lost my hold on you after the crash. I didn't mean to let go of you."

I face Maison, trying not to cry, wishing for his arms to soothe me like they did on the plane.

"Yeah, I'm fine." I manage a swallow and it feels like I was just fantasizing about how my interview with him would go. I was shamelessly flirting with him to gather intel on a story that doesn't seem to matter anymore.

Maison frowns, looking at James. "Can you stay with him? I have to go help the others and salvage anything we can from the plane. Micah's trying to track down a first aid kit in the cockpit. Hopefully, someone will be here soon."

Calm—Maison is so steady and calm. I get why everyone is drawn to him.

"I'm fine," I tell him without glancing up. "I'll stay with James. He was just telling me about his brother."

The rain intensifies, causing a hiss. The sound is so loud, it feels like hell. The plane is broken, battered, and twisted in an unnatural way with the carnage of trees and debris lying in its wake. The rain, I decide, is both a blessing and a curse. It caused this, but is also putting out any fires the crash caused.

This airplane will not be airborne ever again. Rescue is our only hope for survival.

A heaviness expands from my core to every limb as I pull the hood of my sweater over my head and continue to press my hands into James' side. As cries of agony and pure chaos ensues beside me, I close my eyes, refusing to believe what we just endured. What I just lived through.

"It will be okay, London." James' voice soothes me, and I can't help but laugh. He's the one hurt right now, yet he's consoling me. I keep my eyes open and just focus on his dimples, trying to ignore the painful worry coursing through every bone, or his blood seeping all over my hands. I have to keep James alive for his brother.

A tightness forms in the pit of my stomach and it's not because of the corpses lying around me or the sight of James in my arms. Rather, it's the overwhelming sense of apprehension I have for the remaining survivors who only sustained minor injuries. The worst-case scenario is nobody coming for us at all.

CHAPTER SEVEN

Day One

There are a million ways to die. The plane crash that killed thirty-two of my peers is not how my story ends. I won't ever board a plane again, so I suppose I'll find another way. They will have to rowboat me off this island when they finally come rescue us.

We are stranded. Only sixteen of us remain out of the forty-eight people on board. Four of them may not survive another night in their current state, their injuries are too far gone. I'll be the last face they see, even though I didn't know their names. James is still alive, so at least the body count isn't thirty-one. I found out he saved two of his friends by shielding them from the impact of the glass shattering around them. They were in the middle of the plane and should have died. I listened to all his stories from when he was growing up. I feel like I know his whole family intimately. It was all I could do to keep him awake and talking. James is now the one I know the most here. Truly, I am a stranger among everyone here.

Six hours have passed as I write this, and no one's come for us. No cell service, so our phones are useless other than for light, but if anyone ever reads this, especially my parents, please know I tried to call you. It stopped raining. The storm that caused this has passed and we are about to embark on our first day out here. Hopefully, it will be our last. We won't survive otherwise. Someone has to come.

Survivor Count:
London
Jade
Nigel
Naomi
Serena
Micah
Maison
Ezra
Thomas
James
Nathan
Ollie
Jess
Madison
Matthew
Colton

My eyes whip open to blinding light and a shimmering blue sky peaking through the tips of charred birch trees that surround us. I must have fallen asleep after I wrote in my journal because I don't remember the sun coming out. The bright, warm sky contrasts with the blackened horror of the previous night. Even with the light mist that hovers in the air, the rays of sun are a welcome warmth from the cold. I spent the entire night sleeping on the ground, re-living the crash scene over and over in my head. It's the mosquitoes and black flies that awoke me. Buzzing around my ear, biting my ankles and face.

Eventually, James's friends, Nathan and Ollie, came to watch over him. They are alive because of him. They told me to go rest, so I found Jade and Nigel huddled in a nearby tree in the forest foliage. I sat next to them and we just...waited. We passed out leaning our backs against each other because the ground is covered with moss, rocks, sticks, and long grass. We fell asleep, sitting up, from pure exhaustion. Well, some of us slept. In my dreamless sleep, I still heard Jade crying most of the night. I couldn't do anything about it; inside, I was quietly sobbing, too.

The bite in the air is bone-chilling, instantly reminding me of where we are.

The Arctic.

I shift as I look over at Jade, who is lying beside me, shivering on the ground. Her skin is ruddy, her normally shiny hair dulled with caked-in dirt and moss. Her eyes are open and bloodshot, she looks like she's still in shock. I reach my hand up to soothe her. She rises and sits next to me, leaning her shoulder on me. Hugging doesn't come naturally for me—I've never been the affectionate type—but I let her rest on me. It's the least I can do. Nigel is sitting leaned up against a nearby tree with his eyes closed, his expensive argyle shirt ripped, tattered, and bloodstained. All our clothes have blood on them. He's not uttered a word to either of us. I notice his precious bag from the plane is sitting next to him on the ground.

Jade lets out a labored breath and tears start streaming down her cheeks. I need to say something to soothe her. I can't listen to her cry anymore.

"Why did you get into photography?" I ask her.

She pauses, and then her breath evens out. "As a child, I enjoyed drawing beautiful things. But then I realized I was a terrible artist, so I started taking photos instead."

My eyes cut to Nigel. When his eyes briefly open before he closes them again, a shadow of annoyance flickers across his face.

I continue to talk, anyway. "What kind of photos do you take?"

She loosens a breath. "I prefer candid photos of people. It's the most effective method to capture people's true nature in photos. Without all the filters." She glances up at me. "Is that weird?"

Not at all—I get it.

It's the same as my writing. It's the story behind the story that truly matters.

"Maybe you can show me your photos one day?"

The twinkle in her eyes reminds me we all have our reason to live. Dreams, passions, goals—

Jade's passion is photography. Mine, apparently, is digging into people, the same people I am stuck with for the foreseeable future. Even the twins have goals—hockey, it seems, from what I know of them.

Speaking of the twins, one of *them* steps out from behind a tree. "You three need to get up. We are going to talk as a group and decide our plans."

Micah.

He's changed, now wearing his hockey sweater and a pair of loose sweats that hug his muscles. I try not to let my stare linger.

Jade motions to move, and I pull my shoulders back and stay planted on my butt. Micah doesn't get to bark orders at me, especially when we all feel so empty and drained. Nigel gets up as well and walks toward the others with his shoulders slumped. I make a mental note to check on him later.

"Coming, London?" Jade calls a couple of steps behind Nigel.

Micah's dominant presence looms over me, and I narrow my eyes at him. I haven't forgotten the way he treated me on the plane when I was trying to get on it. I want to make a snide remark about saying please, but can't find the words.

"In a minute," I call out to her, but I settle back in my spot and dig my heels into the ground.

He arches his brow and pauses as he watches my clear defiance. I swear a small twinge of a smile forms on the edges of his lips, but it's the blaze in his eyes I really notice.

Amusement? Anger?

I should fear that look. I still don't know what this guy is capable of—he might have caused those bruises found on that dead girl. His voice comes out softer than I expect. "What if I say please, London? Will you get up for me, then?"

For a moment—one moment—he gives me those same puppy dog eyes as Maison; the blaze turning to something softer.

It's enough to make me relent, especially since he addressed me by name. Despite his facetiousness, he acknowledged my existence in a nonthreatening way.

He leans down and puts his hand out, offering me a hand up. I almost want to tell him to suck on an egg, but my muscles are still aching from the crash and the hard hours that followed. So I reach up and grab his hand, letting him pull me to my feet. I didn't notice how weak I was until now, after sleeping outside. The crash had a bigger impact than I thought. I nearly buckle over backward, and he has to catch me. His hockey instincts no doubt, rather than being chivalrous.

His eyes flicker, and his hands hold me, steady me, as I fall into him, but the brooding scowl remains on his face.

"You need water," he informs and stares at my lips. He doesn't look at them in the lusty way Maison did yesterday. It's because they are chapped and dry. "I have some back at the plane."

I didn't notice how dehydrated I am, and I don't even want to think about how much water we have left and what it means if we run out. I will take his offer for some without complaint.

"Thank you," I say meekly. He lets go of me, but the heat of his body lingers. He follows me from a distance, undoubtedly looking at his last name on the back of my sweater. I glance back at him, and just as I suspected, his eyes are drawn to my backside. He flicks his dark eyes to meet mine.

Cocky, so incredibly cocky.

Well, this sweater is mine now, so he better get used to seeing me wear it.

I turn on my heels and stomp off toward where the group is gathered by the plane. Twelve of us standing—four lying on the ground, alive but barely moving. We did everything we could to make them comfortable.

As I walk up, I gasp at the sight that lays before me. It's worse than I thought. The scene's full of horror was concealed by the night.

The blood from the victims is still smeared on the ground, along with the shattered glass and the broken and fallen trees. The trees in the heavily wooded area we landed in are lifeless and resemble charcoal skeletons—nothing like the pictures of Alaska I saw online. I'm not sure if these gnarled fir trees helped or hindered the impact of the landing.

I wish I stayed hidden in the forest because I immediately bend over and gag from the smell and the sight of the plane. Maison is leaning against a tree, his arms wrapped around a trembling Serena when I walk up. It seems like they just got out of bed.

He tilts his head and stands upright when he notices me walking up with his brother. Micah pays me little mind and steps toward Naomi, placing his arm around her. I avoid eye contact with both of them and stand next to Nigel and Jade. I hate the feeling that I'm jealous of Maison giving Serena attention after what we went through last night, almost dying in each other's arms. Like I might want his arms around me at night, keeping me warm instead.

I dismiss the thought. This is not the time or place for these feelings. Not when there are a pile of bodies hidden in the trees twenty feet away.

The boys at least moved them during the night, so they are out of sight, but they are there—all thirty-two of them. A heavy presence that looms over us all, poisoning the very air we breathe with their decay.

"We have to bury them," Micah says. Ezra, who's standing next to him, ignores him and can't seem to take his eyes off a shivering Naomi in Micah's arms.

Ezra—I had all but forgotten about him and his complicated relationship with the twins. The fact his girlfriend of just a few months ago is now in the arms of his nemesis. I wonder if any of them know the situation between their parents.

Ezra crosses his muscular arms. "I'm not wasting my energy on that. Let the emergency crew deal with them when they rescue us."

The rescue team we expected hours ago has yet to arrive. My stomach hollows at what that means. They should have been here by now—they should have been able to pinpoint our exact spot and find us within minutes. It's now been at least ten hours.

"I'm more worried about what to do with them." Ezra jerks his chin toward our injured peers, withering on the cold, hard ground.

Thomas steps forward, his muscled body still wearing the suit from last night. He was the unsung hero from what I saw. He single-handedly carried most people off that plane—dead or otherwise. And unfortunately, his suit bears those scars. He speaks for Micah, stepping right in front of him, as if protecting his friend from some unseen enemy on the hockey rink. "We aren't leaving anyone dead above ground to be eaten by animals. And we can't stay here with them like that," he gripes at Ezra. No love between the two of them, either, it seems.

Ezra steps back and squares his angular jaw, obviously not wanting to be that close to the muscular giant, even though they are all supposedly friends.

"I just mean," he says flippantly, "we only have so much energy right now, and we need to get on the plane to get into those crates. I don't want to sleep on the ground again tonight, and I'm hungry."

"I agree with Micah," Maison says. "We can't have the bodies rotting so close."

Micah dips his chin and shares a look with Maison, who's standing on the other side of the circle beside Ezra, holding a trembling Serena. I get it. His arms made me feel safe when they were wrapped around me, too.

James, Nathan, and Ollie tend to the injured by the plane, sitting a few feet away in silence. Jade and Nigel say nothing as well, keeping their heads down.

"We need to split up," Micah finally speaks, gracing us with more words. Our focus should be on tending to the dead and gathering anything salvageable from the plane. There is enough water for a few days, and we can rely on plane snacks until someone comes.

Micah's in charge—no one's said as much, but I can feel it. They are all deferring to him, hanging off his every word. Even Ezra seems to defer to him, although it clearly pains him.

I disagree with the entire approach.

"I'm not even sure we should stay here at all," I mutter.

Silence. The whole group turns to look at me, including Micah, who doesn't seem too thrilled by my interjection.

"Well, that's a stupid thing to say." Naomi shifts beneath Micah's arms, moving her hand up her body and grabbing his wrist. "Where the hell would we go?" She looks up at Micah, who brushes his lips against her cheek. "I'm not going anywhere, Micah." she says in a whiny voice that makes me want to vomit.

She and I haven't spoken yet. I couldn't bring myself to check on her and Serena while the others were wounded and dying. They just sat there, saying they were scared. Well, we are all fucking scared.

"Let her talk, Naomi," Maison cuts in, and Serena and Naomi share a look. "We are all entitled to have an opinion."

Micah merely cocks a brow. "The floor is yours, London."

I swallow a pit in my throat. "This doesn't seem like the best spot. It's hidden, dead, and rocky, and I don't see or hear any evidence of fresh water. I'm not a survival expert, but I think that should be priority number one."

"We have water," Ezra snipes. "The plane is full of it."

"But for how long?" Nigel snaps back. His body is tense and alert beside me, observing everyone and everything as he does so well. "How long will that water last us?"

Micah hangs back and lets this interaction unfold with that little hidden smile teasing his lips. He's enjoying this...

Ezra's beady eyes narrow in on Nigel. "Watch your fucking tone with me, loser."

"You think popularity contests matter right now?" Nigel scoffs and puffs out his chest. "Do you think the wolves care if I'm a loser? They will rip you to shreds just as easily as they will me."

Pure venom comes out of his lips, enough that Ezra flinches before recovering and steps forward, towering over him.

A primal response...

Maison steps forward and places his hand on Ezra's chest. "Not now, man. Keep it together. Everyone needs to keep it together."

Ezra shudders and steps back, giving Nigel a glaring look.

I did indeed hear those wolves howling through my broken sleep. I hoped it was only Jades crying, and the echoes of agony running through my mind as I remembered our fallen classmates take their last breaths. Those were wolves I heard—and other creatures nearby, likely following the scent of blood. Nocturnal beasts seeing our fallen as the perfect dinner makes sleeping a scary thought.

"What are you trying to say, London?" Maison asks as his eyes zone in on me.

I labor a breath, wishing I could have a sip of the water Micah had promised me. "It's been ten hours and no one's come for us. We have to accept the possibility they might not know where we are."

A sob escapes Serena, who barely looks like she can stand. Maison doubles down on his hold on her. She looks as broken as I feel, though I seem to hide it better.

A foreboding sense of nervousness settles over the group as they contemplate what I said, what everyone must be thinking.

Micah leans back on a nearby tree, taking Naomi with him and pulling her into him. Cocky and confident, like he doesn't have a care in the world. "My dad probably has half the country looking for us right now," he says quietly. "He won't stop till we're found. I give it a day."

Must be nice to be so loved.

I bite my tongue at the stupidity of it. My initial assessment of Micah was he is smarter than that. This plane went off course. Flight trackers should have pinpointed exactly where we are. His narrow thinking will get us killed.

Micah is now watching my reaction. I've never been great at hiding my emotions, which is easy because sometimes I barely feel like I have any. His eyes flicker at me. "We will stay here for another day at least, in case they come searching. Then, if no one comes, a couple of us can go explore."

I dart my eyes between the three boys who are seemingly in charge. If Micah, Maison, and Ezra are leading us, then we might as well kill ourselves right now.

"One more fucking day. That's all I'm asking for, London." He says it like I have any decision-making authority over what we do. "Tomorrow you can go explore and see if you can find somewhere better. I'm not going to stop you." He turns his head toward the four kids fighting for their lives. "But keep in mind we can't exactly move them." They are passed out, but somehow barely holding onto their pulses.

"Now, someone help me move these bodies," Micah barks. "I know it's not the most pleasant job, but we can't have them so close by. We have to find a better spot for them. They will only attract wildlife. The rest of you can help get the crates off the plane and we will assess from there."

The vicious wave of nausea nearly cripples me at the thought of moving those bodies, but even worse is spending one more night next to them.

Thomas steps forward. "I'll help you, man."

Ollie and Nathan, who remained quiet, also step forward. "We'll help you, too. It's the right thing to do," Ollie says, nudging Nathan to go with him.

Maison and Ezra head toward the airplane to evaluate how to get access to the valuable resources inside. The rest of the girls, including Jade, trail behind them. Nigel hangs back and doesn't do a damn thing, but I don't have the time to worry about the dark look in his eye.

I walk over and sit next to James to check how he's doing. Relief washes over me to see his eyes bright, and the fact he's sitting up. Despite his wounded state, he's still tending to the four people gravely injured.

Micah walks over and towers over me, and I glare up at him as the sun behind him nearly blinds me. I'm ready to give him a flippant response, but he hands both me and James a bottle of water instead.

"Here you go, sweetheart." The sharp edge in his voice slices deeper than the rocks I slept on last night. "Drink this sparingly. It's all you get for now."

He slips away to join Thomas and the others waiting for him. I will give him a pass on his clear pissy mood, given the job he is about to do, and try my hardest not to stare at his muscular backside that leaves little to the imagination in those sweatpants.

I check on the rest of the injured; Jess, Matthew, Madison, and Colton—the only ones left breathing, but unconscious. They are all moaning, but there is no visible blood on them. Their wounds are from internal bleeding or head injuries. For a couple of them, all I can hope for is a quick death.

"How are they?" I ask James, who's tending to Madison, who woke up briefly while we were all arguing. His facial expression tells me everything I need to know. They are barely holding on, and I'd be surprised if they lasted a day.

"How are you doing?" I lean down and check on his wound. While exploring the cockpit, Micah found the first aid kits, along with the pilots and flight attendant, their heads hanging in the most unnatural way. At least, that's what Nigel told me earlier, which explains Micah's sullen mood. Micah spared a bandage for James because he has a slighter higher chance of living than the rest of them.

James swallows and gives me a strained smile. "I'm fine. Like I keep telling everyone, it's just a scratch." The sweat on his forehead is building beneath his blonde shaggy bangs, and I worry about infection. He chugs his entire water bottle in one gulp and slumps forward. It's up to him to hold on, but I admire his resolve. His body is strong—all the training he's done for hockey will help him.

I sit next to him and take a small sip of my water, staring up at the fluffy clouds as a breath catches in my throat.

Where the hell are we? And when are you coming for us?

Nothing but a few small, scattered clouds and a blazing sun shines down on burnt skeletal trees that pepper the forest. Thick, gross, ugly woods and slimy rocks, and the faint smell of acid that seeps out of the nearby plane. Alaska isn't beautiful. The landscape we landed on is barren and charred, like a fire blazed through here once, and even mother nature has abandoned it.

Every second that ticks by without the sound of a helicopter gives me less hope that anyone is coming for us. I shift over to Madison as incomprehensible moans come out of her. I offer her all I have—my soft hands—as I rub her forehead and tell her it's going to be alright, even though I know it won't be. It's what I would want to hear if I were dying.

I drown out the banging noises Ezra and Maison are making as they pull out what they can from below the airplane. The other group's progress is unbearable to me... all those dead bodies. I just hope they can find a prettier place to rest them.

They deserve better.

Hunger burns my stomach as James and I sit quietly next to Madison, and I place her head on my lap. Last time I ate was in New Ocean nearly twenty-four hours ago. If Micah has food, he's not offered any to me, or anyone, for that matter. I try to recall how long the human body can go without food. Several weeks, which is probably why Micah hasn't let anyone have anything. But this little twinge of hunger could turn into something much more menacing, and soon.

The moment Madison stopped shaking and died is un-known to me. If there was a death rattle, I didn't catch it as I was lost in my own dark thoughts.

It's when she stops withering, I think to slide my hand to her neck to check her pulse.

There is none.

She is gone.

A cry escapes my lips, and I lean into James as tears flow out of me. I close her open eyelids as her eyes stare right into me. I didn't know her, no personal connection to her, but still, I'm glad she didn't die alone. I consider telling the others, but don't bother.

Instead, I rest my head on James's shoulder and cry, even though he's barely awake himself. For the first time since landing, I let out all my emotions. I cannot spend more time in this place than I need to—

This graveyard.

I will be leaving as soon as I can. I'll find out what we are dealing with, and I'll go alone for all I care.

CHAPTER EIGHT

Day Two

We lost Madison and Matthew last night to the mass grave, which brings our death toll to thirty-four. Colton, Jess, and James are still fighting for their lives. I can't see how they will survive, although we are doing our best to make them comfortable. At least James is holding strong. Micah, Thomas, Ollie, and Nathan came back exhausted and utterly defeated. Micah vanished into the forest and hasn't come back. Maison doesn't seem too worried about him and says he will come back when he's ready.

We have supplies on this island. The crates were fire resistant, and once we figured out how to open them, we found them full of items we can use to keep us alive. Unfortunately, even though they were fire resistant, we still lost five crates to the explosion—the five at the front and back were intact. I documented what we have, and Maison says we aren't allowed to touch anything till Micah gets back. Although he snuck us some bottled water and food from the airplane, just a small bag of pretzels. I'm curious about when Micah was declared the king of the jungle, because I don't remember taking part in any voting process.

Last night was the closet to hell I've experienced. Long, grueling, and cold reminding me how far north we are. Even though the day's are still warm, the nights are bone chillingly cold. I thought I was going to die, at one point. I lost all feeling in my fingers and toes. Nigel and Jade found a spot together, and since Micah never came back, Naomi *cuddled up to Ezra, which I thought was interesting. Maison watched me most of the night after they got the supplies off the plane, but I avoided eye contact with him. I found Ezra and Naomi rooting through my stuff when they found my luggage. They pulled out a pair of my lacy underwear and chuckled between themselves. I snatched it from their hands and told them to fuck off, and they told me to relax—that they were just taking inventory. I didn't speak to anyone for the rest of the day. I slept in the forest alone a few feet away. It was the worst night of my life.*

Supply list:

Crate one: fresh fruits and vegetables, canned goods, pasta, lard.

Crate two: More food and wellness items. Tampons, toothpaste, shampoo, soaps.

Crate three: Fuel.

Crate four: Medical Supplies—first aid kit, pharmaceuticals.

Crate five: Blankets, wire, flashlights, two knives—a large hunting knife, a Swiss army knife—one tarp, a water purifier, a fire starter, flares, a sharpening stone.

With the resources we have, we should survive out here for a while. However, I must remind myself of the secrets these people keep, and the reason I embarked on this journey to begin with. No one here is truly trustworthy, almost like everyone is harboring some sort of secret, and I don't know what they are capable of.

"I'm coming with you," Maison declares, rummaging through the clothes and food piled in front of us. I've just informed Micah of my intention to go exploring, although this shouldn't come as a surprise. What shocks me is that no one besides Maison wants to. I find it hard to believe anyone desires to stay here.

Maison arches a brow at Micah, who standing next to him, as if daring him to object as he repeats, "I'm going with her."

I approached them as they were huddled around the supplies, while Thomas, as usual, stands right next to Micah with Ezra close by. Micah was making a mental checklist of what's available to us. Now that we have resources, I can't stay here for one more minute. There has to be somewhere better.

Maison looks at his brother, waiting for a response, as if he needs his permission to leave. Micah came back a few hours ago, hardly saying a word. The dark gleam in his eye had everyone avoiding him, even Maison, although we are a quiet group today, lost in our own thoughts.

Micah nods and shifts his focus to me, then reverts to Maison. "Fine. You're probably the only one I trust out there, anyway. I think someone else should go, too."

Maison shakes his head. "It's easier if it's just the two of us. Any more will slow us down."

I stand quietly and watch as they interact without even asking for my opinion, though I couldn't care less who comes with me. I need to get away from this airplane and the stench we can't seem to get rid of. I know the bodies aren't too far away, and one more second here might destroy me.

Micah flexes his jaw as Jade and Nigel and the others join us, catching on that something is going on. Serena objects when she finds out Maison's leaving her, and I can't help the little feeling of gratification that he wants to come with me.

Asking no one, Nigel walks up and grabs an apple—it's only one of twelve as part of the fresh produce container.

"Hey." Ezra lunges at him when he notices what Nigel is doing. "You can't just steal fucking food. If I don't get any, you don't fucking get any."

Nigel takes a juicy bite and smiles at him, and I salivate, watching him eat it. Nigel looks the most disheveled out of everyone, his usual thick, sticky hair limp around his sunken eyes and face. Ezra jolts forward but Maison is there, holding his rabid dog back from ripping the shit out of Nigel.

Nigel merely laughs, then saunters off to the woods where he's been hiding.

Micah looks around the group. "This food needs to last us until we're found. Otherwise, we need to go hunting, and I don't think any of you know how to fucking do that."

Maison looks at his brother. "People are hungry, dude."

Micah scoffs and gestures toward the barren woods. "There's plenty of food out here. I saw three muskrats this morning."

The thought makes me gag, especially since he's serious.

"Everyone better learn how to trap and skin a rabbit then," Micah says to no one in particular, "because I'm not wasting this fucking food yet."

Ezra jumps up and gets in Micah's face, and this time, Maison doesn't stop him. "I'm hungry, Micah. Last I checked, you don't own anything, and you don't tell me what to do."

Micah flexes his jaw and stands just a little taller, muscles rippling over every inch of his body. I cower down and watch, far enough away from the two giant hockey players. Tension is coiled up in Micah's body to the point it looks like he's about to burst, but the hatred... the hatred is coming from Ezra.

A cold chill runs through me, watching the two of them, knowing the things I know about their past.

Micah doesn't have to move, he doesn't even flinch because Thomas stands right in front of him. Thomas is a good inch taller and fifty pounds bigger than them both. "Back off, Ezra. What are you going to do? Hit him?"

Ezra's angular face remains fierce, but he says nothing. The whole group is silent—watching, waiting while the two alphas battle it out for their little slice of power. One of which has a massive bodyguard with blind loyalty to him, while the other has his enemy's twin standing behind him. None of it is sensible to me.

Naomi steps forward. "You guys, cut it out. Quit fighting with each other. It won't solve anything right now."

The first words of intelligence I've heard from her.

Ezra shoots her a look, his face softening, his feelings for her clearly etched on his face. He looks at Maison. "I'm already sick of his shit. Keep Micah in check, Maison."

Naomi hesitates for a moment, looking at Micah before she grabs Ezra's arm, her fingers twirling around his bicep. "Come on Ezra, let's go talk."

Ezra smirks at Micah while Naomi leads him into the woods. "Maybe next time your bodyguard won't be here to save you," he spits back at him.

If Micah cares or feels at all threatened, he doesn't show it. Instead, he ignores them and walks over to the food container, grabbing two more apples along with a couple bags of pretzels we salvaged from the plane.

He hands them to Maison. "Ration this because it's all you get. Walk exactly two hours one way and two hours back. If I were you, I'd head due west, and make sure you leave a trail," Micah says to Maison as if I'm invisible. "Your primary goal is to find fresh water."

Maison's throat bobs and he stares at his brother. "Take it down a notch, Micah. Do your breathing exercises and go for a walk."

Maison's challenging him, and it's the first time I've seen him do that—except for when he intercepted Micah's bullying of me on the airplane. Challenging him or... calming him. Micah's fingers are clenched the same way they were when he cornered me.

Blind rage.

Micah nods. "Yeah, man. I know." For a moment, he looks at me, as if seeking my reaction to his outburst.

Since I packed horribly for Alaska, I root through the luggage we salvaged from the wreckage. I find a better pair of shoes and some leggings, and we pack one blanket each, sweaters, and some food.

Jade comes to my side. I've barely spoken to her or anyone since we landed. Her eyes are red and bloodshot, and her face is sunken and gray—not her usual glow—but still, she seems better. At least she's stopped crying.

She wraps her arms around me. "Be careful out there, okay?" I slide my hand around her, relieved I have at least one friend here that seems to care. I'm not sure what Maison's motivations are yet.

I sweep the group to see if I can find Nigel. He's hidden among the trees, looking out at everyone. I jerk my head in his direction. "Is he going to be okay? He's not said much."

A dark hint splashes in her eyes, and her face tightens with worry. "He'll be okay, I think. He just seems to shut down sometimes. I'm staying with him, trying to get him to talk more."

We're all dealing with this the best we can, and I'm keeping with my usual MO to run away. Nigel is hiding in the shadows of the trees as Jade rejoins the group, and I catch his gaze. The dark look in his eye is worse than anyone else's here.

I keep focused on the horizon, beyond the mist, and the thick layer of broken trees and dead foliage. I imagine what is out there as I center my attention on a tiny green plant peeking through some flat, gray-yellow-speckled rocks.

Life—an essence of it.

I'm still alive.

I feel a heavy presence behind me, and I turn to face them. Both twins look down on me after they finish discussing our plans. I don't know who is who—

"Are you ready for this?" Maison asks, stepping forward. His face still holds his normally calm demeanor.

A mix of excitement and fear ripples through me as I look eastward. "I'm ready, but I think we should go that way." I point in the opposite direction from where Micah suggested.

Micah narrows his brows. "Why do you think that?"

Always questioning me.

I fold my arms. "I know we flew over water. I don't know what's east of us. If we walk and find water, chances are, we are on an island. And I believe that's something we should know, don't you?"

He arches a brow, and I can't tell if my response impresses or annoys him.

I flash a fake smile at him, the kind where I don't show my teeth.

Micah ignores me and faces his brother, with not even a hint of emotion. His eyes are distant and dead—deadly. "Leave a trail. If you're not back in four hours, I'll come find you."

Maison nods. "Yeah, I know the drill." He lifts his brows. "Are you going to be okay, man?"

Micah silently broods without answering.

Something's missing between them—that twin chemistry bond I noticed earlier. Yet... an energy so deep and strong, a bond hidden and bubbling beneath the surface. So much is behind those words, it has me frozen as I watch them. Their tension is so thick and obvious, I don't know which one to look at.

Was it always like this? I have spent so little time with them, let alone together.

Maison laughs, unaffected by Micah's mood. "Same asshole, as always. Glad this place hasn't changed you, Micah."

Micah placed thirty-four bodies in their final resting place yesterday. How could that not change somebody? All four of them who tackled that job look like they've seen a ghost.

Micah turns and stalks off toward the plane and the small fire he made earlier. He sits on a dead log, grabs a sharp knife he found in the supplies, and starts cutting the blade off his hockey stick. He angles the blade and slices the stick to a pointed tip.

He's making a spear, I realize, as he blows the dust off and keeping laser-focused, ignoring us and everyone around him.

A complete predator. Why does he need a weapon like that when he's holding a knife?

A soft hand brushes my back as Maison watches me watching him. His face is serious instead of his usual lopsided grin.

I force a half smile, shift my backpack over my shoulders, and start walking ahead of him. It's the most he's getting from me right now. I focus on the rocky ground as I carefully place each foot in front of one another. The crisp terrain slips downward into a valley, and hopefully, closer to water. Maison steps in beside me as we push our way through the slippery ground still sparkling from the morning dew. Mossy rocks, sparse trees, and thick black brush snag our pants. Perhaps one day soon this place will be full of life, absorbing our fallen to create the circle of life. One day, but today is not that day.

The cloudless sky overhead is unforgiving and sweat beads on my forehead as the low sun hits us. The rays up north are strong during the day, at least right now, given it's still summer and I'm dressed in layers. I gather my dark hair into a loose braid that falls over my shoulder, providing some relief from the heat. I keep the rest of my body covered to avoid getting too hot—also because of the black flies I have to swat so they don't steal pieces of my flesh. I also want to hide the mud and blood caked on my skin. Maison doesn't need to see that. As soon as I find water, I am scrubbing myself down from head to toe with the soap I stole from the wellness supplies.

As we walk, it doesn't take long for me to trip on a flat rock, and Maison slides his hand over mine to steady me. I snatch it back.

"You don't have to take care of me, Maison," I snip and immediately regret the harshness of my words as a flash of hurt crosses his eyes.

He tilts his head, his messy hair jostled in the perfect way, his face soft as usual. "Come on, London," he says. "Don't be like that."

Like what, exactly? He doesn't know how I usually act, what makes me tick, or anything about me. I have revealed little about myself to him.

I keep walking, but still feel the tingle from his touch and crave more of it. I should be grateful it was Maison who came with me. Out of everyone, he is the one I would have chosen. I fell asleep the past two nights dreaming of his arms, but they were around Serena instead.

Pure, innocent, pretty Serena, trembling in his arms with fear, and it makes me wonder why he's not with her? Is there a connection to Olivia?

Yup, I'm definitely jealous. The emotion is winding its way through my insides, tightening the muscles in my belly. It's sickening, and I shouldn't be feeling it... It's wrong that I'm so into Maison.

"Did you ever camp as a kid?" he asks out of nowhere, breaking the uncomfortable silence between us.

I step on a root and trip over it, almost falling into a dark narrow hole etched in the rock, splitting it into two. He's there in an instant, catching me and steadying me with his arms. "Once or twice," I say, gripping his arm. I blow out a breath, stepping over it. "I don't particularly like the woods, and it's not something my mom and I did back in Portland." I shudder at not being able to see the bottom of what I almost fell into. I could have easily just plummeted to my death if it weren't for Maison.

He keeps his arm around me, and I let him as we walk over a rough patch of slippery terrain with more black holes. I don't feel like breaking my leg or dying today, so I hold on to him.

We keep steadying ourselves forward as he continues, "Micah and I used to camp every chance we could... ice fishing, hunting, camping, all of it."

Well, that explains their comfort level with being out here, but still, how could he wander these woods with holes in the ground that could suck him down with one false step? I bristle at the sound of his name, and it doesn't go unnoticed. Micah's behavior is confusing and invasive.

"Look," he says, "I know Micah can be harsh, but we need him out here. He knows more about survival than any of us. He will be the one to keep us alive if no one ends up coming. He's experienced out here. He knows how to hunt, fish, trap, and how to survive. He grew up in the wild. He really took to it when we were younger."

Micah had spent the entire night alone in the woods... I'm not even sure he slept.

I tilt my head. "And you didn't?"

A definitive pause. "Not like he did."

My stomach clenches and hunger pains my belly at Maison's words. The acknowledgment that we are in danger and the possibility we won't be found... He senses my hesitation, my fear. "We'll be okay, London. Someone will come for us."

He sounds like me, telling Madison words of comfort right before she died in my arms yesterday.

I stop and face him. "Why did you come with me, Maison?"

He frowns. "I couldn't let you come out here alone."

I cock a brow. "Micah could have since he's so adept at the wilderness. Why you?"

"Maybe I like you, London," he says with a coy smile and cocks a brow. "Is it so bad I wanted to get you alone?"

I draw in a long breath. Those were the same words Chris said to me when he cornered me after a late-night rehearsal, when he slid his fingers along my back, tickling the curves of my body.

I like you, London, he had told me. He was waiting for a chance with me. He planned it, so no one else was around when he kissed me. He could have done more than kiss me if he wanted to...

I shudder hearing those words again and the shooting thrill I got from it because it was so wrong. My obsession with my teacher came after that kiss, never having received that type of attention before. The same sensation pushes through me now, knowing how dangerous these twins truly are.

Deadly amounts of drugs, those bruises on Olivia, half truths, and buried secrets.

"Not good enough," I breathe out. "I've given you no reason to like me, and I'm not even your type. Maison, we're strangers, and you have a girl back there that really wants your attention.

His forehead creases. "I told you, Serena is not my girlfriend. I make sure she's taken care of, but not like that." He cocks his head. "And not my type? What do you think my type is?"

I shake my head. "I know what kind of guy you are, Maison, so you will not convince me otherwise. I've heard the stories."

His dark eyes flash, pupils flare. "*Stories*, London. You know nothing about me or Micah, or any sort of truth. All you've heard is bullshit from people who like to talk too much and write shit about people."

I swallow hard and face him. What does he know about my level of intelligence? "So tell me then, true or false, is there a dead girlfriend?" I pause and wait for him to accept my bait. I need to handle this situation carefully since I know more truth than he is aware of.

"Truth."

I flip my eyes to meet his, my heart racing at this game we are about to play. His face is hard now, like I imagine Micah's would be if I was questioning him. Maison's teeth grind into his bottom lip, waiting and daring me to ask him... like he's getting off on it.

"Was she with Micah the night she died?"

"Truth."

My eyebrows rise along with my pulse.

"Was she with Micah when she died?" A slightly different question.

A pause and he doesn't blink. I already know the answers to all these questions—they are public knowledge. What I am trying to gage is his reaction when I ask him.

"Truth."

Now for the real questions.

I hesitate for only a moment. "Do you and Micah share girlfriends?"

He flexes his jaw, the flare in his eyes hard to ignore. I narrow my eyes, my stomach flipping at the fire flickering in his pupils. I swat a large fly buzzing around me, irritating me beyond belief. I want to ask which one of them hurt her, if it was him who physically hurt Olivia. Mentally, she was obviously a fucking mess, but those bruises...

He moves in closer to me. My breath is heavy, and he leans in and whispers in my ear, "No more questions till you give me something in return, London King. And I told you earlier, I will not answer questions about Micah."

My breath catches and heat thrills down my spine. He moves ahead with grace and ease, as if he didn't just render me speechless. I stand with my mouth gaping open, the whispers of his breath still lingering in my ear.

It was Micah; it had to have been. Maison's hands are too gentle. I felt them on the plane, intimately.

The story is clear to me now. Micah physically hurt Olivia, then lied about it, and now she's dead. Pretty fucking simple.

But what was Maison's part in all of it? Why is he protecting his brother? My entire body is screaming at me that there is more to this story, a level of complexity I don't quite understand.

We walk in utter silence for the next half hour, and I stomp ahead of him despite my swollen feet. I'm mad he wouldn't continue answering my questions, but truthfully, I'm more mad at myself for being so bold with him.

Why would he trust a girl he barely knows with a secret that tore him apart from his twin?

He doesn't attempt to talk, and every few minutes he stops and slips a sock or an article of clothing from his pack on a tree to leave our trail. I pick up my pace and pass him while his footsteps echo behind me. We finally get away from the tundra death patch and into a heavily forested area, green and lush, with just a hint of red and yellow foliage and long grass, reminding me of the season we are heading into. It's wetter, full of life—birds, insects, colorful shrubs, and trees.

After a few minutes, sweat drips down my back. My head pounds from the heat, so I stop and pull off my backpack and sweater. I pause briefly and notice Maison is not behind me as the thick brush and large pine trees take form around me.

"Maison?" I call out.

Nothing but whistling wind and the rustle of leaves. For the first time since we landed, I can finally breathe, as if I haven't had any oxygen since we crashed. The fresh pine in the air and a cool fresh breeze feels like heaven. Forgetting about Maison for a moment, I pull out a pair of shorts I brought with me and slip off my sweats, letting them fall to the ground, stepping out of them one leg at a time. I'm completely exposed now, just my black ribbed tank top and lace panties Naomi and Ezra were teasing me about earlier.

A snap of a twig alerts me, and I spin around and face Maison, who is watching me change. He quickly darts his gaze when I catch him, but I don't miss the gleam in his eyes, or the bite of his lip, or the half smile on his adorable face. My heart flutters and heat pools in my belly at the thought of him looking at me.

I turn from him, bend over slowly, and slip on my shorts. I barely have them pulled up when his hands wrap around my waist, and his fingers find the little sliver of bare skin there.

His thumb rests on my hipbone, and he leans into me from behind. "Why are you teasing me, London?" he whispers and rests his lips on my neck.

I blow out a breath as he digs his fingers in, wiping his thumb across my skin. I close my eyes and let his touch soften me like it did on the airplane. Remembering how safe he made me feel then, and how safe he makes me feel now. The electricity of his lips makes me squirm, and his hands feel warm and inviting.

Then I remember the silent promise I made to myself not to fall for him, how his hands roamed so freely over Naomi during English class, and those same hands all over Serena the past couple of days. I think about all the people who lost their lives and how wrong it is to do what I desperately want to do. I grab his hands and remove them. He's hiding something—Maison Matei is not who he seems. "You can't touch me like that, Maison."

He twists me around, our faces only inches apart. My body locks into place when it seems he is going to kiss me, but instead, he leans his forehead against mine.

He rests his hands on my hips. "Why are you so hardened? Who hurt you so badly that you had to put a shell over yourself?"

I close my eyes, the heaviness of everything weighing in on me.

"You are so beautiful, London," he whispers, and my heart clenches as his fingertips tighten. "And despite what you may have heard or think, I'm one of the good ones."

"They're good, aren't they?" Nigel's words repeat in my head.

His talent is undeniable. He has me yearning for his lips just by saying all the right things—things that would make any girl melt. If Maison's this good, I can only imagine how Micah must be like. The person I am *not* supposed to mention, who seems to excel at everything.

I look up at him. "Maison... I have blood and guts caked onto my skin. We can't do this right now." I feel it cracked all over my arms and wrists, soaked right into my stomach, as if marking itself onto me for eternity.

He smiles that lopsided grin. "Later, then?" A seagull flies by, squawking in my ears. Maison's still holding me. I should push him off me, but I don't—I have no energy to. Then it dawns on me...

A seagull!

My head whips around.

"Maison, that was a seagull."

"Yeah, so?" he murmurs, not catching on. His focus is entirely on me.

I nudge him. "They rarely fly inland."

His eyes light up, and he grabs my hand. "Let's go."

We hurry forward with a renewed sense of energy. I'd give up one of my kidneys if it means we find water. To be able to wash myself...

After a few minutes, the tree line breaks, and a thin shimmering line of blue emerges in front of us. And the smell—the fresh breeze from earlier. So familiar, I hadn't clued in to how close to water we must be. A small rocky beach sprawls ahead, surrounded by large pine trees and a speckled escarpment with various blends of earthy tones. It's a pretty sight, like a private oasis made just for us.

I breathe a sigh of relief, followed by dread that pits in my stomach.

Just as I suspected, water is on both sides of us, with vast, snow-tipped mountains hovering in the distance and a series of rocky islands with fir trees lining the shores as far as the eye can see. A bald eagle cuts in the sky over us.

The vastness of it, the wilderness. My stomach hollows out and my blood runs cold. I'd think it's pretty if it wasn't so terrifying, showing how insignificant we actually are.

The islands all have icy, deep blue water and rocky, unforgiving shores, which means we're probably stuck on an island in the middle of what looks like a fresh-water lake. With that in mind, I have no idea how there are wolves that howl in the night.

Maison steps beside me and I watch him take it in the sight, his eyes flickering all over. "Jesus fuck, look at that," he whispers.

We're not in New Ocean anymore. I'm not even positive we're in Alaska, however, we are definitely in the Arctic.

With a deep breath, I grasp Maison's hand, my chest tightening as I feel the grip of panic take over. "Where are we, Maison? Where did we land?"

He moves his hand around my waist and pulls me in, but not in the sexual way he did earlier—he's scared, too.

The wind tousles his shaggy brown hair, while the earth encloses us like a painting we don't fit in. "Stay here. I want to look around," he whispers. His voice seems out-of-place while a soft wind rustles the trees and the lapping water hits the rocky shores.

He makes his way down a short steep hill, arching his head to both sides as if looking for any lurking, silent enemies. He looks up at me and waves me over.

Once I arrive beside him, he dips down and sticks his hand in the water. "It's fresh. While it's not the ocean, it will be full of fish. Micah will be happy when he sees this. It's a good place to camp, while not too far from the airplane."

The water is so clear, the mountains, rocks, and trees evenly reflect over it. Clear, calm, and inviting.

"The rocks will help shelter us, too," he adds. The entire shoreline is filled with boulders and round stones, with lots of crevices to hide in should we need to.

Crouching, I feel an icy chill as my hand touches the water. These are glacier-fed waters, and I can imagine it frozen and hidden under a thick layer of snow in the winter. A sight I hope I don't have to see.

Maison's eyes are tight as he looks to the horizon with a distant expression.

I nudge him. "Should we go back and tell the others?"

He looks around, then back at me, taking me from head to toe. "We should spend the night here. You look exhausted." I shudder at what I must look like.

I shake my head. "Won't Micah be pissed? He told us to come directly back."

He shrugs. "Yeah, he'll be pissed, but we've been gone for hours. It will take at least that long to find our way back, if not longer. I'd rather spend the night here than in the woods. I can make a fire, so we'll be warm under the stars. We will head back at first light, or who knows, maybe they will come to us."

Warmth, in this context, is rather subjective as I shiver from the cool breeze hinting off the water.

I sit on the beach, resting my legs out in front of me. My entire body aches, every bone, every fibre, every muscle shaking. Maison sits beside me, stretching his legs out next to mine.

I look over at him. I feel like a bag of shit, and of course, he's smiling. He's always smiling.

"What are we supposed to do now?" I ask him. It's still light outside, and dusk won't come for a few hours yet.

He surveys me and silently gets up and takes off his shirt and sweatpants. My face heats as he strips down to his boxers, effortlessly flexing his hard-earned muscles as he moves. His olive skin is still tanned from summer, glimmering with a light layer of sweat. His boxers hang just below his waist, and his hair is tussled above his eyes, which meet mine before he smiles. I can't look away, and he knows it.

Without saying a word, he runs toward the glass-like water, diving right into the shoreline until only his head bobs up and down. The rock cliffs protect this part of the cove from the larger body of water in front of us.

He looks happy, almost childlike, as he swims in one spot. The sun shines down on him as his eyes find me sitting, watching him. The water really does look inviting, especially with him in it. If I didn't know his past or reputation, I'd think he really was a good one, but I can't fall for him—even if he's trying to make it impossible for me to ignore him.

He waves me in. "Come in, London. I won't look."

I shake my head and grab my bag with my soap and shampoo. My skin tingles at the thought of being able to wash and clean myself. To finally get rid of the remnants of the plane crash off me. I stride away from Maison to a different part of the lake.

No way I'm getting naked with him quite yet.

⤙⤚

"Wake up, London."

Wake up. Wake up. Wake up.

The fire is so hot, it's searing my skull, melting my retinas so badly as the smoke takes its death hold on my lungs. I watch in horror as the bodies of my classmates burn and bubble around me. Maison's arms grip me hard, his spicy scent the only source of comfort. But as I behold him, the smile on his face turns nothing short of predatory. The inside of the airplane erupts in flames, and I grasp onto him, terror-stricken, as the plane screeches and shakes as we plummet to the ground. Maison pushes me away from him and rises, leaving an empty cold hole beside me. With a mocking and menacing stare, he walks backward into the flames and vanishes into the darkness, rendering me in shock. It's then I realize it's not Maison I'm looking at, but Micah's devilish features taunting me. Laughing at me as my skin ignites and the flames catch hold of my clothes and hair, and it burns every inch of me. Terror rushes through me as I choke on the ash and desperately try, but unable to, scream.

"London, wake up."

Fire.

I blow out a breath and inhale a mouthful of smoke. I need to remember it's just a campfire and Maison's arms are wrapped around me, and Micah is not trying to kill me. I'm feeling heated, I realize, and the past two nights have been anything but warm, so my body isn't used to it.

My eyes shoot open, the sharp edges of the earth poking through the soft blanket beneath me. It's dark, pitch-black beyond the flames, but as I glance to the sky, a few stars glitter through a thin veil of clouds that reflect off the nearby moon.

I'm still shaking as I come to my senses, and Maison wraps his entire body around me, protecting me from whatever horrors are out there. "Hey, hey, hey, it's just a dream." His voice is soothing, and he brings me back from whatever ugly place my mind went to. My face is covered in sweat, and I am doing my best not to fall completely into him. "You had a nightmare, London," he breathes. "Whatever you just saw isn't real."

I rest my head on his arm, and my heart rages while every nerve on my skin fires up, the pit in my stomach growing. I lay silently beside him, trembling as my terror is replaced by something worse... dread. This is real, very real, and that wasn't merely a dream, it was a memory. A vivid and actual recollection.

"Are you okay?" I feel my abs tense as he whispers, and it's all I can do to not scream like I wanted to in my dream. I manage a swallow, but my throat and lips are as dry as the ash blowing into my face.

"Yeah," I say hesitantly, my voice cracking slightly.

He tightens his hold, his lips grazing my cheek as he reaches over me and passes me a bottle of water. "Take a big gulp of this," he tells me, and I listen to him finishing the rest of it, savoring every drop.

"What time is it?" I ask, looking around, my eyes not yet adjusted to what lays beyond the flame. We fell asleep relatively fast once he got the fire going, which was after I bathed and scrubbed my skin for nearly an hour in the icy lake. I stayed in so long, my skin turned blue. Then I got dressed, and we nibbled on pretzels, which eased the hunger pains enough for me to pass out on the little bed Maison made for us.

His thumb wipes a bead of sweat from my nose. "It's almost morning, I think."

The flames are blazing and beautiful. He must have stayed up all night to keep this fire going.

"You didn't sleep?" I ask, peering up at him.

"No, but that's okay. I wanted to make sure you slept. You've been out a while."

It's the first time I've slept—truly slept since being here. I turn to face him, and he's lying on his side, propping his head up with his hand, watching me, calm and relaxed. He has the same smoldering look as yesterday, and I don't see a monster when I look at him. I don't see what Nigel tells me he is—a guy who tormented a girl and *shared* her. Then again, I'm not the best judge of character. Chris had me entangled in his games for months.

"Is it time to go back?" I ask him, although I hope he says no because I never want to return to that awful place, not for the rest of my life for any reason. I'm done with the airplane, its death stench, and the horrible memories that are still so fresh in my mind. They can rescue us just as easily here; it's not like we traveled that far.

"Yeah, we should," Maison says and my stomach twists. "Micah's probably freaking out that we've been gone so long, but I want to show you something first."

I tilt my head, but his eyes just glimmer in the firelight till he jerks them upward. I follow his gaze and let out a surprised gasp. The clouds have parted and sheets of green and pink dart through the sky. I scramble to sit up to get a better look away from the dancing flame. I've never seen the northern lights before, and never imagined they'd be so bright, so intense. They dance as if singing a silent song—a rhythm, a beat, a pulse of nature. They twist, twirl, stretch, and curve, completely mesmerizing me into stillness and peace I never thought would be possible again. I fall back into Maison's warmth and stare out at them.

"They're beautiful," I whisper, even though beautiful is hardly the word to describe them. They leave me breathless, and I can't help but grin as I'm swallowed up by them.

His fingers nudge the edge of my sweater—his sweater. "I love seeing you smile," he says, watching me instead of the celestial show above us. "We're alive, London. Remember moments like this to remind yourself of that. We survived that plane crash, and we will survive this island. You'll be back to writing your news stories in no time." He chuckles.

He lays his head down to join me and his hold is unwavering as his lips graze my neck.

I flinch as he tugs on the edge of my sweatpants and moves my hair to the side of my face. A scent must be radiating out of me—a primal response to this situation, as his fingers tease the fabric of my shirt. My body bursts with the need to release, for his touch, and to feel good in this moment with the hottest guy I've ever cuddled with like this. The fact he could be dangerous only causes a clench inside me in places it really shouldn't.

His lips begin to suck, his tongue lapping up my neck so softly, I take a minute to realize what he's doing or that he's kissing me.

"Maison," I whisper as the feel of his kisses travel across my entire body. It takes every ounce of control to say his name without trembling while he seems so languid beside me. He presses his hand to my heart and covers the swells of my breast, which seem to have tightened in the anticipation of being touched. It's a painful sensation that brings me nothing but euphoria, and my pulse is beating out of control.

He stops his soft tongue strokes. "Why is your little heart racing so badly, baby? Do I scare you?"

My hands edge toward his hair, desperate to pull it and run my fingers through it. He smells like the shampoo from our bath yesterday—a pleasant scent since my nose is still scarred with phantom decay. My voice comes out unsteady. "Why did you pretend to be Micah in English class the other day? How often do you do that?"

He flinches. "I thought we weren't talking about Micah?" I seem to have struck a nerve, especially since with every mention of Micah, Maison stiffens and hardens.

"I think under the circumstances, it's a fair question," I say pointedly.

He pulls his lips from my neck, leaving a whisper of cold air that tingles against the wetness he left there. "It's something we do sometimes. It's a twin thing. We've been doing it as long as I can remember."

I pull back and look at him, narrowing my brows and letting my hair fall over my face. "Micah hates me. And I don't like the thought of you hating me, even if you're just pretending."

"Micah doesn't hate you, London. He's testing you, finding out what you're made of. And I won't do that again, not with you."

He rests his hands on my hips, placing his head down. His lips are far away from my neck now. "Why does it always seem like it pains him to look at me?" I ask him, ignoring the fact he doesn't want to talk about his brother. "It's like he can't stand the sight of me, and I'm not sure what I ever did to him?"

My question triggers something, a change in him as his body heats, the pressure of his finger shifts, his breath shallows.

He reaches and pulls my hair back, grazing my skin—that wet spot—with his knuckles. "He hates everyone right now; it's not just you. And if Micah doesn't like you, then that just means I get to keep you for myself," he jokes.

"Jesus, Maison." I realize he's kidding, but still... if there is even a margin of truth to those words. I see the way Micah is with Naomi—the way she sits on his lap and he looks at her like a piece of meat. The malice that burns from his eyes when he looks at everyone.

Maison squeezes me. "He treats you like that because you remind him of her."

My body stills, a mix of fear and excitement pulsing through me, slithering over every pore. This is not a joke; he's being serious. He's not spoken about Olivia with me yet; he hasn't even breathed her name or acknowledged her existence beyond my prodding questions earlier.

She's the reason I'm here, stuck on this godforsaken island.

I pause for a second before answering, trying to gage the look in his eye. The light from the sky dancing within them.

Micah loved her.

Maison did, too.

"Do I look like her or something?"

I know exactly what she looks like, and I'm nothing like her. In fact, we couldn't be any more different in our physical appearance. I'm not Micah's type, so it's another reason then.

He snaps back from wherever his mind just went. He dances his fingers over my stomach, up to my beating heart. "I don't want to talk about Micah," he whispers, placing his lips back where I want them.

I shiver as the fire begins to die out. "I am scared beyond belief, Maison. And I'm already tired of being here, and cold."

My nipples are so chilled right now, like pebbles, rock hard against my shirt. He runs his hand down my stomach and up my sweater, touching my bare skin. I tense as he pulls it up. His heartbeat matches my own, but for different reasons. "I want to see that lace, baby," he murmurs, his mouth still latched on the sensitive skin beneath my ear. "Please let me."

I should... I secretly wore it for him. His voice is so desperate, like seeing this lace will make it all better and make his pain disappear.

Such a simple request.

He doesn't take his eyes off mine until I nod. He chews on his bottom lip, and I can't control the slickness between my thighs any longer as his fingers trace the hipbone he likes to touch so much. Then, he slips them lower so he can take a peek at the black lace below them.

He bites at his lip. "Now this," he whispers, and I swallow as he pulls up my sweater, revealing my bare stomach. My heart is still racing as his fingers tickle and dance across my body, and I arch my back so he can pull my shirt up over my breasts. He is so smooth, and my breath becomes so uneven, I nearly choke on it. Guilt-ridden for what I want so badly for him to do.

"Fuck, London," he murmurs, his lips hardly leaving my skin. "You're so fucking hot. You have no idea how much you turn me on."

He presses his fingers into my belly but doesn't move them up.

But he looks. He can't take his eyes off me, and I like all the attention from Maison—until I realize what the hell I'm doing, and I visualize Olivia's cold dead eyes. Until I know for sure he wasn't the cause of those bruises....

"Maison, I can't... We can't do this."

He swallows. His body pulses before he pushes off me, giving me space I don't really want. My pussy is so wet, I have a hard time believing he can't smell it. My true desire is for him to keep touching me further down where the pressure is building so much, I feel like I might explode.

"Okay, London." He moves his hands off me, removes his soft lips from my neck. "What you say goes."

Is that what I want, though? For him to stop completely? "Maison," I whisper.

"Yeah, baby?"

"I just want to feel good for a minute. Just one minute without feeling guilty."

Can't I feel good for just a moment? Even by a person I should fear, someone who has the power to hurt me or share me with his alpha sibling, as I suspect he's done before.

He shifts. "Okay, what do you want me to do? Nothing you're doing is wrong right now, baby."

"Touch me," I whisper.

He knows what I mean and wastes no time moving his fingers to my nipples and cupping my breasts. He rubs and tickles them and makes my skin tingle all over.

"Damn, baby." Even in the dark, I can sense the smile on his face. "These are perfect." His big hands still don't fully grasp them.

I lose myself in the softness of him, the way he explores every inch, as if he's trying to memorize the feel of them. It feels good—hotter than the soft flame burning in front of me, and especially in contrast to the cold, hard terrain around us. My breath lengthens as I shift even closer to him.

He pulls his hand down to rest on my stomach.

"Why did you stop?" I breathe.

"You said one minute."

In just a single minute, everything horrible in my mind slipped away. Who Maison really is, or who Nigel claims he is, or where we are going to sleep tomorrow night, or the horrors of the past couple of days. I dare to move my hand and feel his hard body next to mine. Really feel him, his strength and the lines of his body.

"What next, London King?" he murmurs. I feel the warmth beneath his sweatpants press hard into my abdomen as I try to move as close to him as I can.

I lean up and nuzzle my lips into his, and he flinches. My heart races and skips a beat as I pull back.

Fuck.

Didn't he want to kiss me? He gave me all the signs... I pull my hands off him and squeeze my eyes shut. "Sorry. I shouldn't have done that."

He pulls my chin up to face him and his pupils flare. "Oh, hell yeah, you should have."

He dives in, covering my mouth with his, nibbling on my bottom lip. I let out a muffled moan and enjoy his taste. His mouth tastes as good as he looks. We kiss and nibble on each other for a few minutes, while he continues to explore my chest and I run my fingers through his hair. I knew he'd be good at this, but he is beyond talented.

He shifts his hips into me, enough where it feels like the fire beside us it right inside my belly. "I like kissing you, London," he murmurs. "I haven't kissed anyone since—"

I tense and pull away from him before he can finish the sentence. The tightening in my chest consumes me and a twinge of regret washes over me. He hasn't kissed anyone since Olivia. That was well over a year ago... Not even Serena? I always think of Olivia as being with Micah, but she was technically Maison's girlfriend.

His eyes etch in concern. "What are you thinking about, baby?"

I'm thinking about Micah, but I don't want him to know that. What would he think if he saw us like this? I'm also thinking about that spear Micah was carving before we left, and why he was even making a spear to begin with. Then I remember where we are.

"Maison... we are going to die out here, aren't we?

His fingers find my brow line as a cool breeze washes over us and the first rays of sun streak on the horizon. "I'm not going to let you die, baby. Micah won't let you die, either."

Micah. I really don't want to keep thinking about him right now.

Even though he says he doesn't want to talk about Micah, he brings it back to him constantly. I rest my head on his chest, too tired to fight it.

Eventually I ask him, "How does Micah know so much about survival?"

His heart picks up by thread, a flutter, but I feel it. He holds me for a few minutes, watching the little rays of sunlight streak over pink clouds that hover over the mountains.

Instead of saying anything, he shifts and pulls his arm out of his sweater. So quiet, just the sound of his heartbeat and a soft lap of water hitting rocks. He tugs my hand over my shoulder and up around the curve of his back.

"I want you to feel this," he whispers and moves my hand up and down his back. Beneath a layer of skin is a scar, long and deep. I catch my breath at how big it is, and what terrible thing must have happened to him to get a scar this big. I trace my finger over it and realize it runs down the entire length of his muscles.

"What happened?" I ask him. His heart is beating fast now, much faster than mine.

"I got this when I was eleven. My dad loved to go winter camping and took Micah and I ice fishing. We snuck away, thinking we were hilarious. We thought it would be fun to explore in our snowshoes, but we got lost, and I fell through the ice. This is the scar I got when Micah jumped into the water and dragged me out."

I press my lips together but let him finish the story as he lengthens his breath and continues, "We were stuck out there on the ice for two days. Micah refused to leave me alone, and I couldn't walk or move. By the time we were found, we were both nearly dead."

"Jesus, Maison."

This must be a living nightmare for them both.

"Micah never really got over it. He still has PTSD, and he hates talking about it. He still needs medication to control it, but he quit taking it years ago. He just suffers through it."

My breath catches at the thought of the two of them stranded like that as children. I also remember Micah's fight response, the fire in his eyes with Ezra and the way Maison tried to calm him. "And you don't have PTSD?" I ask him.

"I don't recall much of it, to be honest, though I was unconscious for most of it. I just appreciate my life now and enjoy being alive. I choose to be happy and try to forget about it. I'd rather focus on the nice things in life, not just the nasty memories. Micah remembers everything, though. He kept me alive for those two days, and I owe my life to him. I think he replays it in his mind constantly."

That explains their bond—the weird way Maison seems to resent him, yet remains so loyal.

"So the survival skills?"

"That's just Micah. He never wanted to be weak like that again, so he spent years in the wild—learning it, conquering it, just like he does with everything he cares about. It's part of his illness, but it's also his obsessive personality. It's the same way he is with hockey. So we need him, London. He's our lifeline out here, even if he's a complete dick about it."

I let out a long sigh. "He's just not good at being nice to people. He can work on improving that."

I don't miss the flash in his eyes—the hurt and betrayal that lingers whenever he speaks about his twin. Whatever happened with Olivia that broke them. But I also see glimpses of them. The blinding, unconditional love of brotherhood. Things aren't too far gone that they can't fix what's between them.

My eyes grow heavy again, and pure exhaustion takes over. Maison doesn't offer me any more information and I don't ask. He's told me enough—

Olivia died because of something Micah did, an episode he had perhaps? This confirms it. His illness takes over him. Micah's dangerous and I should stay away from him. But this boy in my arms is someone I don't want to stay away from, and Maison also has a role in all this. I need him to tell me what it is in order for me to fully trust him. My original goal remains intact. Besides trying to keep myself alive, I will find out what really happened between the three of them. I need to know, especially because I want nothing more than to keep kissing Maison Matei.

CHAPTER NINE

Day Three

For now, the beach is our home. Micah tracked us down with the 'breadcrumbs' we had left and brought Thomas and Nathan with him. The others stayed to wait until they returned with further instructions. Micah was pissed—as Maison knew he'd be—but he couldn't deny how much nicer this spot was than the fly-infested airplane, especially with what is rotting so close to us at the other site.

Colton died last night, just leaving Jess and James. I feel horrible for not being there, and for what I was doing instead, giving myself that one minute of pleasure. Nathan said he wasn't alone, that James stayed with him the entire time. The discussion now is what to do with Jess, whether we should just end her suffering. She's holding on by a thread, and James refuses to leave until she's gone. I doubt James can make this trek yet, although Nathan says he's doing much better. Until the situation changes, half of us will have to stay there.

So we've split...

Plane Group: James, Nathan, Ollie, Serena, and Jess.

Lake Group: Micah, Maison, Ezra, Thomas, Naomi, Jade, Nigel, and London.

Serena is staying back with her friend Jess, and she truly believes whoever is searching for us will have a better chance of finding us at the crash site. She may be right, but we've been stranded in the northern wilderness for three days with no signs of civilization beyond our group. No roads, no elec-

tricity, no humanity anywhere. I don't believe they know where we are or how to find us. We need to come to terms with the fact that nobody is coming. So we've split the supplies for the time being, except for the food. Micah said he'd cut the hand off anyone who touches the non-perishables. I don't think he's joking, either. He says we need the food to survive in winter and must learn to live off the land until then. I hope that day never comes. Luckily, the lake we found has plenty of fish, and this part of the island is much prettier than where we were.

"That wood is not going to work for a fire," Micah barks at Jade and me as we walk up with an armful of kindling. He comes out of nowhere to inspect the pile we've spent the last hour gathering in a spot next to what will be our primary fire, as opposed to the fire we will only use to cook food a bit aways away. It was the one job Micah gave us, while the guys gathered other materials and supplies to build shelters. Micah and Thomas went back to the airplane to gather more stuff—suitcases and a few of the supplies. It will take lots of trips, but Micah used it as a chance to check on how the others are doing. They immediately went to assist the other boys with the building of shelters upon their return.

I glare up at him. "What's wrong with it?" We are in the hottest part of the day, the northern late summer sun like rays of fire on my skin, even with the crisp air around me. I've had very little water since the one he spared me the day before, so I'm in a rather shit mood.

He tilts his head, giving me his predatory gaze. "For one, it's wet," he kicks at it with his shoe before he glares at the large branch in Jade's arms, "and you're using a fir tree instead of birch like I told you. If you can't get birch, then look for spruce or aspen. Just make sure it's fucking dry or we will not have a fire at all."

Jade flushes, unlike the silent rage I feel burning under my skin. I understand Micah better now, but that doesn't justify his mean attitude. Right now, we are all dealing with being out here, and he's not special.

"We're doing what we can, Micah," I snip back at him.

He ignores me and bends to inspect the pile further. The wood we found has a mossy, slick texture.

Naomi walks up carrying an armful of dry kindling and smiles at him as she places it down then looks at me and smirks like she's won some sort of competition. She's cleaned herself up, as everyone has. Her hair is pulled back in her trademark ponytail, and she looks natural, clean for once, without all her makeup caked on.

We had decided to split up to cover more ground, also because I'm not sure Naomi knows how to deal with me yet. I'm sure I'm the last person she wants to be stuck on an island with.

I roll my eyes, but keep my mouth shut.

Micah at least softens with Naomi, but he flexes his jaw and walks over a few steps and grabs a large stick anchored beside two rocks. "Look. The amount of wood we need is more than you think. It burns quickly, and wet wood is useless. So no fucking green branches. It's everywhere, you just need to know where to look."

"I asked her to get a fir tree branch." Thomas steps forward, carrying a large log. "I need it for two more shelters I plan to make. Fir branches seem to work the best for insulation since we don't all have a tarp."

One tarp—the second stayed at the plane with the others. It is unclear who will use it, but since Micah is building a shelter with it, we can make an assumption. Micah merely nods at his friend. Only Thomas and Maison can truly communicate with him, something even Naomi seems to struggle with.

The others come over to join us. Maison slides in beside me, causing the entire group to stare at us. Micah's eyes direct right to Maison's hand, which finds the exposed part of my skin between my shirt and pant line. Everyone has questions, I'm sure, but no one asks. Maison and I haven't even talked about what happened between us last night, but his touch calms me, so I welcome it.

It's only when Ezra comes through the line of trees at the edge of our camp that Micah places his arms around Naomi and presses his lips to the back of her head. I swear he's only ever affectionate with Naomi when Ezra's watching.

Micah steps forward, as Nigel slinks in next to Jade, and Ezra stands beside Maison and me. Nigel is out of his funk, it seems, and is helping us set up our new home, and everyone is seemingly getting along.

"Alright, since we're all here," Micah says, "I think we need to establish some ground rules."

"This should be good." Nigel rolls his eyes and plops himself down on a suitcase. Ezra actually snickers at Nigel's snide comments—the first positive interaction I've seen them have. They both seem to have a mutual distaste for Micah.

Micah's face flickers with a mask of arrogance as Thomas comes up beside him like a silent giant. "Do you have something to say, Nigel?" Thomas asks.

"Look," Maison says, waving an arm, playing peace-keeper. "We need to figure out some sort of order of things. Nigel, unless you have hidden knowledge about how to survive out here, I'd suggest we listen to Micah. He's the only one who knows what he's doing." He keeps his other hand firmly in place around my hip, and I subconsciously lean into him.

Nigel merely flicks his hands. "No. No. Please, carry on. I'm so relieved you're here to save us." He directs his comments to Micah, but he glances at my body language with Maison. A gleam hints in his eyes, causing my neck hairs to stand on end. I'm sure living in a society where Micah's in charge is Nigel's worst nightmare. I make a mental note to corner him alone later; I want to know what Nigel is thinking.

Micah scans the group—at Ezra, specifically. Then, for some reason, he rests his eyes on me. "Does anyone else dispute my leadership?"

Silence.

Ezra folds his arms and scowls as his sandy blond hair hangs over his beady eyes. "Let us know what you need us to do," he mutters through gritted teeth.

Looks like we've all resolved to Micah taking charge.

He angles his head down with one arm still wrapped around Naomi in a protective embrace. "Water, fire, shelter, then food. They're all crucial, but that's the order for our survival."

"But I'm hungry, Micah," Naomi whines, and I don't miss the tightness that forms in Micah's eyes. Naomi's whining grates on me too, so I get it.

"I know," he says in a calming way I've yet to see on him. "You'll feel worse in cold or rainy weather without shelter, though. And we probably won't last the night if it turns and snows on us."

I shiver at the thought, knowing snow is inevitable given where we are.

Everyone here has side-eyed the pile of canned goods Micah has stockpiled near the edge of camp. Cans of beans, pasta, sauces, soups, all this processed delicious food just teasing us, while Micah's plan is to catch a muskrat. And I know the lake is full of fish too, which sounds much better.

He looks at Jade and me first. "I need you girls to keep collecting wood, more than you think we need. Keep working on it until it's dark and find the stream that feeds this lake so we can drink from it."

I visibly tense, but Maison squeezes my hip, so I keep quiet.

"I thought this was a fresh-water lake?" Ezra argues.

Micah shifts and curls his expression like it was a stupid question, though I was thinking it, too. "It is, but lakes are stagnant, so more chance for bacteria to form. Even with our water purifier, I don't want to risk it. Our best bet for not puking our guts out is cold water in motion. Something is feeding this lake, and we need to find it."

He moves his attention to Ezra and Nigel. "Ezra, Thomas, and Nigel keep building the shelters. Thomas's idea for using fir trees was a good one. It will keep it in-sulated, and we can put little fires in front of them if you build in a shoot to act as a chimney. Use the moss from the firs as insulation; it will help us retain our body heat at night."

Those steam showers from New Ocean prep would be nice right about now.

A flash hits Micah's eyes, and he stares at his brother. "You need to go fishing, Maison, since I think you're the only one who knows how other than me. And make a big fire. Hopefully, we can use it as a signal in case a plane flies over us.

"Yeah, we got it, man," Maison says.

The scar—that long, deep scar. I can't help but press my hands up on his back. He moves his body closer and drops his hand until it tickles the side of my wrist, then slowly slides his fingers between mine. Micah notices—everyone notices—but I don't care. I only seem to feel good in this place when Maison's skin is touching mine, so I keep my hand gripped on his.

"And what are you going to do?" Nigel asks, finally drifting his attention up from the ground.

"And what is Naomi doing?" Ezra cuts in, narrowing his eyes. "She not going with the other girls?" The primal hatred radiates out of him.

I have to wonder what's running through Naomi's mind as she crinkles her nose at him. She has these two alpha males trying to stake their claim, but it seems she has made her choice. She only has eyes for Micah. Still, I've seen her with Ezra when Micah's not around.

Something's there, too.

Micah's fingers curl around Naomi stomach, that fist he likes to make when he feels *things*. His dark gaze shoots to Ezra with a daring, taunting look. "Naomi and I are going hunting."

It's a miracle that Ezra doesn't jump up and plunge the spear a few feet away right into Micah's heart with the amount of seething rage coming out of him. He's vibrating.

Pure. Primal. Instinct.

And hunger. It's been seventy-two hours since we've properly eaten, other than the crumbs of what Micah has given us.

Maison once again places his hand over Ezra's chest, keeping him at bay. A flicker of amusement seeps out of Micah's eyes, enjoying every chance he can to taunt Ezra.

"Ignore him, Ezra; it's not worth it. He's trying to get a rise out of you," Maison tells him.

With the tension still thick in the air, Ezra stomps to the pile of branches and logs where they plan to build.

Micah snickers, but it's not Naomi who has his attention, despite being in his arms. His eyes continuously stare at my fingers as they intertwine with Maison's. At least his eyes are full of light today, rather than the black void that was in them yesterday. There is something else that lies behind them, which seems more animalistic than anything.

"You remind him of her," Maison told me last night.

Why do I remind Micah of Olivia so much when he has a blonde who looks exactly like her right in front of him? Is it because I'm giving Maison *that* kind of attention?

I squeeze Maison's arm even tighter. I like him, and I will not deny myself just because Micah doesn't approve.

Micah rises, grabs some wire from the storage pile, and pulls Naomi with him in the opposite direction from where Ezra went, but not before he snatches his pointy spear and clasps it firmly with his other hand. A wave of heat flows through me as I watch them and the pure strength in that grip. The heat flows right between my legs. So hot, I wonder if Maison can sense it.

Micah's look suggests they will do significantly more than just hunt.

I throw dry kindling into the pile and return to the near-by evergreen forest. We eventually find some driftwood, branches, and twigs from the odd birch tree, and we collect as many logs as we can before Jade suggests bringing Thomas a few big branches. I spot Nigel building his own shelter away from the others. It seems like Maison disappeared hours ago to go to the lake, presumably to fish. I've not seen him since we all departed to complete our tasks, and I hate how much I already miss him, how close and connected we are, even though I've only known him for a few days.

I feel safe and comforted when I'm wrapped in his arms. When I'm not, I don't, and given our circumstance, I just want to be protected. The thought of his dark hair and cute smile brings a smile to my face, and I can still feel the brush of his hands on my body and his lips on my neck.

Ezra, who is working on his own shelter a few feet away, ignores us as we walk up. Thomas pauses and smiles, wiping the thin later of sweat off his forehead as he anchors a large, prickly branch over a couple larger logs they are using as supports to create an A-frame. His muscles ripple as he works, and he's almost single-handedly built an entire shelter while Ezra struggles to get two sticks to lean up against one another. I'm sure we will continue building and adding to them as the days progress, but the goal is for everyone to have somewhere to rest their heads tonight outside of the elements.

His eyes linger on Jade a moment longer than they do me as we drop the branch to the ground with a heavy *thud*. I sit, out of breath since I am completely and utterly out of shape.

"We found a stream," she tells Thomas, oblivious to the fact that he's checking her out. "It's only seven minutes away, but it's exactly what Micah said we would find close by." Her voice takes on an excited tone and her blush when she sees him tells me she might not be as oblivious to his looks as I thought.

He presses his lips together. "Micah will be happy when he gets back."

Jade smiles at the compliment, as if pleasing Micah is everyone's goal on the island. Thomas's loyalty to him seems stronger than even Maison's, and it was the same as on the hockey rink. When Thomas was on the ice, no one even got near Micah—and given his size, I certainly wouldn't mind a bodyguard like that. Thomas's loyalty to Micah seems absolute, and he's fiercely protective of him. I wonder what Micah did to earn it. It must have been something special.

Jade steps forward and grabs the other side of a large branch to help him hoist it up. "How do you know this stuff?" she asks him.

"Micah showed me before he left," he says as he places the branch down. "We will just layer these branches until it's completely covered, then we need to insulate the top using boughs or moss. It will take a while, but we can just keep building onto it."

I notice Ezra is doing his differently, so is Nigel, and Jade nudges her head toward them. "Why aren't they building theirs the same way?"

He shrugs. "I guess they don't want to do it Micah's way. They think they can build it better." I imagine Ezra's shelter crumbling in on him, and it brings a smile to my face. Nigel is struggling, too, so it's a good opportunity to talk to him.

Thomas moves on to the next shelter, where he already has two poles lined up. "Can I help you with it?" Jade asks him.

He pauses and catches her eye and goes wholly still for a moment. "Yeah." He points at the pile of moss. "Just hand me small pieces so I can start insulating the ground and roof." I can just imagine him ripping that moss off the tree with his bare hands.

She leans over and grabs the flat, flaky square. She's sweaty as the sun is glaring down on us and we've been working hard all day, even though she already stripped down to her tank top and is wearing a pair of tight-fitting jeans. Her curves are gorgeous, and I don't think she realizes how natural and pretty she is. He pauses and watches her, as if noticing her for the first time. She smiles at him shyly, and a brightness hits her eyes that I've not seen in her since we landed. It's the way she looks at Nigel—or rather, it's the way she used to look at Nigel.

Thomas and Jade know each other. They grew up together like everyone here, but they lived in completely different worlds. I wonder how many times they've actually interacted.

Since I'm not wanted, I move over to Nigel, who is still struggling. He's building his shelter next to a small hill, or attempting to, anyway.

I pick up a piece of wood and help him. "What's going on, Nigel?" I ask him casually.

He spares me barely more than a grimace before he asks, "Why is Jade over there helping him instead of me?"

I stare at him and blink a few times, noticing he's still wearing his argyle. "Relax, we're all helping each other. Let's make yours like Thomas and Jade's."

His eyes darken, and he wipes his greasy hair off his face. "Jade is sleeping with me tonight, London," he says in a dark voice.

I press my lips together. "I know…" I say carefully. "How about we follow what they are doing so you can both sleep comfortably tonight?"

While the sun is shining now, we all know the cold evening bite will come, and I realize I have no idea where I am going to sleep. We won't have enough shelters for everyone before nightfall. We follow Thomas' example and prop up logs together, making decent progress.

The wind picks up over the lake, a welcome breeze to an otherwise hot Arctic summer day. Nigel pauses and looks at me. "How is it going with the twins?" he asks, and the way he says it makes my spine tingle.

I dare to look at him as dread hits my stomach. "What do you mean?"

He cocks a brow, his face smug. "Did you hit your head in that crash, or are you just pretending you don't know what I'm talking about?"

I blow out a breath and drop the stick on the ground. Somewhere nearby a crow caws in my ear, prickling my skin. "I hardly see how that matters anymore, Nigel."

He picks up a branch. "Oh, it still matters very much, London. And I see you're making good progress from the way you were pawing at Maison earlier. Tell me, did you fuck him already?"

My eyes widen. "What is your problem?"

He tilts his head. "I want to know how you are progressing with them. It probably won't take long for you to fuck the other one, too, now that you're sinking your claws into one. Micah will get his fill, eventually."

"What the hell, Nigel?" I say roughly, with a bite in my voice—that bark my mom says I have lingering so close to the surface. I wave my arms and gnaw the inside of my cheek. "Look where we are. Why do you care about that anymore? Didn't you hear the wolves the first night? That is more concerning at the moment than an irrelevant story."

He slams the branch down with such venom, it has me stunned. "It has relevance," he spits out. "I want to know what they did to her, and why they're walking around freely while she's buried. We will get rescued, London. We will not stay on this island forever, and life will go on, and I still plan on getting that story written. You better hold up your side, or I will tell everyone why you really came on this trip. I will humiliate you."

My blood thins at the thought of him telling Maison what I was planning to do. Maison won't look at me the same, he won't trust me—and I love the way he looks at me. The hatred that runs through me in this moment is deeper than I expect. Or maybe it's just the hunger thinning out my veins. Regardless, twisted rage pulses through me at Nigel's idle threats.

I go utterly still. "Why are you doing this?" My voice comes out weak, while he gives me that dark stare that tells me he's not bluffing.

"I have my reasons, but please, tell me when it happens... I'd love to find out how Micah worms his way into your pants."

A snap of a twig has me turning to find Jade walking toward us. She pauses when she looks at him, sensing the tension between us. I turn to Nigel and smile sweetly. "I think your shelter's almost done, Nigel. Do you need help with anything else?

He simply sneers and shakes his head, and I turn and walk toward the direction Maison went. I need to find him.

I swear under my breath. This isn't adding up. I have my reasons, but Nigel's intense interest is unclear to me.

Why does he care so much? I'm not buying his obligation to bring justice or expose the truth or whatever flimsy excuse he originally provided me to get me to agree to do this. This is emotional for him—he's connected to this somehow.

"London, wait." Jade comes running over to me. "What was that about?"

I shake my head. "Nothing. Nigel is just a piece of work."

Jade doesn't know what Nigel and I were scheming, and I'm not ready for her to look at me differently, either.

She presses her lips together, clearly conflicted with her feelings for him. "I don't think he's holding up too well here. I'm kind of worried about him."

I sit on a log facing the glistening water and setting sun on the horizon. The vast emptiness, the beautiful mountainous landscape speckled with red and yellow hints of fall, and the thick layer of fir trees lining the rolling hills above. I imagine this lake in winter, frozen, bone-chilling cold. The earth frozen halfway to hell.

My words come out shaky. "Nobody appears to be doing well here."

Jade sits beside me and puts a comforting arm around me. "We have each other, and you have Maison, and Micah."

I shoot her a look.

She sucks in a breath. "You and Maison seem like you're getting close. If you're close with one twin, you're close with the other. That's how they work. Micah will watch over you more than anyone else for that reason."

I shake my head. "I'm not so sure about Micah. He's unsteady and mean, and as you pointed out at school, scary as hell."

"You should have seen Micah and Ezra earlier," she says. "They sat and argued about what to do. Ezra didn't want to come; he said you guys risked yourselves by coming out here, and you had to figure it out yourselves. I don't think Micah sat down the entire time you two were gone. He just... paced. And when he finally sat down, all he focused on was making that spear and wouldn't talk to anyone. So yeah, I think he does care, London. He seems to care an awful lot."

When I found Maison, he had already caught two large fish that now lay dead, wide-eyed, staring at me on the rocky shore bank. Lake trout, he tells me as he stands knee-deep in the cold waters. I don't want to go anywhere near those slimy fish, so I keep my distance and watch him with awe as he catches a third small one.

Enough to feed us for one night.

Somehow, he traps them using bait, and now I can appreciate how often he must have gone fishing when he was younger to be so skilled at it. I watch him, so focused, and his face lights up when I walk over to him, when he finally pulls himself out. He already misses me, despite not being apart for long. My senses dull as I watch him clean himself up and put dry clothes on, and he smiles at me, biting his bottom lip. The mutual attraction between us is unmistakable, and I struggle to hold back the tears welling up in my eyes.

I just found him and already, I'm afraid of losing him. And if Nigel decides to be a dick, my relationship with Maison could end before it even gets started. Maison clams up when he talks about Olivia and somehow, I need to get more information from him. I was so worried about being able to trust Maison that I didn't stop to think about whether he should trust me.

We build a fire at our kitchen spot to prep and cook the fish, and Micah and Naomi joined us at the same time. Her face is flushed, her lips curled in a cocky grin, and Micah's expression is stone cold, as per usual. To his credit, he is carrying a dead rabbit, so they did indeed do some hunting, after all.

He and Maison immediately set out to gut the fish and skin the rabbit, while Thomas and Ezra work on the fire. The food looks bloody and gross, but my stomach does a flip at the thought of eating meat. Our survival out here depends on our fat stores, so we need a lot.

Jade and I decided we are going to forage the forest for berries tomorrow to help round out our diet, and Micah and Thomas are going to the airplane to check on the others. Micah has to teach them how to hunt and survive off the barren land until James is healed enough to walk. If he's even still alive... We have no way of communicating with them.

The sun casts its last rays of light for the day and evening settles as we quietly gather around the fire to get ready to eat. Everyone except Nigel, who keeps to himself, in-sulating with a small fire of his own near his tiny shelter. He forced Jade to stay with him and, of course, she does out of her loyalty to him. Loyalty, I'm thinking he doesn't deserve.

"We have to keep at least one fire lit at all times," Mic-ah stresses as he places the meat on a stick and hovers it over the flames. "It will be our lifeline out here and can help signal our location if needed, especially during snow-fall—which will happen, and soon, given where we are."

"How are we supposed to keep it lit at night, man?" Thomas asks.

Micah sits on a log and pulls it up closer. Maison sits next to him and cooks the fish, the two of them acting like this is the easiest meal they've ever cooked. For a minute, I can't tell them apart.

Micah flicks his head up. "We take shifts. Someone should always be awake, anyway. We'll attract big animals with this food, but hopefully they come to this spot in-stead."

"What if it rains?" Naomi asks.

Naomi has placed herself on the ground between the two of them. Ezra can barely take his eyes off her, and Micah ignores her, his focus only on cooking the food.

Micah flexes his jaw. "We keep the fire lit, no matter what. It's really fucking important. Does everyone understand?"

Silent nods.

We move sites once the food is cooked. I'm sitting alone, leaning back on a log Thomas brought over, away from the others. I have an airplane blanket draped over my legs, and I changed into Maison's sweater because it keeps me warm. Maison heads over to me, and all eyes are on us, including Micah's, as he moves in behind me. I curl my knees in and wrap his sweater around my legs. His heart beats in my ear, and eventually, I lay my exhausted head against him.

Maison's arms around me are all I want, and I'm not trying to hide it. I suppress the nagging pit in my stomach that Nigel can rip this away from me.

"Hey baby," he whispers, and my stomach does a backflip as his hot breath tickles my ear. "I offered to stay out tonight. I want to spend another night sleeping under the stars with you."

I stare up at him and nod. All the feelings of warmth and safety rush through me as his dark lashes and soft eyes glisten back at me. He places a piece of fish in my mouth, which I greedily take, licking a bit of his fingers along with it. He hands me a bigger piece, and I lean back on him and eat, and relief instantly hits my stomach. All day it's been lined with acid laced from the hunger, twinging with worry.

I close my eyes as the heat from the fire hits my face and twilight settles in around us. "And tomorrow," he continues his soft whisper, "I am going to build you and me our own shelter so I can keep you warm every night while we're here."

He wraps himself around me like a shell as the sounds of evening bugs fill our ears.

I glance up at Micah, who is watching us. The shadows hiding his face, but I sense him, watching me like he knows I'm poison. He grabbed a stick earlier and now carves it to the point of obsession as the fire blazes in front of him. Naomi tries to sit with him, but he pushes her away. She sulks by herself while Ezra just smiles.

Micah's focus is unwavering as I watch him out of the corner of my eye. When he's done, he get's up, holds the spear in one hand and heads to his shelter, passing us as he goes. Maison is distracted, but I follow him, unable to look away. Micah meets my gaze right as he walks by, the fire flickering over his face.

I bury my head back into Maison, wishing I could just curl up on him and sleep. And I guess there is nothing stopping me now. Maison squeezes me a little harder and whispers, "I'm never going to let you go, London King." And I don't want him to. I can't imagine a world where Maison isn't hugging me.

CHAPTER TEN

Day Seven

We've been stranded on this island for one week, and I already feel like it's changing everyone. Unveiling our true selves beyond the high school image, after we've been stripped down to nothing. Micah is obsessed with survival—hunting, fishing, making those spears—and is beyond moody. Some nights he pulls Naomi in with him, while other nights he leaves her in the cold, and she ends up crawling in with Ezra. It's exhausting watching them, and sometimes I feel sorry for Naomi. Her life would be a lot easier if she just chose Ezra. Micah seems to just exist to screw up people's happiness with others. Ezra is fixated on Naomi—she's all he can look at. Nigel is a shell of a human. He barely helps and hardly leaves his shelter. He can stay there for all I care; ever since he threatened me, I don't trust him. Jade mostly stays with Nigel, but sometimes I see her sneak off with Thomas, who spends most of his time guarding our supplies for Micah. Micah gave him the job of watching our food to make sure no one steals from it. If Maison's not with Micah hunting or fishing, he's with me. Micah might be the best hunter, but Maison's the better trapper. We sneak away at night to kiss and cuddle until exhaustion takes over. He's not pushed me for anything more yet, although I know he wants to. I'm not ready for that, not when we are trying to survive, and especially with Nigel glaring at us, knowing I'll be crossing a line when I do.

The other camp is surviving, but we lost Jess. She held on longer than I thought she would, but eventually, her body gave out on her. Serena, Ollie, and Nathan are with James until he recovers enough to make the trek—exactly one hour from their camp to ours. They've made shelters there to help them bide their time. Micah and Thomas bring them fresh water every other day so they can survive, and they're doing o kay.

The boys were gone today, and while I was out foraging, I found a stunning cove. It's a perfect little spot about ten minutes away from the others. A place where I can bathe, swim, relax, and read by myself. It's just mine, and it's perfect. I decided to spend the day here.

The early evening sun casts a long, jagged shadow from the overhanging rock cliffs above me as I rest my head on a blanket on a flat rock on the shores. The cove is hidden by thick tree cover and a few large boulders emerge from the water ten feet from shore. I brought a spear with me—Micah had made plenty—just in case I ran into any wildlife while out here alone, even though I'm not skilled at using them. I doubt he will notice any missing, especially since I favor the wooden ones, not the ones he made from hockey sticks and skates.

The vast mountains loom in the distance and seem to sparkle as if a thin layer of snow rests on their jagged tips. A heaviness sets into the thin fresh air around me, and I shiver even though I'm wearing three layers.

I peel off my clothes and slip into the chilled water. I take out my braid and run my hands through my strands, using a bit of shampoo to help get the grime built up in it and let the water soothe me. I then lay out my blanket on a flat rock and dry myself before putting my clothes back on and head back to camp. The darkening sky and hint of rain signal it's time to head back.

Maison will return shortly, but I can't help but feel uneasy when he's away. The mere thought of the potential dangers that surround us—such as the wolves I hear sometime at night or other lurking animals that leave tracks near our site. It leaves me anxious.

The wind cuts into my back as I head to camp. The shadow of the trees pulls me in different directions, so I pick up my pace, not wanting to get lost in these woods, especially since I have shown no one my spot.

I freeze when Naomi's voice cuts through the wind and bounces off the surrounding trees. That had to have been Naomi, because I recognized her shrill laugh. I glance around uneasily, unsure of the direction I heard it.

She cries out again—to my left.

My head jerks toward the source of the sound.

"Naomi?" I call out to her.

I mutter under my breath and switch directions to seek her out. If she's messing with me, I want to put an end to it. I step around a large tree and it's not Naomi, but Micah, who stands in front of me. At least I think it's Micah, definitely a twin, but the shadowed light gives me pause. His body is tense, like he's grabbing onto something, and he's leaned back against a large tree, and his strong hands are indeed gripping the stump. The tempo of my heart picks up when I notice Naomi's blond ponytail and her slim body crouched beneath him.

Micah's eyes are closed, his head tilted back, and he bites his lip with his soft bangs drifting over his eyes. He looks devastatingly hot with his pants slightly lowered, and I can see the cut of his muscles and abs. It's good he doesn't notice me because I can't look away as Naomi takes him deep into her mouth.

I hear that cry, a moaning sound, as he forcefully thrusts to the back of her throat while gathering her hair in his hands. His eyes are still closed as he bangs her mouth. He's not smiling, but clearly, he's enjoying it—I can tell by the way he bites his bottom lip. I watch them, knowing I should look away but can't; instead, I'm fascinated by how intimate they are together.

No... not intimate. Nothing about what he is doing is intimate. He's not even looking at her. He's kept his eyes closed the entire time. If I did that, I'd hope for the guy to show some decency and, at the very least, look at me.

Even though I'm utterly disgusted by him, I keep my eyes on Micah and marvel at how much he looks like Maison. Except, Maison is soft, loving.

Micah's vicious.

He hasn't seen me yet; his eyes still closed, even as Naomi seems to pick up her pace and his hands grip the back of the tree. I watch as his face twists into what I can only assume is pleasure, and his eyes shoot open.

My hands draw down to the line of my waistband as I watch, and I curl my fingers in my stomach right in the spot Naomi is resting her fingers on Micah. I push my fingers farther down, right on my throbbing clit, as a roll of heat develops in my lower belly. I let out a soft, breathy moan. Loud enough, he looks right at me.

He catches me looking at him while touching myself, and he likes it. It's the first time I've seen Micah smile, and I don't stop. All his attention is directed at me as he climaxes, and my own wave of pleasure courses through me. I stand vulnerable, open, raw, and a witness to what should have been a private moment between him and the girl pleasuring him.

Instead, the moment is with me.

His lips curl to that cocky, cruel, and utterly sexy smile.

With my heart pounding a wicked beat, I turn and run before he can say anything. Before he can tell Naomi I was lurking, watching.

I come undone as I flee. The pressure inside me boiling over from what I just witnessed. I can't fathom being on the receiving end of something like that, especially since I didn't know people our age did it. I've never done that before, even with Chris.

Twilight descends as I return to camp, turning the forest into an unknown void. I sigh with relief when I spot Maison and Ezra chatting by the fire—not only for the fact I want his hands on me, but because I worry so deeply whenever he's gone. Although he looks grim, his eyes light up when he sees me.

Nigel, I notice, has also come out of his cave, and sits darkly, not contributing as per usual. Jade is next to him, her face sunken because he's sucking the energy right out of her while Thomas breaks up some of the kindling nearby.

"How are the others?" I ask Maison once I approach them. He immediately pulls me into his chest and curls his hand around my waist.

"Who cares?" Ezra snaps his beady eyes, glaring, his stringy hair greased back behind his ears. "They got to eat, and we didn't. Micah took it upon himself to give them everything he caught today." He looks directly at me. "Everyone needs to contribute more. This is bullshit."

Maison squeezes me and presses a kiss to my cheek. "Dude, relax. London does her part. I'll go fishing tomorrow, and Micah is out now trying to trap something. The other group is struggling and needed to eat more than us."

Is that what Micah was doing? The image of Naomi kneeling below him is seared into my mind—and the mere thought of it sends a pulse shooting between my legs. It's a miracle Micah comes back with anything based on how often he drags Naomi into the woods.

Ezra cuts me a menacing look. "We all need to learn how to get food, including the girls. Where the fuck were you all day, London?"

Maison tenses beside me, and Nigel smirks. This group is bad enough with food, so one day without food and they seem to unravel. Ezra probably knows where his ex-girlfriend is right now, too, which isn't helping his mood.

Thomas walks up behind Ezra. "I didn't see you catch anything today," he mocks.

"Fuck this," Ezra mutters, kicking at the fire. "Everyone, be ready tomorrow. We're heading out early, and that includes you, too, Nigel, you useless motherfucker." He stalks back to his shelter.

I grasp Maison's arm tighter and nudge him. Food is not my concern, although I don't disagree with Ezra—I probably should learn to fish—but Maison insists on doing it for me. Like he's providing for me, taking care of me. His eyes flash at me. "What's up, babe? What's wrong?"

I jerk my head toward the sitting spot he made for us, which consists of two blankets near the fire, leaning on a log. It's also where we usually sleep during our fire night, which is tonight... for me, anyway. Maison will need his rest for the hunt they are going on tomorrow.

I grab his hand and lead him toward our spot, and he raises his eyebrows from the sultry look I give him. My body is vibrating now. I'm acutely aware of Nigel watching me with him, though I've barely spared Nigel a glance since he threatened me. He's bluffing—if he says anything, he'll get outed, too.

He follows me to the blanket. He's been patient since our first night when I wanted to take things slow. He only gets kisses from me at night in our small shelter. My energy is usually low, and the others are just a few feet away. But I'm stupid for not claiming him, for not making him feel good the way Naomi was making Micah feel. If I don't give him something, he may get it elsewhere. Serena is coming back soon, and I can't let it be her.

We sit staring at the fire, and I nestle between his outstretched legs. Nigel, Jade, and Thomas slip away—there's no reason for them to stay awake since there is no dinner tonight   leaving Maison and me by ourselves. Micah and Naomi are still out doing whatever they're doing in the woods.

"What's up, baby?" he whispers in my ear as the sounds of the forest fill our ears with the wind, the trees singing, and the night bugs flying around us. The fire is warm on my face and I lean into him, the pressure now building to the point it's almost painful.

I gaze up at him, and his chestnut eyes flicker in the firelight. I kiss the little spot between his neck and his ear, and his body tenses. "I just missed you today," I breathe. "I don't like when you're away from me."

My hand finds his and I lead it down my stomach, to the band of my sweatpants. He grins and moves his hand lower, his fingers now grazing the pulse between my legs.

"Damn, baby," he whispers, kissing my ear, "I should leave you more often... What has you so riled up? You're so wet right now."

My heat is pooling, and I press his fingers right inside me—anything to get rid of this pressure I feel so deep within me. I lean into him, as if he's not close enough, and I try to absorb his body into mine.

"I want you right now, Maison," I whisper, and I mean every word. This has nothing to do with Micah; I want Maison to feel pleasure. He deserves it more than Micah does. His fingers tease beneath the blanket, and I moan as my hips arch, giving him access to go harder, deeper. I lean up to kiss his perfect lips, and I reach my hand down to the bulge beneath his sweats.

He pulls up and narrows his full, dark brows. "Are you sure, baby? You don't have to do anything you're not comfortable with."

I bite at my bottom lip. "I'm sure."

He grabs my chin and his full, soft, sweet lips kiss me back before he slips his tongue into my mouth. I press my fingers on the spot I saw Naomi touching when Micah's body quivered. I want to explore Maison's body and see his reactions. I reach for his cock and it springs to life in my hands.

His lips twitch into that cute smile as I bring his big erection into my tiny hand and start stroking it. "Faster, baby," he says in a light whisper. "Grip it hard and stroke it."

I take his lead and stroke him. "Like that?" I ask as I nibble on his neck, his ears, his cheek.

His voice comes out rough. "God damn it, London," he moans as my hands move faster, and his fingers slip in and out of me, alleviating my ache for him as my folds tighten around his fingers. His other hand conforms around the swells of my breasts. "When are you going to let me fuck you? I could do so many things to you if you let me."

My stomach tightens and I still my motions, pulling my hand right off him. I can't cross that line with him—especially knowing I was planning to hurt him, to ruin his life more than it already was, when it was his brother who hurt Olivia. Using him to get to Micah—I need to tell him; I need to talk to him about it. Otherwise, he's too good for me, and Nigel will win. The worst thing I could do right now is have sex with him.

He frowns and pulls his fingers out of me, then grips me and leads me on top of him so my back is to the fire, my knees are against the blanket under us on either side of him, and I'm facing his soft face etched with concern. He grips a piece of my hair that's fallen over my face, still damp from my lake dip. "Where did you go just now, baby? Why are you still scared of me? I promise I won't hurt you." He glides his hands along my sides. "Nothing I want to do to you will be painful. You can trust me."

Olivia. He's trying to tell me it wasn't him who hurt Olivia.

I swallow. "Maison... I don't think you will hurt me."

He wraps his arms around me, and I lean into him, aware of how hard he is against me, and how only a few layers of fabric separate me from him. The gold in his eyes shine, and I have to control every urge not to slip my pants down and slide onto him. I want him so badly, so desperately. But I pull off and turn away from him. My face heated and body pulsing, I stare out at the fire and close my eyes. After a few minutes of silence, he says, "I'm into you, London—I need you to know that. I'll take care of you out here, okay, baby? You're the only girl I want."

His hands tickle my belly, and I squirm beneath him. A big smile forms on my face, even though he can't see it. "I'm into you, too, Maison," I say. "Soon... We'll do it soon. I'm almost ready, I promise."

As soon as I tell him what a liar I am.

I'm falling for him—too hard, too fast.

I push down my guilt and enjoy the moment, and he doesn't push me, as I'm nearly lulled into a trance by the fire. I enjoy his arms, the feeling of still being alive and falling in love, despite the hunger in my belly.

My pleasure is short-lived. Twigs snap and footsteps crunch on the rock. Micah and Naomi finally return. Micah walks by us, nudging his brother's shoulder and throws down a squirrel, landing a few feet away, maintaining his expertly crafted mask of indifference at seeing me in Maison's arms. Naomi continues her icy demeanor toward me, barely sparing me a glance as she prances by. "Micah caught us dinner," she says proudly, completely unfazed by what Micah really fed her.

Micah walks over to the supply area, now covered by our one tarp, hidden and protected by bushes and long grass, and tosses a shiny knife on the ground. He jerks his head to Maison. "I caught it, you skin it."

An order from our alpha.

Maison blows out a breath and slightly nudges me to move. He rises, leaving a cold void behind me. He grabs the dead squirrel and heads toward the other site to hang it upside down on some wire we hung a few days earlier. He will be up for a while now, skinning it, but at least we will have something to eat tonight. I sigh heavily at how everyone jumps when Micah barks orders, and Micah merely smirks with amusement.

Naomi sits on Micah's lap, and he wraps his arm around her waist, but he doesn't look at her the way Maison gazes at me. Micah's attention is once again completely fixed on me.

My eyes shoot open as droplets of rain wet my skin and smoke tickles my throat. I jump up from the damp blanket beneath me from the ground I somehow fell asleep on. The moonless, inky sky is like a wall of black around me.

Shit... How did I fall asleep?

Micah made the rule clear, keep the fire lit—simple. It's smart actually, to save the fuel for when we really need it. Maison left me hours ago, for a good night's rest before the boys leave for their early morning hunt.

I jump to the nearby pile of wet kindling, grabbing a piece and throwing it over the charred wood that used to be fire. The rain's pattering down hard around me, causing what's left of the red embers to hiss—simmering heat and smoke rising from the ash.

But the flame went out.

I push at the stick, hoping it lights and catches fire, dreading the fact I might have to wake someone up. The droplets of rain, now turning into a sheet of water, pour down on me, soaking right through my clothes. My chest tightens and stomach twists up as I crouch alone in the night, muttering to myself in frustration for failing to notice the impending storm above me as I now shiver uncontrollably. The last I remember, I was writing in my journal, then grabbed my book to help keep me awake. My eyes must have closed, and I fell asleep sitting up.

I turn to find Maison, but he is already on the other side of the fire, throwing a large stump near it. I didn't even hear him approach through the sound of the rain hitting the ground and the water.

I walk up to him as he crouches, placing my hand on him and running it down his back. He shifts and casts me an indignant stare, and my face drops when I take in whose back I am rubbing.

"Wrong brother, sweetheart," Micah says in a deep voice that makes my thighs clench.

Micah grabs the piece of kindling out of my hand and blows on the fire while poking it until one piece of wood catches hold.

He doesn't falter, flinch, or even acknowledge me as I stand next to him, completely drenched, and the rain pours down on him. Once satisfied with the flame and the rain eases a bit, he finally looks at me. I fully expect his usual hateful glare and a lecture about how I let the fire die, but when I catch his eyes under the hood of his sweater, they are soft. For a moment, I thought I misjudged which brother was helping me. *Maybe it is Maison?*

"Crouch down with me," he says in such a way, I'm instantly reminded it's him—Micah, not the nice twin.

I freeze and falter, so he grabs my hand and pulls me down so hard, I fall into his muscled body. Rather than apologizing for being so brutish, he simply keeps a steadying hand on my thigh as I get on my knees and lean into him. The first time he's ever touched me, and I think about how strong his fingers are—of his curling fist when he threatened me on the plane, and the tiny bruises found on Olivia's neck.

"See that larger log? I want you to grab it."

He threw the bigger piece of wood near the fire. My heart rate spikes at being so close to him, so I try to create distance between us. He presses his hand harder on my thigh, not letting me leave.

"Don't move. It's important you learn how to do this. I can't always save you. Now grab the log. You are going to rebuild this fire, London, not me."

London—he only ever calls me sweetheart, and not in a sweet way.

I grab the log and hesitate, unsure of my next move. I can barely make out his shadowed face from under his hood. "What now?" I ask him as rain drips off my nose.

"Toss it directly onto the embers. Right in the center."

My brows narrow. "Won't that put the fire out?"

"It will protect it from the rain and wind. The fire will burn beneath it. Do it before the ash burns out."

The log is heavy and wet in my hands, so I toss it into the burning pit.

He leans into the darkness and grabs something, a stick, which he then places in my hand. "I stockpiled dry kindling under the tarp. Use it to maintain the fire and keep the wood dry. Don't forget to keep blowing for air."

I pause and hesitate. If he's aware he's still touching my thigh, he doesn't show it.

"Do it," he snaps.

I lean forward, close to the embers, and blow as hard as I'm able, making a wind tunnel with my hands. He does the same until the fire catches, and he tosses a bit of fuel on it from a bottle he has beside him. He finally shifts his hand, but only to grab my waist to drag me up and away from the flames as they take hold and the fire roars in front of us. His lean, athletic body ripples behind me as he maintains his firm grip.

I freeze and catch my breath. As the fire warms my face and the rain shoots down, his tall, muscled body shelters me from most of it. He says nothing; he doesn't move, just his heavy breath in my ear and his heat that pushes right to my core as he presses into my back. The moment lasts longer than I'm comfortable with, and I don't look at him, but I don't push him away, either. Finally, his fingers move up an inch, pulling my body into him slightly.

He rubs that little spot above my thigh, dangerously close to the place I was touching while watching him earlier. His mouth is so close, his breath tickles my neck, sending a shooting pulse of desire through me.

I turn to face him, my heart now a raging beat, and stare at him with a mix of confusion and fear. His chestnut eyes flicker and a smile curls his lips, like a predator eyeing its prey.

My face burns from the memory. I can't turn my eyes away from him—so bold to touch me like this. He knows exactly what I'm thinking about, and exactly what he's doing. A silent tease to remind me I watched him and enjoyed it. My body trembles and I step back, finally pushing his hand off me.

"Micah, don't," I whisper, and he tilts his head as if pondering what to say. Not that Micah's ever speechless, but silence seems to be his message of choice. His eyes flicker with fire before returning to their usual distant and cold state.

He steps away from me, and his face shifts to that of annoyance. "You girls need to practice basic survival skills and how to contribute more than just gathering wood. Tomorrow, while we hunt, make sure you learn how to catch a fucking fish and quit being so useless." He stalks off into the forest, as if he's the predator that truly belongs there.

I blow out a deep breath, relieved he's gone. His heavy presence makes me nervous. Everything about Micah puts me on edge, especially knowing what he's capable of. I've seen it, and I think I just experienced it firsthand.

As the rain eases to nothing but a few faint drops, I make my way to my now soaking wet spot to dry my blanket and damp clothes in front of the blazing fire Micah left me. With my heart rate cooling, I settle in for a long night. Micah won't be forgiving if the fire goes out again.

Maison checks on me without delay. I gaze up at him and smile as he approaches, and I instantly relax, seeing it's him as he walks over in a gray hoodie instead of the black one Micah was wearing.

My pulse picks up slightly as he slides in behind me with a dry blanket in his arms. He's quiet, not saying a single word. My stomach clenches. He saw us; he watched the entire thing, I can tell by the tightness in his eye. It's the same look he has when he talks about Olivia—the distant flash of anger hidden behind his blind love for his twin. An anger I know he is trying so hard to suppress. He just watched Micah put his hands on me, and I didn't push him away.

I sit on his lap and sink my hips right into him, trying to get as close to him as I can. He wraps his strong arms around me, pressing his hand against the flutter in my heart. "Go to sleep, baby," he whispers against my cheek. "I'll watch the fire for the rest of the night."

"London, wake up." Jade softly kicks at my feet.

Dim light pours through the fir moss and sticks that make up the roof of Maison's and my shelter—the one he built for us to live in. My head rests on his gray sweater and it smells like him. I don't really remember him carrying me back, just a brief kiss on my forehead as he left with all the other guys—including Nigel, who was muttering to himself all yesterday about it—as soon as light hinted at the sky, signaling morning.

I rub the sleep out of my eyes, propping myself up. Jade hunches at the entrance, her bright face peering at me, looking refreshed, like she came from a swim.

I am barely coherent, having stayed up for most of the night. Exhaustion seeps into my bones under the mid-day sun and heat, making it difficult to get up. I'm dry and warm and content on the soft bed of boughs that support and protect me from the cold, hard ground. Maison did an excellent job insulating us, having worked on it daily for the six days we've been in this spot. I lay back down in what I now consider one of my safe spots on this island and moan.

A sense of foreboding hits me, like every morning, my muscles lethargic from a lack of proper diet. I survived on meager rations of apple, berries, squirrel, rabbit, and fish. Hunger is a constant tug eating my insides, especially knowing our fresh produce is nearly gone.

"Come on, London," she says in the cheery voice I usually appreciate about her. "Micah warned me to not let you stay in bed all day. Naomi and I are going to attempt to fish. Thomas has been showing me some pointers. I think I can do it." I remember my own failed attempts at it, and Micah's snide comments about my lack of effort since then. She jumps on the bed, tugging at my blanket.

My face scrunches. Jade following Micah's orders bothers me more than him trying to control me from a distance—however, both are irritating. Especially with Micah's roaming hands last night, which I opt not to tell Jade about given her recent fondness of both Micah and Thomas. Jade knows Micah's dark side—she's the one who first warned me about him. She seems to have quickly forgotten.

She sits cross-legged at the end of my bed as I resign to the fact she won't be leaving and change into a T-shirt and new pair of sweats, throwing my hair up into a messy bun.

"Hopefully, the guys have luck catching something big for us," Jade says. "Micah says a deer could sustain us for a while until we get rescued."

Provided we are actually rescued.

Micah made sufficient spears, but I'm clueless about deer hunting. Maison and Micah used to go on hunting trips with their dad. Maison's detailed accounts of those trips assure me they know what they're doing. That, along with the knife Micah carries, makes me think they will get something.

Jade and I walk outside, and cool, crisp air hits my face. It's the coldest day since we've been here, and the sun isn't shining at all. A thick layer of billowing clouds line the sky, with various shades of gray blending into the water. I imagine this is what it's mostly like here this far north, where our daylight will eventually turn into twenty straight hours of darkness a day. Today, a thick moisture lingers in the air, a scent I almost think is snow. Naomi is waiting for us by the fire, her arms wrapped around herself, tapping her toe. Her head whips up as we approach, and she smiles at Jade, but a flash of annoyance hits her face when she looks at me lugging behind Jade, as if my mere presence pains her.

"Glad you could get out of bed to join us," she snipes at me.

"It was a long night, and it rained," I snap back at her, taking in her rather fresh appearance, despite how awful I feel and look. She and Jade must have gone bathing together.

Her eyes flash. "I'm aware. Apparently, you needed both twins to save you."

Jealous. She's jealous Micah didn't go back to her last night; instead, he was too busy digging his fingers into my hipbone.

Jade walks over to our supply area and hands me an apple—the last apple. My mouth waters looking at it. Jade takes a bite of it and gives it to me. "Micah says we can eat this, but we have to share it." I take it and savour every juicy drip before handing it over to Naomi, who finishes it. It takes every ounce of willpower not to tear that apple straight out of her fingers.

She rolls her eyes as I glare at her after her final bite. "What?" she says to both of us. "If it weren't for Micah and me trapping, you wouldn't have meat to eat."

Micah, Micah, Micah—all they talk about is Micah.

My attention darts to the stockpile of food, all that fat and protein stored up in those cans. Given my size, one can of beans would sustain me for a week. Instead, we live off whatever dried up disgusting meat we rip off the bones of rodents. That is all Micah allows us.

Naomi tosses the core into the fire. "We need to fish and contribute."

The fish haven't been biting the last couple of days, which caused everyone's sour mood. Even Maison hasn't caught anything, and he's the best fisher here.

I have no desire to wade into the cold water today, especially with Naomi and the bone-chilling rain last night. So I grab my backpack with my journal and a bottle of water tucked inside. "I'm going to pick berries," I inform them.

Jade sighs beside me. "London, don't be like that."

"Let her sulk," Naomi snips, crossing her arms. "Are you coming with me, Jade?"

The two of them are best friends now, apparently. It won't last long, especially with Serena returning soon. The plan is to check if James is fit for the trip. I'll be happy to see James again—he's the only other male on this island I can stand.

Jade gives me a sympathetic look before they stroll off to the water's edge, leaving me alone. At least now I don't have to hear Micah's name every two minutes. He needs to leave my head. I won't be alone with Micah if he behaves like that again. The games, the fire in his eyes, I'm pretty sure he's out of his damn mind. He knows Maison and I are getting closer, so his hands shouldn't have been on me.

I walk along the edge of the lake toward my hidden spot through the speckled forest. During the past few days, the foliage has turned, the tips of bushes bleeding reds and yellows. I saw fresh berries near where Micah and Naomi were hunting, so I go in that direction.

A couple of hours go by, and I forage all the berries I can. I can't identify the type, but they are orange and look like raspberries. I'm not sure if they are edible, so I don't dare eat them. I'll wait for Micah to inspect them and give his approval. I move onto searching for wood, making my way closer to the camp. I don't want the girls to stumble upon my cove.

A twig snaps, and Naomi walks into view through the shrubs. She's changed into a warmer sweater, her hair pulled back, and her brown eyes are dark as she takes me in. Jade is not with her. "Stay away from Micah, London."

Her voice is threatening, and I realize she was lurking in the shadows, stalking me.

I tuck in my bottom lip as my mouth dries. "I'm not interested in Micah."

She scoffs and crosses her arms. "That's what she said, too, before she sunk her claws into him and ruined his life."

Olivia, the elusive fucking ghost people keep comparing me to. It's like she's haunting me, warning me from her grave.

Don't get involved with these twins...

Either that or she's a jealous spirit, trying to keep me away.

"I'm with Maison," I say cooly, as if she didn't know.

The laugh that comes out of her is ugly, almost guttural. Nothing like the pretty faced girl I see in front of me. "For now." Her jaw clenches and she steps toward me, inching ever so forward. "Maison has the attention span of a puppy. He'll lose interest in you as soon as Serena gets back. He always goes back to Serena. They've been best friends forever. You're nothing but a distraction for him, and you aren't special. Maison's the biggest slut in New Ocean, London."

My chest caves at those words. "That's not true. Maison told me he isn't into her that way," I tell her. And I believe him. I trust him more than Naomi.

Her face turns cruel. "Micah and Maison both seem to have a thing for damaged girls, but I won't sit by and watch another girl destroy them again. So, hear my warnings, London. I can't do much about Maison because he seems into you, but stay away from Micah."

I bristle at her words. Damaged. Is that what I am? I shudder at the truth of that statement.

"Get out of my way, Naomi," I say, trying my best to ignore her harshness. I am not Olivia, but I can't stop the burning in the pit of my stomach. Nigel's heinous words hit me. Last night, Micah made a subtle play on me, just as Nigel predicted he would. Is that how it started with Olivia? He's jealous of his brother's happiness, so he watched her, stared at her under his dark hood, then touched her when he thought no one was looking?

Similar to how Chris was with me.

This is the reason I took this assignment to begin with—shitty male behavior.

No. That makes no sense. Naomi is gorgeous—even if she plays games with Ezra, too. Micah has no rational motive to touch, watch, or want me. Something deeper happened between them all, and for some reason, I remind them of her. Damaged might be accurate.

Everyone on this fucking island is damaged.

I push past Naomi, partly because my guilt is eating me up, and she sees right through me. I barely make it ten feet when she says, "My mom tried to kill herself after your dad left her to rot. I spent four years watching her in a deep depression."

I still at those words, cutting the inside of my soul. As I face her, she accuses, "Your father's choices had far-reaching consequences that affected my family deeply." Her voice shakes with emotion. My father caused me heartache as well. I see the girl I left at twelve, with pigtails and braces, and pain in her eyes from deep wounds.

"I'm sorry," I whisper, and I mean it, before I rush back to camp and the safety net of Jade.

Naomi, Jade, and I are sitting sullen around the fire as the sun settles in its usual pink tones that form and dance among the clouds. Jade talks awkwardly to Naomi and me, oblivious to the tension between us. I push the surrounding dirt with a spear, not a hockey blade spear, the old-fashion kind.

No fish were caught today, and we don't dare eat those berries, despite how appealing they look. The can of beans beckons me in our storage pile. It sits right on top—Heinz beans. That red and brown label will haunt my dreams tonight, thinking about how delicious they must taste.

Then the yelling happens.

The cries from the forest almost cripple me as they flow through the air and bounce off the water and rocky shore by our camp. Horrifying, given I've grown accustomed to the deadly quiet of the northern Alaska wilderness.

The boys are back early, as we weren't expecting them tonight. They didn't even make it a full night, and it's only dusk. They were supposed to stay at the other camp overnight. My heart jumps to my throat when they come into view, and all three of us shoot to our feet. They're all supporting someone, helping him walk. Despite the darkness, I can still discern it's either Maison or Micah, just by the frame of their body as they slumped forward, weakened by whatever happened to them.

I step back while the boys bring him in and lay him on the ground near us. I still don't know who is injured or the extent of it. They all surround him, and as I step toward them, the uninjured twin makes eye contact with me. "Get back, London."

It's Maison who's hurt, and that knowledge makes my stomach twist.

I slam my palm to my mouth as I notice the blood stain around his shoulder, his arm, somewhere in his upper body. "What happened?" I ask no one in particular as Jade rushes up and grabs my arm, pulling me away. I slap her hand away.

"London, get back. Unless you know how to help him, let Micah take care of it."

How does Micah know how to care for him? How does Micah know everything?

Watching from afar and feeling utterly helpless, I watch Micah work as he runs to the storage shelter and grabs the first aid kit. "Ezra, Thomas, help me get him into my shelter," Micah barks orders at them as he digs through items. Clothes, blankets, anything to help him. "Jade, get me some water." Thomas and Ezra both grab Maison and help him walk over to the shelter. He's limping and completely helpless, though he makes eye contact with me. Jade rushes to grab a bottle of water and runs to the shore.

Micah walks by me, looking right through me. "Naomi, I need you," he says instead. Naomi, who is positioned a few feet behind me, runs up to help them, leaving Nigel and me alone by the fire. I don't dare to go close; I just stand frozen, shaking.

Micah doesn't ask me to do anything. It's like I don't exist to him.

Nigel slides in beside me. "What happened?" I ask him.

A vile laugh escapes him, and he simply sneers. "He got hurt, obviously. These jocks are cocky, despite their incompetence."

"How did he get hurt, Nigel?"

"He fought a deer... and the deer won."

My nails bite into my palms and I turn to him. "I'm fucking serious, Nigel. Don't be cute."

No deer is in sight—no deer, just blood. Maison's blood and Nigel looking pleased about the whole situation.

"What is so fucking funny?" I ask him as my eyes drift to Ezra and Thomas coming out of the shadowed wood from the direction of our shelters. Ezra doesn't look pleased, and he stomps directly toward me.

He snickers and whispers in my ear, "Your boyfriend got too close to the beast, London. And he couldn't quite get the job done. We're all going to starve since the deer got away, and your other boyfriend had to save him." His acidic body odor is ten times worse than his vile words.

I shoot him a sharp glare, ready to correct him about the plural boyfriend comment, but Ezra gets right in my face. "This is your fucking fault." He stands at least half a foot taller and his face a mere inch from my nose as hunger ripples from his eyes.

Somehow, I'm responsible for the deer getting away. "What the hell did I do?" I dare to push his chest as rage coils in my stomach. He doesn't budge—not a single inch. He simply casts me a look of pure venom, like he's the runt of the litter who didn't get a scrap of dinner, and I'm a little nearby mouse. He stands hulking over me, baring his teeth.

Thomas is there in an instant, pulling him away from me. "Get away from her, man. It wasn't her fault. She had nothing to do with it."

"Get the fuck off me." Ezra snaps his arm away from Thomas but stands back a few feet, keeping his attention directed at me, like I'm suddenly the enemy. Micah appears out of the shelter with Naomi close behind. Naomi runs to Ezra's side and slides her arm around him, which instantly softens him, but he's still vibrating like a lunatic. Micah's jaw tightens as he takes in the scene—takes in me but says nothing. He doesn't get involved, happy to let Thomas handle it.

Ezra cocks his head at me. "Maison got hurt because he was careless. And do you know why he was careless, London?"

I don't dignify him with a response.

"He stayed up all night with you," he spits. "Apparently, you don't know how to keep a fucking fire lit."

Thomas steps forward, placing himself in between me and Ezra. "Dude, that had nothing to do with it. We had an accident because of our inexperience. None of us know what we're doing out here."

Ezra jerks his head to Micah. "Boy scout there says he does. But he fucked up and let the deer get away because he was out here saving this bitch, too."

A growl leaves my throat. "You can't possibly blame me for this?"

His eyes flash and he wipes his blonde hair behind his ear. "I can and I do. I'm fucking hungry, and now we have nothing to eat."

Naomi pulls Ezra aside and casts me a particularly venomous look, just as Jade comes out from the shelter where she was helping Maison. Her eyes are wide, taking in the situation's hostility, and I push down a wave of jealousy. I want to be with him at this moment.

Micah shakes his head and disappears into the dark. Ezra pauses, his body pulsing with Naomi by his side. "Fuck this," he says, stomping toward our dried food. "I'm eating."

Thomas is on him again, throwing him back. "No, you're not. Micah says we need to save it. We'll try as many times as it takes to kill something." After a few tense seconds, Ezra backs down.

"Come on, Ezra," Naomi grabs his waist and pulls him away. "Let's take a walk, babe."

I let out a shaky breath as Nigel walks up to me, his face like a feline. "I told you, London. You really fucked this one up."

Walk away—walk away and breathe. I turn on my heels and run back to my shelter, where I curl up my knees and quit fighting the tears threatening all day. They pour out of me, my eyes burning from the dirt lingering on my face.

I can't lose Maison, he's all I have here.

My body has a tightness, the vast emptiness that surrounds me pressing in. It consumes... Breathe. Breathe. Breathe. Breathing is all I can do, and at least I have oxygen still filling my lungs. I think of my peers in their mass grave near the airplane. They aren't so fortunate. *Or perhaps they were...*

I let the thought linger. This island is eating me alive, day by day, hour by hour. We are all slowly disintegrating.

I'm not sure how long I'm sleeping for, or if I am even sleeping, when footsteps crunch outside. I'm still sitting in the fetal position with my head dipped in between my knees, when a shadow hovers just outside. I lift my head and Micah crouches down in front of me, still wearing his black hood. I can't make out his face in the night's shadow, but I bet he's scowling.

For once, he actually seems tired and defeated. His body language does, at the very least.

His voice is raw. "Maison woke up. He's asking for you."

I respond slowly and glance around expectantly, like he's really talking to someone else. "Is he okay? What happened out there, Micah?"

A pause before he says, "Yeah, he'll be alright. He's not bleeding anymore. It was just a surface level scratch where the buck got him."

I bite on my bottom lip. *If it was my fault...*

"I'm sorry... sorry if I caused it—"

"You didn't," he cuts me off. "He had a good angle, he just missed. It had nothing to do with you. I fucked it up; I wasn't there to back him up like I should have been."

I catch his face now, the sorrow in his eyes.

"Then Maison fainted," he continues, "probably because of lack of food. Ezra's mad because I called the hunt to get Maison back here."

He nudges forward slightly and I flinch, and his eyes linger on me for a good, long second.

He chose his brother over eating. Even over the wellness of the rest of the group, he chose Maison. This is the part of their twin bond I see so strongly within them. It's there, hidden, but there.

He jerks his head. "Come on."

I scramble to get up and lean on his outstretched hand he offers to pull me up. He keeps his hand gripped on mine as he walks me over the ten feet to where his shelter is. The sun is set now, the night encasing us. I can hear the others at the fire a few feet away as Micah brings me to his brother. A small fire just outside provides ample light and a soft heat. He lets go of my hand and sits with the others.

I crawl straight inside toward Maison, who is lying on the elevated moss bough and a series of airplane blankets.

My heart stops at the sight of him. He's wearing his gray sweater and sits up, propped on a pile of clothes beneath him. To me, it just looks like he woke up from a nap. The soft firelight elongates his dark lashes, and he gives me that cute smile I love so much about him.

I kneel in front of him, every ounce of me wanting to tell him—no, to show him—how I feel about him. "What did you do to yourself?" I ask and cuddle up next to him. He flinches a bit as I accidentally nudge his wounded arm and wrap my hand around him. His uninjured arm pulls my waist to him, and I melt into him as I always do. "It's just a scratch, baby," he tells me. "I'm out of practice. I'll get that fucker next time."

I frown, tracing my finger around his wound. It's all funny to him, but he doesn't understand how wrecked I will be if he leaves me. He cups my cheek, giving me those puppy eyes and lips. "Micah's worried about nothing. I was fine; I just needed a break. We could have kept going."

No, Micah made the right decision by returning. One scratch, one drop of blood can be lethal here.

He presses his lips to my hairline. "Don't worry, baby. I've gone through worse."

He has—we all have. But we survived it.

"Micah wouldn't let me see you," I say, peering up at him.

His hand teases the edge of my sweater. "Micah's protective. And as I told you, he was freaking out. He wasn't thinking straight."

He seemed clear-headed to me, while Nigel and Ezra seemed anything but. They have an animalistic husk, a scent about them that makes my blood run cold.

A similar feeling starts overcoming me—a drive, a need. I lean up and kiss Maison's neck, then move to his lips as I peer up at him and smile. His pupils flare as he arches both eyebrows while I slip my hands on his abs, just above his waistline.

Naomi's sudden laughter cuts into my ears, causing me to watch the entrance. They are only twenty feet away—not one of them a friend. I'm still a stranger to this group. I pull off him, remembering Nigel's threats and the hold on me while my feelings for Maison deepen every second I'm here.

"Stay with me, baby. Ignore them."

"I can't," I breathe.

"Just focus on me."

My pulse quickens as I turn my attention back to him, his eyes only on me. "We're not even in our own shelter."

He smiles and his lips quirk into a grin. "So?"

I don't want to know the weight behind that question. How many girls they've shared? I immediately push Olivia out of my head. I can't focus on a dead girl or her significance to the guy I'm about to sleep with.

Right now, I don't care. I almost lost my chance to experience Maison the way we both deserve. One more day isn't guaranteed anymore.

So I sit up and pull off my sweater—his hockey sweater I've kept close to me from the moment he gave it to me—and strip off my sweats.

Just my lace underwear and tank top now.

I undo my ponytail and let my hair flow down over my chest, which is now rising and falling with quick breaths.

I've only done this once. It was quick and dirty in a cheap motel, which was worse than the ground we are about to fuck on. He left me to go home to his wife shortly after.

I push that out of my mind, too—this is Maison. All my attention is on him.

I straddle him and squeeze my legs together, having zero intentions on leaving this shelter tonight. Micah will have to sleep in ours, or those woods he favors so much, and Naomi can bounce over to Ezra.

Maison stares up at me, his chestnut eyes unblinking as he bites his bottom lip. His eyes drift to my bouncing breasts. "You lead, baby," he whispers. "What do you want me to do?"

I reach for his hand and move it over my chest, and he teases my nipples, which have turned into little bulbs against my shirt.

He reaches up and pulls off my tank top, all while gripping my hip with his healthy arm. His fingers teasing, tickling. I lean over him, and he licks and sucks on each breast. "Are you sure?" he asks as he pulls his mouth away while I grind my clit over his erection.

I lean in and press my lips over his. "I'm sure." I'm absolutely certain.

He flinches as my arm slips over his wound.

"I'm sorry." I ease off him.

He pulls me back, his lips delve into mine, his tongue soft and playful. After a moment, I say, "I can't lose you, Maison... you're all I have here."

He pulls my hair over my shoulder and gazes up at me. "You're not going to lose me, baby. It's just a scratch."

It's not just a scratch, and he knows it—he could have died. We only have one small first aid kit. I shudder to think what could happen if his wound was any worse.

"Keep going," he murmurs. "I can handle a little pain if it means you grinding on my dick like that."

I let out a breathy laugh as I play with the hair resting over his eyes. I admire his perfect olive skin and his messy, sexy hair, which I run my hands through. I swallow, trying to contain my raging heartbeat.

"Fuck, baby," he whispers as he grips my tits and I squeeze my knees into him. "I want inside you so bad." Those words completely undo me. I reach down and grab his erection and help him shift, bringing it out. I grab it in my tiny hand and rub myself on it.

"Maison?" I whisper as the fire crackles outside.

His voice is shaky, his cock throbbing. "Yeah?"

"I don't really know what I'm doing."

He pulls me closer to him, sliding his fingers deep inside me. He kisses my cheek, my neck, my lips. His husky scent tickles my nose. "First," he says, "we need to make sure you're nice and wet for me."

I let out a moan as his fingers press on my clit, and he hits deep inside. He reaches over to his nearby pack and pulls out a condom, slipping it on.

Conveniently, Micah seems to have plenty to spare.

He leans back, relaxed, with his non-wounded arm around his neck, waiting for me. "Then you climb up on me, and you slide that wet little pussy over me. It's that easy, baby, and I promise, it will feel amazing."

I take a deep breath. It's not the most romantic, but it's perfect. Maison is perfect. I couldn't imagine doing it with anyone else.

"Will it hurt?"

A sly grin. "Yeah, probably. You're pretty tight, but it won't hurt for long."

Heat pools in my lower belly, and my body throbs with anticipation as I crawl on top of him.

I lean down and kiss him before lifting my hips and sliding over him.

It hurts as I feel the tip of his cock press through my sensitive, tight skin. I let out a moan as I lean over him and press down, feeling the prickles underneath from the fir tree bedding hitting my knees. I ignore the tiny bite in the air as the fire just outside dies down to nothing but embers and ash.

I'm careful not to put too much pressure on him, and he helps me by arching his hips, meeting my thrusts. I can barely see him now, but I can feel him, every inch. Warm, safe, and just what I need.

After a few painful moments, everything feels good. My insides soften. The ridge of his cock hits me in just the right way as I grind my hips. His eyes don't leave mine as I bite my lip and thrust back and forth.

"Kiss me, baby," he whispers. "I want to feel your lips on me. You feel so fucking incredible."

Our mouths press together as I ride on him. If he feels pain from his injury, he doesn't show it. He grabs my hips and helps me thrust till the heat fills me, and my orgasm builds and rolls through me. I have to cover my mouth so the whole camp won't hear me moan, although they probably already have. He groans as I ride him.

My insides explode as the tension builds, and we climax. I lean forward to feel his hot breath on my face as I drape my body over him for warmth, especially careful this time not to touch his wound. I lay panting beside him, sweating, and I grab the extra blanket to curl up beside him.

"Was that okay?" I ask him breathlessly.

He nuzzles his lips into my neck, still out of breath himself. "Fuck, baby. You have no idea how bad I wanted to fuck you that day I saw you in the towel. All I kept thinking about was how badly I wanted this. How badly I want you."

The day I started spying on him.

I never thought I'd start falling in love with him.

But here I am.

I have to come clean before Nigel beats me to it, because eventually, Nigel will unveil it. Secrets always get exposed.

I don't plan on ever leaving his side, not ever.

Sorry, Micah, Nigel, Serena, Naomi, and everyone else on this fucking island.

Maison is mine.

CHAPTER ELEVEN

Day Twelve

*T*he wind on the island is unrelenting and harsh. The days are shifting, and the temperature has plummeted. Even the daytime has a crispness teasing us of the colder months ahead, should we live to see them. We've run out of fresh food, and the berries I foraged are not growing back, so we share them among the group, eating them sparingly. Not much has happened since the hunt and Maison's injury. Our sole focus is making sure he gets better. The scratch really was small, but his lack of strength from not eating caused him to stay down a couple of days, plus dehydration caused his blood to thicken, which was why his bleeding stopped.

I still haven't told Maison how I planned to expose him and Micah. The timing doesn't feel right. He's only gotten back to being himself today, finally getting enough strength to move around a bit. Micah's been sneaking him food, I'm sure of it, although we are supposed to share everything. I can hardly blame him, though—I would do the same if I could catch anything. I swear, Micah has another spot set up somewhere. He came back with a ptarmigan, a big bird that looks like a chicken. It was fully plucked and ready to roast. It was the best meal we had since we've been here and put everyone in a better mood. We've been sustaining ourselves mainly on fish that the others catch. My job is solely collecting *firewood now, while everyone else focuses on catching food sources.*

All the canned food is still stored, and Thomas watches over it. He hovers around it, as if Micah told him to after Ezra threatened to steal it. They all stare at it while we are at the fire, eating the few precious pieces of food we are afforded. It's not enough. Hunger is driving every minute of our days; it consumes our thoughts, our prayers, our lives. Eating has become our sole purpose.

Alliances are shifting. Maison and I are inseparable—although he is still weak and doesn't move much—except for when I sneak away to my cove. He got sick, like really sick. He spent a full day puking his guts out the day after his injury. When I'm not collecting wood, I'm lying with him, usually reading passages of The Great Gatsby, *since he enjoys it as much as I do. But it's a relief he's feeling better.*

I avoid Nigel altogether now, although he smiles at me sometimes, knowing he has something on me that can ruin what I'm building with Maison. If he says one word about it, I won't hesitate in slicing him with my spear. Thomas and Jade are getting closer, too, and Thomas takes her out fishing everyday. Nigel sees it and isn't too happy about it, but he and Ezra seem to have a mutual hate for Micah and me, which has brought them closer. Naomi is with Ezra a lot, since Micah is distant and moody with everyone, even with her. He spends most of the time alone, trapping. He's an alliance of one, and sometimes I catch him watching me. In fact, he watches me a lot. We've not really spoken since the night Maison got hurt, and I can't get a read on him. I think maybe he's jealous, and I still think about that moment he pressed his fingers into me and what he meant by it. It felt threatening, so I keep my distance whenever he's around.

Micah left today to check on the others near the plane. It's both a stress and a release to have him gone. He's so skilled here, yet I'm petrified of him. We are surviving, but barely. We're left with nothing but waiting and the hope to stay alive.

The sun is finally shining after a few cloudy days. The water is so crystal clear, mountains above shine a perfect silhouette, as if the giants are a part of the lake. The sun's rays sparkle down, like a million diamonds bleeding into the sky. For a tiny moment, I let myself enjoy the serenity of it. Until an eagle flies above me, my silent competition as it circles the same school of fish I have my eye on. I grip my wooden spear in my right hand, and I squat down over a flat rock that juts out a few feet from the shore.

I arrived at my hidden cove earlier, and the stillness of the water is only interrupted by the occasional fish jumping. Maison had a few rough days, but recovered and went trapping with Ezra. Just two rabbits would feed us for a while. It's not even the protein we are after anymore, it's the fat that will keep us alive through the winter. Then, and only then, are we allowed to eat the canned food.

Micah isn't back from visiting the other group, so I thought it was a perfect time to disappear and practice fishing. Others catch fish differently than I do, and I prefer severing it with a sharp point as it seems effective and more satisfying. Calming my breath, I shift my braid to the side as I lunge forward, trying to force the spear into the lake trout I've had my eye on for the past ten minutes finally swims by me.

I miss again. I've thrown this spear nearly twenty times now, and I can't seem to catch anything. The fish swims off, completely unscathed. This time, I plunge into the water up to my waist. Luckily, it's warm enough today that I've changed into shorts and my tank top, and I'm already drenched to the bone trying to fish for the past hour. I'm determined not to go back empty-handed.

"Fuck," I cry out. My legs are numb from the water's frigid temperature and my feet slip on the slimy jagged rocks that make up the bottom of this lake. I pull myself back on top of the rock and dry myself under the sun until I muster up enough energy to try again, knowing I will once again end up in icy waters. I absentmindedly play with the tip of the spear, imagining the sharp edge slicing into that stupid fish. *Useless* was the word Micah had thrown at me the other night, and maybe he's right. But I'm not a quitter, so I stand on the rock, readying myself.

I halt and stare at a cloud puff materializing far away, cognizant of their unpredictability in this area. Maison will be back soon. We've not had sex since the night he was injured. He probably shouldn't have had sex in the condition he was in, but how could he say no to me? I've left him alone since, just cuddles and kisses, and he's not pushed for it. I got my period as well, which was awful, so I made him keep his hands to himself. But I want to feel him inside me again now that he's gotten his strength back.

As if on cue, I look over as a shadow hints the light, and Maison stands against the rock cliff, wearing his gray sweater and an amused smile playing at his lips.

He finally found my secret spot, and I wonder how long he was watching? I can picture my wet T-shirt being transparent, and the nothingness I'm wearing under these shorts. He notices, his eyes meeting mine briefly before drifting down my chest.

I turn from him playfully. "You could help me rather than just standing there, you know?" After a moment, water sloshes behind me and I feel him jump on. The rock is barely enough for the two of us, so he presses himself against me and reaches his arms around me, gripping the hilt of my spear. My body tingles as he rests his hands over mine.

"You're doing it all wrong," he says, and his breath tickles my ear. I press my ass into him, and he stiffens a bit before reaching down and pulling me further into him. He's probably surprised at how bold I'm being, but I'd let him fuck me on this rock if he wanted to, which is exactly what I plan to do. Screwing Maison feels just as good to me as food.

I bite my lip, and my insides heat at the thought of it. "Am I now?" I ask coyly.

"You're holding the spear the wrong way. Hold the shaft with two hands, not one." He moves my hands to different points. "It's not badminton."

He lets go of my hands and grabs my waist, bending me over, crouching me down. "You need to bend your knees; you're too straight up. Throw with your body as much as your hands."

My chest rises and falls as the tension builds between my legs. "What else?" I pant, barely able to control my breathing with him so close.

He wraps his hands around my tummy, pressing his fingers into my torso. "Throw from here." I close my eyes and bite my tongue as the strength of his hands pulse through my entire abdomen. "Open your eyes, focus on your target."

I do as he says and find one larger fish, right as it's about to pass me. He doesn't let go, and my knees weaken and tremble. He must know the effect he's having on me, which is why he's trying to distract me.

Bastard.

"Be still," he whispers.

I calm my breath, my eyes never leaving my target, even though my heart beats uncontrollably.

"Throw."

With all my abdominal strength, I forcefully thrust the spear down with both hands. It nips the fish I was aiming for, injuring it.

"Grab it! Grab the fish, London," he says excitedly.

Driven by adrenaline and hunger, I jump into the cool waters and grab the slimy fish, next to the spear now floating in the water. It's a big one, about ten pounds. I carry it as it flops for a moment, before it's dead and limp in my arms, and I carefully move toward the shore. Maison is already behind me when I toss it onto the slippery rocks. Its big eyeballs stare right at me while I wash my hands and turn to face him, driven by a different primal need now.

That was the most exhilarating thing I've done since I've been here, and it was because he taught me how to do it. I don't let him react or stop me; I lift onto my toes and press my lips on his neck, enjoying his soft stubble, before sliding my tongue into his mouth.

He responds the way he usually does, nibbling and playing with me, sliding his hands to my lower back. I deepen my kiss, and he meets my passion with equal vigor.

"Lift me up," I demand and jump up a few feet, hoping he catches me. Which he does with no problem and grips the fleshy part of my ass with his firm hands. I press myself into him, wrapping my legs around him. I nibble and bite at his neck and ear, and he tickles my bare legs. I love how small he makes me feel wrapped inside him. "Take me to that rock over there." He enjoys playing our little game where I give him permission bit by bit, till he gets the entirety of me.

I run my fingers through his hair, and he carries me over to my flat rock on the edge of the shore. I keep my lips on his neck, moving them back to his mouth, and he presses me down to the cold ground. The uneven rock beneath me scratches into my back, but I don't care.

I want him inside me, right now.

I moan as I run my hands up his gray sweatshirt, tickling his hard abs, while teasing the string of his sweatpants, ready to pull them down. "Touch me everywhere." I tease his neck with my tongue. "I want your hands all over me."

He slides his fingers up my shirt. "Like this?" he whispers as he glides his fingers over my breasts and teases them. My whole body pulses as I lift my shirt and throw it onto the ground beside me, exposing my entire chest to him, my legs sprawled out with him in between them.

"Yeah, like that," I breathe out as his soft fingers tingle every bit he contacts.

He pulls away and my eyes meet his. His pupils flare and he grabs my fingers and pulls them down with his, right along my belly and down between my legs.

"I want you to touch yourself," he says as his hands circle the apex of my thigh. "I want to watch you."

I take in his messy, sexy dark hair, cherry lips, and the bit of facial hair he has growing. I breathe deeply, feeling my slickness between my legs and absorb his heady scent. My jean shorts are irritating, rubbing up against my clit, so I undo my top button and slide them down while arching my back as he continues caressing me. As I stroke myself, his thumb finds its way inside me as our fingers intertwine. I close my eyes and bask in the feeling of his hands, the refreshing Alaskan air, and the tranquility of the natural surroundings.

My lips crave his so I lean up and kiss him, then catch my breath as my orgasm builds and I wrap my hands around his neck so I can feel every hard line of him. "Fuck," I moan as I continue rubbing, knowing he's watching and likes it. I move my other hand to my breasts and tease my nipples, wishing he would touch them instead.

His fingers still rest on my hipbone, so I pull them inside me and nudge him on top of me. I wrap my legs around him and squeeze so he can get them deeper, and I tighten around them, trying to get him as close to me as possible. I let out a soft moan as another wave of pleasure rolls through me, and I push my hips into him.

His face brushes up against mine, his lips tickling my cheek. "You fucking like that," he says as he pulls his thumb out of me. I feel his wet fingers on my belly. "You want more of that, sweetheart?"

Something's wrong...

I run my hands up his back and over the muscles of his shoulder and freeze. "Micah. Get off me."

He lets out a dark laugh as I pull my lips off him. "Your legs are wrapped around me."

A twist pulls in my stomach as my thighs grip him tight, tense and pulsing. Almost like my body hasn't caught up to my head. I release the tension between my legs and roll from under him as he steps back and gives me space. He towers over me as I scramble to find my clothes.

"Why did you do that?" I bark at him as I grab my shirt and slip it back on, doing the same with my shorts.

"Do what? You kissed me."

I shoot him a look. "I only kissed you because you were pretending to be Maison."

Narrowing his eyes, his mouth twists. "I never once *pretended* to be Maison. *That* was all me."

Liar.

I ball my fists, taken aback by his stark denial. "Yes, you did. You're even wearing his sweater."

He scoffs. "If I was acting like Maison, I would have caught that fish for you, and spoon fed it right into your fucking mouth. And as for the sweater, I borrowed it. Is that so wrong?"

I blink and my heart rate spikes. Why is he denying it?

"Why the hell are you here, then?"

He gives a half shrug. "I was exploring the island. I saw your pathetic attempt at fishing, so I watched you for a few minutes. You asked for my help, so I gave it to you." He bites his bottom lip, giving me that same flickering stare as before. "Apparently, you were quite... *appreciative.*"

There he is. The Micah I know and hate. How did I not see it?

Oh god. He got me off, and he knows it, too.

I meet his dark stare with a flat one of my own. Every line in my body tenses. "Is this what you did to Olivia?" I ask him darkly. "Did you wear Maison's sweater?"

His jaw tightens. He takes a step forward and I flinch, but I keep my icy gaze on him. Watching him, studying him like I was supposed to be doing all along.

Patterns, connections, subtleties.

His fingers, his kiss, the guidance on how to catch that fish, and how he made me do it all myself.

Fuck.

It was him the whole time, and I just didn't see it. I got distracted.

He knows who I am and who I thought he was. "How far would you let it go if I didn't realize it was you?" I ask, feeling very exposed with how much skin I'm showing, my ass cheeks still burning from where he grabbed them.

"I did nothing you didn't specifically ask or want me to do. And based on your reaction, I think you liked it."

I'm well aware of how on fire my body is. My pulse is still raging.

I want to shut my eyes, and shut him out, but I simply stare at him instead, looking as beautiful as the boy I'm falling for. Except it's not him, it's not Maison, and they are so very different.

I wrap my arms around myself as a cool breeze flushes through the air. Those puffy clouds are closer now, darker with shades of gray as they twist and rumble above us. "You could have stopped me." I tell him, not that I was giving him much of a choice.

He gives me that smirk, the only heartless smile I ever see on his face. "And push away a beautiful girl telling me to do naughty things to her? Why the fuck would I do that?"

A flush of warmth runs through me as I take in his words. My tongue and eyes emit heat and fire. "You don't deserve Maison as a brother. He's better than you, Micah, in so many ways."

Accusations lace every word. I can see how Olivia fell for it. Diabolical, Nigel had called him, and I agree as Micah just stares at me with a cool indifference. I almost can't feel my heart as it flutters so fast.

"I don't disagree," he says, observing me.

Then his inner rage bubbles to the surface as his eyes flash and he reaches into the pocket of his sweats and pulls out a knife. He opens it and the blade flashes in the sunlight. He walks toward me, and I flinch, half expecting him to do something to me—grab me by the neck and slice me open. Maybe he will kill me like he's done before.

Instead, he pushes past me, barely brushing against my skin. "You know nothing about me, London," he says in a deadly voice as he steps toward the fish. He bends over, muscles rippling, and places the fish in the calm clear waters, cleaning it.

"I know enough," I mutter. It was either Micah or Maison who hurt Olivia. I am incapable of imagining Maison hurting someone, and I refuse to believe I can be this wrong about somebody.

Micah looks at me with sharp eyes. "You know nothing about your boyfriend, either. He's not the golden boy you think he is, sweetheart."

My skin crawls, every inch buzzing at the way he says it. Unfiltered, unflinching, raw emotion. It's the most real moment we've had together.

He drops his knife into the water and cleans it. I can't rip my eyes from him now, and I can't speak, as he takes the knife and runs it along his sleeve. So sure of himself, every motion he makes is fluid and confident. He ignores me, as he's so good at doing. And with precision and focus, he skillfully makes an incision along the fish's belly to the throat. I watch as he slides the scales apart and the guts spill out of it, and I try to keep what little I've had to eat in the past twenty-four hours in my stomach. He takes his time and scrubs the inside of the fish as I stand silently behind him, watching him work. I suck in a breath, trying to lower my heart rate, willing myself to move, to get away from him. Instead, he rises, leaving the guts spilled out on my rock, meeting my eyes as he passes.

"I hope you enjoyed the show, London, because next time, you're gutting your own damn fish."

He stalks out of sight, into the woods and the veiled mist forming from the impending storm, leaving me cold, alone, and reeling.

It's only when he's gone that I let out a deep exhale.

How could I have not seen it? The way he touched me, so calculated; Maison never touches me like that. Maison's softer, not so forceful. Micah knew exactly what he was doing. Everything about him just hits differently. What buttons on my body to press. He wanted to get me off.

I was right about Micah. He is not a good person.

I genuinely thought it was Maison I was kissing earlier, but Micah knew who I was, and what's happening between me and his brother. He let me kiss him, knowing I was confused. He's messing with me, plain and simple.

He's not entirely innocent, and I know I made a serious mistake. And now I can't stop thinking about how he called me beautiful.

Micah leaves and I do my best to clean the fish guts he left behind. I wash my hands and lay back on the rock, severely annoyed by how quickly they attracted flies. The storm blows over, merely skirting me, but still kicks tiny drops of rain on my face before a hint of sun drops through a tiny hole in the clouds like a fan casting a streak of pink across the now boiling waters.

I can't move yet, not until I can get my heart rate under control. I'm unsure how to face Maison after what I did.

My heart and mind race with desire that I desperately try to control.

I was so into Micah that I almost had sex with him. How did I not know? How did I not *feel* it? I was blind to the fact that his hands were clearly not Maison's. His touch, the flicker in his eyes, and how badly I wanted to put on a show for him.

He used my physical attraction to him to his advantage, to play with me and paw at me, as if I'm nothing but a ball on a string. But it was his comment about Maison that bugs me the most. Maison never held his brother responsible for what happened to Olivia—not like that, not in that way.

I rise and wipe the dirt off myself.

Enough is enough.

It's time to have a real conversation with Maison. I need to know exactly what occurred between them and Olivia.

After this, I have a right to know.

It's nearly dusk by the time I walk back, carefully stepping through the wet moss and rocks. Once I arrive close to camp, I stop in my tracks as voices cut through the woods. A female laugh echoes through the forest, and it's not Naomi or Jade.

A rush hits me as I realize the others are here. Micah must have brought them back and didn't think to mention it. As I approach, my eyes immediately draw to Maison, who is sitting in our spot with Serena. Her head is on his shoulder and his arms are around her, and I immediately suppress the jealousy that tightens my insides.

Friends. They are just good friends.

After what I just did, I can't be upset with him. I watch him for a moment before anyone notices me. He's smiling and looks alive. It's nice to see him up and back to his regular self after two full days in bed—yet another clue it wasn't his mouth I shoved my tongue inside.

Three rabbits hang from the string a few feet away near our cook site, evidence of their successful trapping today. That, with my fish, means we will eat well tonight. Micah is busy already tending to them, and pointedly ignores me, even though his eyes graze me as I walk up. He's the only one who notices me as I hide among the thick woods, and he barely spares me a sidelong glance before going back to skinning whatever animal they had trapped earlier.

I'm cold and bitter, so I slide into my shelter unnoticed and change into sweats and Maison's hockey sweater. Micah's not the only one who can make a fucking point.

I finally join the others, walking in as casually as possible, even though tears burn the backs of my eyes.

Maison shifts when he sees me, as if he knows he's being a bit too handsy with Serena. His eyebrows rise as I walk up, wrapping my arms around myself as a cool breeze hits my face. He knows something is wrong.

James, along with the others, is busy constructing two new shelters for the four newcomers. Nigel and Ezra sit to the side, engrossed in their own conversation yet again, and I suddenly feel like an outsider among this group—or rather, more than usual.

Naomi's busy snapping pieces of wood for the fire, and her head whips up as I approach. Her eyes flicker and my heart tightens as she looks at Micah, then at me, and hands me two water bottles. "Micah needs you to fill these up from the river." Her tone is flat.

Her eyes are electrifying, eyebrows arched, and lips tightly pressed. It's a look I would give to someone if I suspected they had just hooked up with the guy I'm seeing.

She knows something happened—I can *feel* it. Our conversation, her warnings and threats, all of it in her eyes as she hands me the bottle.

I quickly snatch them from her. "Why doesn't Micah tell me himself, then?"

With her hand on her hip, her brown eyes flash. "He told me to ask you when you got back. He's obviously busy."

Micah's concentration on gutting the rabbits a few feet away is broken only by his occasional glance up at us. His face is stone cold.

I snap my gaze across the fire where Maison is still chatting with Serena. He's watching me now. In fact, everyone's looking at me, except for Micah. The daylight is fading quickly, so I twirl on my heels and head toward the river, happy I have an excuse to get out of there. I'm barely at the twist of trees when I hear Maison's voice.

"London, baby, wait," he calls out. I swallow and face him, a look of faint worry etched on his face as he runs his hands over my arms. "What's wrong? Are you upset I was talking to Serena? I've told you many times that I'm not into her."

I try to put out the image of Serena smiling, leaning into him, twirling her hair, or the fact this island would be easier for everyone if I wasn't on it. He'd be with Serena, I'm sure of it. She's a gorgeous brunette—not as pretty as Naomi, but pretty enough. They are both bright and shiny, and I'm just a dark cloud.

I shake my head. "No, it's fine. I'm happy they're here. Hopefully new people will brighten the mood."

"Then what is it, baby?"

I press my lips together as tears form in my eyes. Instead of saying anything, I just fall into him. The weight of everything crushes me, and I can't look at his beautiful face while feeling this guilty.

He grabs my chin and forces me to look at him. "Is this about your fishing lesson?"

My stomach tightens. *He knows... He fucking* knows.

I shake my head. "I don't know what you mean?"

He runs his hand through his hair, trying to tame the wild strands that keep falling into his eyes. "I know Micah didn't catch that fish. He told everyone you did, so I assumed you were with him."

He's watching me, waiting for my reaction. His eyes darken with resurfacing feelings, and now I question what that dark look really means. This is the first time I have ever imagined Maison causing harm to Olivia. It was Micah who sowed that idea in my mind, and it took root like a weed. His words were so malicious that they made my ears burn just hearing it.

Maison embraces me tightly, enveloping me with his muscular arms. His body feels just like Micah's, every muscle hard and firm. Even now, my body still tingles from the two intense orgasms Micah brought me using just his fingers. In Maison's arms, I feel tense and on edge, my whole body coiled.

He looks down at me, his lips pursed at my clear discomfort. "What did he say to you, London? I know he said something. You wouldn't be this upset if he didn't."

I swallow a pit in my throat and grab his hand. "Maison," I whisper, taking in a deep breath, "I like you."

He leans down and kisses me, and a tidal wave of guilt washes through me, knowing where my lips just were. "I know," he whispers back.

I sigh. "I like you a lot."

He squeezes my hand and leans into me, pressing his forehead against mine. "I know, baby," he says again. "I like you, too. What has you so upset? What happened with Micah? Because if he said something that hurt you, I'll kill him."

I press my lips together. "He didn't." The lie rolls off my tongue easier than it should, and I have no idea why I'm protecting Micah right now. I should tell Maison and make him face the consequences.

He joins me as I keep walking, and we walk together through the twisted forest. The sound of our footsteps echo as we crunch through the fallen leaves beneath us.

He doesn't allow me to go far before he pulls me back. "Then what is it, London? Talk to me, baby."

I loosen out a breath. "Micah killed a girl, Maison, and no one seems to talk about it. Yet, somehow, I'm supposed to put all my trust in him."

His eyes flicker, and he opens his mouth to say something, but I stop him by placing my fingers on his mouth. "Please tell me about her. Help me understand him better."

"It was a car accident, London. It was all an accident. He didn't mean to kill her." He turns his head from me—so many more words lingering on the tip of his tongue.

I bristle. "Why was he with her to begin with, Maison?" I say louder than I should. So loud, it slices through the vast forest around us, cutting through the trees and rippling the leaves. "I thought she was your girlfriend."

I watch as he freezes in his tracks, slowly turning toward me with a deadly look in his eyes. His head cocks and he stares at something behind me. "London, come here," he hisses.

The rustle...

I turn to face the sound, and what has Maison's eyes so wide. Yellow eyes and gray fur stare back at me—a cat of some sort that has my body frozen in place. It blends in so well, only its eyes really give it away. Maison walks up slowly, grabbing my hand and pulling me back as I stand frozen in place.

"Step back with me, baby," he says in a quiet, alert voice. "Just walk slow."

I take a trembling step backward, keeping my gaze locked on the feline. It takes a step forward toward us, its muscles gleaming, its dark fur shining in the dim light. Maison's grip on me tightens as a small cat, weighing only twenty pounds, approaches us. The feline inspects us curiously, its yellow eyes fixated on us as it blinks and sniffs, almost as if it's considering us as a potential snack. "Don't move," Maison whispers, as though he's aware of my desire to flee.

The creature stares us down for a few tense seconds, its yellow eyes dancing in the dusky light before it carries on, disappearing back into the woods, and I can breathe again.

"What was that?" I ask Maison as he hugs me, and in an instant, he feels safe to me again.

"I think that was a lynx," he whispers. "Super rare to see them. We should go back and tell the others it's close and make sure we clean up after ourselves tonight. We need to leave, in case it returns."

I grab his hand before he can start walking and slide my fingers through his. "Maison, why won't you talk about her?"

A slight squeeze of his fingers and a pause. "It's the past, baby. I just want her to stay there."

It's not the past... whatever past tensions between these brothers linger. It's clear all over their faces, every interaction, every dark look Maison gets when she gets brought up. Olivia's ghost hovers around him constantly.

I flex my jaw. "I don't know what kind of history you and Micah have with girls, but I am not like that. I am with you and you only, so please keep Micah away from me."

He's quiet, lost in thought as he replays something in his mind.

After a moment of hesitation, he finally speaks up. "Micah's complicated, London, and I owe him so much. We owe him our lives out here. I don't think we would survive out here without him."

A surge of adrenaline rushes through me as I recall Micah's fingers inside me, with no hesitation, despite my relationship with Maison. It seems as if he feels entitled to me because of it.

"You shared her with him, didn't you?" I ask pointedly.

His lack of anger or concern tells me everything. *He knows something happened with Micah and me, but he's too scared to ask about it.* I want to be furious at him, but the look of utter sadness on his face gives me pause.

"It's complicated, baby," he whispers, wrapping his arms around me. "My relationship with Micah is complicated, but just remember whose sweater you're wearing right now. You're *mine*, London. What happened with Olivia was a mistake, and she's in the past."

"Did you hurt her?" The words fall out of me before I can think about it. "Before she died, she had bruises... That's why they were trying to charge Micah, isn't it?"

His eyes narrow. "Why would you ask that?"

Because I know the truth, and I'm spying on you.

"Answer my question, please. I need to hear you say it."

He pulls my head into his chest. "I would never hurt anyone, especially someone I love. Micah would never hurt anybody, either." He presses a kiss into my brow. "Neither of us are going to hurt you, baby."

It takes every ounce of control not to rip my clothes off and fuck him on the forest floor. Any ounce of desire for Micah from earlier is gone.

Maison is everything.

I press my lips to his; I nibble on his lips, his neck. He gives me his full attention and his hands drift to my lower back.

"London," he whispers. "Can I ask you something?"

I turn my head up at the very serious look on his face. "What is it?"

"I want you to be my girlfriend."

I nearly choke on my spit, and I can't help but laugh. But then I realize he's being serious and my heart fills. "I thought I already was?"

"I want to make sure *you* know it."

The smile on my face hurts. "Yes, Maison, I will be your girlfriend."

He wraps an arm around my shoulder. "Good answer. I'll do anything to protect you, baby. I hope you know that."

Happiness swells in my chest as we head back to the others. It's a small sliver in the pit of my belly that upends the full bliss of this moment. My lies still haunt me.

As we make our way back, we see Micah sitting by the fire, his silhouette flickering in the glow of the flames. Holding hands, we approach him, and he looks up. His eyes linger on my hand, tightly laced with Maison's. His jaw flexes as he grabs a stick and starts making another one of his damn spears.

I was right about Micah; and I won't trust him merely because Maison tells me I should. Maison obviously has a blind spot when it comes to his brother and the loyalty is clearly not reciprocated.

For whatever reason, he is trying to drive a wedge between me and Maison. Olivia's death may have been unintentional, but he's far from innocent.

Micah study's me, and he flashes a smile, reminding me how I nearly fucked him a mere hour earlier, and worst of all, how much I liked it.

It's a good night.

Despite Serena's longing glances at Maison, I'm glad to have the rest of the group with us. Having more people means more help, more intelligence to keep us safe, and a bigger divide between Micah and me and the other members of the group I don't like. I truly admire James and his leadership qualities that our alpha and everyone else here are lacking. Respect mainly.

The others finished the beginnings of their shelter, while Micah and Naomi prepped and cooked supper for everyone. Nigel and Ezra were even helpful and didn't complain about using extra energy. I also noticed the two of them talking more in general, in a friendly way, that makes my skin crawl. We are all together for the first time, gathered around the fire eating, consuming the necessary fat and protein to prevent feeling miserable for the next few days. Although, hunger still holds a constant place in my life.

After we eat, Maison and I cuddle in our usual spot where I sit between his legs and lean my head back into him with our blanket wrapped around us. My gaze drifts to the stars, casting a faint glow across the clear night. Jade pops over to chat with Maison for a few minutes, telling us all about how she helped Thomas construct the new shelters. The rest of the group appears worn out after their trek today, but there's an undeniable sense of energy that's pulsing through us—the highest it's been since we arrived. Though there's a hint of frost in the air, I feel warm as I lie still, my attention solely on Maison's heartbeat as I watch and listen.

Nigel keeps staring at me, and I don't care anymore. If he wants to tell everyone my secret, he can go for it. He'd only expose and ostracize himself from the group. But the guilt eats at me, and I have to suppress this nagging feeling that somehow, I will lose Maison.

Naomi's positioned right between Ezra and Micah, each barely sparing her a glance and she cuts a glare at me every chance she gets.

Let her look.

I suppose that's the consequence of jumping between two guys. In the end, they both lose interest in you, although Ezra signals for her to sit with him. He bends down and whispers something in her ear, and she smiles and leans into him. And I can't help but wonder what Micah's reaction might be.

Nothing, apparently. He's laser-focused with that knife in his hand, etching a sharp tip out of wood. And for what? It's not like we don't have enough of them. He makes them every damn night.

Suddenly, Ezra stands. "Now that everyone is back, it's time for a group meeting." Micah's attention snags as he briefly stops his woodworking and arches a brow. Likely because of Ezra taking charge when everyone knows who we will actually listen to. Micah holds an amused smirk for a moment before drifting his attention down to his task, evidently ignoring Ezra's attempts at leadership. Ezra continues anyway and circles the group, "We should investigate the island to determine the situation we're really dealing with. This may not be the best spot."

Chatter erupts from the group, especially the four who just arrived. "We just got here, man," James speaks for his group. He's sitting with his knees up, and his back against a log, with Ollie, Nathan, and Serena close by. "We're staying put for a few days, at least. That airplane spot was brutal. Someone else can go." I catch Serena give him a look, and one I recognize. It's the same look she gives Maison, and I stop to wonder... He's not that much younger than her, only a year. He's intelligent, strong, and has earned respect. He wouldn't be the worst guy to hold on to here, plus I'm happy it's not Maison on the receiving end of that longing look.

I grip Maison's leg and shift beneath him. "Did you know about this?" I whisper.

"Just let him talk, baby."

Ezra grimaces his mouth at me. His hair is longer now, greased down and wiry as it hangs over his twisted, angular face. "Stop fucking whining. It's what's best for everyone. Let's resolve this before winter comes."

Naomi grins, and I consider suggesting Nigel go with them. I don't disagree with his premise, but telling anyone they have to go out there? Leave the safety of our numbers and sleep in the forest when temperatures are plummeting?

It's savage.

I narrow my eyes and shoot to my feet. "I found this place, so I've done my part, Ezra. I don't have to listen to you."

Maison stands up with me. "If London goes, I go."

I glance at Micah, who's barely lifts his head. He blows on his spear and a cloud of dust forms around it.

Ezra shakes his head, keeping his scowl firmly planted on his face. "No, we can't risk anything happening to you, Maison. We need you to hunt, and she's expendable." He gestures toward Jade, who's now moved over to sit with a sulking Nigel. "You two are expendable as well."

"Expendable. Is that what we are to each other?" I say, trying to stay composed, but a blinding panic takes over, for myself and those who get stuck going.

A smile spreads across Ezra's face. "Micah and I discussed it; it's what's best for everyone. The three of you contribute the least."

Micah. Of course it was Micah, and he won't even look at me. Is he retaliating because I pushed him away at the cove?

Micah finally stands, apparently interested in participating in this conversation. "Colder weather is coming, and if we aren't fully prepared, we won't survive out here. We should look for a better spot on the island. We have to look for caves, anything to help protect us from the elements." He shoots a look to Ezra. "We won't force anyone, but we need two people to step up."

Ezra glares back at him. "That's not what we just discussed."

He shrugs. "I changed my mind, and London has a point. We have no right to force people."

Huh? I'm... right?

"Yes, we fucking do, man," Ezra says, waving his hands. "This is *our* island. What we say goes, and this isn't a fucking democracy. We need to step up and take charge. Tasks won't always be as enjoyable as gathering wood and berries."

Micah faces Ezra, half an inch taller, just as intimidating. "I'm in charge," he snaps, "*that* is what we all agreed on. You would be fucking dead already if it wasn't for me. And I said, I changed my fucking mind."

Ezra steps forward, his rage blazing. "No, we wouldn't be dead, and we wouldn't be stuck eating rodents, either." He points at the storage area a few feet away, covered in the tarp and meticulously organized, as if someone is keeping inventory. "The food can sustain us until we're rescued."

Maison's sitting stone cold beside me as Ezra glances at him for help. Ezra then faces Micah, his head a mere inch from the other. But Micah doesn't back down; in fact, he seems to double down on his resolve. "Does everyone not agree with that?" Ezra says, looking at the rest of the group. "Why are we letting that food go to waste when we're starving?"

My heart tenses. It's not the time for them to fight while leading us. My shoulders stiffen, and Maison squeezes my hand, hinting at me not to get involved. Another crack in leadership within the two alphas, it seems.

I can't keep my mouth shut. "It's not *our* island actually, it belongs to someone, the US government most likely, unless we landed in Canada."

It's Naomi who speaks this time. "Shut up, London."

I swallow hard and meet her eyes as she runs her fingers along her ponytail, daring me to say something. "We still have to follow the regular rules of society and learn to govern ourselves better. Show more respect to each other than I've witnessed."

Silence bites at the group, and I feel sorry for James, Ollie, Nathan, and Serena, who all watch us in what looks like a mixture of horror and intrigue.

This is how it's been here. Fucking miserable.

After a few tense moments, it's Ezra who ends up backing down. He sits next to Naomi, while Micah turns and faces the group.

Silence—not one word uttered by anyone after that little performance. He shoots a look at Maison and me as I stand tense in Maison's arms.

"We aren't forcing anyone to go," Micah says, "and you aren't going, Maison, because we need you to stay here and trap."

Nigel stands and shakes his head, then makes his way back to his shelter. I take a moment to inspect him. His sunken face shows the toll of twelve days living off the land. I wonder if I look the same, and the thought makes me shudder. He pauses when he realizes everyone is looking at him. For a brief second, I think he is volunteering as tribute.

He arches his brows. "What? Do you all think I'm volunteering? That is fucking laughable." He tugs at Jade to come with him, because it seems like she belongs to him, catering to every little whim to please him. "Come on, Jade, let's go."

Jade stands, her eyes wide, and she darts them around the group. "I'll go," she says meekly, ignoring Nigel. "I'll go explore the island."

"Don't be fucking stupid, Jade." Nigel sneers. "You're not going anywhere."

It's Thomas who stands now, after remaining quiet near Micah. He rises like a feral animal and gets right in Nigel's face. "Don't fucking speak to her like that."

Nigel is half the height of Thomas, and doesn't so much as flinch. The hatred coming out of Nigel's eyes sends a shiver down my spine. "She doesn't know what she's doing out there. So sit down and put a muzzle on it."

Thomas takes a deadly step forward, and I worry for Nigel's life. Thomas's fingers are curled as his whole body tenses. I think it's wonderful how he's sticking up for Jade, but the thought of Jade going out there makes my nerves shake. She'd be less prepared than I am, although she has taken to learning the survival skills better than I have. Nigel sneers, seemingly unaffected by Thomas's reaction, almost as if he's plotting something.

Jade rubs her shoulders, darting her eyes between Nigel and Thomas. Her old friend—only friend she really had in school—and Thomas, the guy I think she is falling for. Nigel knows it, too. "It's okay. Ezra's right, I've probably contributed the least out of everyone."

I grind my teeth and mutter under my breath, "Ezra's an asshole."

Maison leans down and whispers in my ear, "London, stop. You're not making this any better. We have to let this play out."

"I'm going with Jade," Thomas says. "I'm not letting her go alone, and I don't trust anyone else with her."

Nigel remains eerily silent, and I want to tell him he's the one who should go since he's literally contributed nothing. He pivots and strides toward his shelter, emerging shortly after with Jade's bag in hand. He hurls it at her feet and declares, "Take it. You created this mess, now you must accept the consequences. I'm not watching out for you anymore, you stupid bitch."

Bold move on Nigel's part, considering the brick wall in front of him that looks like he wants to murder him. Ezra and Naomi are grinning now, finding this whole situation rather amusing. And Micah continues his blundering silence.

Thomas picks up the stray clothes Nigel threw into the mud and wipes them off. His eyes shoot up to Nigel, his voice low. "I'll break your face if you talk to her again."

Nigel cocks his square head. "Whatever."

And off he goes, clearly not volunteering to help with anything whatsoever. If he wasn't such a calculated asshole, I'd feel sorry for him.

Micah rises and slaps Thomas on the back. "We'll chat tomorrow about a route I found. Travel for one day and stick to the shoreline. You two will be fine."

I have to get Micah credit; he handled this well. I'm unsure how I would have reacted if they tried to force me to go. Maison squeezes me again, and I'm tempted to pull away. I wish Maison would have more to say to Ezra. Micah's the only one who will ever stand up to him.

Say something, Maison. Stick up for people.

It's Ollie who's speaks next. "What if they don't come back?" The younger guys seem to avoid getting involved, and I can't really blame them. It's only been ten minutes, and we're already at each other's throats.

"Then God fucking speed," Ezra snipes from the side.

With tensions simmered, the group goes back to talking amongst themselves. Jade and Thomas move to the other side of the fire and strike a deep conversation, while Serena sits close to James and leans into him. Maison and I cuddle, watching the fire in silence.

Out of the corner of my eye, Micah rises and grabs Naomi's hand while she's sitting next to Ezra. He pulls her back to his spot, placing her on his lap, where he pushes his tongue down her throat.

Micah's eyes draw to mine when he notices me watching them.

Shit.

I shift my gaze immediately and squeeze Maison's hand. Not that I care. Micah can make out with whoever he wants. It's just.... he's barely looked at her for the past week, and I figured he lost interest. And I can't help but feel it's more to agitate Ezra than anything else at this point—or maybe even me. My cheeks heat at the latter.

Drawing my eyes to Ezra, I jump slightly when I see him staring right at me instead of watching Micah and Naomi like I assumed he would be. A dark, chilling stare in flickering firelight.

Jesus.

Maison's hand rubs down my arm. "Ignore him. He pouts whenever he doesn't get his way."

"What is wrong with him?" I whisper, still watching Ezra, and his beady eyes not blinking.

Micah and Naomi disappear and a pit forms in my stomach. I'm aware of what they'll do—he would have done the same thing with me if I had let him. That same mouth sucking on hers was sucking on mine, touching where he shouldn't with his fingers. I'll never understand how he can be so complacent with sex, like it doesn't matter to him. It's just... physical for Micah, completely void of any emotion.

Maison's voice jolts me back as if he senses me watching him, like he knows the dark thoughts swirling in my head. "Ezra gets pissed at Micah. They've always had a bit of a rivalry, ever since we were kids. Micah is the team captain and always wins. The girls like him, our parents are richer, and he's much better looking."

I roll my eyes and can't help but smile at the last comment. If Maison knows anything about Ezra's parents going bankrupt because of his father, he says nothing.

He pulls me up. "Enough about Micah. They'll get past it, they always do. Let's go to bed, baby."

I follow Maison to our little home and crawl in with him as he lights us a small fire outside our shelter. We pass Micah and Naomi on our way, and my chest tightens at the sight of them making out. It's not like I haven't seen the two of them kissing before, because I have—a ton since we got here. But now, I think I might be jealous, although I don't want to admit it.

CHAPTER TWELVE

Day Fourteen

If I can explain this island in one word, it would be quiet. The silence is almost as suffocating as the vast expansiveness that lays around us. Except at night, that's when we hear the wolves. I woke up last night, terror erupted through me, and I cried out—screamed. A raw, horrific, blood curdling sound I didn't know I was capable of. It hurt my throat for hours after. Panic, fear, dread, hunger. These feelings consumed me when I reached for Maison, who wasn't there. When he came back to me, I could barely speak. I thought he was gone and I was alone. He had to calm me down after I shook for hours. Now I'm petrified to leave his side.

Everyone has retracted into themselves. In two weeks, the island left us as empty shells of ourselves. The weather is horrible—it rained the last two days—and except for fishing and trapping, we've all kept to ourselves. Maison's the only optimistic one, like any moment an airplane will swoop in and save us. His optimism is why I'm falling for him. He will find a silver lining in anything, no matter how awful. Micah's obsessed with keeping the fire going, hunting, making weapons, and just keeping us alive. He won't sit down. He prowls the campsite like an ax murderer. He's agitated all the time, and he won't look at me. It's like I don't exist to him. But then again, Micah barely speaks to anyone. When we do make eye contact, I keep thinking about his hands on me, which only makes me feel guilty. Kissing Micah at the cove made me feel the way I did with Chris—where my body was alive, but my mind knew how wrong it was. Giving my body what it wants but nothing of what it needs. Making me feel so fucking alive it hurt. It hurt so much. And then... and then it ruined me.

We are going to die out here. Deep down, we all know that. If the world hasn't found us by now, they are not going to. Any glimmer of hope I had was gone when Jade and Thomas left this morning. With winter coming, and with it the snow, ice, and darkness, we will have no hope until spring... if we make it that far.

Maison's soft arm grazes over my stomach as I curl into him. His sweet smell of body wash tickles my nose. I smile as I shoot my eyes open and appreciate the closeness of him. The soft streaks of light tease the roof of the otherwise dark shelter, barely big enough for the two of us. I lose myself in Maison's messy hair, his soft facial hair that now lines his chin and face, and his dark lashes that go on for miles when his eyes are closed.

The thing about the wilderness is we create our own schedules, and today I have no intentions of leaving this bed. Maison must agree since he won't open his eyes, but I know he's awake from the little smirk on his face. He lets me fuss over him, and I slowly wake him up with my hands, kisses, and soft strokes. It's the same attentiveness he gives me that has me falling for him more with each passing day. I'm eager to have sex with him again and forget about Micah.

As I wake up, I realize something is wrong. My icy breath and crystals hang in the air, and the ground beneath me is colder than usual, despite all the insulation Maison built beneath us. I shiver, even though I'm under the blankets with his body heat, and looking at the ground next to us, I find a thin layer of white just beyond the opening. It brushes the ground with a soft, brilliant white.

"Maison," I whisper, nudging his arm. "I think it snowed."

His eyes open, and he shoots up. "Shit. It did. We should get up."

I pull him back down to me and force his arm back to where it was on my belly. "No, we shouldn't." I kiss his nose. "Let's not rush to get up. Micah's just going to put us to work. I don't want to deal with snow, and you're so warm."

My chest caves in on itself at the thought. Snow—and it's only late September. My hand trails down his stomach and I push myself closer. It doesn't take much to convince him to stay. I turn away from him, so my back is into him, and his erection presses right into me. We lie for a few minutes like this, and I think he's fallen back asleep because of his soft snores. After a few minutes, I nudge him, anything to help me distract from what's waiting for us outside.

"Maison?"

"Yeah, baby?"

"Where would you have taken me?"

He shifts behind me. "What do you mean, pretty girl?"

"I mean, if we didn't go on this trip, and the plane didn't crash, where would our first date have been if you had given me the time of day at school?"

A pause, which is adorable. "I was going to ask you on a date during that interview you promised me."

I elbow him in the ribs. He lies. My social standing at school wouldn't have allowed him to ask me out. "You were not. I was awkward and mean."

He nibbles on my ear. "What do you mean, you *were*? Your awkwardness and cruelty are why I like you so much. I'm a sucker for punishment, baby."

I turn to face him, and his pretty dark eyes flash with amusement. I frown as a tightness rises in my chest. It's time to tell him why I came on this trip.

He matches my frown with one of his own and presses a kiss to my brow. "It's true, baby. I wanted you the second I saw you blushing in that cafeteria. What do I have to do to show you how much I want you? I'm falling so hard for you, London King."

I bite my cheek and close my eyes as a coppery taste fills my mouth. I imagine Micah's hands inside me as I withered and dripped in pleasure beneath him, bearing everything for him. That, and Nigel's smug fucking smirk as he threatened me. The two people who can ruin what I'm building with Maison.

Heat balloons in my chest, despite the cool air around me, and I'm about to kiss him when Ezra's voice cuts through the air like a sharp knife. "Everyone, get the fuck out of bed. There's work to do."

I groan as Maison jumps up like a dutiful pet, and he urges me out of bed. I quickly pull on a few layers of clothes and pull the hood up over my head before crawling outside. I'm almost blinded by how bright it is. The sun shining over the snow, the crystals, the frost wrapped around every branch. It shimmers over every rock, making the water shine a brilliant blue. It looks like a holiday card, and if I wasn't so terrified of it, I'd say it was beautiful.

The lingering sick feeling I constantly carry hits me full force. Jade and Thomas are out there somewhere. They left yesterday, so they would have spent the night in this.

Ezra and James stand by the water, discussing their plans, probably debating how to handle this, especially with some of us missing. Ollie and Nathan are busy tending to the fire. Nigel, of course, is nowhere in sight, and neither are Naomi and Serena. I expect to see Micah somewhere, but I wonder if he even spent the night here. Ever since our interaction at my cove, his distance has increased. Like he can't stand the sight of me and avoids all of us. He's certainly not leading us like we need him to. Little by little, and day by day, Ezra is taking over that role.

Maison nudges my arm. "Stay here a second. I'll find out what's happening."

I join Ollie and Nathan by the fire and warm my hands over the flames. The humid air is already seeping into my bones. Micah emerges from the woods, and his eyes meet mine briefly as the others walk over. He gives me no hint of emotion, and I can't help but notice the wildness in his eyes. Like being here, with us, is not natural. The wilderness, being alone in the woods, is where he belongs, where he's happiest. Sometimes he seems more out of place here than I do. I wonder if he spends the night alone because it's a place no one can hear him scream. As if his pain doesn't exist as long as no one is there to hear it.

The other boys join us at the fire, and Naomi and Serena emerge from the woods as well, holding wet kindling. Ezra paces as he begins his tyrannical speech, "We need to prepare for winter. These shelters won't last long-term; they're shit. Also, we need to hunt bigger game. No more small prey. We need to go after deer."

"What about Jade and Thomas?" I ask. "Are we just going to leave them out there? We should go after them. Send a small group to find them and bring them back."

Ezra cocks a brow. "Don't be stupid, London. We have to look out for the betterment of everyone, not just one or two people."

Micah steps forward, causing Ezra to twitch and snap his head at him, clearly not enjoying being interrupted. "We can't afford to lose anyone. They have to figure it out for themselves. I gave them a route; they will be fine."

I fold my arms. "They weren't prepared for weather like this. They have no shelter, nothing. They could die out there, and your plan is to just... leave them? We can get by on fish and rabbits for a few days; we need to find them."

"We could all die out here," Naomi snaps, walking over and standing next to Ezra. She too looks less like herself day by day as her pretty face loses some of its plumpness. Her cheeks sink in onto themselves, and even her blond hair looks duller, less golden.

For the first time, Micah's eyes soften and he actually looks human, like how he looked and felt when I kissed him. Then I remember it's his best friend out there, too. He'd be a monster if he didn't care a little. "They volunteered to go, London," he says to me. "They knew what they were getting into. I've taught them everything I can."

Maison walks up and places his arm around me. "Come on, babe. Thomas is strong, and Jade is smart. I think they will be okay. I bet they will be back tomorrow."

I don't like it... any of it. We should go after them.

My eyes find Micah, his eyes shadowed under his black hood. "Is this the kind of group you want to lead, Micah?" I say, finally looking at him. The first real words I've uttered to him since the incident. My icy coolness toward him is met with equal animosity over the past couple of days, making it very easy to avoid and hate him. I'm not sure if Maison's noticed the clear tension between us, but I make sure Maison knows he's the one I want every chance I can, and that Micah sees it.

The twins exchange a glance, and Micah seems unfazed by the comment. Instead, his eyebrows arch. "We'll need extra wood for the next few days to keep the fire lit. Can you handle that, London?"

I nod, then roll my eyes. "Fine."

Fuck this.

Without uttering a single word, I extricate myself from Maison's arms and trudge into the dense woods, where I come across Nigel lurking in his shadowy corner of the world. I assume he's only come out to scavenge for food since he hasn't interacted with anyone since Jade left. I head down the shore away from him, grateful Micah sent me away. I have to take careful steps as the snow has made the ground more slippery than normal, and my feet crunch atop the thin layer still not burned off from the sun. Most of the snow has melted or is melting.

I take nearly an hour to calm down my raging nerves, but I find dry wood underneath a few fallen trees. At one point I even rip bark off a dead tree, pulling it so hard my fingers bleed. I repeatedly return with wood, keeping my head down as I add it to the pile. I saw Naomi and Serena doing the same earlier, so I guess it's nice to know Micah wasn't specifically picking on me.

Hours go by, and I'm nearly drenched in sweat by the time I'm done. My knees are weak, and I can barely walk as I approach the camp from my last trip.

Naomi is standing alone by the fire, everyone else off doing something or resting, I'm assuming. She's holding something, and my stomach drops at the sight of my leather-bound journal in her hands. She's flicking through it, reading every fucking word.

My words... my private words.

This is low, even for Naomi. I've kept that journal hidden in my bag, hidden from Maison, Nigel, everyone. She must have snooped through my stuff. I drop the wood and run up to her. "Give that back, Naomi. Right now. I'm not kidding. Give that back."

Her eyes narrow and she lifts them to meet mine. Then, to my absolute horror, she reads it out loud. "This is the first journal entry for my story about the twins. Although, I don't have much to say since yesterday when Nigel gave me this."

I cut her off before she can say anything else just as James, Ollie, Nathan, and Serena come walking up like a perfectly timed fucking disaster. She keeps reading, and I stand utterly still as Naomi raises her voice, trying to catch the attention of everyone.

"I tried not to stare at them, and I have no idea how I will find a way into their world, especially with Naomi always around. She won't let me near them. So I just observed the best I could and slipped into the school office to see if I could order a school uniform that actually fits me."

James stands forward just as Maison walks around the bend and into view, Micah close behind him. My stomach is in my throat and my heart is beating out of my chest as everyone stops what they are doing to listen to her.

"That's enough, Naomi." James steps forward, but it doesn't matter. The damage is already done. She flips through a few pages, but I suspect she's already read most of it and gives me a predatory look. "Oh no, this is just getting good," she says with a vicious snarl. I look directly at Maison—at least, I think it's Maison. They look so damn fucking alike. Naomi zeros in right on Micah and continues reading. "Kissing Micah at the cove made me feel the way I did with Chris—where my body was alive, but my mind knew how wrong it was. Giving my body what it wants but nothing of what it needs."

She drops the journal and raises an eyebrow at Micah, who, like his brother, is fixated on me. We're in a circle with me as the focal point. Even Nigel came out of his den with his crumpled argyle shirt hanging off him. I'm glad about it, too. This is as much his issue as it is mine.

"What's going on, Naomi?" Maison asks her, darting his eyes between us.

She purses her lips at him. "Ask your girlfriend, Maison. Apparently, she came on this trip to spy and expose you and Micah about Olivia." She turns her focus to me. "Or are you Micah's girlfriend now, given you fucked at the cove?"

I swallow bile down my throat, and I literally have nothing to say. Every truth, every thought, feeling, and fear is out there for everyone to hear.

Maison narrows his eyes and shakes his head. It's the look I've been dreading this whole time, where he sees me differently. "London, what is she saying?"

"Maison..." my voice cracks, "it's not what you think."

Naomi waves the journal around. "Yes, it is *exactly* what we think. You wrote it out pretty clearly, London. You came on this trip to write a story about them, then all you do is fuck them behind their backs. You're just as bad as she was."

I'm pretty sure my breathing has now stopped, my lungs caving in.

It's Micah that steps forward, looking me up and down. "London and I didn't fuck, Naomi."

She shakes her head, her eyes blazing with equal parts anger and sadness. "Well, according to her diary, you did *something* with her."

I only half hear them. My eyes are directly on Maison, who shakes his head and draws his eyebrows together. I look at him, pleading and completely broken. "Fucking unbelievable," he mutters, unable to face me.

"Nigel made me do it," I scream, and I know I just sound desperate. I had every chance in the world to tell him. Both twins watch me now, their expressions confused. "Nigel wanted to write this story. He convinced me to do it, but that was before I knew you, Maison. I never would have agreed now."

"Shut it, London," Nigel spits with more energy coming out of him than I've seen in days. "I had my reasons for doing it, but what were yours?" He cocks his head. "Oh yes, you fucked your teacher and had to leave town because of it. You wanted to ruin two strangers' lives to get into a prestigious school."

I shake my head at him, tears forming in my eyes. That little girl I used to be, in my ballet outfit—twirling, prancing, innocent. I had dreams.

"What? You think I didn't look you up?" Nigel says indifferently. "I knew what kind of girl you were before you even started at New Ocean Prep."

Maison turns and walks away, but not before facing his brother. A moment that embodies two years of pain. "You're a fucking asshole, dude," he mutters to Micah, then he turns his back on me, on everyone, and walks off into the white-dusted forest. And it's all I can do to squeeze my eyes shut and drop to my knees.

He. Walked. Away.

A crunch of twigs and snow has me out of my hazy sleep a mere second before strong hands wrap themselves around my mouth. So strong, they stifle my breathing as at least one other person drags my feet and pulls me out of my shelter, raking me right over the cold rocks and snow. I touch the ground briefly, surrounded by the veil of night, and looming shadows of gnarled trees before they pick me up again, shoving their hands over my mouth. This time wrapping a cloth of some sort around my face and head.

I can't even scream as I wither and panic beneath their iron grip.

"Shut the fuck up, London. Don't make this harder on yourself."

Nigel.

Fear winds it's way through my gut, freezing me as I realize I am severely outnumbered and my memories of the night come swirling back. Maison never returned or checked on me, and neither did Micah—not that I expected Micah to. I finally fell asleep after crying alone for hours, trying to figure out how to face him—face both of them.

The hands gripping me are strong. Nigel's not carrying me—his weak ass body couldn't bear my weight—which means Ezra's the one who hauled me over his shoulder. Then I hear Naomi's laugh as he throws me onto the forest floor. My mouth chokes on mud as my face meets the ground with a heavy *thud*.

I cry out when the poorly placed gag falls out. "What are you guys doing?"

Naomi kicks me in the teeth while the other two loom above. I try to cry out, I try to scream, "Maison!"

Naomi bends down and grabs me by the hair. "Don't try to scream, London. Don't fight the punishment, and it will end faster. I told you not to fucking mess with them." She throws me back down again.

They couldn't have taken me far. "*Maison,*" I cry out again.

The crack of her foot to my head whips me to my side, pain radiating all the way down my spine. Blood trickles down my nose, and I can taste the metal as it falls into my mouth.

Naomi circles as I curl into a fetal position, trying to protect my head. "I told you; they can't hear you," she growls. "Accept your punishment and don't lie to us again."

I close my eyes as mud and dirt seep into them, preparing myself for what's to come. My mouth is already pulsing and split, my heavy breath and beating heart the only sounds I can hear. My punishment, apparently, and Naomi is the judge, jury, and executioner. So I let her have me.

"It didn't have to be this way, London," Nigel says darkly. "You just fucked up again."

Through swollen eyes, I see his sneering lips under the moonlight. "Fuck you, Nigel," I cry before the three of them kick me in the ribs, and Naomi unleashes her fury. She hovers over me and punches and kicks me more times than I can count. My shirt rides up, my belly scraping against the hard ground and rocks beneath me.

When she's done, I lie alone and in pain on the forest floor, where they leave me. Maison's promise to protect me a mere day earlier is the only thing I can focus on.

"I'll do anything to protect you, London. I hope you know that."

And I think to myself, Maison is nothing but a fucking liar.

It's often said to trust your instincts, that trust can take years to build and mere seconds to shatter. And some-times, you realize you never should have trusted at all. Unfortunately, every time I've put my trust in someone, I've been burned. In the past, I would have preferred to believe a sweet, deceitful lie rather than face the bitter truth. But now, all I have left is that bitter truth, which scorches my throat as I swallow it. I've come to realize that the only person I can trust is myself. I trusted Maison, and he abandoned me. My gut was right, guys are all the same. Maison wouldn't even let me explain, and he let them hurt me.

I stayed on the ground, cold and alone, before the early morning streaks of light bled into the morning sky. My body hurt all over, searing pain in my ribs from Naomi's brutal kicks. I reveled in the pain; it reminded me I'm still alive. It fueled me forward asI crawled my way back to my shelter, packed my bag with some clothes, and made my way over to the storage area. Thomas, of course, was not there to guard it, so I stole a spear, a couple cans of beans I've had my eye on for days, a lighter, and a bottle of purified water. Then, for good measure, I dumped water over the fire that was left unattended. It's coals still burned red, sizzling and cracking from the wet wood. A final fuck you to everyone here—especially Micah.

If anyone had watched me, I'm sure I looked nothing short of barbaric. Mud was still caked on my face, dried blood on my lips, my hair unruly. I took pleasure in stealing as much as I could fit into my pack. It should be enough until someone comes. I am banking on someone coming; otherwise, I know I will die alone out here.

If the others follow, let them hunt me. I'd rather die alone than spend one more night with any of them.

I left the camp quietly. Slow and steady, I now make my way through the forest, which is dimly lit by the early morning sun. A hazy mist circles the air, and I was frozen to the core, but I refused to give up. I kept following Micah's trail markers through the frost-covered wilderness toward the airplane. My senses are now listless and dull as I focus on taking one step at a time, almost like I'm dead inside and just trying to make it to the plane.

I take almost two hours to make the trip, and it's only as the sun burns high in the sky that I finally notice the landscape changing. Back to burnt, crisp, dead trees and tundra with very little greenery.

The graveyard.

The brush tightens around me, and it's completely silent when I finally see the charred tip of the airplane wing. My blood pounds through every hurt muscle as I take in the sight. The plane looks as animalistic as I do. Its exterior is ashen and dusty, blending into the blackened landscape around it. And the flies, so many buzzing around me. But it's the smell that has me keeled over. The pungent stench of decomposing bodies overwhelms me, and I cry deeply at the horror of it all. It was easy to forget them when all I could focus on was survival. But now, being here again, the entire crash comes burning into my memories as if I'm living it again.

I can't stay here long, but I can't walk anymore, so I make my way to the airplane, over the slippery rocks and mud left from yesterday's snowfall. Even the snow, it seems, wants nothing to do with this place, as there is a very little remnant of it.

The stairs hang down, inviting me through the open airplane door. I haul myself up and into the back door, where Nigel, Jade, and I sat when we left New Ocean. I immediately throw my pack down and ignore whatever else is on the airplane with me. I'm scared to check if Micah and the others removed all the bodies, although I have to believe they did. I curl up, grateful for a moment to rest out of the elements and my thoughts immediately drift to Maison.

Maison. I hate him, and miss him, and I wonder if he even knows I'm gone.

I dare to stand and look in the bathroom, at the mirror inside. Through the dust and ash, I see the image of myself, and it's worse than I can imagine. I don't recognize the person staring back at me. I have the same sunken cheeks as the other girls, and my hair is caked in mud and blood, falling over my chest while my collarbone protrudes out, showing how thin I have become. I pull up my shirt to properly inspect the damage done to my body, and below a thin layer of grime, the red scrapes and purple bruises are already forming.

I draw my hand to my hip bone—the one Micah likes so much. The layer of fat that used to surround it is gone. I doubt it would entice him so much anymore because I look like death reincarnate, not at all womanly, and super dirty. I'm not sure where to find fresh water, so I know I can't stay. I'm so used to my daily baths in the fresh lake to clean myself.

I grab my spear and run my thumb along the edge, and I think of how satisfying it would be to jab this in Naomi's leg. Which is exactly what I plan if she ever touches me again. Placing the spear down in front of me, the gentle howl of the wind outside lulls me into an almost sleep. My eyelids are swollen and heavy, and I have no sense of how long I've been sitting in here as I drift off to blissful sleep.

Then a hand brushes up against my cheek and I flutter my eyes open and gasp.

"London." The familiar voice has my heart lurching.

My heavy lids take on his concerned face. "Maison?" I whisper.

He cocks his eyebrows and shakes his head.

I scramble up, lean back on the window, and reach for my spear, which is long enough I can jab it right in Micah's belly. "Leave me alone, Micah." I glare at him with my mud-caked hair hanging right in my face like a feral cat. Unease almost cripples me as he stares at me as an amused smirk plays at his lips from the pointy spear I have jammed in his belly.

I'm sure I look like a vision.

"Come on, London," he says, taking in every cut, bruise, and streak of dried blood. "We both know you will only hurt yourself with that spear."

I turn my eyes from him, highly annoyed by how utterly sexy I still find him. He removes the spear softly but firmly, displaying his dominance.

"Where's Maison?" I ask him, as it seems like he is alone.

He ignores my question. "What happened to you?"

A guttural cry escapes me as I recall every kick, punch, and the suffocating hands over my mouth. I push it out of my head so I don't burst into tears. Never in my life have I experienced such violence. "Your girlfriend happened to me," I spit. "And Ezra, and Nigel. The people you call your friends."

Micah swallows, his jaw flexes and eyes flash. "They're not my friends."

I slump over now in full defeat, knowing my backpack is full of his precious stolen food. I swat a couple flies away as they buzz around my face. To my surprise, he reaches his hand out. "Come on, we have to go."

I wrinkle my nose. "I'm not going anywhere with you."

"Well, you're not fucking staying here." Before I can protest, he pulls me in his arms and lifts me up. I'm like a leaf to him, so tiny, wasted away to almost nothing, while he still seems strong and thriving. I have no energy to even fight him. He grabs my backpack and spear, and says nothing as he carries me out of the safety of the plane.

"Where's Maison?" I finally ask him, keeping my head down and in the crook of his arm. His muscles flex beneath me as he carries me.

"When we realized you were missing, he freaked out. I wouldn't let him come with me to look for you. He doesn't think straight when he gets like that. I promised him I would find you and bring you back. He's pretty fucking mad at me."

As he should be. "I'm not going back, Micah."

He takes me away from the airplane, away from the stench and flies that surround it. He carefully steps over each death hole in the earth as we pass them. "Yeah, you are, London. It's comical you think you will survive even one day out here alone. These cans of beans you stole are cute, but how were you planning on opening them?"

I silently seethe at his point. I have no clue how to open a can of beans without a can opener—although, if I were that desperate, I'm sure I could have figured it out.

Micah continues, ignoring my bristling, "We're heading back, but I'll find you a nearby place to rest for the night."

I scoff as he carries me even farther into the dense brush, not the way I came in. He's taking me to where James and the others stayed. "Why do you even care?" I finally ask.

His hard muscles still beneath me, just for a moment, but it was a flinch. He stops and looks at me, and I focus on the bob of his throat. "That shouldn't have happened to you," he admits. "I shouldn't have let this happen to you."

I choke on a cry I can't control. "No, you shouldn't have. You shouldn't have done a lot of things to me, Micah."

He has no smart response for that.

Even when I try to be strong, I'm weak. Eventually, I let my head rest on him and close my eyes. We don't say another word while he carries me to wherever he is taking me. Dizziness buzzes in my head, and my muscles tremble. I've barely eaten, my energy depleted.

Utterly broken.

It feels like we're walking forever, but I'm not sure how long it is. I think I even fall asleep in the lull of his arms. When we arrive, it looks as though a fire was recently burning, the beginnings of one anyway, with embers burning in ash. He must have come here first to prepare the site—fixed the half-broken shelter to the point where it looks sturdier than the ones we have back at our camp and set up a proper fire.

He places me down, and I can't help but notice other supplies here as well. Useful items, mainly wire for trapping, lots of spears, and clothes—an abundance of them. Micah's mark is evident all over this place, almost like he lives here. The rushing sound of water nearby validates my suspicions.

I watch as he moves around the site with familiarity and ease.

"You've been staying here. This is where you disappear to every day," I accuse when he finally makes eye contact with me.

He didn't take me to the other camp like I thought he would; he took me to his home. He's clever about not arousing too much suspicion by occasionally sleeping at the other camp. He spends more time away from us, so I assumed he was like a sleepless vampire who prowls the woods at night. Micah's not merely surviving on this island, he's thriving out here, while the rest of us are shrivelling away and ripping each other apart.

He looks at me, that pretty face void of emotion. "Don't tell anyone," he says in his deep voice. "We're heading back to the other camp tomorrow. Maison and Thomas will search for us if we don't go back, and I don't want anything unguarded there."

Jade and Thomas—I had all but forgotten about them.

"They got back this morning," he says, tossing some wood on the fire. "Unfortunately, they didn't find much. Most of this island is like this. I think you found the best spot."

A wave of relief hits me that they made it back safely. At least I'll have one friendly face back there. And I disagree. I think this spot Micah found is perfect. It's by a small meadow, a speckled escarpment to shelter us from the biting wind, and is next to a clean water source. The surrounding fir trees are among the prettiest I've seen here.

I keep my head down in the shelter as he takes a can from my backpack. He blows on the fire and get's it burning with a piece of small dry kindling. His heavy presence lingers over me as he works. He takes the can of beans and starts making small cuts into the lid, eventually squeezing it so the lid pops off. He moves to heat the beans over the fire, but I rip the can out of his hand and start shoving those beans into my mouth with my fingers while he watches me with amusement as I stuff my face. I forget to offer him any until I've almost finished the can. Of course, he refuses, and I don't say thank you—after what I endured, it's the least he can do.

When I'm done, he takes the can from me and walks over to the nearby creek, filling it with water. He then holds the can over the fire until it's hot enough, even he flinches.

I watch him, stone cold, as he crawls in front of me and arches his brown eyes in a soft gesture of neutrality. I raise my chin as he reaches out for me. "What are you doing?"

"I have to wash you up with hot water. Cuts and scrapes can easily get infected. Trust me, you don't want to deal with that."

He doesn't wait for my response. He pulls my sweater off, leaving me in my ribbed tank top. I lean back, aware of how close to me he is, how exposed I am to him again, and how his presence makes me so nervous. He only focuses on my wounds as he dips a spare T-shirt into the hot water, gently lifts my tank top up.

I flinch when the heat hits my skin. "Relax, London, it's just water. I'm only cleaning you."

I nod hesitantly and lay back, deciding to enjoy the slight burning and sizzle on my skin. His hands are like they were before, soft but pointed, skilled. He wipes me, starting with a nasty cut on my belly. So attentive, giving my cuts just as much focus as one of his precious spears.

It doesn't take long for my body to react, for that heat to build in my lower belly. I jolt and he stops just as his hands rub against my ribs. "That's enough," I tell him. "I can do the rest." I don't want him to notice the reaction I have to him, or the wetness building between my legs.

He nods, as if understanding the exact reason he needs to stop. "When you feel better, go for a swim to clean off the rest of the dirt. It will help." He rises and steps toward the river.

"Where are you going?" I ask, suddenly afraid to be alone, as if I didn't just run away into the wilderness alone with no plan.

"I'm getting myself dinner. Just rest, you'll be fine," he says and stalks off.

I listen to his advice and head toward the nearby spring and rub every part of my body. I'm quick about it, mainly because the waters are icy and I'm not exactly sure where Micah went off to or if he's watching. When I'm done, I dress in layers and grab some extra clothes Micah has stored here. I wrap myself in blankets and lay down on the comfortable bed he's made himself.

When he returns a couple of hours later, the sun is a low haze in the sky, hidden behind the thick brush of trees around the camp. I dozed on and off, waiting for him to return, realizing and dreading where he will need to rest his head tonight.

I hear him fussing and can vaguely stay awake long enough to know he's skinning and cooking something nearby. Eventually, he stokes the fire, flames bursting to life and heating my face and toes. He hesitates before joining me inside, crawling in next to me. I shift a few inches away, giving him lots of room before my teeth start to chatter despite the heat from the fire. He wraps his arm around me, tucking a blanket around me, and I immediately pull away.

"I can't let you shiver," he tells me, keeping me close. "Shivering burns calories, which you need right now. I'm not going to touch you like that again, London. I promised Maison I wouldn't."

They talked about me. I wonder what they said and how Maison's feeling about it. I hope Micah clarified some things. I want to bring up the story, bring up Olivia, but I don't dare. And since he's not bringing it up, either, I don't bother. It hardly feels like it matters anymore.

From pure exhaustion, my body relaxes and conforms to his, and immediately, the warmth makes me feel better. Before I close my eyes to sleep for the night, I shift and ask him the question I'm dying to know. "Micah?" I ask in a low voice. "Why do you hate me so much?"

His lips brush against the back of my head. "I don't hate you, London," he breathes, and a beat of silence goes by before I hear him say, "and that's part of the problem."

CHAPTER THIRTEEN

Day Eighteen

Micah brought me back two days ago, and I still refuse to talk to anyone. Jade moved in with me for the time being after I ignored Maison's attempts to talk to me. My bruises are still raw and visible—a reminder of what this group is capable of—and my body feels like it's eating itself. Micah still retreats to the forest, but spends every night here now. I think to watch over me, though he won't say so. He ignores everyone, including Naomi. Maison punched Nigel for what he did to me. The only reason Maison didn't turn on Ezra was because James and the others had him pinned down before he could do anything further. His fury reminded me of Micah's primal rage, a side of Maison I had never seen before. It's like I don't really know him—or either of them, really. Nothing is as it seems. Everyone realizes the gravity of our situation. I worry about what will be left of us when they come.

I wring out my hair and slip my clothes back on. Winter's first blast is behind us, with warmer weather the past few days. I felt strong enough to leave the camp for the first time since the attack. Desperate for a cleanse, I slipped to my retreat and dove into the chilly waters before soaking up the late evening sun. The warmest time of day is when the wind stops and the heat retains in the air. I sprawl out the flat rock, laying my leg out in front of me, staring at the water and mountaintops above the dusty horizon. The mountains feel so close today, like I can reach out and touch them.

Footsteps draw my attention toward the tree line where Micah emerges. I am certain it's Micah, as Maison is not aware of this cove, and I have always kept it a secret from him. Micah is the only one who knows about this place, and I can easily recognize him from his broody expression. "What do you want?" I ask, shifting my gaze back to the mountains.

I've avoided Micah since we got back, but for different reasons than Maison. Maison, I'm still furious with. Micah... Well, I confess I might have been wrong about him from the start. But it's easier for me to pretend to hate him than to admit he's not a complete asshole. I jump off the rock, pull my hair back into a ponytail, and try to walk past him. He grabs my wrist, his eyes blazing into me as he pulls me back to him.

I snatch my wrist from his iron grip. "Let go of me, Micah."

He squeezes harder, which catches my attention. "I want you to hit me, London."

I scoff, thinking he must be joking. Then I remember I've yet to even experience Micah's laugh let alone him making a joke. "Enough games, Micah, let me leave."

"Hit me," he repeats and lets go of my wrist. He stands before me like a mountain, immovable.

I place a hand on my hip. "I'm not going to hit you."

He takes a step closer, his face only inches from mine. His hair is longer now than when we first arrived, his bangs falling over his piercing, dark eyes. When he looks at me like that, I can't tell him apart from Maison, and it freaks me out. I have to look away.

"Come on," he taunts. "Let's see what you can do, and don't pretend you haven't thought about hurting me at least once since we've met. You've wanted to slap me ever since I made you touch yourself."

Adrenaline courses through me, and my face heats. "Is this your way of apologizing? Because a simple sorry would suffice." As I try to pass him again, he grabs my arms. I feel like I'm about to burst into flames.

"Stop it, Micah. I'm not playing this stupid game with you."

He arches his brows. "You're lonely, afraid, and angry. You won't hit Maison, and you can't hit Naomi or anyone else, so... hit me."

I turn away from him and cross my arms. "Don't be fucking ridiculous."

With lightning speed, he grabs my hands, twists me around, pushes me up onto the side of the escarpment, leaning into me with one hand just inches from my face. "Fucking. Hit. Me," he growls.

"What the hell, Micah?"

"You're weak, London. Maison made you weak by protecting you all the time."

So that's what this is about. He's trying to toughen me up?

Fuck him. I'm not doing this.

I try to wiggle away, but he slides his hand on my waist. He grabs so hard at first, then nuzzles his fingers in. Heat pools between my legs and my heart hammers out of my chest. His touch leaves me stunned and motionless; I might even like it, but then—

Rage boils through me.

"Stop it!" I scream and slap him across the face and damn, it feels good. I barely make a dent in him, but he loosens his grip and steps back, flashing his teeth. A real smile forms on his lips, one that actually meets his eyes. "That was good. Do it again, harder this time. But don't be so fucking pathetic. Stick up for yourself, London."

I curl my fists and hit him again, this time giving him everything I have, and as I make impact with his chest, pain sears through my wrist, right up to my shoulder blade.

"Damn it," I cry out, holding my wrist with my other hand. Punching Micah is the equivalent of punching a steel wall.

He's so bloody strong.

He nudges me toward him and gently grabs my waist, pushing me down until I bend my knees. My body jolts to life as he positions one hand over my wrist and wraps one arm around my waist. His fingers tease, although I'm not sure he's meaning it that way. It's the same as way when he taught me how to fish.

"Remember what I showed you before? Use this stance. Hit with your core, not your arms."

He steps in front of me, this time placing his hands out, giving me a target. "Try again."

Controlling the shake in my hands, I lean into the punch this time, connecting with his hand as hard as I can.

"Better. Do it again."

I connect with even more force.

"Again."

I keep pounding on him until I can't see or think straight, completely losing myself, forgetting everything but pounding the shit out of Micah's hands. I punch him so hard and fast, eventually tears well up in my eyes. But it feels amazing to release all that pent-up energy I've been dying to get out, despite the fact it drains my limited energy reserves.

I finally stop and sit down, pulling my knees into my chest. Barely phased, he sits beside me as my chest rises and falls with heavy puffs of breath. "You feel better?" he asks casually, keeping his focus on the haze in the sky.

"Why did you do that?" My is voice is unsteady, and I rest my head on his shoulder because it's too heavy to keep upright.

He inclines his head toward mine. "You need to know how to fight. You're strong, London, your mind is sharp. But physically, you're weak, and Maison can't always be there to protect you. Protect yourself on this island because no one will do it for you. If you're not strong here, you won't survive long."

I gaze up at him, half expecting him to be watching me. To my surprise, he's still looking over the horizon, like he's a million miles away. I'm acutely aware of how close we are sitting, his dangerous energy swirling. His leg grazes mine and the place his muscular thigh touches mine is pulsing.

We sit in silence for a few minutes, and he lets me lean on him while his fingers curl in and out of a fist. It reminds me of the airplane when I thought of him hurting Olivia.

Do I still believe he's capable?

"Maison's the stubborn twin, you know," he says suddenly.

My head pops up. "What?"

He chuckles under his breath. "Everyone thinks I'm the difficult one, but I don't hold a candle to how fucking stubborn he is."

What is he saying? I don't react to him, afraid he'd decide to stop talking. I've never heard Micah open up like this before.

He swallows sharply and continues, "Maison leads with emotion, not logic, and acts on instinct. He is a good defenseman and brother, but he reacts in the moment rather than thinking things through. He's also not a fighter, he's always been a protector, but he's pig-headed sometimes, and that will be his downfall. He went three months without speaking to me after Olivia died."

Olivia.

It's weird hearing her name from his lips. She was real—and he was in love with her. Maison kept this part of the story from me.

His eyes find mine. "And you're stubborn, too, just like she was. He's complicated, London, more than you realize. Try to forgive him."

Funny, that's the same thing he says about Micah.

I hood my eyes, suddenly feeling very guilty about agreeing to dig up dirt and write a story on him. It was obviously a painful experience for both of them. My voice nearly cracks, and I can't even look at him. "Micah, about the story..."

He shakes his head without letting me finish. "You don't owe me an explanation. I get you had your reasons." He stands up to leave. "Meet me here tomorrow. I'm going to bring you food because you're too fucking skinny. Let's get some meat back on your ass."

In typical Micah fashion, he disappears into the woods.

My pulse quickens as I watch him walk away with the same sexy swagger he had when I first saw him, like he can do no wrong. Maison's swagger is identical, so it must be a twin thing. I place my hand on my ass, indeed feeling how bony it is, then trace my fingers up to the spot Micah likes to touch. My skin stings like little lightning bolts. I hate how much I like him touching me there.

I pull my knees into my chest.

Stubborn. What does he know? I'm not stubborn.

I close my eyes. It's almost three days of constant pining on Maison's part to get my attention. Maybe he deserves to have me at least hear him out. The problem is, when Maison apologizes, I know I will forgive him, and I'm not done being angry.

I stand and head back to the camp. When I arrive, Naomi and Ezra are to the side. Micah sits alone, staring into the fire, ignoring me even though I know he sees me. He's always aware of me, I've decided, even when he takes great effort to pretend like he isn't.

Anger pulses through me as Serena stands in front of Maison, who's sitting on a log, leaning back and chatting with her. His eyes draw up when he notices me, and she twists around only to see me approaching. Without hesitation, I push her out of the way.

"What the hell, London?" she cries out. "We were just talking."

Maison looks confused and cute as hell when I sit on his lap, inviting his arms around me.

I blink at Naomi, who rises as though she intends to stand up for Serena. Micah looks up and glares at her, and Ezra and Serena, which gives her pause.

That's right, you won't do anything, Naomi.

Maison moves his hand up, massaging the back of my neck, which instantly relaxes my shoulders. I lean in to kiss him, drawing it out, making sure everyone can see it. I nibble on his lips and tease my tongue inside his mouth.

When I'm done kissing him, he whispers. "Hey, baby. I missed you."

"I miss you, too, Maison. And I'm so sorry for everything." I grab his arm, pulling him up to his feet.

I want to get away from everyone, so I grab a bit of food and pull Maison toward our shelter and lie down.

He slips in beside me as if he never left. "I had no idea Naomi would do that to you," he blurts out. "I would have stopped it if I did. I went to the woods for space, returned, and left again. I'm sorry, baby, I just had to think. You never came out, so I slept in Micah's shelter. I checked on you, but you were sleeping. I was going to come in the morning, but then... you were gone."

He's so apologetic, my heart melts, feeling the weight of his remorse. I lean into him, so familiar now, his skin, his heat, the lines of his body. "You left me, Maison. You didn't protect me when I needed you... like you said you would."

Pain flashes through his eyes as he stops and stares at me, his full lips pressed together, and for a brief second, I can't bear to see him hurt. I stop breathing.

He's so beautiful.

"Jesus, Maison. Can you stop with the charm for one second and let me be angry? I have a right to be angry."

"Why didn't you tell me?" he finally asks after a few seconds of agonizing silence. "About Nigel blackmailing you? I would have kicked his ass as soon as I found out."

I finally turn to meet his smouldering look, and his chestnut eyes flicker. "I didn't think you'd understand. And I'm still not clear about what happened with Olivia. You never talk about her, Maison."

"You'd be surprised what I understand. Are you going to tell me who Chris is?"

I take a deep breath. As mad as I am at him right now, he still deserves an explanation. "He was my teacher. He pursued me when I turned seventeen, though I knew it was wrong."

I look over at him. His jaw sets and eyes narrow. He says nothing, so I keep going. "We snuck around for a bit. Nothing crazy."

"Did you... did you sleep with him?"

I cast my gaze downward. "We made out after my rehearsal, in school hallways after hours, and in his classrooms. It was pretty scuzzy when I look back at it. He was married, while I was a naive girl in love. We only had sex once, in a hotel room, right before my eighteenth birthday. His wife found out about it shortly after finding his hotel receipt in his emails."

"How old was he?"

"Twenty-three."

"Jesus, London."

It feels good to get this out, so I close my eyes and continue, "I was in the school play, and they needed a dancer. I saw the way he looked at me, so I danced for him. He cornered me after rehearsal one night and put his hand under my shirt, and I let him. I had never received that kind of attention before."

Maison shakes his head. "What a fucking scumbag."

"I thought I loved him. He told me how smart I was, how I was destined for great things. He gave me a top grade in English when I probably didn't deserve it. He got fired, and I got labeled as a home-wrecker and a slut. I had to leave... I couldn't stay at that school anymore."

He loosens his breath. "I'm sorry that happened to you."

"Don't be. I'm glad I'm away from him. I couldn't see it, but it was the best thing for me."

I raise my eyes to meet him. "You were my first, Maison, in every meaningful way. I'm sorry I lied to you. I should have trusted you and told you, even when Nigel threatened me." His eyes flash at the mention of Nigel. "Nigel hates Micah," I say. "Why is he so invested in this? Did he know Olivia?"

He shakes his head. "No, no way. He was just some loser nobody cared about. He's just bitter cause he doesn't have any fucking friends."

Nigel's more involved than Maison thinks—his hatred for the twins runs deep.

I open my mouth to speak, but Maison interrupts my train of thought. "Micah doesn't want to admit it, but he's lost control of the group. They made a choice without including him. Don't blame him for what happened. There was nothing he could have done to stop it."

My heart skips a beat at the realization of what that means. If Micah is not in control, that means Ezra is, or worse yet, Nigel. And that's much worse than Micah being in charge—at least Micah shows some remorse.

"Are you two better now?" he asks. I'm assuming Micah and Maison have hashed things out regarding what Micah and I did at the cove. If only I could hear that conversation.

"We've talked," I tell him.

He caresses his fingers through my hair. "No one is going to hurt you again, London. Micah and I will kill them if they do."

Maison doesn't know about Ezra and what his parents did, otherwise, he wouldn't put so much blind trust in him if he did. I don't feel like bringing it up, but I know it's just one more secret that will unravel this island if I don't.

Maison takes my pause as an opportunity to slip his tongue inside me, and I'm still so tired I can barely move. And he's warm, so warm. He moves his hands along my belly as he likes to do and rests his lips on my neck.

"I'm sorry," he whispers.

I lay still in his arms and close my eyes, putting everything out of my head. I plan to wrap my legs around him all night and not let go till morning. Everything else can wait till tomorrow.

I crouch behind a boulder, keeping myself steady while my spear rests on the ground in front of me, ready to grab it at a moment's notice. I wait for Micah at the cove, having removed a layer of clothing to keep myself more agile. My hair is freshly braided after the quick dip in the lake, and the sun hides behind the clouds, dusting the water a dark gray.

Micah's been teaching me how to hunt. Well, more like how properly use the wooden spear I've taken a liking to.

He will visit me today at the usual time, and my tummy grumbles at the thought. My energy is better now. Usually when he comes, he brings me smoked meat—and I've long suspected he brings Maison food, too. Perhaps it's only because he doesn't want me to tell anyone about his secret camp spot, but I also think it's his way of apologizing. I don't ask questions, I just rip my teeth into that rabbit like it's the last supper.

I look forward to his visits more than I care to admit for other reasons. He's teaching me other things, like how to fight, punch, kick, and throw. If Maison knows about it, he doesn't say anything—not that Maison and I have done much talking. Our making up has lasted a full week, and we're always touching each other. With the weight of our secrets finally off our shoulders, we can just exist and be together. He barely lets me out of his sight, but the boys are planning another big hunt—which makes my stomach clench.

The thought of them both leaving me has me thinking all the darkest thoughts. I need them to take me with them.

Today I have a surprise for Micah. As I hide from behind the tree line, I angle myself so I can have full access to the rocky shore. I'm hoping he falls for my trick. My heart races when I see him, and he stalks toward the beach with his head down. He arrived, just as I predicted, and once he realizes I'm not there, he turns his head from side to side.

Ha.

I creep down to the next rock while his back is turned. The soft waves of the water lapping against the rocks hide my sound and the wind hides my scent.

He looks right at me, but I'm already well hidden again, and I can still see him. His expression hardens, then a half smile forms on his lips. I have to suppress the swell of pride I get when he reacts like that.

That smile... Micah never smiles.

He takes a couple of calculated steps in the other direction, his body rigid and ready, wearing his hockey sweater. He doesn't know where I am, but he now knows I'm coming for him.

I creep down to the shore, getting much closer, timing the breeze perfectly as I crunch over the rocks. I duck beneath a boulder just as his head turns.

"London, London, London," his voice is barely more than a whisper, but it carries right to me. When his head turns away from me, I pounce. He blocks my punch, but I surprise him for once. I kick him, connecting right in his gut and jump at him, in a full offensive attack, using all the moves he showed me the past week.

He pushes me back, then turns and faces me with his eyebrows arched. He likes this game as much as I do. I keep pushing at him, and we spar for a few minutes. He let's me punch and kick him, only blocking my hits enough so I don't hurt him, not that I really could.

I lean into my last punch, targeting his face, and just as I expect, he blocks my hit. My other hand ready, I whip my spear around and shove it into his side, digging in just enough to let him know I won.

I grin. "I got you, Micah."

The corner of his mouth quirks up. He grabs my wrist and the spear out of my hand, twists me around onto the ground, and presses his body on top of mine. My hands in his iron grip above my head while he props himself up with his other hand.

Fuck, he's strong and fast.

"No, you don't," he grumbles as he takes in my now heaving chest, glistening with sweat. Only a loose tank top between us, and my nipples are now hard under my shirt.

He pauses, his hand still holding my wrists as I lay beneath him, waiting for him to do something else as I catch my breath.

He's so close to me, I feel his heartbeat, and it seems to match my own.

Why isn't he letting go?

His eyes trail up to my neck, my lips. His expression is unreadable, hidden behind what I know is a wall of emotions waiting to break free. His lips are just one inch from mine, and a week ago, I would have pushed him off. With him following me to the plane and keeping his hands off me, all I can think about now is his hands on me.

I shift my hips as his erection pulses on top of my inner thigh. I can barely resist grabbing it. He's incredibly turned-on right now, and I'd be lying if I didn't admit that I am, too. He shifts his hips to meet mine, and instead of tensing like I should, I relax, just as I did when he carried me, broken from the plane, and as I did that same night when it was the two of us.

He's not touched me since, except for sparring. I close my eyes and open my hips so he can dip further into me, waiting for him to kiss me—*wanting* him to kiss me. His body is like fire on top of mine.

Fuck. What am I doing?

He needs to get off me.

He lets go of my hands and I let them drift to the hard lines of his back. When he doesn't kiss me, I dare to open my eyes, and a flicker of hesitation rolls over his face.

Or perhaps it's pain.

He always looks so sad, and I remember what Naomi was doing to him—her mouth wrapped around him, his face contorted with pleasure as she sucked him off. I want to experience making him feel that way—to pleasure him with my mouth. The only time I haven't seen pain in his eyes was when his hands were inside me on this rock, or when he was looking at me when he was with Naomi.

The silence between us feels painfully long. Eventually, he grazes his fingers over my lips, and a surge of electricity runs through my body.

"Micah," I whisper. Without thinking, I wrap my teeth around his fingers and tease him with my tongue. A silent invitation for him to do more. His body is crackling above me, so alive. He keeps his fingers steady for a moment before his eyes flicker, and he pulls them away, pressing himself up and peering down at me. I sit up, leaning back on my wrists, and I swallow a pit in my throat.

Fuck. Fuck. Fuck.

Why did I do that?

He reaches down and helps me up, looking me straight in the eyes. "I think you're ready," is all he says, and then he walks back toward camp with ease.

Ready? Ready for what?

I watch him walk away, moving like Maison. Is that the sole reason for my attraction to him? From the outside, he's Maison, but he's so different.

Maison is sweet, gentle, and warm. Micah's withdrawn, moody, and cocky beyond belief—everything I despise in a guy. And yet, when he looks at me, my insides explode. His touch still gives me the same jolt as that first lunchroom encounter when I saw him for the first time.

At the fire, he tested me, and I didn't pull away; instead, I stayed there because I liked it. He attempted to do more, and I freaked out. He was into me, but I didn't see it because of Maison. I hated Micah when I really didn't know him, either.

I trust him now and crave the moments he comes alive with me. So badly, I want to see that part of him again, but I know he won't, because I told him not to and because of Maison. I misjudged Micah entirely. He's a good one, and now I desperately want to know more.

"Everyone needs to be involved," Micah informs the group congregated around the fire for supper. "It's prime hunting season, and it's pathetic we haven't caught anything. We need to put our shit aside and harvest a buck. Everyone has to go."

I've spent the last ten minutes listening to the group snarl at each other about this hunting trip—mainly Micah and Ezra, while the others watch and listen. I trailed in behind Micah a bit ago, hoping no one noticed we were together. I immediately found Maison, sliding my fingers over his thigh as I sat next to him. He grabbed my hand, interlocked his fingers with mine, and pulled me closer while a tidal wave of guilt washed over me.

"We may need to split up," James says, with Serena right beside him. James sometimes seems like the only rational one out of our group, definitely the most level-headed. Ever since Maison's clear loyalty to me, Serena's kept her distance from us both, and the longing stares between her and James don't go unnoticed. If it weren't for the fact she's best friends with Naomi, I could almost imagine us becoming friends. Jade is next to Thomas, the two of them also inseparable since Nigel's temper tantrum. Clear alliances are forming, and a major shift is in the air.

Ezra grimaces as Naomi sits on his lap and jerks his head toward me, the fire casting a retched shadow across her face. For a pretty girl, I've never seen anyone so ugly.

"I am not hunting with her," Naomi says. "I don't trust your little girlfriend. It's dangerous, and she's already stolen from us once, which you did very little about, Micah."

I can't help but smirk at her. Not only did Micah not get mad at me for stealing food, but he let me eat those beans I was salivating over—he actually fed them to me. My eyes draw to Micah, who I noticed has not been doing a great job of ignoring me as he usually does. "Fine, I'll take London with me. I'll take Thomas and Jade, too."

Maison wraps a protective arm around me. "No. No way, London is not leaving my side, bro. I don't think it's too safe having the girls come with us. I got hurt the first time we attempted this."

Butchering a deer with his bare hands, he means.

Micah cocks his head and merely throws a log into the fire. "The girls need to learn to hunt and obviously, I assumed you were coming with me, too. The rest of you can split off however you want, but that's my group; London and Maison are with me."

I suppress the tingle in my stomach from Micah, claiming me like that. Jade, I notice, is also beaming. Micah has that way about him, and I'm finally understanding why Naomi is so smitten with him.

"Suit yourself," Ezra snipes. "As long as I get Naomi; she's better, anyway."

Micah shakes his head. "London's better. She's quieter, less intimidating. That's what makes a good hunter."

Naomi visibly bristles at his dig and glares at me. She's not uttered a single word to me since she hurt me, and I'm thinking she's regretting what's she did now that Micah is icing her out, too. Getting out of this camp and making a kill sounds much better than sitting here. The group Micah chose is perfect, and I don't want to leave them... either of them.

Ezra lets out a huff. "What the fuck do you know, Micah? You grew up a rich kid, just like me."

"You're not rich anymore, are you?" Micah snarls. "I know a hell of a lot more than you."

Ezra jumps up, tossing poor Naomi onto the ground. "What the fuck is that supposed to mean?"

Micah is unflinching when Ezra gets right in his face. "You know exactly what I mean."

I sway slightly, knowing exactly what he's talking about. Maison squeezes me, noticing my clear reaction, and narrows his brows. He doesn't know the extent of what I know, and I wonder how much he knows. Obviously, the three of them know something.

Ezra's jaw squares and he stands up to Micah, looking like he wants to rip him apart. "Leave my parents out of it, man."

Maison sits up straight. "None of that matters right now, Micah. Let's focus on getting through this and leaving whatever shit we have at home there."

Naomi sits, wide-eyed, looking up at her boyfriend. "What are they talking about, Ezra? What happened to your parents?"

Micah and Ezra stand toe to toe, nearly identical in height and weight. Micah has a slight edge, though. He's older, and more skilled at everything. Ezra would lose if it came down to a fistfight.

He shakes his head and softens his eyes at her, clearly uncomfortable at the turn of conversations. "Nothing, it doesn't matter, babe. Micah's dad's just a fucking asshole. But we're all used to the Matei family getting away with murder."

Maison jumps up so fast, and before I know it, he's right in Ezra's face. "That's not funny, dude," Maison spits at him, with anger seeping out of his eyes. Now both twins are peering down at Ezra, and I have to give him credit, he doesn't flinch, either. The whole camp is dripping with testosterone and tension, but it's nice to see Maison finally sticking up for his brother in a way he hasn't since being here.

Thomas stands and pushes himself into the mix. "We haven't eaten properly in days. We're all hungry and pissed off. We need to chill, all of us, and focus on the hunt. We need to end this bullshit, or none of us will feel better about our situation."

Nigel finally emerges, his smirking face relishing in the chaos and upheaval. James, Ollie, and Nathan just shake their heads, and after a few tense seconds, the three boys sit down.

Three distinct groups now.

James let Ezra have Ollie because I think he felt bad since Nigel is refusing to go. Ezra gave Nigel a pass, which has me wondering who really is pulling the strings between those two. Nigel and I haven't spoken yet, and I refuse to look at him. The hunting trip isn't the time, but I will make him pay, eventually.

Seeing me nestled comfortably and safe in Maison's arms, Micah rises and heads to his shelter. "Everyone get some fucking sleep, then. We leave when the sun rises."

Ezra follows him out, dragging Naomi with him.

Maison yawns and pulls me up. "Come on, baby, let's go to bed. Micah's going to work us tomorrow, so we should get some rest."

Once we crawl in, I curl up next to him but struggle to get comfortable. The ground seems colder and harder tonight, somehow. After a few minutes, I dare to ask him. "What happened between your parents and Ezra's parents? Why does Ezra hate Micah so much?"

Maison's quiet, contemplating, as if trying to decide how much I should know. Then he says, "His dad owed my dad a bunch of money. It was for a business investment, and Ezra's dad didn't perform. Our parents cashed it in last year."

"So why doesn't he hate you, too?"

"Because I don't torment him about it like Micah does. But I told you, baby, they've always had it out for each other. This isn't anything new."

No, but now we live in proximity with two people who seem to hate Micah. When all your possessions are stripped away from you, and you're broken down to bare humanity, emotions are all we have.

Maison pulls me closer as I shiver. Fall is here and the frosty nights are hard to ignore. The first snowfall was just the beginning, and even the lake water bites harder than before. Winter is not just looming in the distance, it's basically here. This situation will soon look very different, as fall in Alaska is brief.

He turns me around to face him, pushing my hair back from my eyes, his eyes etched with concern. "I'll make us a little fire, baby, don't worry about the hunt tomorrow. I promise I won't let anything happen to you."

My heart flutters with a mix of guilt and worry.

"I know you won't," I whisper back. "Micah's been teaching me a few things with the spear. I'm not as pathetic as I was before."

"I know."

Wait... what?

My mouth twitches. "You didn't say anything. You knew Micah was teaching me this past week?"

"Yeah, baby, he told me. I knew you'd come around on each other." A knot fills my belly, and I let out a deep breath. I wonder if he realizes how much my perception of his brother has changed. With their history, would he be okay with it?

I watch Maison now, crouched down, making the fire. The temperature has plummeted from this morning, and his breath teases the air. His hair is much longer now, his facial hair, too. He looks rugged and handsome and mine. Once he's done, he lays back down with me and rubs his hands on my back, and I push Micah out of my mind. I'm simply reacting to a person who looks identical to the one I'm falling in love with.

"I want you to stay close to me tomorrow, London. Micah's reckless and will try to push you. He won't protect you the way I will. Promise me?"

I wrap my hands around his neck and kiss him as he studies my face. I turn from him, giving him a brief nod, hoping he doesn't notice my hesitation. I want to believe him, but he wasn't there the first time, even though he's trying his hardest to make up for that. Micah's been teaching me the importance of taking care of myself. If it were up to Maison, I'd be under his watch twenty-four-seven. He'd take care of me and spoon feed me fish, as Micah had once so cruelly said.

"Maison?" I let out a whisper. "What are your goals, beyond hockey? Like, what do you want in life?"

He chuckles. "To live through winter."

I elbow him. "What would you have done after graduation if not for the Olivia situation, and if you weren't stuck with me now?"

What defines Maison Matei when Micah is not there? Why am I falling in love with Maison beyond the physical? Why does he get a dark look whenever I mention Olivia?

The twinkle in his chestnut eyes is what I want to hold on to right now. "I don't know… I guess what everyone wants." He tickles my ribs. "A hot wifey like you."

I press my lips together. "A trophy wife, Maison, really?"

He stills the circles he's been drawing on my back. "I'm not complicated like Micah, baby. I don't have grand ambitions." He grabs my hips and pulls me on top of him, and I let myself sink into him. "Is there anything wrong with wanting someone to take care of and protect? I like to take care of the ones I love, London."

My pulse quickens as I lean in and press my lips into his. I press my whole body into his, releasing all the pent-up tension I had with Micah earlier.

"There is absolutely nothing wrong with that." I feel his teeth through his smile and the wolves howl outside, causing me to tremble like I always do whenever I hear them. Maison pulls his hand up from under my sweater and runs it along my back, right over his last name. He traces his fingers over the number before moving them down to the base of my spine.

"Don't worry about the wolves, baby," he whispers. "Focus on me and what I'm telling you." My heart hammers with the seriousness in his eyes, not the usual lopsided grin I'm used to. "I love my brother more than anything, even though he's complicated, and I've also hated him more than I ever have over the past year."

I press my lips together and I pull my fingers over his brow. "I know you do, Maison. Your experience must have been difficult. I can see how it would make things hard to get over." I still have no idea what that was because they won't tell me—all I ever get are half truths and avoidance.

"I owe him so much, but sometimes, it just pisses me off how much I have to cater to him." I part my lips to say something, but he leans up and whispers in my ear and what he says shoots chills right up my spine, "I can see the way he looks at you, London. Just remember though, baby, Micah doesn't do feelings the way I do. When you fuck him, make sure you don't fall for him."

CHAPTER FOURTEEN

Day Twenty-five

*E*veryone is raw and retreated, like they've all found their little part of the wilderness to call their own. Even Jade and Serena, who are usually so bright, are listless and dull. Splitting for this hunt is good. This camp is draining me, it's degrading my soul. Maison's going to give me to Micah. It's like he's prepping me for it, giving me subtle hints that he's okay with it, even though I'm not sure he really is. I don't know if I am ready or what will happen to my heart if I allow it. I'm not one to be shared for the amusement or needs of others. I just wish I knew what I needed or wanted, although I'm thinking it might be bits and pieces of both of them.

We leave for the hunt today, and I feel good about it. I wish I could get rid of this nagging feeling something bad will happen if we don't come back with anything, although, something bad will likely happen, anyway. Almost thirty days on this island, and I've not even seen an airplane other than the one we crashed in.

Please pray for us.

The woods seem thicker than usual—heavier and denser. A layer of thick colorful foliage glazes the ground as our footsteps crunch over it, spoiling the natural beauty with each step forward. The three of us will hunt where deer graze in the thickets. Micah, Maison, and I are alone in the forest, as if no one else exists.

Realizing how good of a spot it was, Jade and Thomas stayed back at Micah's camp—we decided to spend the night there. They are making a shelter to rest their heads and will trap on their own nearby and will wait till we make our kill so Thomas can come help us bring it back.

The trees are almost barren, though dashes of red and yellow still linger. A mist hangs in the air today—so thick I can almost choke on it—and its constant chill wraps around my bones. The air is stale, making it hard to differentiate between the sky and earth, causing me to trip. Micah shot me a menacing glare to be quiet.

Maison and I hang back, walking carefully and slowly following Micah's lead, as if he's a wolf sniffing out dinner. I'm not sure what he's looking for, but we aren't allowed to speak, or even breathe, lest we make too much noise.

In front of us, Micah is gripping something I've not seen before today. Part of an animal I suspected he killed and has secretly been feeding Maison and me for days. His knuckles are nearly white, gripping it. A deer antler, I think, but I call it his bone weapon. Watching him with it, I can't help but think nothing is sexier than a guy wielding a bone weapon.

He also made a spear for me last night in his shelter and gave it to me this morning before we left. He made sure it was nice and pointy, and I can imagine him making it, sitting alone in his shelter, after our almost kiss, carving it for me. And I can't stop daydreaming about that almost kiss between each crunchy footstep that must be driving him crazy.

Maison's words hang heavy in my ear, and every time Micah looks at me, my body jolts at the thought of it. But then my hunger and fear take over, ruining my fantasies of him, and even keeps me from admiring the beauty of the landscape that surrounds us. Micah is not focused on me today—he wants to make his kill.

We pass a few squirrels and rabbits, which Micah ignores—nothing less than a deer will do today. We didn't come out here for smaller game, and I know he secretly wants to make a bigger kill than Ezra. We walk for what feels like hours and Maison stays close to me. I grab his hand for comfort, mainly because they are in way better shape than me, and I don't want to get lost. Plus, those wolves I hear at night are stuff nightmares are made of, and I don't wish to come upon one alone.

The forest eventually becomes settled and quiet, with just my heart and the slight crunch of our footfalls sounding around us. I pause as my knees weaken, and Maison, who hasn't stopped holding my hand, turns and looks at me, giving my hand a squeeze as I meet his eyes.

Under no circumstances are we to talk; Micah made that perfectly clear.

"Micah, man. London needs a break."

I'm just about to protest when Micah's hand shoots up, and Maison and I both freeze.

The signal.

Micah sees something, so Maison and I immediately crouch down as we were instructed. We wait for him to signal, surround the prey, and one of us will kill it. I don't want Maison doing it—I already told him that. Plus, we all know Micah will be the one to do it. It's like he was built to survive out here.

He was made to kill.

Micah motions again, this time waving me over. Maison nods, but his worried expression cautions me to be extremely careful. He hesitates, but eventually releases my hand, and I encourage him with a smile.

I approach Micah, who is looking at the ground. Micah doesn't look at me; instead, he pulls me down to a low crouch. It takes me a second to understand what he's looking at. It's an animal print, and from the looks of it, a fresh one.

"Do you know what animal that is, London?"

I shake my head, all too aware of how close we are, every body part touching me, and how Maison must be watching.

He draws a circle in the mud around the print with the tip of his bone weapon. "Do you see that X?"

My heart races as I imagine the massive creature responsible for leaving such a huge paw print. Two small sticks lie in perfect symmetry across the indent in the dirt.

"The X means it's canine," he continues.

I shoot my head up. "Like a wolf?"

"Yeah," he mutters. "Probably the one serenading us every night. It's fresh, too. Stay here. I don't want you to move. I want to find out if it's a whole pack or a loner."

A lone wolf like Micah, I realize, and here I always thought he was an alpha.

He rises and waves Maison over, and he disappears into the brush. I'm so tired, and the thought of Thomas and Jade cuddling by a fire makes me envious. It's not long before Maison's by my side again, and Micah comes back, and my whole body grows weak, lightheaded. I can hear the boys talking, but it's like my mind can't quite register.

"Just one I think," I hear Micah say. "It may be a stray. I don't see evidence of an entire pack."

"You okay, London?" Maison asks as my wooziness intensifies. "Micah, man, I think she needs a break, or water... something. Look at her, she's pale as fuck."

I shake my head to snap out of it. "I'm fine... I'm okay. I think I just need a bit of water."

And I could really go for a cheeseburger right about now.

Micah pulls a bottle out of his pack and hands it to me, just as my dinner order walks by.. A doe and fawn pause twenty feet away to graze. We duck down as the boys notice them, and I inhale sharply.

Micah motions for us to stay where we are and crawls toward it, keeping low to the ground, his weapon in hand. Maison rests his hand on my lower back before leaving me, getting into his position. "You got this, baby. Move to the left," he whispers, and I tighten my grip on my spear.

Once Maison moves to his place, I follow his lead, but my foot catches on the slippery ground beneath me. I fall forward on my hands, dropping my spear, and take in a fistful of mud that splatters up on my face.

Fuck! The deer shoots it's head up and bolts off like lightning before Micah can reach them.

"Damn it, London," Micah blurts out.

I pull myself up and wipe my mud-covered hands on my pants. My chest tightens and face drops. "I'm sorry. My foot slipped."

He slams his weapon on the ground. "I fucking had them. You need to focus, London. Be fucking quiet, just like I taught you."

Maison approaches from behind, grabbing my face and inspecting me before slipping his arm around me. "Take it easy on her, Micah," he warns, and my heart sinks. He thinks I'm weak—they both do.

Micah's eyes flash with anger. "You can't coddle her all the time, Maison. She needs to learn." I'm also not thrilled with how they speak about me as if I'm not standing right in front of them.

The two of them are glaring at each other, and Micah cocks his brow as the tension between them thickens. Tension or something else, but it seems like they are having an entire conversation through their eyes.

"I'll do better next time," I blurt out, swallowing a lump in my throat.

Micah ignores me and addresses his brother, reminding me why I'm supposed to hate him. "It took us three fucking hours to find those deer. There were two of them, for fuck's sakes." He stomps off ahead.

Maison rubs my shoulder. "It's fine, baby. It was your first try. We'll find another deer."

I sigh and stare off in the direction Micah stormed off. I'm mad at myself for screwing up, but mostly because Micah's disappointed in me.

"Try to keep up," Micah yells back at us.

Maison narrows his brows as I breathe, trying to calm my nerves. My legs and arms are shaky, and I don't know how much farther I can go. I give him a tentative smile and keep walking.

"Yeah, we're coming," Maison mutters behind me and quickly finds my hand.

We walk for an hour, then stop briefly for a bite to eat—more dried meat Micah had in his pack. Micah sits on a fallen branch, resting his elbows on his knees before looking at me as I take tiny little breaths, crouching down.

"We can't go much farther today," he says, taking a good look at me, his gaze resting on mine. "Another hour, then we head back to camp."

We don't want Thomas and Jade to search for us, so we informed them to meet us an hour before sundown. I can already tell Micah's mood will be complete shit if we go back with nothing.

Without saying a word, he rises and keeps going, staying a good few feet ahead. He surveys the forest with predatory eyes, bearing the weight of the world. And it kind of is—we need something big to sustain us. Plus, his leadership is in question. Slowly, over the past couple of weeks, his hold on the group has slipped. Like either he just doesn't care, or Ezra is really taking over. Micah doesn't seem to fight it as much, either, especially since he's built a home elsewhere.

Micah finally stiffens and lifts his hand, and my stomach twists. Micah turns back to look at us, and waves me over. I try to let go of Maison's hand, but he doesn't let go this time. "You don't owe him anything," he whispers.

My eyebrows arch. "I want to, Maison. I'll be okay this time." I reach up for a quick kiss before he can argue and slide over to Micah, who's crouched ten feet away from us. I join him so I am eye level with whatever he is looking at, letting my spear rest on the ground.

The buck is twenty feet away, a silent beauty. Micah shifts and hovers above me, resting his head on my shoulder.

"Do you see him?" he asks.

I nod, watching the big creature and acutely aware of Micah pressed in behind me.

His voice is a mere whisper. "I'll aim for the heart, right behind the shoulder, and I'll kill it quickly."

I hold my breath as the deer silently moves toward us. "Stay here, London. Block it in if it runs." He reaches his fingers down my arm and squeezes my hand, causing my whole body to tremble. "Remember everything I've taught you."

Focus.

Keep my breath steady.

His lips graze my neck and for a moment, I think he might press them into me. Instead, he slides away, leaving phantom tingles I feel all the way down to my stomach.

I check back for Maison, who is not in sight, but I know he's close—watching me probably over the buck. We've got it cornered; I just need to not mess up again to end this.

Micah glides over to the buck, his bone weapon in one hand, his knife in the other. My heart is in my throat as a guy, not even twenty years old, is about to take down a deer with his own hands. I can't take my eyes off him as he circles and stalks his unknowing prey.

God, the way he moves...

Maison might have the edge on fishing, but Micah was born a hunter. A silent stalker—patient and deadly. Maison told me they did this every fall with their dad, which I'm guessing is why Micah feels so at home out here.

Micah gets so close to it, and it has no idea. Every heartbeat in my chest is drumming as I watch him silently dance around his prey, angling, edging closer and closer.

Micah's a few feet away from it now, mere seconds from killing. The buck notices him at the last second, but it's too late. In one swift motion, Micah leaps up and jabs the weapon right into its heart, then swipes his knife across its throat for good measure.

The animal dies on the spot. It's a clean, swift kill, and humane as possible given the circumstances. He leaps out of the way as the buck falls.

"Yes, Micah!" I jump up right at the same time Maison leaps up, too, smiling ear to ear, and runs to his brother, wrapping his arms around him. Then they both start yelling at the top of their lungs—raw emotion running deep in both of them. Screaming and dancing around like they are fucking animals. Their love for each other is heartwarming and beautiful. I can imagine this is what it used to be like between them—before Olivia happened. Playfully jabbing and wrestling like children and giggling like schoolgirls.

Maison's eyes find mine, and he frowns, standing up and alert. "London, watch out," he cries out, leaping over to me. I hear it before I see it—a swirl of fur and sharp growls. A furry animal comes lunging at me, and I lift my spear and jab it hard into the chest of what is attacking me.

A small yelp fills the air before deafening silence.

Just as quickly, I'm thrown off balance by a six-foot-two hockey player as he pushes me out of the way before the animal can get at me. We land hard, but he takes all the impact, and I know by the way he's gripping me with his entire body wrapped around me, it's Maison who saved me. Blood splatters all over my face. As I glance up, Micah pulls out the spear, finishing the kill with the knife. One final yelp and the beast is dead.

Wolf blood... A small silver wolf attacked me.

We stare at the lifeless deer, then at one another. The only sound is the wind rustling the leaves above.

I was mere seconds from getting ripped apart by that thing, and I'm only in one piece because of Maison. He protected me as promised, and now I want to hold on to him forever.

Micah's the one to break the silence. "Fuck yeah, London!"

My heart is in my throat as I lay on the ground with Maison on top of me, my breath heavy. He rolls off and helps me up, and I stand up, shaky and frozen, unable to believe what I was seeing.

Not one, but two kills.

A wolf... I killed a fucking wolf.

According to Maison, Micah can skin these creatures—something he reassured me whenever I panicked at the sound of their howls at night. That's better than eating it even. Its silver fur is thick and soft, and I can only dream about wrapping myself around it at night.

I secretly hope Micah skins it for me.

I jump up and wrap my legs around Maison, running my fingers through his hair.

"Are you okay?" he asks me.

I bite my lip and lift my chin, nodding. Micah's watching us, his face gone from happy to completely unreadable. This time he bites his lower lip, and a look lingers in his eyes. I've never felt this alive before. Even though it's Maison's body I'm wrapped around, it's Micah I can't rip my eyes from.

We make it back to the campsite and, despite my legs buckling beneath me and Maison carrying me back, my heart is pulsing with excitement. Luckily, we weren't too far away. Micah knew the way back, as if he's prowled every inch of these woods and memorized every leaf, stick, and gnarled tree. The boys took Thomas to help with the kills, leaving Jade and me alone for the first time in a while.

Jade and Thomas made the beginnings of a shelter about seventy feet away from Micah's. Close, but not too close, and made up of fir tree limbs and moss, just like the others. They must have spent most of the day making it. She's still working on it as I approach her, and I realize I've not spoken to her much the past week, and not at all about Nigel or her growing relationship with Thomas. Admittedly, the twins have been distracting me, and I am too tired at night to talk to anyone except Maison. After a short lie down in Micah's shelter, I venture out to find Jade. One shelter—Micah, Maison, and I will share tonight. The thought of lying with both of them makes my stomach heat, especially after Maison's cryptic warning the night before.

When I step outside, I look around, just as the sun sets, darkening an already cloudy day. I love the campsite Micah's picked, I've decided, much better than our other one that's now tainted with my bitterness and anger. And the sound of the nearby fresh-water stream soothes me. The small meadow is peaceful and sheltered due to the nearby escarpment and opening in the trees. It's serene and perfect, and every part of me wishes we can stay here instead, far away from the others. Right now, this is the closest place to anywhere I've considered home since I got here, except for my little cove.

Jade gives me a tight smile as I approach, busy layering moss over the roof as Thomas taught her so well to do. She's brighter than I've seen her in a while. Her glow is back, her hair pulled in shiny loose curls that hang around her face, and her body looks lean and muscular. Most likely because she's not anchored down by Nigel anymore, but she looks healthy, happy, and strong. She's not spoken to Nigel since the incident—nor me really, come to think of it.

"Why didn't you tell me about Nigel's story?" she asks, crossing her arms as she inspects me. Direct and to the point, and my heart sinks at the thought of me not noticing she's been mad at me for a full week.

I press my lips together. "Can we go talk while we find wood and bathe?" I'm aware I still have wolf blood splattered all over me, but I was too tired to do anything about it when we returned and Maison forced me to lie down. Plus, Micah gave me clear instructions when they left to gather more dry kindling when I woke up.

She pulls back slightly, then steps forward, grabbing her bag and signals me to follow.

"I'm glad you're here," I tell her as we approach the clear water creek, and I peel layers of clothes off my body. The melody of water echoes in my ears as I dip my toes in and start washing myself in the freezing waters. She joins me, and I tell her everything—my sordid past, my connection to Naomi, everything I know about the twins, Ezra's father's embezzlement, the drugging, the car accident... all of it. She listens as she's so good at doing, not interrupting, not judging, just listening.

"Do you believe Nigel?" she finally asks. "Do you think he's telling the truth about the twins lying about what happened with Olivia?"

My stomach twists as I wring out my hair and pull my fingers through it. "Truthfully, I have no clue. At the time, he had no good reason to lie about it. Neither of them will talk about her with me, so I honestly don't know what to make of it anymore. I can't imagine either of them being capable of that."

She shakes her head. "I can't either, not anymore, and Thomas is so loyal, he wouldn't align himself with someone who would do that. I feel like they're so genuine. I don't think Micah poisoned her, London; I really don't."

Neither do I, but I don't tell her that. Thinking of the alternative is ten times worse and is a place I don't want to go to in my head. Maison is my sunshine on this island, and I'm not ready to view him as anything different.

I squint and gather dried kindling as we move down the bank. I suddenly think of something I've not thought of before. "Do you know if Nigel had a connection to Olivia? Why was he so involved in something that had nothing to do with him?"

I've long thought this was personal for Nigel, but I always thought it was because of the twins. Not once—not even a single time—did I think it was actually Olivia. My pulse throbs at the thought of it.

Jade's eyes turn to saucers. "Honestly, now that you say that, he mentioned a half sister to me once. He mentioned her a few years ago when he moved here. She was only his half sister, I think. He said he wasn't close to her because she had issues, and they lived in completely different towns. He never brought her up again, and I never would have made that connection."

I freeze and my blood runs colder than ice.

Her mouth gapes open. "You don't think..."

I purse my lips. "There is no question in my mind. Fuck, no wonder Nigel's so tortured and destroyed. He used me, and now he's angry and stuck with the people he thinks killed his sister. He had proof, Jade. Irrefutable proof about what really happened."

"What proof? Like she didn't die in the car crash?"

"Fuck," I yell out, ignoring her question. I grab a rock and hurl it at the water. Nigel had no reason to lie—everything he told me was the truth. Which means one twin poisoned Olivia, and they are both lying about it. Now the question is, will I actually do anything about it?

Jade walks over and places a gentle arm on my back. "I'm sorry, London. It sucks you are messed up in all this. You shouldn't have moved to New Ocean. You probably would have been better off staying in Portland."

I can't help but burst out laughing at that thought. Of course I would have been better off. I'm trapped on an Arctic island, surrounded by enemies.

Exhaling, I perch on a rock at the escarpment. "I'm not sorry I came to New Ocean," I tell her as she pulls up beside me. "I wouldn't have met them otherwise, and I wouldn't be falling in love with them."

A deep long pause. "*Them*, huh?"

As I look at her, tears form behind my eyes and I quickly cover my mouth, realizing my mistake. "Yeah," I whisper as the cry catches in my throat at the enormity of what I'm saying to her. What I've not wanted to admit out loud. "Both of them."

"Oh, London," she breathes out.

CHAPTER FIFTEEN

The boys don't make it back till an hour after sunset. Jade and I have the fire going, and we both know it will be a long night with no food. We won't eat that deer today, and all we have is some leftover smoked animal meat Micah left for us to chew on.

It's not enough, it's never enough, but the taste helps me pretend and eases the feeling of my stomach eating itself. They finally finish hanging the carcass, and the ambient temperatures should help keep the meat from spoiling for the few short hours before the sun rises and the boys can do what they need to prepare it. I'm not sure what they did with the wolf—it took all their strength to just bring back the deer.

I'm sitting alone, feeling content, when the three of them come join us, and Maison takes his usual spot next to me. It's calm now, like before a storm, and I can finally relax for the first time since arriving. As Maison curls up behind me, he slides something into my hand under the blanket.

A bottle of sorts.

I narrow my brows and look at it, and my eyes widen when I see the familiar logo of Jack Daniels. I look up at Maison, who simply grins and arches his brows.

He wraps his hand around my stomach. "Come on, baby. Remember how I wanted to see what you were made of?"

Jesus.

He raises his brows higher, as if daring me to drink it. They must have gotten these from the plane and neglected to tell anyone else.

Fuck it. It can't possibly make me feel any worse, although I've not been much of a drinker. I guzzle the whole shot down in a single gulp, and nearly spit it right back out as the burning drizzles down my throat and into my already queasy stomach.

"Damn, baby." He laughs, and in the corner of my eye, I see Micah sitting across from me, taking his shot. Once the stinging goes away, my insides fire up, and Maison hands me another.

Looks like we are having a party tonight.

The second goes straight to my head, partly because I barely have meat on my bones, but I like the feeling of how numb it makes me. I ask for one more drink and relish it as Micah and Thomas discuss their deer butchering plan, and Maison and I cozy up to each other.

"Take it easy, baby. You don't want to get poisoned," Maison whispers to me.

His words strike like a knife in my heart as I imagine him pouring something into a drink and handing it to Olivia, poisoning her.

I push out the thought... *Not right now.* Maison would not be capable of that. Nigel had it wrong; he's a despicable person who assumes others are as wicked as he is, and I refuse to think this way about my boyfriend.

Eventually, Jade and Thomas tell us good night, leaving me alone with Micah and Maison. Ignoring the nagging feeling in my belly, I sip on the third shot until my vision blurs, and I suddenly have the urge to dance. I rise and stand in front of Maison, shredding my sweater, leaving me only in my tank top and loose sweats as the fire rages behind me. I sway my hips over him, landing them at his eye level, and he immediately places his hands on me, tickling the drawstring of my pants with his thumbs. I give him a little show, knowing Micah is right behind me. Arching my back, running my hands through my hair, I smile down at Maison, liking the thought of Micah watching.

I dance... For the first time in a year, I dance. It feels good to let go. Letting life happen to me again instead of fighting it—hating it.

Maison rises and joins me, sneaking around to the back of me, placing his hands around my mid-section. I sway to the sound of the fire and close my eyes, enjoying the feeling of his warmth and safety behind me, letting my hair flow with the wind. It takes no time to feel a hard body in front of me. I stop swaying for a moment and take in Micah staring at me—my lips, my chest, all of me. I know exactly why Maison gave me the shots as I see the flicker in Micah's dark eyes.

Maison's lubricating me, and it's working.

My vision blurs and I close my eyes, knowing they won't let me fall, enjoying the heat on my face and the beat of my song in my ears as I replay a soft melody I used to dance to. Something I didn't realize I missed so much.

Hands grab me from behind, and I turn around, leaning up to meet Maison's lips. I kiss him hard, slipping my tongue inside his mouth as his hands reach down and grip my lower back. We sway and I pretend we are somewhere else, like at a club in the city where we can leave to go home after and spend the night in his bedroom, not the hard, wet forest floor. I turn around and press myself into him, the edge of my reality and senses dulled.

I dance like I used to when I liked to be looked at. I'm hyper aware of both of them now as I run my hands over my curves. Micah steps toward me and grabs my waist, saying nothing, but I can feel his desire for me.

I finally get to feel him.

We dance for a few minutes like this. I press myself inside each of them, arching my hips to make sure I touch each one. Maison's hands slide down the front of my sweats, and I gasp as I feel his fingers slip inside me, pushing the fabric of my thong to the side.

"Fucking hell, baby," Maison whispers, leaning into me. "You are so wet for us. We both want to fuck you right now. Will you let us do it together?"

Heat pulses through my veins as Micah steps back, waiting for my response, which I don't give.

I knew this was coming... I was warned from the beginning.

Am I ready for this?

Maison leads me into the shelter, and I crawl and lay back on my arms with my knees up and face them as they light a fire. A soft blanket grazes my thighs.

"Take off your clothes, baby, right down to that sexy lace. Let us look at you." Maison looks almost predatory as his eyes flicker off the fire, and I barely recognize him. This is a dominant side of him, never how he usually is, and I wonder if it's because Micah is here, too. In fact, if it wasn't for his gray sweater, I'd think it was Micah barking orders at me.

I do as he says and strip down to my thong, grazing my hand right over my flat stomach and twisting my fingers through my hair that rests on the swells of my large breasts.

Maison crawls in around me, twisting and pulling me between his legs with my back pressed over his hard cock. The scent of whiskey is fresh off his breath, which may explain the sudden personality change.

"You're going to fuck me first, baby."

I tense and sit up as Micah faces me, crouching in front of the shelter, watching us—his dark eyes hidden by shadows. But his gaze penetrates me.

"I'm nervous," I whisper, and I wonder if Maison is too, or how long he's known this would eventually happen.

Maison playfully nibbles on my ear. "Don't be nervous, baby. We aren't going to hurt you. I've never hurt you before. We're both good at this."

My heart beats faster, and I bite my lip, my eyes finding Micah's.

"He won't come in unless you tell him it's okay," Maison says, trying to calm my nerves.

I watch Micah's full lips, thinking about what they taste like. What he would feel like inside me. I give a subtle nod, giving Micah permission to come inside. This is my chance to find out what Micah's like, to see what he's made of. I've only been dreaming about it all day.

Micah crawls in, and my entire body pulses with anticipation of what will happen next. The slickness between my thighs drips out of me.

I dig my fingers into Maison's thighs as my heart beats out of my chest, and I realize I'm about to be with two guys at once—something I never thought I'd do.

Maison senses my hesitation. "It's okay, baby, relax. Tonight is for you."

I deepen my breath. "I don't know if I can do this," I whisper and look up at him. "Do you want to do this?"

Does he really want to share me?

Micah pauses and Maison grabs my hands, linking them in between mine. "We share everything, baby; we always have."

Realizing this is what I want, my breath deepens. I've dreamed of it for days, every time I'm near them. "Okay," I breathe. "What do I do?"

He squeezes my shoulder and wraps his arm around me, pinching my tight nipples and cups his hand over my breast as his cock springs out.

"Sit up and take off those panties," he demands, then helps me slip them down my leg while I discard them somewhere beside me.

I lean forward on my hands and knees, my ass and pussy right in his face while I wait for his next command. He slaps my ass, making me cry out. "I want you to slide on my dick and face him," he growls.

I know Micah is there, even though he's shrouded in darkness, waiting for his turn, watching my every move.

This is so new. Maison is never like this when we have sex, and never so dominant. I know how sweet he usually is, and it's terrifying, given what I suspect he's capable of. But it's also the mysteriousness of it all I find incredibly hot, my body on pins and needles thinking about it. He teases my clit for a moment before grabbing my waist and slides me onto him.

I'm so wet, it takes very little till he's deep inside me. The force of his cock is different in this position than I'm used to, and it hits my spot so intensely, I moan as he thrusts.

His hands are so warm and soft on my back, it helps me relax into it.

Micah, who has barely blinked—watches me—waits for me.

Then I grind and I clench.

Grind.

Clench.

"That's it, baby," Maison whispers, his voice laboured as I squeeze myself around him, trying to make my pussy as tight as possible. "Now I want you to kiss him."

Micah's in front of me in a second. His head tilts as if needing my permission to get any closer. I lean up to him, inviting him in, as Maison's cock hits me hard with each thrust. Micah grabs my chin and I press my lips into his, opening my mouth slightly, letting his tongue slip in. Maison's hands cup around my cleavage, and I let out a loud moan as a wave of pleasure wraps around me.

Micah's kiss is different, not as soft as Maison's. It almost feels desperate, like he's been waiting for this. I nibble on his lips, wanting to know what he tastes like.

I lose myself in him for a few minutes, forgetting about everything else, even Maison. Just his mouth, the same mouth I woke up fantasizing about this morning.

Maison thrusts harder, reminding me he's still there. My orgasm builds and I pull away from Micah and close my eyes, letting the waves of pleasure take over me. Once it passes, I open my eyes and Maison lifts me off him, pulling me back between his legs. My breaths are short, and I take a moment to recover.

I gaze up at Maison, who's waiting patiently, his face as serious as I've ever seen him. "What now?" I whisper as Micah kisses my cheek and neck from behind. His kisses are so fucking soft, it makes my heart burst with shame for how much I like it. For wanting both of them as badly as I do.

Maison's cock is still hard and throbbing. He never finished.

He leans back and pulls me with him, his erection digging into my back. I still can't take my eyes off Micah, who hasn't taken his eyes off me, either.

Maison whispers, "I want you to spread your legs wide, baby, and let him fuck you while I hold you."

Jesus.

I lie back, completely exposed and at the mercy of Micah. The flicker of the fire outside casts a shadow across his chestnut eyes, his wild hair falling over his face. Micah and I are doing this, but we are doing this on Maison's terms, and it seems like Micah might not be the dominant one in this particular situation.

My nipples harden as Maison reaches around, touching one of them, playing with them between his fingers. Micah crawls over me, slipping down his pants, pulling out his rock-hard dick. I reach out and trace my fingers down his abs, his mouth only inches from mine. And he feels so good.

They both do.

With Maison's warm body beneath me, Micah kisses my stomach, tracing his lips right up to my breasts, taking one of them in his mouth.

I let out a moan as Maison's fingers trickle down to my clit, pressing hard. Micah stops and looks at me, grabbing my waist and pulling me into position.

His eyes flicker to his brother. "Is she broken in?"

Such a Micah thing to say in this moment, and my vagina clenches, wondering what he means by it.

Maison chuckles. "Yeah, brother. She's broken in."

A gleam hints on Micah's shadowed face as he looks at me, finally saying something. "Good, because I'm not nearly as fucking gentle. Hold on tight, sweetheart."

He leans up and kisses my mouth, grabbing his cock with one hand, while Maison kisses my neck, sucking on it with little laps of his tongue. Marking me as his, while his brother is about to fuck me.

My desire for Micah burns inside me, but I love the feeling of Maison's possessive lips on me, even though he's the one allowing this. I didn't push for it, I wouldn't have. I would have stopped at my silent teases and the memory of Micah's hands on me at the cove. But I want to know what Micah feels like while knowing it's him I'm kissing, even if it's just this once. He traces his cock over my clit before pressing it deep inside me, and he doesn't hold back in the slightest.

He fucks me, hard and fast—with fury.

I feel like I'm going to explode all over as he thrusts hard, and my body completely gives into him. I can't control the sounds coming out of me—I'm sure Thomas and Jade can hear. He hits deeper and deeper until I can barely breathe. Maison's body keeps me steady and in place, although I couldn't move even if I wanted to.

I arch my head back as he thrusts with as much force as he can without completely breaking me. With Micah inside me, I reach my mouth for Maison's lips, wanting him to know I'm still thinking about him.

Maison kisses me and wraps his arms around me, pulling my legs up and allowing Micah to go even deeper. I pull my lips from Maison, and my eyes find Micah's, pulling him in as my orgasm builds in my belly. I want to experience all of Micah at this moment. He presses his lips to mine while reaching down, pressing on the spot he knows drives me crazy. His kiss is hard and hot, and I don't want it to end as my insides explode and waves of intense pressure course through me.

He pulls out of me, still rock-hard.

That was insane. Out of this world, mind-blowingly good. Micah's just as amazing at sex as he is at everything else.

I lean back on Maison. My chest rises and falls as I gasp for air, my eyes stuck shut, sweat beading on my forehead. After a few seconds, I open them, finally feeling like I can breathe again.

It's Micah's sexy face that greets me. "Did you like that?" he asks me. "You want more, London?"

I press my lips together and nod weakly, although I don't know how much more I can handle. But I'm determined to satiate these boys tonight.

"Good. Now turn around."

The power shifts, and it now seems like Micah's in charge. And I know with that performance from Micah, Maison will want another turn. Facing Maison, I get on my hands and knees as instructed. Before I do, Micah grabs my hair and gently tugs it over my shoulder and kisses my neck. Chills shoot up my spine and my body pulses in aftershocks of pleasure.

I turn toward Maison to look at him. His cute, lopsided grin is back, and I love it. It's the Maison I'm used to. He reaches up and kisses me, and instead of sliding me on top of him like I expect, he shifts and joins his brother behind me. "We're just getting started, baby," he whispers. "We can go all night."

One of them grips my hips and enters me from behind for round three. His cock slides right into my g-spot, making me moan before taking my body into complete euphoria. I have no idea which twin it is, nor do I care in the slightest.

Cool air sneaks around me and goosebumps rise on my arm, jolting me awake. The first signs of morning trickle into the shelter, and I know the fire still has hot embers as smoke seeps into my nose. I'm dressed in the clothes I threw on before passing out from utter exhaustion in between both of them.

I swallow hard, remembering what I did last night. I'm too comfortable to care, as one of them is curled up behind me, with his arm draped over my waist. The other is missing. I am not yet prepared to face the day, so I relish in the moment while the effects of the alcohol from last night take over.

I suspect it's Maison holding me; Micah probably got out of here as soon as the light hit the sky. He will need to tend to our deer, and I doubt he wants to watch Maison and me during our morning cuddle routine.

They fucked me in five different positions, each taking me multiple times before my body just couldn't take it anymore. Eventually, I lost track of who was who. Before last night, I didn't know what an orgasm was, or that it was possible to feel so good. I still feel the aftershocks of pleasure between my legs.

When I was aware of who was inside me, Maison did a good job comforting me, assuring me what I was doing was okay, and making me feel safe. With Micah, I was never sure what I was going to get, but he was softer as the night went on, and I'm pretty sure he kissed every inch of my body. I've never felt so safe or taken care of. And I know I can't let it happen again—I can't be physical with both of them—my heart and body can't handle it.

And my heart is with Maison—he's better for me.

I open my eyes and face him. He's already awake, staring at me. His beautiful chestnut eyes watching me sleep. I bite my lip and a smile forms on his lips. My stomach tightens and I go wholly still when I realize I can't tell them apart. I assumed it was Maison by the way he is holding me, but that's not Maison's smile. Who am I looking at? Why can't I tell them apart?

I reach my arm up and drag it along his shoulder.

No scar.

"Micah," I whisper.

He presses his lips to mine and pulls me into him, and I jolt back at the suddenness of it. "Shh, don't say anything," he whispers against my lips.

My heart shutters as he cups my cheek. I lean in and lengthen the kiss, deepening it. We make out like this for a few minutes, and I let his hands explore me as he gently strokes me with his tongue. I kiss him till my lips are swollen and heat pools through me. I reach my hand up his shirt and feel his hard abs, his chiselled waist, and the dips down to the apex of his thighs. He shifts me around and slides his thumb into my waistband to slip my sweats down to my knees. I help him by kicking them off, naked once again beneath these blankets. I hesitate only for a second before his knee is nudging my thighs open.

"Open your legs, London," he murmurs. "Please."

I close my eyes and let him guide me, his hands gripping my hips and pulling me up, knowing Maison must be close by and could crawl in and see this.

I feel his cock enter me from behind, and even though I'm raw and sore from the night before, I'm already wet. He fucks me slow, steady and intimate, our bodies mingled together, his thumb rubbing that spot while he fills me.

He was completely different last night—rough, aggressive, and treating my body like his only release. Last night, he just fucked me. But this... this is something different.

I softly moan as he kisses my neck, moving my hair away from my face. I grind into him and arch my back, and he slides in and out of me. My breath lengthens and I savor the moment, enjoying every line of hard muscle on him, how wet and turned-on he makes me. It breaks my heart, because this has to be the last time we do this.

"You feel like fucking heaven, London," he whispers, pressing a kiss to my ear. "I wish you were mine."

I hitch a breath, but don't respond. My heart and everything tightens, and I grip his muscled legs so hard, my fingers turn white while he picks up the pace while nibbling on my neck and ear. He finishes faster than I thought he would, which makes sense since I'm not even sure he finished last night. He withdraws and ejaculates onto his blanket to avoid getting any on me. Part of me wishes I could look over my shoulder and watch him in this moment, but I don't. If I did, I think that would be my undoing.

When he's done, I pull my sweats back up and dare to look at him. His soft lustful gaze from earlier is now void of expression.

Back to the Micah I'm used to.

I blink at him, and a wave of shame pours through me. "I have to go find Maison," I tell him.

His eyes flicker, but he nods, as if he also knows what we just did is a betrayal of sorts. "Yeah, I know," is all he has to say about it.

I scramble to find my clothes and head outside. Once there, I see Maison about thirty feet away, peering down into the water. I walk up to him and place my hands around his athletic frame. He grabs my hands and turns me to face him.

Sadness radiates out of his eyes. He just heard everything Micah and I did. He must have left knowing that would happen—he let it happen. The little flicker he sees when his mind wanders off, and I know it's connected to Micah and me. For whatever reason, he is allowing his twin to fuck his girlfriend, encouraging it even. The bit of shame I have grinds much deeper. Maison is my boyfriend—he's the one I want, even with my doubts about him and his true involvement in Olivia's death.

I step on my tippy toes and force him to look at me. "I love you, Maison," I tell him softly and kiss him. He kisses me back, even though my lips are still swollen from making out with Micah. I mean every word, and I remember whose hands kept me warm and safe on the airplane, on this island, and every day since.

I have to remind myself which brother I'm in love with. It's not Micah...

Not Micah.

CHAPTER SIXTEEN

DAY THIRTY THREE

Imagine every thought, feeling, or emotion known to humanity, and then multiply your hunger, thirst, pain, desire, rage, love, and fear by a thousand. That's how living on this island feels. Closing my eyes leaves me feeling completely drained, but the moment I open them, I'm surprisingly alert. Hunger consumes my thoughts until the thirst takes over, and I can't think of anything else. When I'm mad, I can imagine what it feels like to kill someone—the rage is all-consuming—and when I love, I love with intensity. Every part of my body ignites with flames, my heart feels like it's about to explode, and my soul seems to want to escape my flesh. It almost doesn't feel real, like it's happening to someone else, and I'm floating above watching it unfold. The possibility of each day being my last increases my intensity for everything. We've been on this island for over a month—long enough for the world to believe we are dead, and that's exactly what is going to happen. I'm scared, and deep down, I really miss Micah, and I can't see how we will survive this.

We spent one more night at our camp before heading back to the others. We were all exhausted and passed out silently after the guys were gone most of the day. Thomas and Micah carried the deer back with us over two trips. The wolf was never mentioned.

The twins were noticeably tense when we got back. Jade arched her brows at me when she came out of her shelter in the morning, but had the good sense not to ask questions about it.

It's like Olivia's ghost possessed me. I am a living, breathing reincarnate of her, and I'm bringing out the worst emotions in both of them. I can feel it. They wanted it—I saw the desire in their eyes when we hunted—and it was planned. For whatever reason Maison gave my body to his brother, and now Micah will barely look at me. We've made a truce of sorts with Ezra, Naomi, and Nigel, and James and the others are already somewhat neutral. No one has the energy to argue anymore.

Nigel is worsening by the day—the husk is taking over everyone. Jade and I decided it was best not to say anything about of our suspicions of his relationship with Olivia, but I watch him like a hawk as every part of his humanity looks like it is being stripped away from him. Hour by hour, day by day, we're all losing our sanity.

As we push mid-October, the days are getting shorter, the nights longer. Most days I don't even want to get out of bed. I force Maison to stay with me as long as he can before he encourages me up, and I find dry wood. It snowed again, a couple of times, so we are all miserable but holding on to what's left of warmish weather. At night, I can't be alone—that's when this island scares me the most—so I hold on to Maison tightly, since Micah frequently goes missing to be at his preferred camp, I'm assuming.

Alone.

When he is here, Ezra bosses him around, which is completely unnerving. Life was easier when I hated Micah. Sometimes I wish I still did, because anything is better than this. Micah doesn't do feelings—and he's only proved Maison right. Yet the emotion bled out of him, it bled out of both of us. It's the side of him I didn't think existed. Since we returned a week ago, I've gone to the cove a few times, hoping to see him.

Even now I'm sitting, waiting... like a fucking idiot, because he's not coming, even though he knows I'm here. I move like he's watching me, every motion, hair twirl, lip bite, every time I bathe myself. I wait until the sun dips down under the mountains before I head back to camp, feeling alone and defeated.

Returning, I notice Naomi, Serena, and Jade chatting by the fire. Naomi and Serena ignore me, but Jade waves me over. Naomi and I don't speak, and Serena and I barely interact since she spends most of her time with James, and I have no desire to chat with them. I also don't go because a shadow flickers to my right, and I see the outline of Micah heading into the woods toward the creek.

All the boys went out trapping earlier, as we've already devoured the deer. I'm not even sure why he is here. No one else seems to notice, so this is my opportunity to follow him. I'm desperate to find out what's going on in his head.

I pretend to head to my shelter, but I cut into the trees instead, my spear steady in my hand, and I hover behind him all the way to the creek. Silent as a mouse, or in this case, the predator, like he taught me. Despite the crunching underfoot, he remains unfazed. At one point, he pauses and looks around. Something triggered him. I sigh when he keeps walking, as I'm not ready for him to see me yet.

When we arrive at the creek, I hide behind a nearby tree. Not too close, but close enough I have a full view of him. His back is to me as he leans over, filling water bottles.

My plan is to attack him when he fills the last bottle. It's when his mind will be focused on something else, giving me a chance to get him when he least expects it. My heart pulses. The last time I did this, he played along. Will he this time? I know he likes this little game we play, and I miss it—I miss him.

Finally, I see my chance, and I leap out from my hiding spot and lunge toward him. At the very last second, he whips around and grabs me.

"Nice try, London," he says, gripping my wrists hard.

Instead of giving in, I twist my body and kick him, but he stops me with his knee and slowly pushes me down to the ground. I can't stop him, he's too strong, and he's not letting me hit him like he usually does. He cocks his head to one side and frowns, keeping a firm grip on my wrists. "You've lost your edge. I heard you following me thirty seconds after I left."

He lets me go, leaving me on the ground, and turns his back to me.

Jerk.

I prop myself onto my wrists. "What the hell is wrong with you?"

He picks up his water, keeping his back turned to me. "Go back. You shouldn't be here with me."

So, he is avoiding me, but I'm not going to let him ignore me.

"So that's it," I spit at him. "That's all I get from you; all the energy you'll spare for me?"

He shakes his head and walks away, leaving me on the ground alone.

Pathetic.

And so I scream, "Why won't you talk to me? After all those things I let you do to me, I deserve better than this."

He pauses and rubs the bit of facial hair growing from his chin, making him look closer to twenty-five than twenty. "Go back to your boyfriend," he rasps. He takes one more step, which is the final straw for me. My hand finds a nearby rock, and I stand and hurl it, hitting him square in the back of the skull.

Perfect fucking aim—he should be proud of me.

He turns around in two slow steps and faces me. Pure rage steals out of him. He shifts his head and actually cracks his neck like some sort of lunatic.

Oh shit...

I quickly cover my mouth and see the spear two feet away on the ground. I'm helpless as he stomps toward me, grabs me, and shoves me onto a tree stump. "Why did you do that?" he spits out. His mouth is so close to mine, I can almost taste him.

Because you won't talk to me, you won't look at me, you won't train with me when I clearly followed you to do just that. Because I can't seem to get any sort of emotion out of you. I can't stop thinking about you, and when I do things that surprise you, I know it turns you on.

"You said I lost my edge," I whisper instead of saying all the things swirling in my head. I feel the heat of his body so close, and every emotion I was looking for now blazes out of his eyes and right into me. My knees weaken as he leans down and moves closer, his lips hovering over mine.

With my body frozen in place, he grabs my waist, pushing his body onto mine. With my heart in my throat, I close my eyes as he draws his head down. A few seconds go by.

An inch—a mere inch—and I could have his mouth on mine.

I finally whisper, "Micah, I can't."

A pause, then he says, "Why the fuck not?"

I open my eyes, my body shaking and breath shallow.

He shakes his head and leans up to my ear. "Every part of your body is screaming at me to touch you right now."

"Micah, I'm with Maison."

"I'm well aware."

"I can't do this with you both."

He curls his lip. "Then why did you stop me just now? When I was trying to leave? Why aren't you with him right now?"

"I'm worried about you."

He tilts his head, keeping me trapped inside him. His jaw flexes. "I can assure you, I'm fine."

A tightness wraps around my chest and heart as he stands so close. I want him—I want him so badly, it hurts my skin. But I shouldn't want him... I have no reason to want him.

Fuck.

"Micah. I'm confused."

He leans in closer, his strong body all I can process. "Bullshit. That's complete bullshit. I know you want me, London. You want me to grab your mouth and kiss you right now. You want me inside you again. You want my hands on you, to watch you, to pay attention to you. Well, here I am, sweetheart. I fucking *see* you."

His hand reaches up my shirt, teasing my stomach with his fingers. My muscles clench with each soft stroke. He hovers his hand and draws his gaze down to my mouth, making every inch of me quiver. He restrains himself from kissing and having sex with me against this tree, like I know he wants to.

My words come out as a sob. The world around me goes white—no gray—then a swirl of colors.

"Micah... I..."

He grabs my hands and pulls them up around his neck so our mouths are so close, his heart beating so close to mine. He swallows before saying through gritted teeth, "Do you think I want this? Do you think I chose to have feelings for my brother's girlfriend? Because I don't. I don't want to want you. I've gone down this path before, and I nearly lost him over it. I fucking *hate* the way I feel about you, London."

A sob escapes my lips and tears flow out of my eyes in one wet blur. He hates the way he felt about me. But he feels, even if it's apparently hate.

Hate—such a strong word.

I hate it, too. I need to clarify exactly what he's referring to. Enough of this bullshit. I look up at him, my eyes blazing. "Micah, did you really kill Olivia?"

A silent, deadly pause and he pulls back. "Why the fuck are you asking me that?"

My hands fall to my side. "Because I need to know, and I want to hear it from you."

He keeps his head down, his eyes locked to the ground. I'm worried he's going to clam up again, close off, but he parts his lips. "It was an accident. That's all you need to know."

My breath shallows, and I lose the ability to breathe. "Or was it Maison?" I ask softly.

He closes his eyes, as if reliving every single second of what really went on. He gives me a pleading look, not wanting me to press this.

Finding my nerve, I keep going. "Did Maison drug her? Is that how she really died?" I'm pretty sure my heart has stopped beating now. I know the truth just by his reaction. Every dark flicker from both of them over the past month. Their tells were in their eyes the whole time.

He stands with his shoulders slumped over, still close to me, and bites his bottom lip with so much sorrow in his eyes. What he says next shocks me to the core. "He doesn't know... He thinks I killed her in the car accident, and that's how she died. I let him think that; I let everyone think that. I created the narrative."

He doesn't know?

"But..."

His lips twist, and I can only imagine tears pouring out of him by how much pain he's in. The realization of it sickens me—Maison drugged her. He gave her a lethal dosage of something to control her, and it killed her.

He's capable of killing someone. And Micah took on that pain and sorrow, sparing him from that realization. Everything is clicking into place.

Micah looks at me now, his eyes dark with all that sadness. "It would kill him if he knew the truth. He's not a bad guy, London; he just did a terrible thing. It's easier for everyone to think it was me, and I deserve it for betraying him to begin with by even being with her at that moment. But she was so messed up when I found her, I couldn't... I shouldn't have even been with her."

The image of him with her stains my mind. "You fucked her when she was like that?" I can't help the level of disgust in my voice. What kind of guys have I fallen for?

He dips his chin and keeps speaking, despite the look of horror on my face. Obviously, he feels good about finally getting this out. "I was sleeping with her for weeks. She drank a lot. She came to find me after she broke up with him and threw herself at me. She died right after we... I didn't know. I didn't know until...." His voice catches and I place my fingers over his mouth for a moment, stopping him from saying it. I can't hear it. I don't want to picture him with her, or Maison, for that matter.

"What about the accident?" I ask him.

I watch the bob in his throat. "I faked the accident. I didn't know what else to do. My dad's lawyer and I talked about it after they found all the shit in her system and started investigating me for murder. When I admitted everything, my dad found the shit in his room. Maison messed around with drugs a bit, here and there, but I never touched the fucking stuff. It was either me going to prison or him. My dad couldn't imagine his golden boy being in prison, so he paid a lot of fucking money to make it go away. He pulled in some major debts over it.

Ezra—his dad fucked over an entire family for it.

I shake my head, my body trembling. "I thought it was you. I was certain it was you."

His eyes glaze over. "You wanted the fucking truth, sweetheart, well there it is. Now go back to him, and don't tell him what I just told you. Promise me, London."

My hands squeeze into fists and the world collapses in on me. He has no right to ask that of me. I try to speak again, but I choke on my words. I try to scream, but all I do is suck in air as chills run through my spine as I fall to the ground.

What is happening to me?

"London?"

Micah's voice is soft, calling for me.

I can't breathe.

The world blurs.

His soft hands are on me, shaking me. "London... London. You're having a panic attack, and you just fainted. Breathe."

I slowly regain my focus, but my chest rises and falls at a rapid rate. I can't control it. Micah is crouched down in front of me, his eyes wide.

He looks like Maison. Is it Maison? I close my eyes, and let my head hang heavy as Micah grabs me and lifts me, wrapping his arms around me.

My body is limp in his, like I'm intoxicated. My senses dull. He cradles me in his arms and I'm floating, like I'm not really in my body and am watching this all unfold as someone else. It's all too much, this whole island. It's all just a dream. One fucked up hallucination.

He cradles my head into his chest as he walks. My eyes shut tight, his heartbeat against my ear. The rhythmic beating of his chest calms me, so I focus on that as I slowly come back into myself.

Eventually, I let out a moan, and he rubs his fingers against my forehead.

"Shh. Don't speak," he whispers.

My breath deepens, and he stops and puts me down. I don't know how long he carried me, but my legs are still weak. I open my eyes and find him. His expression is tight, his eyebrows narrow as he keeps his arms around me.

His effect on me is debilitating. Just being in his presence takes away my ability to function properly, to think straight, to take a simple breath of air. I finally feel the courage to say something. "I'm not strong, Micah. I can't deal with this." I dart my eyes away from him, feeling like I might topple over. I hate him seeing me like this.

Weak. Pathetic.

I can't handle anything without breaking down.

"You're not weak, London," he tells me, pulling my hair behind my ear. "I think you're the strongest girl I've ever met. Maison and I are just really fucked up."

I squeeze my eyes shut right before we cross the tree line to camp. Maison's back from trapping and seeing him sitting there, looking at me, his eyes tight with concern as I probably look like a heaping mess once again. I don't know how to face him right now, but it's Nigel's sunken face that sickens me over everything else. His ripped argyle shirt sticking out from under his hood, and his stupid fucking bow tie he still likes to wear for whatever reason.

This is all his fault.

"Micah," I barely choke out a whisper as all eyes shift to us, "you can't trust Nigel."

"What did you do to her?" Maison asks as Micah carries me back to the group. I can barely walk, feeling so weak and utterly exhausted, my mind shattered.

Everyone's sitting around the fire, their faces grim, hoods pulled up to their eyes. Sitting. Waiting. Surviving.

Micah looks at his brother, who bolts over to us. "I didn't do anything to her. She just fainted." Micah places me in Maison's arms, who picks me up, acting as if I'm made of glass.

Maison refrains from asking why we're together. The tension between them is thick, thicker than I've ever seen it, but at least I understand it better.

Maison thinks Micah killed Olivia, and Micah only ever protected Maison. Yet Micah's DNA was all over her, inside her, when she died. Micah's not telling me everything, but he told me enough...

He has feelings for me. Feelings that are wholly reciprocated.

"Come on, baby," Maison whispers, "let's get you to bed."

I fall into him and walk away from Micah. I need rest. The overwhelming emotional and physical response I just had over both of them almost killed me.

Maison takes me to our little home—our shelter, the one I've spent countless hours with him in, getting to know him, falling in love with him, and now it feels like I'm in the arms of a stranger. I don't know Maison Matei at all.

He crawls in next to me, his hands comfort me, his body warm as always. I lie on him and let him rub my shoulder, all the tension releasing, but the thought of him drugging Olivia makes me tense and bile rises into my throat.

He knows I'm not okay, he senses it. His fingers are tentative and his breath falters. I don't want to talk about it, but I have to. I have questions. "Don't be mad at him. It wasn't his fault," I finally say.

His finger's pause and tighten around my collarbone. "Why were you with him, baby?"

I tense up. "I followed him to the creek... he didn't know I was there."

I'm not going to lie to him—too many lies are being told on this island. His lips graze my cheek, and he pushes himself around so he is over top of me, leaning both arms just over me. My heart's pounding now, just like it did in the beginning, when I was unsure of him, unsure if he was capable of hurting someone. I stare up at the roof of the shelter, every branch and piece of moss he made for me—for us. He traces his finger along my collarbone. "You're *my* girlfriend, baby, or have you forgotten that?"

My lips curl, and I push his fingers off me. "I haven't forgotten, but have *you*? You just shared me with him, Maison. If you were so concerned about Micah, then why did you do that? Clearly, it bugs you."

He tilts his head and his pupils flare as he hovers over me. "I shared you with him because I love him, and I knew he needed you that night. It was wrong... I know it was wrong, but I wanted him to experience you the way I have," he slides his hand up my back, "and you didn't seem to mind too much, baby."

They share everything.

Heat flushes through my body. "Is that why you shared him with Olivia? Because he needed her?"

That has him at a loss for words.

I watch him carefully, so carefully. Every facial expression, every twitch, I watch him re-live every decision.

His face drops, and any anger I have simply drops with it. He looks broken, tired, like we all are. He rolls off me and places his arm around me. I dip my head into the crook of his arm and close my eyes as tiny sobs release from my throat.

"I warned you, baby," he whispers. "Micah doesn't do feelings. Don't fall for him; he's only going to hurt you. He's projecting everything that he did to Olivia onto you. I wanted him to feel good for one night, so I shared you with him because we're all hurting on this island. That's why I shared her with him, too. He's fucked up, baby... he's always been fucked up."

Half answers—half truths from both of them.

Blaming each other.

I swallow a lump in my throat. Is that all I am for Micah? Then why are my feelings growing exponentially for him?

I turn to face Maison and press my lips into the worry crease on his forehead. My love for Maison is strong, too—even though I desperately want to hate him. "I followed him because I was worried about him. He's withdrawn, like we're losing him."

This seems to appease him in this moment, but he still studies me, his brows drawn together, watching the confusion on my face. "This is how Micah is. He has highs and lows. He went months barely speaking to anyone after Olivia died. If something doesn't go his way, he breaks down."

I pull my lips away from his. "Those few months, when Micah barely spoke to anyone, was that when you weren't speaking to him?"

He blinks a couple times and rests his hand on his head, leaning up on his elbow, and cocks one eyebrow. "Why are you asking that?"

"Answer my question, Maison."

He hoods his eyes and shifts uncomfortably. "I was mad at him. He never had to pay for what he did to her. Even if it was an accident, he shouldn't have been with her that night. Our dad just made it magically go away. Micah's never held accountable for anything."

Stubborn. Maison is stubborn. And... stupid. Does he really not realize what he did?

I arch my brow. "And he beat himself up every day about it, I'm sure."

Maison presses his lips into my forehead. "Let him deal with this. He will come around."

I close my eyes, a numbness overcomes me, and I can't talk anymore. He rubs my forehead, wiping his thumbs over my eyelids, which lulls me to a near sleep. His chest rises and falls beneath my head, and a few minutes of silence passes between us.

"You can go to him if you want," he says darkly, just as I'm about to pass the threshold into sleep.

I open my eyes and turn my head up to him, my pulse racing. "What did you say?"

"I'm sure he can keep you as warm as I can."

I purse my lips, shaking my head. "Maison, stop." Why is he saying this? He's the one who invited him into our relationship, not me. I could have avoided my weird physical attraction to him. What did Maison expect? They look exactly the same. But I have Maison, and I don't need both of them. I could have stayed away from Micah, continued ignoring him. "It can't happen again," I whisper. "I'm with you, Maison."

He squeezes me tight. "Good answer, baby."

CHAPTER SEVENTEEN

A gut-wrenching scream pierces a hole through my ears and jolts me awake. Maison and I both shoot up, and he grabs me, holding me back as I instinctively lurch forward.

"Stay here, baby," he whispers. "I'll find out what's going on." He jumps out of the shelter to investigate the cause of the screaming.

"Fuck no," I mutter and follow him out into the chilly night. Freezing, moist air hits my face as traces of morning hint in the sky—early morning, still night, still bone-chillingly cold, even with the clear night sky seeping it's light down on us.

The whole group is already out there, minus Micah, and a large body is on the ground, withering in pain. It doesn't take long for Micah to join, his bone weapon tight in his hand.

I take a few seconds to realize it's Thomas on the ground in a lifeless heap with a lot of blood pooling around him. Only a two-hundred-and-twenty-five-pound hockey player could make a sound like that.

"What the fuck is going on?" Micah barks, seeing his friend withering in pain. The group surrounds Thomas, while Micah approaches with a look nothing short of predatory.

Ezra, Nigel, Ollie, and Nathan all hover around him. Naomi has a sobbing Jade in a choke hold. Micah closes the distance between him and Ezra as I run up to Maison, who stops a few feet away, looking equally confused at what's going on, but doing nothing to stop it.

The three hockey players turn to face Micah, creating an impenetrable wall between the two friends. Nigel, I notice, slinks to the shadows with a smirk on his face. James and Serena walk up with puzzled looks on their faces.

"Get the fuck back, Micah," Ezra barks. "This has nothing to do with you. Nigel caught Thomas stealing food on his fire watch, man. He needed to learn a fucking lesson not to steal from the group."

Micah's dangerous glare shifts to Nigel, who appears responsible for the situation based on the twitch of his lip.

"What the fuck did you do to him?" I cry out and try to run to Thomas.

Maison's on me in an instant, holding my arms back. "Baby, please calm down."

I try to wiggle out of his grip, but it's pointless. He's not letting me move. Maison is obviously siding with Ezra on this.

Ezra shoots his snarled look to me, then back to Micah, who's gripping his bone weapon so hard, I'm surprised his hands aren't bleeding. Ezra fails to recognize how good Micah is with that thing, or how sharp it is. I wouldn't want to be on the receiving end of Micah wielding it, especially wielding it with fury.

Ezra's voice is unhinged, centering his attention on Micah, who's staring at him with a deadly calm. "Thomas took food, Micah. Nigel caught him eating two cans of beans. That's three cans now that have been stolen from the rest of us. We didn't think you'd do anything about it, so we decided as a group on a punishment to teach everyone that stealing will no longer be tolerated." He points at Micah, and I realize Ezra's holding a bloody knife in his hands. The big one—the only other knife not in Micah's control—the one that could sever a leg.

"What punishment?" James asks, stepping forward and glaring at his two friends standing next to Ezra. I'm relieved to know at least James wasn't part of this—which means Micah has at least one ally in the group.

Thomas moans from the ground, his voice catching an octave through the pain he's clearly in. "They tried to cut my hand off," he wails in agony. They obviously beat the shit out of him too, before they cut him—or whatever they did to him.

"Jesus Christ," I mutter, trying to wiggle out of Maison's arms to go to him. His hold on me only tightens. "This isn't a punishment, this is brutality," I say to whoever will listen.

But no one does.

It breaks my heart seeing him like that—it's how I was when they did that to me, and they got away with it. Thomas, of all people, doesn't deserve it. They are doing it to get to Micah.

Micah steps forward. "Get the fuck out of my way, Ezra. I will not hesitate to fuck you up if you don't." Micah's eyes show no fear, despite being severely outnumbered and facing a larger knife from Ezra. "Or you, or you." Micah points his bone weapon at Nathan and Ollie, who both flinch a little. Micah tilts his head, making his neck crack once again. I wonder if it's just from the rock I hurled at him earlier, but it has the desired effect of making him look psycho.

Everyone is unraveling; we're nothing but hungry, angry, irrational teenagers about to tear each other apart over beans. Food I hated eating growing up, but Heinz beans are more valuable than gold on this pretty little island.

A flash of anger sweeps out of Ezra's eyes, and he swings at him, connecting his fist right in his mouth so hard, Micah's head whips to the side and blood spurts out of his nose. I cry out and keel over, as if I got punched in the gut, too. And Micah just takes it, not even fighting back.

"What are you doing?" I scream, looking at Maison. "Why aren't you doing anything?"

He squeezes my arm. "We have to let this play out, babe; it's been brewing for a couple of weeks. This is Micah's fight. He has to win if he wants to stay in charge."

Barbaric. This island is making us savage.

Naomi still holds Jade in a chokehold, but even she can't watch this. Although, I'm sure if Micah wanted her back, she'd drop Ezra like a dirty hat. Serena and James stand off to the side, unsure of what to do, either, with James not being in on the inner circle of whatever group decisions were just made.

"This is wrong, so fucking wrong," I sob, and I can't take my eyes off Micah, his body rigid. "Maison, do something."

"I can't, baby; otherwise, they will turn on us."

"He's your *brother*, Maison."

He tenses behind me, the truth of those words hopefully hitting him.

Ezra laughs, circling Micah, who is silent with an electric current surrounding him. Thomas is down, barely coherent now, and not there to back him up as he usually is. I have no idea how badly they hurt him, but from the looks of it, they made their point in spades, and Micah is truly on his own.

"You can't take us all, Micah," Ezra taunts. This seems to give Nathan and Ollie a bit more confidence as they both stand straighter.

Nigel sits back, watching... smiling.

Micah jerks his head to Thomas, then at me in Maison's arms, planning... assessing. "We'll leave," he finally says, his jaw tight. "Let Thomas go, and we'll walk away, and we won't come back."

No. No. No. I don't want him to go.

Nathan and Ollie look at James, who shakes his head, signaling them not to interfere while Ezra considers. James looks pissed, his jaw tensing from the control he's losing, too. At no point before have the younger guys gotten involved in the seniors' fucked-up dynamics.

Ezra steps aside. "Fine, get out of here. But you're not getting any supplies; you already have enough. We know about your secret camp, and all the shit you have hidden." He kicks Thomas's face, making me cringe. "This fucker already ate two cans of food, so he's had enough. If you try to take more, it will be a problem."

Nigel steps forward, slicing me a look. "And your bitch girlfriend already had her fair share, too, so I'd say you had enough."

Maison's reaction to Nigel makes me cringe. Referring to me as Micah's girlfriend, it was purposeful, no doubt, and Maison tightens his hold on me.

Nigel crafted everything carefully, as if he planned this for a while. And I've played into it, almost making it too easy for him to tear us apart.

"Get off me, Naomi," Jade finally pushes Naomi, who lets her through, and she immediately runs to Thomas's side. Naomi glances at me, her eyes narrowed, waiting to see what I will do.

Thomas gets up and lunges at Ezra, holding his bloody hand, which is curled in his chest. He can barely stand straight. Thomas looks directly at Micah, his eyes pained and pleading. "I didn't eat that food. I was set up." Thomas glares at Ezra's beady little eyes and flexes his jaw. "You didn't have to cut my fucking palm."

Ezra grimaces. "You'll be fine. It was just a warning scratch. And it was Micah's idea." He laughs darkly.

That empty threat Micah made. The punishment for stealing food, forever marking Thomas as a thief. As if we are living in nothing more than the Dark Ages.

Thomas grunts and lunges toward Ezra. Clumsy, without his usual athletic grace, and Ezra merely steps out of the way. Nigel just snickers, his greasy hair falling right over his eyes under his dark hood. Ezra is nothing but a puppet—an extremely strong, hot-headed puppet.

I cringe, seeing how hard the bigger guy falls. Ezra turns and kicks him in the ribs, and Thomas cries out in pain. And that's when Micah bolts, taking Ezra down, pressing his arm down hard on Ezra's neck. I've never seen such strength, every muscle rippling, every fiber of his body holding Ezra's head down to where Ezra's eyes might pop out of their sockets, and Ezra drops his knife. Micah presses his bone weapon into Ezra's temple.

The knife now sits only inches from Micah's grasp, and I'm pretty sure Ezra stops breathing. A vein pops dangerously out of his forehead.

Micah lifts his gaze to Thomas. "Run."

Without hesitation, Thomas flees, the guys parting to let him stumble through. He grabs what he can from his shelter, and Jade follows, and the two of them disappear into the forest. Ollie, Nathan, and Nigel surround Micah, each holding a spear, ready to pounce on him. My heart hammers in my chest. Taking down Micah will not be as easy as Thomas, and they know it.

"Get off him, Micah," Nigel says dismissively, waving his hand as if this is boring to him.

"Maison," I plead. "Please, do something."

"Micah will be fine," he whispers. "I'm more worried about everyone else."

Ezra reaches for the knife, but Micah doubles down on Ezra's neck—to the point Ezra starts to turn purple now. Completely helpless under Micah's pure strength. Micah only loosens his hold when Nathan and Ollie crowd him. He jumps up and grabs the knife, and the guys fall back a couple of steps. The last time I saw Micah in this stance, he took down a buck with his bare hands.

Ezra rises and faces Micah, sweat dripping down his forehead, his beady eyes gleaming as Nigel tosses him a spear.

All these spears Micah had made... only to be used against him.

Nigel steps forward with his hood hiding his face, his bow tie perfectly in place. "Just go, Micah. You can't take all of us. We will hurt you if you try to sabotage this group any more than you already have."

The overlord speaks.

Micah twists his bone weapon. "I can fucking try," he fires back, completely unfazed by the threat in front of him. James sits neutral with Naomi and Serena, who all watch in horror. Even Naomi, I'm assuming, didn't expect it to get to this level.

Nigel was behind this whole thing; I know it by the way he's watching it all unfold exactly how he planned it. Who knows what kind of bullshit he's been feeding Ezra, knowing the deep hatred Ezra has for Micah under the surface. Using it to his own advantage to gain control of everything.

Nigel clicks his tongue as the three other boys step up behind him, clearly choosing a side. "We can all avoid more unpleasantness if you just leave, Micah. Go die on the other side of the island. We've all had enough of your brooding bullshit."

My hand squeezes into a fist as Micah backs away. His eyes flash to his brother, then to the pleading look I'm giving him.

"This is bullshit," Micah says. "You're all on your fucking own now." He slips away into the dark forest as more light illuminates the sky. He doesn't spare me a glance, not a single glance.

Ezra yells toward him, "If you come back here, we will cut your hand off, too."

Jesus.

The group stares at me, and the silence that follows is nothing short of terrifying. I realize it's because I'm shaking uncontrollably, so much so, that Maison finally loosens his hold on me. Tears well up in my eyes, and I wiggle out of Maison's hold with full intent on following Micah.

I can't be here... not without Micah.

Maison quickly realizes what I'm planning and grabs my hand. "London, stay with me, baby. Don't follow him. He did this to himself. You and I shouldn't have to pay for his mistakes."

I bite my lip, "Maison, you don't understand..."

His words are pained as he spits out his next words, "No, you don't understand, because you don't know us. You don't know him like I do. He thinks he's above everyone and can act however he wants and get away with hit. Ezra's right to be pissed at him. He's the one who fucked up, not me. Let him sulk in the forest."

"Maison, you don't mean that."

He lowers his head, then raises his pained eyes to meet mine. "Yes, I do. He ends up ruining everything he touches..." a silent, painful pause, "including you."

The words strike as intended, ripping a hole in my heart.

I open my mouth. "What does that supposed to mean?"

He shakes his head. "Stay away from him, baby. I mean it. It won't end well for you. He'll poison you... he poisons everything he touches."

With all my strength, I push myself away from him. I ball my fists and strike him... I hit him hard. "Like you poisoned Olivia?" I shriek. "You shared her, then when she fell in love with him, you poisoned and killed her, Maison. So don't stand here and blame Micah for everything."

The viciousness of my words surprise even me. In no way did I mean for them to come out like that.

Or... my stomach drops, *in front of everyone.*

He stands there and shakes his head. His eyes flash with sadness and... love. He still loves me, even though he's losing me.

I know he's hurting right now, but how can he be so stubborn? I wipe the tears streaming down my face as Ezra and Naomi walk over and stand in front of me, placing themselves in between me and Maison.

"Don't hit him again," Naomi threatens.

"You," a guttural noise releases from me, "are the ones who tried to cut off Thomas's hand." I purse my lips and glare at them. "Micah did nothing wrong. He was just defending Thomas."

"Oh, don't be so dramatic." Naomi stands with her hands on her hips and head tilted. "We weren't actually going to cut off his hand, London. We were teaching him a lesson—the same lesson you needed to be taught. Don't come here spreading lies about our friend group and our history. You weren't even there."

Our history? What the fuck was your involvement, Naomi?

What about the next time? Or the time after that? Where is the line between riotousness and pure evil? They tread that line. They drew blood—they made me bleed, too. And these are Maison's friends? The people he's aligning himself with over his twin brother?

Ezra's nostrils flare as he wipes sweat off his brow. He's shaking, probably because he knows how close he was to Micah killing him. Micah scares him, as he should. Micah would fuck him right up; he's the strongest guy on this island.

He yells to the rest of the group, loud enough for everyone to hear, "Micah's a liability. He can't come back here.

If anyone follows him and helps him, they are on his side." He flits his eyes to me. "Do you understand that, London?"

I take two steps back and stare him right in the eye. "Loud and clear."

Without looking back, I stomp back to the shelter. Maison follows me, desperation pouring out of his eyes.

"London, wait." He grabs my waist and pulls me to him. My entire body stiffens beneath him. I can't even look him in the eyes. My whole body sinks into him. I give up fighting. "You let him leave. How could you let him leave?" The sobs shake out of me.

His lips graze the back of my head. "It's for the best. When he gets like this, he is dangerous, even to himself. He's unstable. Micah's sick, baby—he doesn't view the world the way you and I do. I don't want him hurting you, too. I can't lose you, London."

Like he lost Olivia. Like they both lost Olivia. Is that all I am to both of them? A proxy to her?

"He was helping Thomas! How is that unstable? He's the only person on this damn island who's actually thinking clearly. We are not above the law, Maison. Hurting people with a knife or beating them in the woods is not right." I turn to face him. "We can't kill each other, Maison."

"Look around, London. No one is here but us, and no one's coming, either. This is our island, and Ezra's in charge. Thomas fucked up, that's it."

Ezra is not in charge—how does he not see that?

"I don't want to be a part of a group that will stand by and allow this."

His nostrils flare, that darkness again hinting in his eyes. "You can't leave. I won't let you."

Fire ripples under my skin. "You won't *let* me? How about you don't have a fucking choice?"

He rubs his hands through his hair while I whirl around toward our shelter. I grab my pack and start throwing whatever I can inside. He stands back and lets me, watching as I ready myself to leave him. I dare to look at him again, his eyes so pained now. He shakes his head. "I can't protect you if you leave. You're going to be on your own."

I reach out and cup his cheek. I run my hands down to his chin, his facial hair soft under my skin. "I don't need you to protect me, Maison. I need you to step up and do the right thing for your brother."

He sits and slumps forward, and it breaks my heart. "You're making a mistake. He's fucking gotten to you. I don't know what he told you, baby. He killed Olivia, not me. I should never have let him have you. This happens whenever he sinks his claws into people—he destroys them. No one loves him like I do, but he's sick, baby... He's always been sick."

He truly doesn't understand why I have to leave, or what he did. Or how much his brother loves him, has sacrificed for him... or how much I love him, despite everything. So much guilt between them, and they've never even talked about it.

I crouch in front of him, pulling his head up. I need him to understand; I need him to quit being so stubborn. "We have to get him. He has no one. Come with me, Maison. He needs you more than me. We can figure this all out."

He taps his feet and twists his mouth. "No. I'm not cleaning up his fucking mess this time. I'm not protecting him on this one."

I stand and fold my arms. "Fine. But I have to go, then."

His jaw tightens as a swallow bobs in his throat. "Why am I not enough for you, London?" he asks, his voice raw. "Why am I never enough? I would have given you everything."

I close my eyes as the tears sting through them. "Don't say that, Maison," I whisper. "You're perfect. You have no idea how perfect you are."

"Then why are you going to him when I need you more? He makes everything about him. If you choose him right now, we are over. I mean it, London."

And I believe him. Maison is not the type to say anything not true to his heart—that's what I love most about him. He's real, honest, and sees the beauty in everything and everyone, which is why this is so hard. His mind is clouded. This island has darkened him, Olivia darkened him, and Micah tried to take that on for him.

I turn to him and press my lips to his. He immediately softens. "I love you, Maison," I tell him as his brow tightens with a tortured look in his eye.

So dark, so brooding.

Right now, he could be Micah. I turn around and run. When I get to the tree line, I turn back as a chilly wind hits my face. He stands still and watches me. His silhouette shines against the silver sky. I run into the forest, leaving his light and a big piece of my heart behind me.

CHAPTER EIGHTEEN

I didn't think this through.

I have no clue where Micah's camp is. I thought I did, but I've wandered this forest for a while, and it's only twenty minutes away. I'm going in circles, and I swear I am seeing the same tree. I even saw a footprint at one point that matches my own.

I sit numb against a thick fur tree, my stomach clenching at the thought of getting stuck out here, even for one night. I pull out my pack and assess my situation more closely, since I packed everything in a wet blur. I have the sweater I'm wearing, an extra pair of sweats, tiny pajamas, and a piece of dried meat I took from Maison. I have no supplies other than my sharp wooden spear I now carry around with me everywhere, almost as if it's a part of me. I'm completely and utterly at the mercy of the forest.

No one's looking for me this time. Micah won't know I came after him, and I don't see any sign of him, or even the sign of the creek anywhere, just the thick forest of dead pines. If I could find that creek, I could follow it till I find him.

My body shivers from the cool morning breeze. The sky's barely getting heated by the sun after just a month here. It's so cold, my hands go numb. Maybe it would be easier if I just died right here, right now. All the pain would go away, and this would be over. Instead of offing myself with my spear, I rub my hands together, trying to get feeling back into them.

I slip my fingers into my pack and grab the bit of dried meat. It's the only food I've had in at least twenty-four hours. Maison handed it to me right before I left, and my heart twinges at the memory of it, of his face when I left him. *He didn't say he loved me back.* A rush of anxiety flows through me, and I whimper at the thought of leaving my safety net on this island. How I left Maison hurting. But Micah needs to know he's not alone before I go back. In the meantime, I suppress the urge to scream for him.

Wait—

I rise, let my spear drop to my side, and let out a blood-curdling scream so loud and strong, it ricochets across the forest and echoes back to me. I scream so loudly that I almost faint, realizing I should have done it sooner.

Nothing happens.

Micah doesn't magically appear in front of me.

I fall back on the tree and slump my head down between my hands, willing myself to eat. I must doze off because a few minutes go by, and a little noise causes my eyes to jolt open. A little critter is eating the last of my food right out of my hands. The squirrel must have smelt my food, it's white stripes and wide eyes nibbling away without a care in the world.

I know, little guy. I'm hungry, too.

I let go of it and it scuttles a few feet away, and I contemplate for only a second before I grab its tail, my spear, and I sever it, killing the furry creature in one swipe. This island is pushing me, making me do things I never thought I would.

Once it's bled out as much as I think it's going to, I grab the squirrel and wrap it in one of my shirts and stuff it into my bag. With uncertainty, I gather strength to keep going. The thought of sleep motivates me to move faster. After about five minutes, I finally hear a trickle of water and I blow out a breath. At the very least, I can wash my hands.

When I lean down, I feel a prickle on my skin, like I'm being watched. I snap my head up and look around. "Micah?"

I feel his heavy presence.

He steps out, his black hood over his eyes. I'm startled as he appears unexpectedly before me. His chin is dipped down, his hair fallen over his eyes.

He jerks his head to my pack. "Nice kill."

So, he was watching me.

I press my lips together, annoyance circling my insides that it took him so long to let me know he was here. But there is so much pain in his eyes, I can't be mad at him.

"Why are you here, London?" he asks in a raspy voice.

The words in my head are heavy on my tongue. I never thought about what I would say to him when I actually found him. And now that I have found him, I just want to pass out.

"I came for you, Micah," I breathe out before falling to my knees. I'm utterly exhausted, broken. I don't even know if he wants me here. He's certainly not acting like he does.

He walks over to me with slow, steady footsteps. He stands in front of me and nudges me. I rise my head to look at him as he bends down, pulling me up and wrapping his arms around me. I crumble into him.

"Tell me it's okay to kiss you," he whispers as he holds me.

I swallow, and apparently, that's a yes to him, because he grabs my face and thrusts his tongue so hard inside my mouth, I feel it between my legs. The kiss is hard and deep and desperate, but soft at the same time. Despite feeling like a piece of shit for doing it, I could kiss Micah forever and would never get enough of it. His mouth feels so good. I forget how cold, tired, and miserable I am. I forget how kissing him is hurting someone I love. I'm just dizzy, intoxicated, and fuzzy all over. It's how I felt when he first kissed me on the rock—when I thought he was someone else—and I haven't felt it since.

"How did you find me?" I ask him.

He snickers, keeping his hand gripped on my ass. "I think the whole island heard you scream. And... well." He nods to the right, and I see his shelter outline fifty feet away.

For fuck's sakes, I was so close. He grabs my pack for me and pulls out ahead of me, leading me over the slippery rocks of the creek bed, keeping a tight hold on my hand.

"You could have said something," I bite out at him, keeping my hand firmly gripped on his.

He angles his head and gazes back at me. "I had to make sure you were alone. I didn't want to startle you and get hit by a rock again."

He didn't trust me...

"How's Thomas?" I ask as we pass Jade and Thomas's shelter. No movement at all from the inside, and I don't see them anywhere.

"He's okay. I wrapped his hand, and he's resting," he mutters, "just like you're going to do. You look like shit, London."

Yeah, I feel like shit.

We walk to the front of the shelter, where he has a little fire going, as if waiting for me. It's calm, quiet, and just the two of us, and he has an ample amount of blankets. It's perfect, and the warm bed I've been dreaming of the past three hours beckons me.

He stops directly behind me, his dominating presence heating my back. I can't help it; I turn and press myself into him. He responds by lifting me up by the waist, and I wrap both legs around him and shove my lips to his.

He flexes his jaw and smiles, mumbling over my lips, "This is the opposite of resting, London."

"Micah—" He draws my lower lip between his teeth, his hands gripping the meaty part of my ass. I pull on his neck, resting my cheek on his. "I still love him. I need you to know that."

He pauses for a second and blinks, pulling back for a moment to look at me. "I know. I love him, too, London."

That's all I needed to hear.

I grab his chin, sliding my lips back onto his, leaning up and biting his lower lip. I'm sick of holding back with him, so I don't. I explore his mouth, nibbling on him. He lets me take the lead, resting his hands on my hips as my legs drop, and I focus on my kiss, exploring his tongue, his lips, his teeth, every part of his beautiful mouth. After a moment, I pull back, my eyes wide and willing.

Before he can do anything, I push him and his foot slips. All six-foot-two of him topples back so hard, I hear branches snap beneath him.

He simply arches a brow. His pupils flare as he watches me get on my knees and pull at his drawstring. My fingers find his cock already throbbing, so I slide my hand down and pull it out, and a gleam hits my eyes.

"I want to make you feel good," I whisper. "And apologize for throwing that rock at you."

I really want to pleasure him with my mouth.

He spent the first night we were together making sure every inch of my body was taken care of, but now it's about him. He needs to know he's not alone.

I part my lips, ready to slide my tongue on the tip of him. "I want you like this."

He smirks at me. "Do you know what you're doing?"

I peer up at him through my lashes, suddenly feeling very self conscious. "I thought... I thought this was what you liked?"

His brows arch. "It is... but have you done this before?"

A flush hit my cheeks. In all the days with Maison, he never pushed for this. Maison always let me take it slow.

"No," I admit. "Is it... is it hard or something?"

He chuckles. "Not really. It's hard to screw up."

I turn my focus down, and I lift his shirt and kiss his pecs, his abs, his V-shaped muscles near his hips. I explore every inch of him. I try not to think if Maison, but it's hard. They look exactly alike, but Micah has an edge, even in the way his body twitches in anticipation of me wrapping my mouth around him.

But something is... off. This isn't how he was with Naomi. "You don't like this?" I ask him.

He wraps his hands around my neck, pulling my hair through his fingers. "Why would you say that?"

My voice is shaky. "You're acting different with me than you were with her."

The night I watched him. He watched me watch him as he finished with her.

"Because you're not Naomi, London. I could never treat you the same as her. So don't try to be her."

Not in a million years do I want to be like Naomi, so I push her out of my thoughts, mad at myself for even bringing her up.

I'll show him I can do this...

I start by flicking my tongue against the tip of his cock, swallowing the little bit of cum that squirts out. And instead of taking him deep and hard like she did, I lick him like an ice cream cone. He moans and wraps his hands around my head, pulling my hair to the side, playing with it as his cock swells inside my mouth. I lick and lick, and suck and suck, until he makes the face I am waiting for.

I awkwardly look away from him, remembering how hard he fucked Naomi's face, and I wonder why he's not doing that to me.

Before he comes, he pulls my head up. His voice is hard and raspy. "I want to see you. Keep your eyes on me, sweetheart, and that mouth right where it is."

He stays locked on me as he quivers, and I suck and swallow every drop of what comes out of him. "Fuck, London," he murmurs, biting hard on his bottom lip, his mouth and body twisting with pleasure. He grips my hair so hard as he releases, I think he may pull it out. It pleases me so much to make a guy like Micah come undone. Knowing I caused it... knowing how lethal he is. When he's done, he pulls his sweats up and lays me on top of him. His breath is heavy as he leans back with me in the crook of his arm.

I don't say anything, but there is nothing to say. We both wanted this, we both craved this, and couldn't move forward with any discussion until it happened. He licks his bottom lip and flicks the sweat off his brow as his hands slide up and down my body.

He's not done with me. He traces his fingers up my shirt, cupping my breasts, pinching them, playing with them. He draws a line down my stomach with lustful intent.

I fidget beneath him, stopping him and curling up so small. I hate to admit what I'm about to tell him, but the guilt will eat at me if I don't. I'd hate for him to think I've already betrayed him so deeply.

But I did...

"Micah, I think I really fucked up..."

His fingers are still beneath me. "For fuck's sake, London, I told you not to tell him."

This angers me beyond belief...

I'm beyond sick of people telling me what to do.

I whip my head up. "You had zero right to request that of me, Micah. Maison has a right to know. He should know what he did and come to terms with it—you both do if you're ever going to truly heal from it. That is not what I fucked up about. I don't regret telling him for one second. The lies between you two are destroying you both, and you're taking me down with you."

He pauses, considering. His body twitches and jaw clenches.

I lay my head down on him and he rests his hand on my back, laying wholly still. His other hand goes right back to my chest.

"What happened?" he finally asks.

I tremble, recalling every word. "I said it in front of Nigel when I was upset. It was right after you left, and the words just fell out of my mouth."

His lips graze my head, and he softens. "It's not your fault... none of this is your fault. But what the fuck does Nigel have to do with it? Why is he so involved?"

I look at him, tears stinging the back of my eyes and worry hitting the pit of my throat. "I think Nigel was Olivia's brother."

He bristles. "Why would you think that?"

I peer up at him, the hardness piercing out of his dark eyes. I hate how Olivia is here right now—it feels like she's in the bed with us. Her ghostly presence involving herself in every aspect of my relationships with these boys.

She's worse than Naomi.

"It was something Jade told me. Nigel mentioned a half sister to her once, and honestly, she forgot about it, because he never mentioned her again. She was from Douglas Cove, and it would make sense. His investigation into you was borderline obsessive—he prompted me on day one of school to look into you. He knows about Ezra's parents' debts, the amount of GHB in her system, and that's how she died. He just didn't know it wasn't you who actually killed her. I said it out loud... and then I left Maison there with him." The tears shake out of me now as Micah just listens. "I think he's deranged, Micah. He lied about Thomas."

I don't know if Micah regrets doing what we just did now that he knows what I did, and I'm scared to ask. But I notice his fingers are no longer fondling my breasts.

Emotion takes over and pressure wells up in my chest. I can't control it, and I let out a soft sob and tears flow from my eyes. He wipes them away with his thumb, and I lift my gaze to meet his. "I'm sorry, Micah."

His jaw flexes and eyebrows draw in, and he squeezes his hand around my waist, even though he seems absent as he peers outside, flexing one of his hands into a fist. He says nothing for a few minutes. "We'll get him back," he finally whispers. "I promise you we'll get him back, and I'll cut that smug smirk right off Nigel's fucking face."

It's then I notice the knife glistening in the corner of the shelter, the one he stole.

And I shutter, because I don't think he's joking.

***

"Thomas was set up," Jade tells me when I finally emerge into daylight. After our chat, I fell asleep and when I woke, Micah was gone. I rooted thorough the shelter and saw he had a pile of clothes in the corner—girls' clothes. He stockpiled a ton of them for me. I find a new pair of comfy sweats that fit me perfectly.

As soon as I saw Jade, I ran to her and wrapped my arms around her tightly, not wanting to let go for at least ten minutes. My squirrel is hanging clipped to some wire, completely skinned and ready for roasting. A large pile of kindling is right beside it.

I scrunch my face. "I know he was, Jade. I don't think Thomas took anything. He wouldn't betray Micah like that. It had to have been Nigel, trying to weaken Micah, and it's working."

Poor Thomas still hasn't come out since I've arrived. He's slept the entire time, with Jade fussing and checking on him every ten minutes. The tightness and circles under eyes signal her tears and grief, and I know Jade's worried about him.

She shakes her head and closes her eyes. "What happened to Nigel? When did he turn like this?"

"How well did you really know him, Jade? I mean, you didn't know much if you didn't know his sister died. How do you hide something like that? Nigel is obviously not a good person—I doubt he ever was." The island is revealing our primal instincts and stripping us of everything else.

She swallows, contemplating. I'm sure it's hard hearing someone tell you that you know nothing about your best friend or what they are capable of.

"What about Ezra?" she asks, grabbing the squirrel and severing it, like eating critters for dinner is the most normal thing in the world. "Is he just doing this because of the debts, or Naomi?"

I reach down and grab a piece of kindling and crouch, blowing on the embers. The moisture is heavy today, precipitation is coming and I want the fire prepped for it. "Ezra has a high school complex. I don't think he realizes that high school doesn't matter anymore. Plus, he's stupid and easily manipulated. Nigel is playing him like a fiddle. I don't know what Naomi's deal is, but nothing adds up right about her."

She swallows and wraps her hand around herself. "I guess, but the others turned on him, too."

"James didn't," I cut in. "I have to assume Nathan and Ollie sided with who they think would win."

"What about Maison?" she asks softly.

My heart shutters at the sound of his name, and I visibly tense. She pauses, too, staring right into my soul. I'm sure she heard Micah and me earlier while I was sucking him off. I'm sure she heard me last week while I was fucking both of them. It's not like we were attempting to be quiet.

I shut my eyes and shake my head. If I talk about Maison right now, I will break down. She's quiet, focusing on cooking our dinner, and I stare out at the stream trickling nearby.

I forgot how much I like this spot. It's hidden away near a stream, a little escarpment with various earthy tones and the meadow. It reminds me of a place I used to camp with my parents before things went south between them. Despite only going once or twice, it became a fond memory I held on to.

The one night I spent here was also the best night on the island. In one night, this place felt more like home. It feels like home now—it's just missing one really important person.

After an hour, Micah returns with upholstery in his arms. Upon seeing him, I instantly relax, not that I was pining for him or anything. He journeyed to the airplane and appeared to have ripped the seats. It's for insulation, he informs us. He plans to rebuild the roofs and siding of the shelters to help keep them warmer as the colder weather approaches.

He's withdrawn, stone-cold and barely looks at me, completely in his head like he is ninety percent of the time. The only time I see him come alive is when we are intimate or I'm challenging him. It's a part of him I've seen so little of, but that's the part of him I'm falling in love with.

He sits alone at the clear other side of the fire and starts making a new spear. I wish he'd show me more, give me more of the side of him underneath his hard exterior. It makes me question if he truly has feelings for me at all.

Or maybe this is just how he is, and I have to live with it.

I try not to stare as he shifts his attention to getting the fire roaring. We share the squirrel among the three of us, saving a bit for Thomas for when he wakes up.

A cold breeze sweeps right through my backside. I'm not used to sitting alone; Maison was always behind me and would be right now if he were here.

I already miss him.

Micah's oblivious. He just sits there with his knife, by himself on a log, satisfied with what he's doing.

"Do you think they will come here and find us?" Jade asks, breaking the uncomfortable silence.

Micah shakes his head. "I don't know why they would. We have nothing they want, and I doubt any of them will want to face me and chance getting their legs diced up. If they are after the knife, I would love to give it back to them properly." Unleash his fury, all that pent-up tension bursting at the seams.

The sun sets and evening settles in around us. Jade heads to bed, leaving me and Micah alone. I see no good reason to stay up anymore, so after making eye contact with him, I rise and, without saying a word, I turn my back to him and crawl into bed.

Once inside, I nearly jump to the roof when my hands touch a soft, thick blanket beneath me. I can't stop the smile that spreads across my face.

It's my wolf... my wolf blanket. Micah skinned and made it for me and snuck it in here without me noticing. When he did that is beyond me, but it's perfect. I run my hands over the thick fur and curl up over it, pulling the airplane blankets on top of me. It's the most comfortable I've been since arriving here.

After a few minutes, Micah finally crawls in beside me. I relax as he wraps his arms around me, his hands finding my waist and belly. I was wondering if he was going to come at all. As close as I thought we were, there is a distance between us, like he doesn't know how to act around me or if he's allowed to touch me without my distinct permission.

Or perhaps it's guilt—as I certainly feel. He probably feels like he just lost his brother.

I turn around and face him. "Are you okay?"

He stiffens slightly at my question. "I'm not like Maison, London. I don't do pillow talk like he does."

Ouch. There's the asshole.

I shake my head and turn away from him. "Fine, we don't have to talk. I'm tired, anyway."

After a few minutes, his body relaxes and his lips touch the back of my head. "I'm sorry," he whispers. "I'm just not him."

I turn to face him again, my lips trembling and my heart beating out of its chest. "I know exactly who you are, Micah."

He lies there for a second as the fire dims the light between us. "Do you regret coming with me?"

I swallow a pit in my throat. "No. But I do miss him." I feel him tense, but I need to say this. "Nothing about you is simple, Micah. You're not as easy as he is."

He rubs his fingers along my hairline, his eyes not leaving mine. "Yeah, I know."

I grab his face and cup his chin with my hand, his growing stubble tickling my fingers. "But not for one second do I regret coming for you."

He doesn't respond; instead, he presses his mouth into mine, parting my lips, gently teasing his tongue inside. I moan and he pulls me closer. After a few minutes of him biting, nibbling, touching me all over, he pulls away and I feel him reach for something.

"What are you doing?"

"Hold on."

He slips back beside me and sticks something small inside my ear. Music suddenly fills my ears. Music is something you don't really appreciate until it's gone. It's purifying—it fuels me as much as that squirrel. Every note, every lyric, hits my soul. I have no clue how he has battery in his cell, but I'll call it some sort of miracle. That's what Micah is capable of—he makes miracles happen. Maison was right about something. Micah is just as good at keeping me warm, and I love feeling him breathe, and I fall asleep to the music with Micah wrapped around me tight.

CHAPTER NINETEEN

I wake up to crying. Agonizing screams that cut right into our shelter, reverberating over the meadow and bouncing off the water. It sounds like Thomas is right in the shelter, with how debilitating it is. Micah and I both shoot up. The sun's not even up yet, still the darkest part of the night.

"Stay here," Micah says, rising out of bed and grabbing his bone weapon.

I'm sick of being told to stay put, so of course, I wrap myself up with blankets and follow him out and wait, shivering. It feels like the temperature dropped at least ten degrees since the early evening. The fire is nearly out, and my icy breath wraps through the surrounding air. I blow on the embers, trying to get them burning again.

After a few minutes, Micah emerges from the shadows of the meadow. "Thomas isn't doing well. His hand is bad," he says as he approaches me. "Jade is asking for you."

His eyes are tight as he crouches next to me—the same tightness he gets whenever he's worried.

Keeping the blanket wrapped around my shoulders, I head over to their shelter. Micah stokes the fire, adding a few more logs to get it going again.

When I arrive, Thomas is on the ground, withering in pain. Jade is lying beside him, crying and wiping his forehead. I step around their small fire, embers still burning ash.

I crouch down, lean in, and try not to choke on the sweaty smell. "What happened?"

"I don't know," Jade says, sitting up with tear-stained cheeks. "We were sleeping, and he started moaning and burning up."

I grab his wrist, pulling off the shirt he is using to protect his wound. My heart skips a beat. Even in the dark, I can see the redness and swelling. His body heats the entire shelter. "His palm is infected."

She sits up and grabs his other hand, wiping the sweat from his forehead. "Yeah, I kind of thought so. What do we do?"

I sigh. "Let's try to keep the wound clean. Give me a few minutes, I'll talk to Micah."

I head to the stream, tiptoeing through the dark. I grab one of Jade's shirts and, surprised by my strength, I tear it in half and dip the two pieces into the cold water. I rush back to them and place one on his forehead and use the other one to clean his wound.

Thomas isn't coherent. His eyes are closed, and he's shivering, even though his body feels like he's in the depths of hell.

They slashed his hand, like we are in the Dark Ages, and now he's dying.

A hand tickles my back while I'm bent over, laying a cool cloth over Thomas's forehead. Micah crouches behind me and places his head on my shoulder. I turn to face him and grab his knee to keep me stable. "We need the medicine from the first aid kit, Micah. We have to disinfect it. We have some, don't we?"

Micah scowls. "We do. I used some antiseptic on Maison when he got wounded. But there is no way they are going to give me anything... not after I pressed my arm in Ezra's throat."

I adjust the blanket over my shoulders as the cold wind sends chills down my bones. "We have to get it. Maybe if we explain the situation?"

Micah snorts. "Sure. I'll just walk up to Ezra and tell him I need to steal his medical supplies. Remember, they're the ones who did this to him, London."

I press my lips together as annoyance cuts through my chest. I don't need his sarcasm right now. "So, what do you think we should do?" I snip at him.

He reaches up, massaging the back of my neck, and his eyes soften. "I have to sneak in and take it."

My eyes widen. "No. No way. I'm going with you. I am not separating from you again. Wherever you go, I go."

Micah lets out a sigh. "I'm not sure that's safe."

I cross my arms. "Since when do you care about safe?"

A quirk of his lips. "Good point. Are you sure you're up for it?"

"Yes."

He nods in approval and that bloom of pride swells over me. "Ezra will probably have the supplies guarded. At least, that's what I would do if I were in charge. Somehow, we'll have to distract them or hurt them. But either way, we grab the medical kit and leave. Quick in, quick out. Hopefully, they won't even know we're there."

"Won't they be expecting us?"

He shrugs. "The fact we've only been gone one night is in our favor. They may not expect us so soon."

I pull my blanket up. "I don't know, Micah... I have a bad feeling about this."

Terrible, actually.

He pulls me aside, away from Thomas and Jade, and wraps both hands over my arms, gripping me and snapping me back into focus. He leans forward, his breath tickling my ear. "We have to do this, London. Thomas will die if we don't get those supplies. Do you understand?"

I close my eyes, my heart twinging at the enormity of it. So much death already, I can't deal with anymore. "Yes, I understand."

"Try to get some sleep. We'll leave in a couple of hours when we can see better."

My mouth gapes open. "We aren't leaving immediately? He needs our help now, Micah."

He arches a brow. "And if you or I get hurt in the forest, or lost? We can't help him if we're both wandering around the woods."

"You wander these woods all the time," I counter.

"Not toting you with me. I'm not willing to risk it. Plus, we still need to come up with a plan for when we get there. So get some rest; Thomas will be okay for now. Jade is with him. She won't leave his side."

Despite my yawn, I sit by the fire instead of lying down, hating how right he always is. "Fine, but I can't sleep."

I've not slept since I left Maison—not really. Just a few hours in Micah's arms, but even then, I prefer warmth from the fire to the cold of the shelter, so I sit just outside it. I know Micah won't sleep now, either, since he's doing his pacing thing.

The cool air wraps around me, but I quickly warm up as the fire crackles. Micah circles the meadow, grabbing pieces of wood, doing anything he can not to relax. Finally, he comes and sits with me, stretching his legs out, pulling me inside them. My body vibrates. The way he's positioned reminds me of how Maison would hold me. He knows this—he watched us for weeks. I close my eyes for one second, leaning into him, pretending he's Maison before snapping myself out of it.

It's Micah.

As if reading my thoughts, he rests his head on my shoulder. "I know you miss him. I miss him, too, but we're not going back for him this time. Do you understand?"

I don't know how to talk about Maison with Micah. Even bringing his name up feels like a betrayal, but I caused their rift, and I can't even imagine the pain Micah feels about this situation.

He moves my hair out of the way and kisses my neck. "I can pretend to be him if that makes it easier for you."

I whip my head up and narrow my eyes. "Stop it, Micah."

A lopsided grin forms on his lips. "Are you sure? I'm good at it, baby."

I dig my nails into his muscled legs. "Stop it right now."

A pulse hits my lower belly, and his erection thickens beneath me.

Fuck.

Fully aware of how messed up I am for being turned-on, I grind my hips into him. If he's into it, then so am I.

Leaning up to his ear, I nibble on it and whisper, "On second thought, let's go lie down."

We departed at the first sign of morning, just as we said we would. We left Jade with clear instructions to keep the wound clean, the shirt we are using for a bandage fresh, and to do her best to keep Thomas's fever down by keeping him cool. We promised her we'd be back as soon as we could. By morning, his condition had worsened to the point it rendered him unconscious. He was barely coherent as his body shut down on him.

A scratch... a scratch did this to him. Out of all the things that could hurt him on this island, *we* did this to him. Our lies and desperation.

Part of me wishes we could just explain the situation to Ezra. He was, after all, the one who cut him. We should give him a chance to redeem himself. I can't see how he would want him to die. Would he want that kind of blood on his hands?

Micah refused. He said Ezra wouldn't believe him, and it would only hurt our chances of getting what we need to save him. And maybe he's right. Our situation on this island is deteriorating as fast as Thomas. Everyone is desperate, hungry, and not thinking straight.

Especially Maison.

Somehow, Micah and I have become the villains. That's the story they will tell, should they have the chance.

We make it as close to the camp before taking a break. Micah moved quickly on the way here, and I kept pace without a single breath of complaint. We walked for nearly a long while in dense trees and brush, my legs and body aching the whole time. I didn't dare suggest at any point we were lost, even though I think we were.

Finally, we found the camp and now crouch in the near-by woods.

Of course, on the one day we need to hide among the shadows, the sun is raging over both the lake and sky, shining down on us.

"We may have to split up," Micah says, hovering beside me, "to get a good look at what we're working with." The vapor of his breath lingers in the air. It may be sunny, but it's bloody cold, as every day is, now that we are pushing November.

I hate the thought of splitting up, but he may be right. "Where's our meeting point?"

"Our cove."

My heart tingles.

Our cove. Since when did it become ours? I viewed it as mine, but I guess it's now our place.

A shaken breath leaves my lips. "Okay."

He rises and places his hands on my shoulder and gives it an encouraging squeeze. "You circle to the right. I'll go to the left. Stay out of sight, just look around and leave. Remember everything I taught you, and for the love of god, London, stay fucking quiet. Thomas needs you."

I close my eyes and nod as he stalks off with grace and confidence, looking utterly sexy with his bone weapon in hand.

He was different again this morning, back to his brooding self, after another round of mind-blowing sex where he kept calling me baby. He turned on the twin thing, and while it was royally messed up, I secretly enjoyed it. Probably more than I should have, especially since Thomas was lying so close and in pain. I think it's part of his sickness, as Maison called it—the hot and cold his brother knows so well. But now I'm thinking maybe I'm just as sick as he is.

I see it now, in a way I didn't before, like he's only ever alive when he's hunting or fucking. He lives in a dark place in his mind, and I want to help him escape it. Remind him life isn't so bad, and I'm here with him, and I'm not planning on leaving. And that he can fuck me as much as he needs to so I can see the side I love all the time.

I hitch a breath to calm my shaky nerves, not thinking I'd be back here quite so soon. Only twenty-four hours since I fled, and now I'm back sneaking around, hunting them.

It feels like war.

But it's a war they started, and I have to remind myself of that.

My hand runs down my thick, dark, muddied braid that lays over my shoulder. Seemed an appropriate hairstyle under the circumstances, to bring out my inner Katniss. I wish I had her bow and arrow and knew how to use it, but I guess a spear will have to do. I'm on my own now—Micah won't help me, and Maison won't save me.

I approach the tree line and pause when smoke tickles the back of my throat. The main fire is ahead, my old shelter to the left, and the glistening lake in the distance. I hardly recognize the people in front of me. Everyone is so dirty and skinny. A few of Micah's original spears lay strewn about—the ones made of hockey sticks and sharp skates. Everything else just looks primitive, barely human. The once-neatly stacked supplies are now in disarray and picked through. Open cans lay strewn about, and I can't believe those fuckers ate some of the food.

Nathan and Ollie sit slumped over, looking utterly miserable. The two younger guys are half the size they used to be, although I think everyone is. If they are the only two sitting between us and the supplies we need, this should be no trouble. They have no idea how angry Micah is or the direness of our situation. I've long said I would never want to be on the opposing side of Micah, and they were stupid to turn on him. He won't quickly forget the two of them shoving a spear in his face.

Nigel is sitting alone by the fire, picking at his nails, his hair greased down under his hood. I only see his side profile, which is enough for me. Nigel is evil, regardless of any valid reason he may have for his anger. Seeing him sickens me, so I move on, desperate for a glimpse of Maison, just so I know he's okay. Not that Nigel could do much, but he's manipulated a lot already, so I'm sure he's planning something.

If I can find Maison and just talk to him, then I know he will help us. And hopefully I can convince him to come with us.

I keep moving to the left, staying hidden in the trees toward the shelters. Ezra and Naomi walk toward me, so I spin back and hide behind mine and Maison's shelter. I'm only two feet away from them as they walk by, and my blood freezes when they stop just in front of me. If they were smarter, they should sense me. My heart is raging, and I can't keep my breath in check. But a small breeze rustles the forest, hiding me.

"Fuck, you're sexy," Ezra croons, and his voice is like sandpaper in my ear. I've never understood his friendship with Maison. How could Maison be friends with someone who hates his twin so much?

All I hear is the sound of their kissing and moaning, and I wonder where Ezra's hands are. At least it's not Micah she's kissing anymore. I'll never let her near Micah again.

"Where do you think their camp is, anyway?" Naomi asks between her panting.

"Why? Are you planning on making a visit?" Ezra snipes, and I don't miss the heavy undertone.

Naomi huffs. "Ezra, please. Can we just move on from Micah? I made a mistake; I should never have broken up with you for him. It would just be nice to know how far away they are. It's unnerving having them around."

"Who fucking cares," Ezra says acidicly. "They'd be stupid to come back here. If I see him again, I'm going to kill him. And if you ever talk to him again, Naomi, we are done."

Micah must have humiliated Ezra by taking him down so easily. Micah would have crushed his lungs had it not been for Ollie, Nathan, and Nigel. Ezra's ego is going to be an issue.

"I swear, London is more toxic than Olivia ever was. She's fucking destroying them. That's what this is about, Ezra. You've known Micah your whole life. We know nothing about her."

Ezra's voice raises to the point I nearly jump. I can only imagine him screaming in her face. "Yeah, well, he's been an asshole his whole life, Naomi, and he gets away with murder. They deserve each other. Don't get sucked back into his bullshit, or I'll toss you into the fucking forest, too."

"Okay, Ezra," Naomi begs. "I promise I won't ever talk to him again. If I see him, I'll tell you immediately." I can only imagine how horrible Ezra's making her feel, and it brings me nothing but delight. "What about Maison?" she asks.

My heart skips.

"We just need to keep his mind off them, keep him distracted."

Distracted? Distracted how?

Naomi gives out an evil little laugh. "Don't worry, we're trying. I have Serena working on it. By the time she's done, he won't even think about the little slut, but she feels bad, like she's betraying James. We have to watch out for James. I don't trust him."

I grip my spear so hard, my knuckles turn white. I'm so close to her, I could easily turn and gut her. Instead, I stand ghostly still and try to ignore the intense jealousy I feel at the thought of Serena touching Maison. I'll get caught, and Thomas will die. Naomi will have her moment of reckoning, but this isn't that moment.

They finally move on, and I let out a deep sigh. To my relief, she and Ezra head back toward the fire, giving me perfect access to root through her shelter quickly. It sounds like James might be someone we need to talk to. I still have hope for Maison. He knows where our camp is and hasn't said anything.

I creep back to my original spot and lie on my stomach.

I listen and watch.

The first voice is Maison's, and my stomach wrenches when I see him. He looks relaxed but sad, sitting in our regular spot. And he's sexy as ever, wearing his tight-fitting sweats with one knee up. He looks cuddly, like I could just walk up to him and sink my hips into his and everything will be okay. If only I can get him alone. I know I can try to talk some sense into him. Ezra and Naomi are across from them, their faces tight and grim from the fight I just heard them having. Now that I have a better look at them, they both look like utter shit. Naomi's once plump face is skinny, void of any color, and they are all oblivious to the fact Micah and I are buzzing around them like hornets, while one of our classmates may lose his life. After a minute, like some holy miracle, Ezra and Naomi wave Nigel over, and the three of them walk toward the creek.

Plotting, no doubt.

But they left Maison alone, and his adorable face is so sad, it breaks my heart. I want to reassure him about Olivia and bring a smile to his face. I want to tell him I forgive him, even if I don't truly understand it.

Fuck it. I'm going to see him. He and Micah will have to figure their shit out. I'm not giving up this opportunity to get to him.

I don't think; I react, hopping to my feet like a gazelle. I leap toward him and am basically mid-air when strong arms wrap around my waist and a hand goes right over my mouth.

I didn't even hear Micah coming.

"Let's go, London," Micah whispers in my ear and plucks me away, keeping his hand firmly planted to the point I can barely breathe.

I wince when he picks me up and carries me into the cover of the forest, ready for the shit I know he's about to give me. He doesn't put me down, he doesn't let me speak; he carries me all the way to the cove, all while I grip my spear, imagining myself poking him with it.

When he finally puts me down, I whip my head at him and my nostrils flare. "Why did you stop me?"

Micah's eyes are dark, and I hitch a breath at the intensity of them. "Are you regretting your decision already?"

He seems to have this weird ability to know exactly what I'm thinking, especially with Maison. I blink a few times before narrowing my eyes. "He was alone. He could have helped us get the first aid kit."

"Liar. I told you this wasn't about Maison. You could have fucked this all up, London. I saw Serena. She was ten steps away from him, not to mention Nathan and Ollie, who were literally watching."

"If I had been quiet, I could have forced him to come with me."

Micah shakes his head. "We can't trust him right now, not when he's like this. You have to do better tonight. We're not here for Maison, we're here for Thomas. You can't get distracted like that again. Keep your fucking wits about you."

"I know, Micah," I snip. "It's just..." The tears flow out of me now, the pressure of the past two days hitting me so hard with the realization I lost Maison. I realize the impact of that decision now. Clearly, I still love him.

He softens his intense, angry glare, and I can barely look at him as he stands behind me and wraps his hands around my waist. I know this type of affection isn't natural for him, so I appreciate the gesture.

My breath hitches, and I lean my head back into his chest. "I want to get him back," I breathe.

He flinches at my inner turmoil, and I know it hurts him, even though he's utterly wrong to think that my loving Maison means I don't love him, too.

More even.

His hand squeezes mine. "We will, but not today. Thomas needs the medical kit. Right now, nothing is more important than that."

I nod. He's absolutely right. Now isn't the time, and I've been selfish enough on this island. "It's just Ollie and Nathan watching over the supplies."

He keeps his arm around me, but his face is distant. The awkwardness of this situation must be weighing on him, too. "Yeah, I saw that, too."

"So, what's the plan?" I ask.

"We'll hang here for a few hours till they eat, and their guard will be down."

"How will we get in? I don't want anymore bloodshed, Micah. That doesn't make us any better than they are."

He shrugs. "That's entirely up to them, but I can't let Thomas die."

My foot kicks at a rock and I stare at the lake water, the waves crashing onto the shoreline and the sun sparkling over the water. Micah presses his lips into my back as we stare out at the ice-kissed mountains. His lips graze my neck, causing my insides to stir.

Sometimes he seems to distance himself from me, and at other times, he can't keep his hands off me. The game we constantly play.

"What do you need from me right now, London?" he whispers.

I turn to face him. The urge to kiss him is strong, but at this moment, it feels wrong. Like the weight of what I'm doing and who I lost comes crumbling down. Micah's lips feel like fire even from a couple of inches away.

Warming me. Igniting me. Fueling me.

Reminding me why I'm with him right now instead of Maison. Instead of rising to meet his lips like I desperately want to, I fist my hand and I hit him. His eyebrows rise as my fist connects with his chest. I hit again and again till I can't move anymore, and then he lets me lay my head on his lap and sleep until nightfall.

We wait till the sun dips just below the horizon, leaving the clouds in the sky speckled shades of blue and pink. We have enough light to see, but not clearly. Dark comes quickly with short sunsets this time of year. From there, once we get the medical kit, we have no real plan. We hope for the best and to avoid getting caught so we can bring Thomas his medicine.

I crouch down, watching poor Ollie and Nathan. This time, James is sitting with them. Micah doesn't think the first aid kit is there; he thinks it's in Ezra and Naomi's shelter, although I didn't see it when I was in there earlier. I don't dare look at the others, even though I can hear their muffled voices and Naomi's shrill laugh.

Right as I say this, Ezra walks up to the supplies and grabs the bag we need and carries it to his shelter and leaves it. It's almost comically easy. He must think it's somehow safer from Micah's clutches in there.

I shift, ready to run and grab it. Quick in, quick out, they might not even realize it's missing for at least an hour. We decided I was the best one to go. If I get caught, Micah has the chance of rescuing me, and I know in my heart Maison won't hurt me or let me get hurt. If Micah gets caught, it's game over.

My heart drops when a figure moves toward us, and immediately, I recognize Nigel's stocky build moving toward the shelter, sitting on the ground in front of it. My lip curls at the sight of him.

Micah, who's hovering a few feet away, cuts toward me, sensing my hesitation at the wrinkle in our plans. He presses his hand on my lower back, hinting for me not to move. He grabs my hand, and we creep back into the woods, out of sight.

I breathe out a sigh of frustration. "It's Nigel," I whisper when we are safely out of earshot.

Why did I think they would make this easy? Of course, they will keep their supplies guarded.

Micah flexes his jaw as a gleam hits his eyes. "I can fucking take Nigel."

My eyes shoot up. It's not all the time Micah seems out of control, but the sudden flash of anger reminds me of what he is actually capable of. I wonder just how close that version of him hides just below the surface, waiting to bubble up.

I place my hand on his. "Obviously, you can take him, but he will just sound the alarms if he sees you."

He tilts his head. "What do you think we do then, London? Tell me what our options are."

I think for a second. "We have three, from what I can tell. We wait Nigel out, and hopefully, he gets bored with watching an empty shelter and goes to bed. The second is for you to handle him, the way I know you want to. But that will just get the attention of the entire group, and we risk everything. Or I'll distract him, get him to leave his post, and then you sneak in and grab the bag."

He quirks his brow. "Then you'll be caught, and what makes you think he won't sound the alarms if he sees you?"

A darkness shutters through me. "He'll be happy to see me alone. I think he's been waiting to get me alone. He'll lose the opportunity to fuck with me, and if he cries out, Maison will hear, and he won't want that."

I'm going to use Nigel's dementedness against him. I'll flirt with the devil if it saves Thomas.

My eyes find his as I sense his hesitation. "Trust me, Micah. I'm coming back to you. Even if they catch me, I will find my way back to you."

He hoods his eyes. As good as he is in hiding his emotion, even he can't hide the flare in his eyes.

He needs reassurance.

I wrap my hands around him, and he bends his head down, resting his forehead against mine. "I won't blame you if you want to stay," he tells me.

This time my lips find his, and his stubble tickles my cheek. "Stop that," I murmur. "I promise."

And it's a promise I hope I can keep. Although, I wonder what I'll do when I see Maison again. Can I really walk away from him twice?

He squeezes my arm, but his face is unreadable. "We need to do this fast, while everyone else is eating."

"Yes, I know the plan."

I turn away from him and lead the way back to our original hiding spot. I squint at Nigel, still sitting there, alone.

Good.

Without saying another word, and before I lose my nerve, I step over to Nigel, a few feet away from him, close to Maison's shelter. I'm loud and clunky, purposely breaking a few twigs beneath my feet.

I pause for a moment as other voices carry from the fire. I shift my focus toward where Micah was hiding, but he's gone. Nigel hasn't noticed me yet. A heat fills my belly as I step toward camp, silent as Micah's taught me so well. I need to see Maison again, even if it's just for a second.

I hear him, and he's laughing, as if he's simply on a camping trip and I didn't just tear his heart apart.

The sound of Serena laughing sickens me as I walk up and see her sitting next to him, in my spot, cuddling with him. A pit of anger boils in my stomach.

Two nights. That's how long we've been separated, and it looks like he is doing just fine without me.

His face is hidden beneath a gray hood, but I see his body language. I can't tell who's reacting to whom. Or perhaps it's both? And maybe it's too late. Even if I wanted to come back, would he even want me? Do I even have a right to be upset with him right now?

"Well, well, well..."

Nigel's slimy voice fills my ears, and my stomach coils.

I whip around. "Nigel."

He crosses his arms and his oversized jaw tightens. "What are you doing here, skulking about? Pining over your ex already?"

I swallow a pit in my throat, but I hold his steady stare and his eyes flick to my spear. He's stupid enough not to carry one around with him. "I'm not skulking. I came back," I tell him.

He tilts his head. "Really. Broke up with your psycho boyfriend already, did you? Let me guess, he ripped you up between the sheets? I've heard he can get quite violent when he has sex." He arches his eyebrows, enjoying this way too much. "But you like the broken ones, don't you, London? Although, apparently, the golden boy has quite the skeletons in his closet, too."

I curl my lip. "Don't be sick."

Micah's shadow flickers in the night as he sneaks through the shelters.

So he was there? Did he see me watching Maison?

Smug satisfaction quickly replaces my sense of worry. If Nigel thinks he's in control, Micah will have more time.

Nigel clicks his tongue. "Please, tell me what it is about that guy that has every girl dying to spread their legs for him. I'd really like to know."

I dart my eyes to the fire when I hear Maison's laugh. Nigel has a vicious smirk on his face when I glance back at him.

Nigel chuckles at my confused expression. "You're too late. It took Maison no time at all to move on from you. And who can blame him? You're nothing but a cheating little bitch."

"Fuck you, Nigel."

"Oh, please do. I would love that. Apparently, every other guy on this island gets their turn."

I inch my way away from the fire and away from Micah. Nigel follows the bait as we slink back into the woods.

Nigel narrows his brows, taking one forbidding step after another.

I dislike the look in his eyes.

I step back and he mirrors every single movement with a predatory gleam in his eye. He really has lost his mind. "I know who you are, Nigel, and your relationship to Olivia. She was your sister, wasn't she?"

That snaps him into place.

His eye twitches and he pauses his menacing walk, and I revel in the fact I just caught him off guard. He thinks he's so fucking smart.

I can't help but smirk. "Olivia," I remind him, as if he could forget her name.

He deepens his tone, confirming everything. "Is her death funny to you? Or are you just satisfied with yourself now that you've taken her place as their plaything?"

I bite the inside of my cheek. I should be respectful to the dead, even if it seems like she's still alive. "We can talk about it, Nigel, like normal people. You don't have to punish them for it. You obviously loved her, but it doesn't have to be this way."

"She was a fucking disaster," he scoffs, "but she didn't deserve to die the way she did, with absolutely no retribution. And now here I am, stuck in a lawless society with her killers. If you could get back at the teacher who fucked you, what would you do? If you could peel away his sanity, layer by layer, would you do it?"

Sweat pools over my hairline, despite the freezing air around me. My voice is calm and steady. "It was Maison who killed her. He gave her those drugs, not Micah. But it was an accident—no one murdered anyone. You have no right to condemn them."

His eyes betray his true emotions, and it is abundantly clear he has not let go of his strong animosity toward Micah.

He blares his teeth and lurches forward. "Micah was the one with her, you stupid skank." The voraciousness in his voice makes me step back. "Don't tell me you think he's innocent. You are lacking all the intelligence I thought you had if you think for one second that he didn't hurt her, too."

My eyes whip to where I know Micah is and wonder if he's hearing this. I can't help it, and it's enough for Nigel to notice the sudden change in my behavior.

"Are you trying to distract me, London?" he asks, looking around. "Where is Micah? Is he here with you?"

"No. I'm alone." It's a terrible lie, but it seems to appease him.

He snickers and I stay wholly still while he inches closer to me.

A few more minutes... that's all I need before I can end this.

He reaches his hand for my shirt and I step back as he tries to pull it up. Rage builds in my stomach as I recall the first day of school; I slap his hand away.

His lips twists and his eyes flash. "That was a mistake. You have no friends here. I just want to see what has these boys all crazy for you."

He lunges for me again, but this time I'm ready for him. I grab his head and knee him so hard in the stomach, he's on the ground in mere seconds, withering in pain.

The trick Micah taught me weeks ago.

I circle and stand over him, pressing my spear right into the soft part of his neck. "You will not touch me ever again," I spit out. "Do you understand?"

His eyes widen, clearly not expecting me to defend my-self like that. For a tiny moment, I wonder what it would feel like to dig the spear into his neck.

To make him bleed.

To make him pay.

To fucking kill him.

His face turns back to that self-assured grin as footsteps fall behind me. I freeze, knowing I'm fucked.

"What the hell?" James says, and I blow out a breath of relief.

I turn to face him as Nigel sneers up at me from the ground. "Grab her. She's trying to steal from us."

Nathan and Ollie are with him, and the two other boys look to James for direction.

"He's dying," I blurt out, ignoring Nigel, who's getting himself back up. "Thomas is dying. His cut is infected."

They look at each other.

"She's lying," Nigel sneers.

"I'm not. He's hurting, and he needs medication. If you try to stop me, you are killing him." I give them a pleading look. "Please, he needs his wound cleaned. He could die. This is Thomas we're talking about. I'm not the enemy here."

After a few agonizing seconds, James gives me a nod and steps aside. "Go."

Nigel takes a step forward, but then Ollie and Nathan grab him, stopping him. Nigel's eyes flash. "You can't let her leave. Ezra and Naomi will be furious with you." Nigel waves a dismissive hand. "Never mind, I'll call them my-self."

James slides over with just as much finesse as Micah would and grabs Nigel with ease, wrapping his arm around his back, covering his mouth with his other hand. Nigel withers and tries to scream, but he doesn't stand a chance against the bigger hockey player, even if he is younger.

James looks at me. "Grab what you need. We'll cover for you the best we can."

I bite my bottom lip. There is hope for this group, yet.

"Thank you," I whisper.

I take a few steps forward, but pause and turn back to them. They all stare at me in the dark, Nigel radiating anger. "You don't have to stay here, you know. You have options." I turn and run as fast as I can back to Ezra's shelter, where I'm hoping Micah is waiting for me.

When I arrive, I freeze. He's nowhere in sight.

Where are you, Micah?

My chest rises and falls, my breath filling the surrounding air. The sun is all the way set now, leaving only the outline of the shelters and the silky lake ahead of me.

Swallowing a pit in my throat, I carefully make my way to the cove under the moonlit sky, avoiding tripping in the dark. I just hope Micah is waiting for me when I get there.

But for reasons I can't explain, I know he won't be.

He wasn't there when I arrived, and fifteen agonizing minutes go by, and I still have no idea where Micah is, or why he didn't follow our plan. I sit on the flat rock and place my head between my legs, listening to the soft lap of the water in front of me. The silence is beyond unnerving, especially as it's only my dark thoughts keeping me company and the deep veil of the forest behind me with branches that seem to whisper.

All my worst fears swirl in my brain.

They caught Micah.

Thomas will die.

Maison doesn't love me anymore.

If Micah doesn't come back, I truly don't know what I will do. I suppose I'll go back to the main camp and beg them. I'll beg them till my knees are raw.

Finally, I sense him before I hear him. Every nerve fires when soft footsteps echo against the rock. I can barely make out his tall frame as he walks up to me, holding a bag in his hand. He's tense and doesn't look or acknowledge me. Annoyance quickly replaces my initial wave of relief.

I snap my head up and shoot to my feet. "Where were you?"

He ignores me and tosses the bag onto the ground and roots through it.

I step toward him, balling my hands into fists. "You didn't follow the plan. You had me so worried."

Silence. Just his brooding, dominating presence taking over the cove.

"Fucking say something, Micah!" I scream out.

He snaps his head up so fast. "You didn't follow the plan, either. You got fucking distracted, London."

I tilt my head, pressing my lips together.

What does he mean by that?

My voice comes out as a shudder. "I did what I needed to do. You got the kit, did you not? And here we are, together again... So what is your problem?"

He's leaning over, inspecting the contents, pointedly ignoring my question. His hard eyes flit up to mine. "Maison's not into Serena. You didn't have to spend five minutes gawking at them."

I let my arms drop to the side, my stomach in my throat. "I wasn't gawking at Maison and Serena; I was distracting Nigel, and it worked."

He turns his face up at me and arches a brow, as if not believing a word I'm saying. I'm glad it's dark so he can't see my cheeks burn. "He's just upset, London. This is how he acts when he's hurt—he pretends nothing is wrong. He's been doing the exact same fucking thing since Olivia died. He postures, it's what he does."

His words are a gut punch to my stomach. It stings, and he knows it, which is why he said it. I shake my head and push out the twinge in my stomach. The guy I've spent the last two days having passionate sex with is consoling my broken heart over someone else. This couldn't get more bizarre. And Micah's acting as if it's no big deal, as if he doesn't care.

Who's posturing now?

My words come out heavy. "Maison can do what he wants to. I have no right to be upset with him."

Micah cocks a brow. "I'm not sure what you're worse at, being quiet or lying. Although you seem to be pretty good at lying to yourself."

I loosen a breath while he continues with his back turned to me. "Micah, that's not fair. Everything about this situation just hurts. And I can't turn off my feelings for Maison. Love is not a light switch; it doesn't work like that. Are you going to at least tell me where you were?"

Even in the moonlit night, I see his jaw flex and the heartbreak on his face. "I had something to do." His body is tense, like he's trying to restrain himself.

He's mad at me... No, he's furious with me.

I fold my arms and hold his stare. "Fine, can we just go back?"

"No."

"Why the hell not? We have what we came for. We need to get back to Thomas."

He jerks his chin. "Same reason as before. I don't want to deal with you getting lost in the dark woods." He throws a blanket at me. "Morning will come in about six hours, so get comfy."

A full twenty-four hours since we left. I'm exhausted, starving, and don't know if I can endure another night outside. I fold an extra sweater to use as a pillow, and I lie down on the cold, hard rock, trying to decide what's worse, the icy air above me or the stone-cold rock beneath me. I decide the latter and drape it over me, and immediately shiver. A rock.

Micah is making me sleep on a rock, in October, in Alaska.

Asshole.

A surge of anger pulses through me, and I can't help but feel like this is some sort of punishment, and I won't be getting any sort of sleep.

I turn to look up at him while he hovers over me. "My life was easier when I hated you, you know," I bite out at him before curling up, facing the faint reflection of the stars over the lake, my icy breath a stark reminder of the winter looming.

After a few minutes, he lays down beside me, and slowly, he presses himself closer and closer till his whole body is wrapped around me. He leans into my ear, sending a sharp chill down my spine. "I haven't even started making you hate me yet, sweetheart. Wait till I fucking do, and see how you feel then."

My lip trembles, and I inch away from him and lie sinfully still as every fiber of him heats my backside. I refuse to answer him; I refuse to acknowledge his presence, even as he runs his hands up my sweater and warms my skin. His hands are so big, they cover every inch of my tiny back and curves.

I refuse to respond to Micah's mood swings right now, not when I did everything he asked of me. So I give him icy silence, not even a flinch, as those fingers move toward my lower back and he massages his knuckles into it, rubbing my skin in the most delicious way. I bristle, refusing to give any sort of hint that I like what he's doing. Eventually, I ease just a little, caving into his warmth. I get lost in his soft circles before he digs his fingers into the apex of my thigh with more force than he ever has before.

I jolt, opening my eyes while my entire body lights up, and he presses his fingers in harder, sliding down to the wetness building in between my legs. He knows exactly what he's doing, and I'm not here for it.

"Stop it, Micah."

With one fluid motion, he grabs me, whipping me on top of him like a rag doll so my legs are on either side of him. His erection presses hard between my legs.

"Stop it..." he says in a mocking voice. "What? Am I not allowed to touch you anymore?"

My body ceases, my eyes narrow, but he doesn't let me go. I gasp at how forceful he's being.

"Not when you're like this," I say, trying to pull away from him. He grabs my waist harder, pressing me closer, pulling me in, biting at my bottom lip. A surge of heat pools in my stomach.

He stares into my face. Even in the dark, his eyes burn into me. Something is different, like a flip switched inside him. He's here, but not here, a shell of himself. His dilated pupils make the whites of his eyes shine in the moonlight.

I stare at him, daring him to keep going, keeping my lips pressed together. He runs his hand over my hips, keeping a firm hold on them as he reaches his other hand around and grips my ass. He pulls his legs up so I'm trapped within him and arches his hips. "What are you going to do, sweetheart?" he taunts. "Run back to Maison?"

I shake my head and bile hits my throat. "Micah, what is wrong with you? You need to stop. Is Maison the reason why you're acting like this?"

Maison must have triggered him, caused this manic behavior.

He presses two fingers over my lips. "Shh, baby, don't say his fucking name right now."

My heartbeat flickers as he grabs the back of my head and tugs me to him, pressing hard kisses into my neck and face. He's never kissed me like this—ever.

"Micah," I gasp, holding my breath and hating how much I like it—his need for me.

He trails his hand down to my waistline, slipping his fingers inside me, circling my clit, and rubbing me for a few seconds. He pulls his hand out, wiping my wetness on my cheek and sliding his fingers toward my mouth. I part my lips, letting him. "Seems like you're into it," he whispers while a tense throbbing hits between my legs.

I quit fighting it. I want Micah to want me more than the air he breathes—I want him to suffocate.

My pupils flare and I match his grinding motions. "I'm not into it, I can assure you."

Of course, my body says otherwise.

"That was incredibly hot," he murmurs into my earlobe.

It puts me over the edge. "What was?" I breathe.

He runs his hands down my side. "You, kneeing Nigel like that. Then watching you press that spear into him while he wiggled on the ground like the fucking swine he is."

Oh, that. So he was watching.

I soften slightly, letting him kiss my neck and face. He reaches his hand up my shirt, cupping each of my breast, my nipples like pebbles between his fingertips. His breath is heavy and desperate as he lifts my shirt and takes each breast into his mouth.

He shifts beneath me, pulling down his sweats and shifting his cock out.

"Take off your sweats," he demands, the heat in his voice taking over me. "Slide that pussy over me, sweetheart. You are going to ride me and show me how much you fucking want *me*."

His eyes are blazing with need as he slides down my pants. He then centers me over him and presses me down on top of him as he thrusts inside, giving me no grace. I yelp and moan, and my body tenses.

"Take it in deep, London," he growls. "You're going to fuck me so hard right now."

This isn't right. He doesn't seem like himself, let alone the indecency of us doing this again while Thomas is suffering. And he never speaks to me like this.

Something is seriously wrong with him.

But I'm dripping wet, my body responding to every single touch. Even though every ounce of me is screaming no, I can't resist him when he puts his hands on me, and he knows it. But if this is what he needs from me right now, then I will give it to him.

I arch my hips, letting myself wrap around him, taking him deeper inside me. My nipples are painfully swollen as he grabs and plays with them while I grind on top of him.

"Is this what you want right now?" I moan, rolling my hips as he squeezes my waist.

He pulls his hands off me and rests them behind his head, but he matches every movement. "Yeah, sweetheart. It's what I fucking want."

Sweetheart.

I seriously hate when he calls me sweetheart. This is the part of him I don't understand—the part that equally turns me on and scares me. A side Maison doesn't have. Maison would never demand this from me the way Micah is right now.

I pant as the edge of his cock hits deeper and deeper. If we were trying to be quiet, we are failing. I'm surprised the entire camp can't hear me right now. He watches me for a few minutes as I rock back and forth, grinding and fucking him just like he wants me to. His eyebrows narrow—so much emotion radiating out of him. I close my eyes and relax into it. It's so easy getting lost in him. His hard abs, soft skin, and muscled thighs... his lethal hands on me.

He grabs my chin, forcing my eyes open. His chestnut eyes flare. "Say my name."

"Micah," I whimper.

"Say it again, louder."

"Micah. Micah." I choke out his name.

"Good," he says. "I want it to be crystal clear who you're fucking tonight."

Jesus, Micah. So this is all about Maison.

"Yes, Micah," I moan, running my hands over the hair falling over his eyes. I trace my fingers down the ridge of his nose, cup his cheek, and tickle his stubble, feeling every inch of his face. "I know it's you, Micah. I know it's you."

He comes undone.

He grabs my hips and starts thrusting so hard, my insides might explode. I fall off him, my pussy slipping from his cock because I can't keep up with him. He swears under his breath and sits up, spins me around and slams me into the hard rock beneath him. His body falls into me with his full force.

The impact slams my head right into stone, nearly paralyzing me. It sucks the breath right out of my lungs. As I catch my breath, he enters and repositions himself by holding one leg and cradling my lower back.

"Micah, stop... you're hurting me." My voice is barely an audible noise, my vision blurs and my lungs are on fire from when he slammed me. His lips slip over mine, suffocating any chance I have of telling him no, or how much pain I'm in. My eyes roll back as my orgasm crests and his lips suck on mine till they're swollen, and he continues fucking me harder than ever, pulling my legs up higher, crushing them into my body. He gives me no reprieve, even as we edge over the rock and my back scrapes on its surface as my sweater rides up my body, his hand sliding over my neck, bracing me in place. Not enough to choke me, but enough to let me know he's in control right now.

He literally fucks me raw.

And I take him with every single thrust. I reach over and pull the sweater under my head to at least protect it from further injury, and as he pulls his lips off me, my body tenses and throbs with anticipation of more release.

"Say it," he whispers, then sucks on my neck, leaving his mark all over it. The scrapes on my back and head throb just as hard as the orgasm that edges through me.

His name rolls off my tongue. "Micah."

He pulls out of me before releasing and collapses his body on to mine, both of us gasping for air. With my eyes closed, we lay in silence for a few minutes, until he reaches his mouth to my ear.

"I love when you say my name," he whispers. "I fucking love you, Olivia." And just like that, my entire world goes black.

CHAPTER TWENTY

I picked the wrong brother.

I realized what I am to Micah last night, what he needs me for. And I can't be that for him. I can't be his dead girlfriend, or whatever the fuck Olivia was to him.

After he said those devastating words to me, I rolled off him, closed my eyes, and tried to go to sleep on the wretched, freezing hard ground. I was numb all over, my fingers, toes, my heart slipping into a cold steel. I let him hold me only because I was frozen. His body kept me warm while my teeth chattered so hard, I thought they might fall out. He didn't say anything to me after, he just pulled me into him like he owned me.

I would have given him everything, surrendered my entire self to him, fully chose him. But I don't mean anything to him at all. Maison's warning rings through my head.

"He'll never love you the way I can."

"He'll hurt you, baby."

"He's sick…"

Did I really think I was different? The girl who can change him? I'm nothing but a girl of convenience—he only wanted me because his brother had me and neither of them properly dealt with what they went through. It's his fucked-up way of getting back at Maison.

Micah rustled me awake as soon as the first ray of light peeked above the mountains. The cherry sunrise reminded me of the first morning at the lake, and I held on to that memory the whole walk back as my chest ached for Maison.

Tension is palpable as Micah and I hike back to our camp. My feet crunch on the forest floor as I keep a comfortable distance behind him, monitoring that bone weapon of his while I grip my spear. I refused to speak to him when we woke up. My lips remain tight now as he leads us through the woods back to camp, even though he keeps turning back to check on me, motioning me to hurry. I can't walk fast. Every muscle is aching from the lack of food and water, my head pounding from where he slammed me into the stone. My wounds are still open as they graze across my sweater. I'm pretty sure my entire back is scraped up.

I startle when he whips around to face me. "Why are you acting like this?" he asks me, and I'm shocked at the anger seeping out of his eyes.

I cross my arms, my mouth gaping open. *How is he possibly mad at me?*

He blocks me, refusing to let me pass him. "I don't understand you, London. Why can't you give me my fantasy when I gave you yours? You were more than happy fucking me while I was acting like *him*."

I suck in a breath.

Maison. This is all about Maison.

I shake my head and keep walking, refusing to even look at him. He's not getting anything from me anymore. He lets me pass, but his overbearing presence behind hits me like an electric current. He purposely walks close, as if reminding me it's him I'm with right now and not his brother.

I stop and face him, and he bumps into me. As his body presses into mine, the corner of his mouth twitches like he's enjoying this.

So cocky.

I cut my gaze right to his face, my eyes slightly swollen from the silent tears coming out of me all night. And he stares at me like he has no emotions at all. "This is over, Micah. Whatever this weird physical connection is between us, it stops now."

A mirror of his old self shines in his eyes. "Suit yourself, sweetheart," he scoffs and takes a step back.

I fold my arms and jerk my head to the medical kit over his arm. "I'm serious. I will stand by you right now to help Thomas, but as soon as this is over, I am going back to him."

His mouth twitches and his eyes flicker. "Yeah, you fucking think so? I guess we will see if he even takes you back. You're tainted goods to him now that you chose me over him. You're mine, baby. Whether you want me is irrelevant now."

His words slice through my skin like a razor-sharp knife. I take a few deep breaths to calm my trembling nerves and nauseousness swells through me. I never should have let it get this far with him.

I lean up to him, giving him a taste of his own medicine. His body twitches as I press into him. "You want me to act like Olivia?" I breathe, sliding my hand over his stomach. "Does that turn you on, Micah?"

The vein in his neck pulses.

He's sick—he really is sick.

"I did a good job already, asshole," I growl. "If the bruises and scrapes you gave me last night are any indication."

His eyes flicker—*life* finally comes out of them. He swallows a bob in his throat as I slide my hand down to his pant line. A smile plays at his lips.

"You hurt her, didn't you, Micah? The bruises on Olivia's body were from you, not Maison."

His silence and corresponding frown are the only admission I need. After a moment, he says, "I guess you really did you your homework before you came on this trip." He throws his arms up, waving that damn bone weapon so close to my face. "You wanted me, London? Well, here I am. This is me; I've never pretended to be anyone else, and don't fucking pretend you didn't love every single second of it. Your pussy was salivating over me last night."

I ball my fist. "Nothing of what you showed me last night was you, Micah," I scream. "I don't know who the fuck that was, but that version of you is an asshole. I *hate* that person."

I turn and stomp away from him—I can't even look at him. I hate him, and I hate how my body reacts to him, like I have no control over it.

I hear him scoff behind me. "Yeah, well, I'm the asshole who's keeping you alive, London."

Relief hits me as the camp finally comes into view, the little trickle of the stream hitting my ears. Immediately, I see Jade sitting alone by the fire, her head between her legs. My pulse quickens.

Something is wrong.

Her head whips up when she hears us approach, her eyes red and puffy.

"What happened?" Micah asks, running to her.

I immediately follow him.

Jade rises, darting her eyes between the two of us, likely sensing the massive tension between us. "He's not well. He got worse after you left yesterday. He's just convulsing and moaning, then he just went limp. I... I can't get him to wake up."

Micah and I run to his shelter and see Thomas lying lifeless on the ground, heat radiating from his body. Micah kneels down and grabs his wrist, pulling off the wrap and hands it to me. It's full of blood, sweat, and... something else.

I cringe and gag at what's beneath. His whole palm is red and swollen. It looks like the infection spread into his fingers, like a spiderweb into his wrist. But the worst part is the black and purple skin right where the cut on his palm is. The pus is seeping out of it. The smell of rotting flesh... it's putrid.

It takes everything not to pass out from the smell alone. Micah's jaw flexes as his eyes find mine. "He has sepsis."

My chest tightens. "Can you fix it?"

His face pales. "I don't know... I need to clean it and get a better look at what we are dealing with. Can you grab me some water?"

I nod and immediately grab a water bottle and head for the stream. When I get back, Jade is behind him, standing just outside by her small fire, her arms wrapped around herself. She's shaking, with tears flowing out of her eyes.

"Can you help him?" she asks between sobs.

Micah turns to face her, his eyes soft, and he steps outside the shelter, grabbing her arms. "Listen to me, Jade. The skin tissue on the cut is dead. We have to remove it, or the infection is just going to spread."

I suck in a breath as the realization of what he's saying hits me.

"What do you mean?" I ask slowly. "Like, cut off his hand?"

He nods, his lips pursed together.

Jade whips her head up. "No. No... there has to be another way. We can't... We can't do that to him."

Micah pulls her into his arms. "We have to, Jade, or he will die."

The dark edge he had when speaking to me in the woods has vanished, and she crumbles, sobbing into his chest. He holds her for a moment, letting her tears dampen his shirt, but his eyes are on me the entire time. Watching him hug her is surreal, and it tugs at my heart.

This is the side of Micah I am falling for—too bad it's not real. He gently places her in my arms and turns to Thomas, grabbing the medical kit, rooting through it, and pulling out everything he needs.

"Come on," I whisper to Jade. "Don't watch." I take her to our shelter and lie her down. She immediately curls up on the wolf blanket and sobs.

I run back to Micah, who's rooting through the medical kit. He stops and runs his hand through his hair when he notices me. He's strong and confident, but a tightness surrounds his eyes as he holds the massive hunting knife in his hand.

"Are you sure about this?"

He tilts his head and I catch a glimmer in his eye. "No, I'm not sure of anything anymore. But if I don't do something, he probably won't last the night. His organs will shut down on him."

I swallow. "There's no other way?"

He looks at me with deep sorrow in his eyes.

"What do you need me to do?"

He flexes his jaw and flicks the little bit of hair covering his eyes. He reaches into the medical kit and cleans the blade with an antiseptic wipe. "I need you to hold him down."

Jesus.

Worry coils my insides, and I close my eyes. My body shakes—the same trembling from before, only a thousand times worse, and for a completely different reason. My body and mind haven't yet recovered from my fight with Micah.

Little speckles of light shine around me. I take small breaths to contain my dizziness and when I open them, Micah is crouched beside me. I realize I'm swaying as the earthy shelter swirls in front of me, and I nearly topple over into the fire.

He places his hand on my shoulder, steadying me, running his hand down my braid. His fingers tickle my cheek. "I need you to be strong, London. Okay?"

The world goes utterly woozy as my knees tremble, and I topple over. He places his arms around me, pressing my head into his chest. His heartbeat is the only thing that brings me back. I fight a tear as it runs down my cheek as I try to be strong for both of them, but my energy reserves are running dangerously low.

Micah presses his lips against my forehead. "Do this for Thomas, London. Just a couple of minutes and it will be over. Do you trust me?"

The stress of those words.

Trust Micah... after what he did.

Calling me Olivia to hurt me. He physically hurt me, and I think he hurt Olivia, too, then lied about it, and slept with his brother's girlfriend for reasons I can't even fathom.

"Yes," I whisper.

I scoot over to Thomas, softly placing his head on my lap as Micah readies himself to amputate his hand. He pulls out some gauze and places it nearby. He crouches behind me, pulling Thomas's other hand, and urges me to the other side of Thomas's large frame.

He pushes down on Thomas's non-wounded arm. "Hold him down like this. Use all your strength and keep his arm and body contained."

His words pierce through me, and my stomach tightens. Thomas is five times my size, and it's comical to think I will have any real impact on him. My heart rate evens, and Micah doesn't let go of me until my body is completely calm and relaxed. I press my body down on Thomas and dare to look at Micah.

In this impossible situation, and despite my earlier hatred, I want to make him proud. I can do this for Thomas—for Micah.

I hold on to Thomas as hard as I can, pressing my whole body into him. The hint of silver flashes from the blade in Micah's hands. Knowing Micah's style while he hunts, I know he will be hard and fast.

Thomas is completely comatose; his limbs are limp—strong, but limp.

I close my eyes as Micah kneels in front of him. I don't need this visual haunting my dreams. Thomas's entire body convulses, and he screams out in pain—it's then I know Micah has started.

"Hold on to him, London, don't let him go."

Keeping my eyes closed, and using every ounce of my strength to hold him down, I press on his convulsing body.

Thomas screams—a gut-wrenching scream that nearly deafens me—and his body flails, his arms smacking me straight in the arm. Micah kneels on his chest, and the noise I hear next I can assume is the crunch of the bone, a grinding noise as metal meets flesh. A warm liquid splatters against my face. I just hold on and breathe.

My eyes open when Thomas's body eases, and his breathing regulates. Sweat pours down his forehead as Micah wraps Thomas's arm. He hoods his eyes and sets his jaw as he focuses on finishing his task.

I wipe my face—my fingers are blood-red.

I swallow and lean back, wiping my hands on the dirt and my sweats, then take those same hands and gently run them over Thomas's forehead.

Thomas has passed out again, completely unconscious, and I don't even know if he's alive. I want him to know we're here and doing our best to save him. My eyes flick to Micah when I hear him shuffle. He's crouched down, watching me at the entrance, his expression pained. Beyond anything I've ever seen in him.

"We have to take turns keeping watch on him," he tells me.

I nod. "Is he going to be okay?"

He looks away and shakes his head. "I don't think he'll last the fucking night." Micah jumps up and leaves the shelter, stalking off into the forest.

I'm alone with Thomas now, so I continue rubbing his head while listening to Jade's sobs. I focus on the wind and the trees and the crackling fire outside. A few minutes later, from the nearby woods, Micah's scream pierces through the air. The anguish in that cry rips me apart. I barely make it outside before I throw up what little I have in my stomach and dry heave the rest of the morning.

I don't know how long I was in with Thomas, it could have been one hour or several. My mind is woozy, so I focus on my breath. I'm not even sure when Jade's cries ceased. Eventually, I stopped hearing anything at all, as if Thomas and I were the only people left in the world.

My fingers steadily check his pulse, just to make sure his heart is still beating. The fire just outside had long burned down to ash. My fingers freeze, and only Thomas's burning body beneath my fingertips provided a warmth to my otherwise entirely numb body. I'm also immune to the stark temperature drop and freezing air around me because my numbness has nothing to do with the frozen air.

My head whips up when Jade crawls through the shelter to sit next to me and moves Thomas's head from my lap to hers. Just as I've done for the past couple of hours, she immediately checks his neck for his pulse. Her eyes are distant and dead inside, just as I assume mine must be, but she lets out a sigh of relief when that small pulsing sensation hits her fingers. A stain of blood pools on the ground next to me, smearing across their bed—a visual reminder of the heroism that happened here today, and the savagery that caused it.

I avoid it and sit cross-legged near the entrance. Moving him away from the stench requires Micah's help, and he is still missing.

Jade's puffy eyes rise to meet mine. "Is Thomas going to live?"

I swallow, keeping my focus on the blood-soaked bed next to Jade. I'm not sure what to say, Micah wouldn't even confirm it. So I force a smile. "He's okay for now, Jade. That's what we have to hold on to." My voice is raspy and raw from puking my guts out earlier, my body still shaking.

"How could they let this happen?" She looks at me, noticing the mud, blood, and sweat on my body from the past twenty-four hours with Micah.

I meet her stare. "I can't even make sense of what is going on right now, Jade." The layers of complexity even she doesn't realize the depths of. At this moment, I just want to shelter her from it. She doesn't need the burden of what's happening between Micah and me, or between Micah and his brother, or between the twins and the rest of the group. Secrets and lies will destroy us.

She sucks in a breath, her hand trembling as she caresses the forehead of a comatose Thomas. "You can go to him if you want," she tells me. "I'll be fine with him for a few minutes. Go clean yourself up."

Jesus, I must look that bad.

I give her a tight smile. "I'll be back soon. We'll clean up this mess, I promise."

Secretly, I'm eager to find Micah. He's been gone for hours, but I know he didn't go far. Not when things are this bad, and when the others are pissed we stole from them. I have no idea what I will say to him. We broke up a mere minute before he had to cut off his best friend's hand. If breaking up is even what you want to call it, I'm not even sure we were really together.

When I step outside, the mid-afternoon sun momentarily blinds me, and a northern wind seems to blow right through my clothes. I walk across the meadow to my shelter and grab some extra clothes and my pack, where I keep a small bottle of shampoo and some soap. The sun hits my face, and it's truly the first warmth I've felt in days, so I revel in it.

Once I'm at the stream, I bend down and place my hand in its shallow waters and wipe the blood from my fingers and face. I slowly peel off my clothes and dip them into the water, ringing out the blood the best I can, then I place them on the bank to dry. The smell of rotting flesh still lingers in my nose. I'm not sure I'll ever get that scent off me, and I'll certainly never forget it. I pick up my tank top and see dried bits of blood on the back side of it. That blood is all mine, so I wash it in the river, too.

I ignore the goosebumps rising from my flesh and fully submerge myself into the stream, letting the cold water completely engulf me, enjoying the stinging sensation on the scrapes on my back. It gives me a moment of utter blissful relief as the stream washes away the dirt and grime all over me. I unbraid my hair and fully immerse myself, bathing for the first time in days, and I can't scrub my skin hard enough.

My stomach still hurts, so I place my hand on my flat tummy, then move my fingers to my hipbone and ribs protruding from my skin, feeling what little meat I have left on my bones. I've probably lost at least ten pounds since I've been here. I slide my fingers down between my legs, where that aches too, and wash myself the best I can, letting my hair now fall over my chest. I lean back, letting the sun dry the top part of me. I'm not sure if Micah's watching me right now, but I hope he is. I want him to stare. To see what he can't have while simultaneously giving him a show.

Torture and tease.

Punishment and pleasure.

I honestly don't know which one.

I move like he's watching, arching my back, rubbing and washing between my legs. After ringing out my hair, I let it hang down over my chest and lie back, letting the sun dry me. I close my eyes and listen to the song of the birds nearby. The buzz of the forest and the glorious silence, but Thomas's screams still linger.

"Do you like what you see, Micah?" I whisper after a few minutes and in no particular direction.

I open my eyes and he's there, a few feet away, leaning against a tree. His hair is wet, and he's shirtless, his sweats hanging just below his cut waistline. My heart stops at the sight of him. He glistens, even with the dark aura that surrounds him.

How long was he watching me for?

He remains silent and watches me, giving me space. I rise and slip out of the water, and I move toward the clothes I placed out waiting for me.

His eyebrows furrow and he hoods his eyes as I reach to put on my shirt. He places a hand on my back and my entire body freezes. He softly rubs his fingers of over the cuts, as if just realizing he's the one who caused them.

I turn to face him, quickly sliding on my shirt, and his dark eyes flare. "They don't hurt that much," I whisper. Truthfully, I'm used to the physical punishments this island has given me—I'm immune to the pain now.

I almost welcome it.

Emotion floods his face as he bristles and balls his fist. I flinch as he turns and curses as he slams his fist into a tree. "Fuck!"

I'm on him in an instant, wrapping my arms around his toned back as he leans into me, shaking and letting me hold him. My heart breaks for him, for what he had to do. His entire body is tense. "Micah, this isn't your fault. You didn't do this to Thomas, you know that. The only reason he is still breathing right now is because of you. You saved his life."

After a few minutes, he stops trembling and leans up to stare at me, coiling my wet hair in his fingers, his pained eyes drifting down my cold nipples protruding out of my shirt.

My breath grows heavy, craving his touch, slickness already forming between my thighs from my visceral reaction to him. His fingers slide down from my face, but I grab his hand before he can go any farther. I'm still so mad at him, I could burst.

I'm met with a cold, hard stare. "I was wrong not to come back to Thomas earlier," he admits. "We should have left when you wanted to. We could have stopped it."

I shake my head, rubbing his hand with my thumb. "You couldn't have known how bad it was. You made the right call. Thomas would be dead if we got lost, hurt, or delayed. You didn't do this to him, Micah."

A moment passes, and he flexes his jaw, reaching his hands around my back before resting them on my hips. "If we had just come back, I wouldn't have hurt you the way I did."

"They are just scratches," I mutter, although the goose egg at the back of my head throbs dangerously.

He presses his lips together and leans his forehead against mine, his fingers gripping me so hard. "Do you still love him?"

My chest rises and falls with heavy breaths. I keep my head down, worried I will fall apart if I look at him.

Why is he asking me this right now?

He cups my face and pulls my head up, forcing me to look at him. "I asked you a question."

I let out a trembling breath. "Yes. At least, I think so. I don't know if I can turn something like that off. Feelings don't work like that." I pause for a moment. "I just miss him."

I refuse to lie to him, even if this isn't what he wants to hear.

His voice is raspy, unwavering. "Do you love me?"

I bite my lip and his hand still pulls at my chin. "Yes, I love you, Micah."

He dips his head, and I press my hand against his ripped chest.

Did I really just admit that?

"I can't share you," he finally whispers. "I can't share you with him the way he shared you with me."

My eyes squeeze shut. "You won't have to. I won't be with both of you like that again."

When I open my eyes again, his brows draw together. "I don't mean physically. I can't be with you if you still have feelings for him. If you're with me, you're mine. Completely."

I let out a sob. "Do you even want me? Because you've given me no indication that you do. I'm not her, Micah. I'm not Olivia, I'll never be her. If that's what this is all about, the only reason you're attracted to me, then I can't do this." I just splayed my heart on the table, and he hasn't even responded, just that stone-cold look of disdain.

He goes wholly still. His abdominal muscles ripple beneath my hand, words hanging off the tip of his tongue. Finally, his lips brush against my cheek. "I'm addicted to you, London, and not in a good way. My addictions aren't healthy, they never were. I was addicted to her, too, but I never loved her. I only said that to hurt you.

"Micah—"

"She was never that person for me, and you can't be, either. You need to go back to Maison; he's the better twin. I'll just end up destroying you. I can't be who you need me to be, the loving fucking boyfriend Maison is. It's not who I am."

A cold wind slices through me, and I shiver more from his admission than anything else. I can't be out here much longer like this. I wrap my arms around myself. He reads my physical cues as he always does and pulls me into him.

My breath hitches, the air thick between us. "You're wrong," I whisper with tears flowing down my face, but I'm not sure he hears me.

His eyes are so pained as he takes me in, completely shattered beneath him. "At first, my father thought it was me who killed her," he says suddenly.

I freeze looking at him, my heart pounding as he recalls those painful moments that destroyed him. He is finally telling me.

"The moment she died, and for days after, my dad was going to let me burn over it. And then do you know what happened?"

I shake my head as the tears burn my eyes, all his pain radiating out of him.

"He found irrefutable proof that I had nothing to do with it. All signs were pointing to Maison, especially when he found the drugs in his room, and the online transaction of when he purchased them. Only then did my father take action to get me out of jail, and he completely ruined Ezra's family to protect Maison. My dad moved mountains to make sure Maison never saw the inside of a jail cell. Maison still thinks she died in a car accident that I had caused."

He pulls away from me and glares down at me. "For once, I need someone to choose me, to make me feel like I'm fucking worthy of being on this earth. He's the better twin, London. Go back to him." He lets me go and slips into the woods, into the shadows of the trees where I worry that one day, he won't come back should his darkness finally consume him.

I fold to the ground. "I already chose," I whisper to myself in a sob, but he's already gone.

I already chose you, Micah.

I wake up to the fire sizzling and gusts of swirling wind, so cold the snow is flying sideways, directly into where I'm sleeping. My fingers and toes are numb beyond comprehension, despite wrapping myself up in as many layers as possible, including my wolf blanket. My body feels like it might break. As I regain consciousness, I instinctively feel for Micah, and my heart lurches as I realize he's not come back yet.

After Micah left me at the creek, I composed myself enough to go back and help Jade clean the mess in her shelter and watch over Thomas. I changed back into my filthy sweats and worked on helping Thomas until the long shadows of dusk hit the sky and neither of us felt any good reason to stay awake after the temperatures plummeted.

This storm came out of nowhere.

Goosebumps fill my skin as I do my best to blow at the fire that is no longer burning. Slowly, the snow is wiping out the fire and ash and any sort of flame that could keep me warm. The heavy snow pours while the glacial wind whistles in my face. I can't see two feet in front of me from the whirling snow. I give up on the fire and lay back, curling up in a ball, shaking, trembling, and praying Micah will come back soon.

Finally, snow crunches outside and Micah kneels down. His lean frame is hunched down, and by some holy miracle, he gets the fire lit again. The snow is so bright outside, I can see him clearly, as ice crystals hang off his sweater and face. I don't help him because I can't move. My body is stiff, the chill settling into every bone and nerve, even my hair is frozen.

He crawls in with me. The fire flickers off his face as he quickly changes into a fresh sweater. When he finally gets a good look at me, his face twists with worry as I sit, swaying back and forth, trying to keep myself together.

"Fuck, London. Your skin is blue. Come here."

I want to yell at him, ask him where the hell he's been while Jade and I cleaned up blood all afternoon and tended to a dying Thomas. Not to mention, I haven't eaten in days. My body is eating itself. I have no fat to keep my body temperature warm.

He crawls over to me, placing his hands on mine, feeling how cold my skin is. Even his touch hurts me, but the fire just outside is helping as the heat defrosts me. He wraps the wolf blanket around me even more and covers his body over mine, heating my face with his hands.

"Are you okay?" he whispers.

"Yeah," I shutter out through chattering teeth. His skin to skin contact instantly makes me feel better.

"Are Thomas and Jade okay?" I ask him in barely an audible whisper.

His hot breath is welcomed against my skin. "Yeah, I just checked on them. Thomas is still unconscious, but alive. Their fire is going, and I showed Jade how to keep it going during the storm. Hopefully, it passes quickly."

I spend the next few minutes shivering in Micah's arms, watching the flames as they seduce me to a near sleep. I think about Maison and hope he's okay, wondering how he's feeling and if I'll ever see him again. I close my eyes and wish only for a second that they were Maison's arms around me instead of Micah's. Admittedly, only because of how much easier Maison is to deal with, and he never would have left me alone during a storm. I wonder if Micah is thinking about his brother too, or my plan to go back to him. He must be, even through all their pain and hurt, every decision made by both of them is because of the love they have for each other. I have to bring them back together.

They are better together, and better off without me.

Micah crawls off me only when my body stops twitching. Without speaking, he retrieves a can of beans from his pack—beans he stole the night before, along with a few more he could carry in there. It won't be enough to last us through winter.

He makes the can of beans, and we share it between us, eating with our fingers. It's enough to satiate me, even though it sits like coal in my stomach, and I almost vomit it right back up.

He lies down beside me, and at least the temperatures have increased and the snow is blowing in a different direction. He won't look at me, won't speak to me. I think he utterly hates me. My teeth chatter again, so he pulls me back into him, where I instantly melt.

A beat of silence goes by. "You were so strong today," he tells me.

My eyes shoot open at his unexpected compliment and happiness bubbles up inside me. I hate how much I love his acclamations. It's quickly followed by a feeling of dread. Tomorrow will come—and tomorrow scares me. Just like every day on this island scares me. Just like Micah scares me, and how my feelings for him scare me.

"Micah?" I whisper.

"London."

"What happens now?"

His body shifts and his leg presses into me. "I don't know, but right now, it's time for you to go to sleep."

I want nothing more than to drift off into emptiness, knowing Micah is safe beside me, but I still can't feel my extremities. "I can't feel my feet," I whisper to him, not that he can do much about that.

I'm wrong.

He shifts to the other side of the bed, takes hold of my legs under the blanket, and removes my socks. I scramble up on my elbows to get a good look at him, trying to catch what look he has in his eye right now. He doesn't meet my gaze, but he rubs my toes, massaging each one until feeling comes back to them.

"You lied to me, Micah," I finally tell him, as he does all he can to avoid eye contact with me.

His eyes flicker up. "What do you mean?"

"You said you never once pretended to be anyone other than yourself, but you did. In English class, you and Maison switched personas. You were watching me the same way Maison looks at me."

He focuses on my feet, moving his strong fingers to the arches, digging in, bringing feeling back to them. "That was all me, London. That was me, looking at you for the first time. I was checking you out. It was the first time I really saw you."

Heat rushes through me as I think about him walking in, seeing me, then side-glancing and smiling. I lay down and don't speak as a roller coaster of emotions flood through me.

The duplicity of my thoughts —

Micah, Maison, Maison, Micah.

My emotions shift rapidly from bliss to terror and rage within seconds. Hunger, thirst, and feelings of lust and love that only dreams are made of.

I love him. And I hate him. I love both of them.

And Micah doesn't love me back—he made that perfectly clear.

But right now, at this moment, I'm exactly where I want to be. I'm next to the strongest guy I've ever met. Who's selfless, protects others, and is showing me how strong I am. How to protect myself at all costs, to protect myself from him. I despise him beyond measure for how he makes me feel, and I love him so fully, my bones ache. It's all I can do to not burst into tears as he continues rubbing my feet for nearly an hour.

I'm scared of losing him and scared to keep him. I'm just plain fucking scared.

He's right here, yet he's not mine.

Micah Matei is officially too much for me to handle.

CHAPTER TWENTY-ONE

Day Forty-five

I realize this morning that I lost track of time here. The tree foliage suggests mid-November. As I write this, things on this island have digressed to the point I'm not sure how we are going to come back from. I've not written since Naomi tainted my journal by reading it. I hate to admit how scared I am to write again. Writing makes it real. I'm also scared of what I will admit to myself. I'm not the same person I was when I landed here, and I'm not sure who I'm turning into. Since writing my last entry, I've fallen deeply in love, nearly killed someone, and helped cut flesh from bone. The last two days have been the hardest of my life. What frightens me the most about this island is the darkness within people. Micah is not the enemy, but he scares me the most. He's strong but fragile in so many ways, and I worry his darkness will consume him if I'm not here to bring him back. Please, for anyone who may read this, make sure the world knows that Micah is the true hero on this island, and not the cause of what happened here. Because... I think this pretty little island is going to kill me.

When I woke up this morning, I choked on the cold, crisp air that filled my lungs. We are in a freeze, but Micah doesn't think it will last. And when the snow melts down a bit, that's when we really need to hunt—although frost still clings to the trees' tips and branches. It's utterly frightening knowing such a simple element can turn my fingers blue and cause me a slow and painful death.

Micah actually lied down with me this morning, something he's not really done before. Once he checked on Jade and Thomas, he came back, threw some kindling on the fire, and cuddled with me, making sure I stayed warm. It's peaceful lying with him, just being with him, without fucking all the time—especially when we don't talk. Although I read him the first few chapters of *The Great Gatsby*, and he informed me it was boring as hell. Like he's read anything better.

He never sits still long enough to read, and I wonder if the snow is the only reason for it. It's like our bodies can't be away from each other, like a magnetic field pulling us together. I feel his need, his attraction, his intensity. The way his lips graze my skin while he sleeps. Or when he traces tiny circles on my shoulder with his finger when he thinks I'm sleeping.

I can't think of anything better than having him next to me. I want to press my lips to his and make love to him. My insides freeze at the memory of his last words during intimacy, and I stop myself.

I watch him now, broody and quiet, as Jade, Micah, and I huddle around our fire, and he guts a fish. There's a thick, heavy tension among us, like mist over a stream. I swallow a lump in my throat, wishing he would give me something, anything, to let me know he cares beyond his need to keep me alive. Jade came to sit with us earlier, the heavy bags shimmer under her eyes and she's not spoken a word. Micah left us for a bit to fish, and we warmed our hands on the fire. An hour later, he actually came back with one, which only makes me more attracted to him, if that's even possible. Micah can truly do anything.

My threat to leave him was only yesterday, and I truly don't know what I will do. It's like my heart is split in two, and I can't be with either of them fully. But I can't bring myself to leave Micah, not yet... I'm not sure ever, even if we are not right for each other. Maison needs to come to us, I've decided, and I'm determined to make it happen.

They need each other more than they need me, although I'll give them each a piece of me if they need it, too. I know in my gut this isn't over. I was about to stick a spear in Nigel's throat, and Ezra's threat to Naomi was real. Maison doesn't know the real danger he's in by being with them.

All three of us jump up, heart rates spiked and alert, when a loud moan echoes from Thomas's shelter. Micah throws the fish and launches himself through the thick snow across the meadow while Jade rises to follow.

"Let him go," I tell her. "He's the one who needs to deal with this." To explain to his best friend why he cut off his hand.

The scream that comes out of him next will haunt my nightmares for the rest of my life.

"My hand!" he cries. "You cut off *my fucking hand!*"

Jade falls into me, crying and shaking. I can't imagine waking up realizing you have a limb missing. What that would feel like....

"This is a good thing," I tell her. "Thomas is awake. It means he's healing, Jade."

She wipes her tear-stained eyes and stares out into the forest. "Thomas is alive because of Micah," she says after a few minutes. "I can't believe what you both did for him. I never did properly thank you for it, either."

I bite my lip and dart my eyes to where Micah disappeared, looking at his deep footsteps across the glistening field. "It was all Micah," I whisper. I can't take any credit—my eyes were closed the whole time.

"He really is something special, London. Hopefully, you can sort out whatever is happening between you."

I guess the tension between us is quite obvious.

My head whips as a shadow flashes in the nearby trees. My body is tight and alert, and I jump to my feet. "Did you see that?"

Jade pauses and looks around, narrowing her eyes. "I don't see anything..."

My heart pulses. I know I saw something move. I press my finger to my lips, gesturing Jade to be quiet.

We are not alone.

"Micah! Micah! Someone's here," I whisper-yell in his direction as panic takes over my body. I'm at my limit, but we won't let them take anything from us without a fight.

Micah emerges from the shelter and narrows his eyes, his body tight and ready to pounce, just as two people appear from the tree line.

James and Nathan.

I grab my spear and Micah's bone weapon, and hand it to Jade. "Get this to him, now," I whisper. "Then go hide in Thomas's shelter." She runs through the snow, tossing Micah his weapon, which he slices right out of the air. I walk slowly and meet Micah in the middle of the meadow, and we face them together. I trust James, but Nathan and Ollie betrayed Micah, so I understand his lack of trust, even though they helped me escape Nigel.

"I don't want to hurt any of you," Micah yells as the two of them stand ghostly still about twenty feet away, "but if you take one step closer, I guarantee, I will make each of you bleed." He takes one step in front of me, subtly shielding me.

They both freeze and look at one another. James steps carefully toward us, his hands up. "We're not here to fight, Micah."

Micah nudges me. "Go with Jade and make sure no one gets in that shelter."

He hasn't yet hidden the first aid kit, I realize—a mistake I can tell he's regretting. I pause for a moment before walking toward where Thomas is fighting for his life, keeping my eyes fixed on Micah.

"Then what the fuck are you here for?" Micah yells.

"We just came to talk." James steps forward, facing someone who once saved his life, now looking at him like an enemy.

"Why should we believe you?" I yell at James, who darts his pleading eyes to me.

"Because we risked a lot coming here, and there is a lot you need to know," James says without so much as flinching. Micah flexes his jaw. I believe them, that they are not here to harm us, but I'm not the one they need to convince, and I will follow Micah blindly with however he chooses to handle this.

Micah lowers his bone weapon. "Fine... come forward. But where the fuck is Ollie? I swear, if you try anything..."

James walks toward him while my heart pounds out of my chest. The only thing between the first aid kit and James is me and my spear, and while I'm quite proficient at using it, I also know James would obliterate me.

"Ollie didn't come, man." James keeps focused on Micah, and I focus on James. He looked so boyish back when I sat with him after we crashed, but he doesn't look that way anymore... He looks as if he's aged five years, very much a man, now just like Micah.

Micah glances at me, a silent plea to stay alert and keep my wits about me. He knows I have a soft spot for James, but this island is changing everyone—desperation can kill the human spirit, killing any decent parts of it. None of us are immune, and every one of us are desperate.

Micah steps to Nathan, ignoring James right beside him, and hurls him to the ground with one solid push. James does nothing to stop it. Nathan asked for it when he pressed a spear into Micah's throat. He needs his retribution.

"What the fuck, man?" Nathan cries out as Micah drives his knee into his chest.

"Thomas almost fucking died because of you," Micah spits at him.

I stand alert, my adrenaline bursting at the seams. The last thing we need is for James to get involved. As strong as Micah is, I'm not sure he can take both of them.

"I'm sorry, man," Nathan pleads. "I didn't know. I didn't do anything to Thomas. It wasn't me who cut his palm."

Micah grabs him by the collar. "Exactly. You didn't do *anything*. And do you know what I had to fucking do yesterday because you decided not to do *anything*?" He shoves Nathan down into the snow, letting go of him. "What London and I had to do?" he corrects.

Nathan shakes his head, his eyes pleading to James, who, to my relief, stands back and watches, letting this play out.

Micah cocks his head. "I'll tell you. His cut got infected, as we couldn't access the first aid kit in time. The tissue on his palm turned black, and the infection spread up his fingers and toward his wrist. London had to hold him down while I cut off his hand because of his severe fucking infection." He turns and pushes Nathan again, who had just barely gotten back on his feet. "That was the consequence of you not having the fucking balls to stick up to Ezra. And so, I ask again, why should I trust you?"

Nathan runs his hands through his hair and says nothing for a few awkward seconds.

"I'm sorry that happened," James says in a low voice.

Micah merely scoffs and dips his chin. "Yeah, well, not as sorry as Thomas is right now. He's barely hanging on to his life." He looks at James now, ignoring a trembling Nathan. "Where is my fucking brother? Is that how you found us?"

My insides explode at the mention of Maison.

Something flashes in James' eye. "That's exactly what we need to talk to you about, Micah. They are planning to attack you," James says. "They convinced Maison to give up your location. That's the only reason we know where you are right now. We came to warn you."

Micah snaps his head up and drops his weapon to the side. His body slumps forward. "When?" he snarls, and the sound of his voice is nothing but pure venom. I approach him now, slowly. Something's not right. Maison wouldn't have voluntarily given up his brother's location. He wouldn't have turned on Micah like that.

Nigel had something to do with it.

Fuck.

We really need to get Maison away from them.

"I'm not sure when," James admits. "I'm not exactly on this inside track with them. Especially since I let London leave a couple of nights ago. They just want the first aid kit back, man." I wonder if James knows the true depths of what's going on and how little this actually has to do with the first aid kit.

I walk up, standing next to Micah and placing my hand on his rigid back. He tenses and turns from me, walking over to the fire. Jade peeks her nose out to see what's going on, and I wave for her to join us. Micah sits back, swiping his finger along the tip of the bone weapon. His mind is probably envisioning using it on one of them.

I get it... I was so close is sticking my spear into Nigel's neck. The only reason I didn't was because James had stopped me. I wonder if I should have just killed Nigel when I had the chance.

Micah won't look at me, and I know exactly why. He's quiet, contemplating, musing about all things Maison.

James and Nathan sit tentatively next to us as we gather around our small fire.

"So why are you here, then?" Micah asks. "Do you want to come live with us or something? Because I'm not exactly looking for more company."

James shifts while his soft blond bangs hang over his face, his cute dimples more pronounced than ever. "No, we just want what's fairly ours. A third of the food, and a knife, and maybe a few other supplies we can negotiate later. We'll start over somewhere close, and I promise we will leave you alone. No offense, man, but your group of friends are pretty fucked up."

This causes the tips of Micah's lips to curl up, but he doesn't look up from his weapon, his eyes distant.

"And what about Ollie?" I ask, grabbing the fish we had all but abandoned and start smoking it over the fire.

James shrugs and kneels to warm his hands. "He's made his bed. He thinks he's better off with them than with us, which was his choice. Look, man, our aim is to survive and eat. We don't want violence. I have no personal issue with any of you, and I don't want to get involved in this shit you have going on."

Micah lifts his chin. "I'm afraid that's unavoidable. If you think you can go sweet talk Ezra into giving you any-thing, then have at it, but I highly doubt they are going to just give up their food."

"But they are planning to attack us," Jade says, sitting and curling her knees beside me. "What do we do about that? They are going to come for the first aid kit. They will want that more than anything. Maybe we should just go hide somewhere else. This island is big. They won't find us."

"I don't hide," Micah scoffs, "and I already ran once. I'm not doing it again. Ezra can barely hunt to save his life, and Nigel is useless at everything. Maison will be their only life source for food. The medical kit is important, but when it's subfreezing temperatures, it's not what will keep them alive."

My eyes find his. "So what do you propose we do, Micah?"

Micah looks up at the sun, positioned halfway through the sky, and the snow crystals in the air that gleam from it. "We leave now. We attack before they do. With the snow, they won't be expecting us. We get in, steal what we can, and we leave. If they try to stop me, I'll hurt them, and without a fucking bandage to patch up their wounds, I doubt they will want that."

I grab my spear and rise, a sharp ache pulsing at my chest. "And what about Maison? What if he tries to stop you?" I snip at him. "Are you going to hurt him, too? We are just high school kids, Micah. This isn't war." I stomp toward the river, whipping one more glare at him on my way.

A storm is coming, a worse storm than anything this island can give us. I push down the sensation that this may be one of the last days on this island that every one of our original survivors will remain breathing. My gut is telling me this won't end well for any of us, but what choice do we have?

Once I get to the river, I walk downstream and crouch, trying to catch my breath. I'm tired... Micah wants me to go into battle, but I am exhausted. And worse, a battle against someone I love.

His heavy presence looms behind me before he wraps his arms around my waist, pressing his fingers into my stomach. Just like the first time he ever touched me, my eyes close and tears sting against them. I didn't think I had the energy to cry anymore, but I was wrong.

"He made his choice, London," he whispers, grazing my cheek. "We need the food to survive the winter. You don't have to stay with me. Now's your chance to go back to him if that's what you want to do, no questions asked. But make no mistake, I'm getting my fair share of the food."

I whip around and jab the spear into his belly. "And what if I choose Maison? Will you hurt me, too?" I croon at him.

He shoots his eyebrows up, a smile forming on his lips as his eyes graze down to the spear digging into him. One small jab or motion from me and I'd have him.

He bites his bottom lip and keeps his eyes blazed into me, even though I'm digging the tip into his chiseled abs. I wonder how hard he will let me poke him with it before he finally admits it hurts him. "I would never fucking hurt you, London," he says eventually.

I tilt my head. "But you don't care if I stay or go?"

He has no response, just that menacing stare that makes me want to punch him, then fuck him silly.

I jerk my chin, but don't relent on my spear. "Take James with you. Why does it have to be me?"

He dips his chin, finally swatting the spear away. "Because right now, I don't trust anyone on the island except for you. It has to be you. You're the only one I want by my side," he says. "And we aren't high school kids anymore, London. High school kids don't cut each other up in the woods. We stopped being high school kids the moment that plane crashed. The sooner you realize this island is hard, and you have to do shitty things to stay alive, the better chance you won't be dead by January."

I aim the spear right at his pretty face. "You are infuriating, Micah."

He bites his lip, looking up and down the length of my body like he wants to rip me apart. "Yeah, well, so are you, sweetheart."

CHAPTER TWENTY-TWO

"Do you know the plan?" Micah asks, resting his chin on my shoulder as we crouch a few feet away from the enemy camp. I suppress an eye roll. We've only gone over it a thousand times on the brutally cold walk over here.

Quick in, quick out. Just like last time.

"Yes," I whisper and blow a breath into my palms, but worry tugs on my insides.

Cold crystals hang in the air, and despite the many layers I have on, my bones still ache from the freeze. Micah says this isn't even the beginning of how cold it will get here and that I have to get used to it, but I'm not sure I can... it's unrelenting.

Snow encrusts the entire lake as it begins its seasonal deep freeze. The forest is enveloped in white silence. It took us forever to walk here, and I can't feel anything beneath my calve muscles as my legs are completely covered in snow. The sun is about to set. No matter what happens, we will have to find our way back in the dark.

With one hand, Micah takes my hands and kisses the back of my head. I close my eyes, steadying a shaking breath. "You got this, London," he whispers, and I resist the temptation to turn around and kiss him. Instead, I lean my head against his chest and focus on his heartbeat while I try to contain my own.

It's then I see the first of the shelters to the left of us. I almost didn't notice them, completely hidden and buried in plain sight. The shelter I shared with Maison has a coil of smoke rising from the ash in the small fire pit in front of it.

"This is your last chance," Micah says, as if reading my mind. "I'll drop you off if you want to stay."

I reach my hand to grasp his leg, avoiding the knife in his other hand, and squeeze it. It's exactly what I need at this moment. "I'm not leaving you, Micah," I whisper, and I mean it.

I decided this morning, in all finality, that I'll never turn my back on Micah. But this island is just better with Maison, and while I won't leave Micah, I'm not abandoning Maison, either. I'm bringing him with us, whether Micah wants me to or not. I think Micah wants him back more than he admits. After all, he wore his gray sweater today. My heart startled earlier when I saw him leave the shelter before we left.

He dressed like Maison.

He squeezes me one more time before letting me go and creeps up closer, taking the lead. The sharp curved hunting knife sits menacingly in his right hand. Micah decided not to bring his bone weapon on this trip, opting for the big knife instead.

I'm thinking this whole plan is just insane and could end up incredibly violent. But then I remember how good those beans were... and all that other delicious canned food that is rightfully ours. We are only taking our fair share of it, and they should be grateful for that.

I stand back, my spear ready, adrenaline powering my every limb. Micah moves a few feet and crouches. His knife flashes in his hand. I'm not sure how far Micah will go if pushed. Micah's not like the rest of us—his mind works differently. I admire how strong he is, lean, agile, and comfortable in the wild.

He stops and stares at the shelter, his head whipping back to me. Something is off. His body is tight and alert.

"It's empty," he says.

I tilt my head.

Huh?

He leaps to the next shelter a few feet away and slips his head inside. He turns back to me, and a flash of fear escapes his eyes before he opens his mouth and jumps up to a crouch.

He shouts at me without hesitation, "London, you need to run!"

The next few minutes are a complete blur. My blood heats, and adrenaline completely takes over as I run blindly through the snow, keeping my grip firm on Micah's hand. Everything around me is a whirl of trees and dim shadows bouncing off the snow as the sun begins it's evening descent. He stops suddenly, and I keel over, trying to catch my breath. Running in the snow is nearly impossible, but something spooked Micah so badly that I let him drag me into the woods.

"What happened?" I gasp as my muscles threaten to buckle beneath me. That fish is all I've had today, and even then, Micah ended up sharing bits of it with James and Nathan.

Micah stops and turns to me, rubbing the back of his neck. "The camp is empty. They were expecting us."

I narrow my eyes. "Are you sure? Maybe they left for our camp already. James said they were planning to attack us?"

We left James, Nathan, and Jade back there to watch over our stuff and Thomas, while Micah hid the first aid kit somewhere. He refused to tell me where.

He turns in a complete circle, looking around at the empty threat of the forest, and the hidden lurking enemy he's so certain is there. I see nothing—the only evidence of humanity is our cold, silky breath. There is no sign our former classmates are hunting us like he seems to think they are.

He flexes his jaw. "They are here somewhere, London. Ezra's not the type to run and hide, either."

Everything is too quiet, unnervingly so. I look around and try to distinguish where we are. We only ran for five minutes, but nothing looks familiar.

If it were up to me at this moment, I'd give up, but Micah has that look in his eye. The hunt is just beginning…

"What do we do now, Micah? Let's just head back. This was a bad decision." Despite being on the brink of collapse for days, I'm still holding on.

He tugs the backpack off his shoulder. "We stick to the plan. I'll go in alone and grab what I can and come back for you. You'll be safer out here. When we get back, we can regroup on how to handle the others."

A wave of panic slams into me.

Fuck, I don't want to separate from him.

I shake my head and my eyes widen. "No, Micah. Please don't leave me here."

If anything happens to him, I'll have no way to find my way back. And if they are here somewhere, hiding, lurking like he thinks they are…

He looks down at my trembling hands as I grip my spear, but I'm sure I look anything but fierce right now. His eyes soften as he takes me in, the very real fear pouring off my face. "The plan was never to separate," I hiss. "You wanted me by your side, Micah, remember? Abandoning me in the woods was never the plan."

"Look around us; look at the snow. Do you see it? Do you feel it?"

I grind my teeth. A sinking feeling consumes me. "Yes, I see the snow," I say dryly.

"Get used to it, because it's not going anywhere. It's only going to get worse, that much I can promise you. I want you fucking alive, London, don't you understand that by now?"

I stand back and blink at him—at his intensity, the sharpness in his chestnut eyes.

How did this turn so wrong so fast? They knew we were coming; they were expecting us, and we walked right into it.

Micah's face is dark as the shadows of the tree's shift, but his presence only serves to embolden me through the resolve I see in him.

"Please just trust me, London. Wait here, I'll be back for you. Don't move from this spot. Without food, we won't make it through winter. I have to do this."

His eyes gloss over, and he spins on his heels and is gone, moving with such precision, gliding over the snow, before I can protest any further. He leaves me truly and utterly alone again. I'm getting so bloody sick of him doing that.

"Fuck, Micah," I whisper and hold myself in position because I have no other choice.

I trust him—with my life, my heart, and every bone in my body, but that doesn't take away the fact I've never been so frightened.

More than the plane crash, even.

Every whisper of wind makes me jump, and I turn slightly to keep track of my surroundings. They are here somewhere; I can feel them, watching me through the tapestry of shadows. I know because Micah says they are, and his instincts are spot on. So what do they care about most, stalking me or protecting their food and supplies?

Because Micah's coming for them.

A dark laugh spreads through the snowbank and chills my spine.

Of course, it would be Nigel watching me. That steel voice, the image of him crouching somewhere in his tattered argyle. He finally materializes from behind a tree, a dark hood covering most of his face. No argyle, but that bow tie is firmly in place, although slightly crooked.

He takes a menacing step forward and gives me a feline grin. "Tsk tsk, London. I knew Micah was stupid, but to leave you so wide open and vulnerable... This was almost too easy."

I curl my lip at him, my hand firmly placed on my spear, deeply regretting not taking him out when I had the chance. "What are you going to do, rip my clothes off again, you sick fuck?" I spit at him, noticing how he too has lost too much weight.

"You fucking wish. No, we have other plans for you," he says darkly.

Naomi emerges from where Nigel was hiding and slides up next to him. Her platinum ponytail has lost all its shine, and she looks nothing like the bikini-clad cheerleader bullying me at the beach. I almost feel bad for her, but then I remember I doubt I look much better.

I narrow my eyes at her, watching every move as she beholds me with such venom. "You look like shit, Naomi. Is Ezra not taking care of you? He's no Micah, is he?" I'm baiting her, but I can't help it. I'll never forget the feeling of the three of them holding me down and hurting me.

Her eyes harden like liquid clay, and she tilts her head. "Why are you doing this?" she asks, and I'm quite taken aback by her question. "Why are you attacking our camp?"

"They are doing exactly as Maison said they'd do," Nigel chimes in and my stomach tightens. "He told us Micah wouldn't wait to steal from us, that he'd try right away. Ezra and I didn't believe it, but here you are. The first aid kit wasn't enough? You have to take everything?"

I tighten my stance, ready to pounce if they take even one step closer to me. They won't want to risk it, and I won't hesitate this time. "Do not, for one second, pretend that you give a shit about Maison's well being, Nigel."

Confusion runs over Naomi's face as she darts her eyes between Nigel and me, not following. I glance at her, the hesitation within her. It's only for a second, but her muscles tense. She may hate me, but I know deep down, she cares about the twins, especially Micah. "You don't know, do you, Naomi?" I ask her. "Who Nigel really is?"

He hasn't said anything about knowing Maison killed Olivia; he's biding his time... smart motherfucker.

"Naomi, get her," Nigel barks out.

Naomi is lightning fast and on me in an instant, but I'm ready for her. I smash the spear right in her face and dig it into her side before she tackles me and knocks me to the ground. Blood sprays out of her pretty nose, and I lose my grip on my weapon. "You fucking bitch," she spits out. I fight to get away, but she's got the advantage. She keeps her knee pressed into the back of my neck and leans down, whispering as I eat a face full of snow, "I used to train in martial arts to help me with cheer, in case you were wondering."

She has my left arm twisted right behind my body and pain sears down my spine. But despite the pain, I can't help but chuckle at the fact I at least marred her pretty face.

Nigel steps up, wearing dark, thick-soled boots, and I keep my eyes wide open, trying to scream, but she's crushing my lungs. The spear is two inches away from my hand. If only I can grab it...

Nigel bends down to pick it up. "Is this what you want?" he taunts. "What are you planning to do with this?"

I don't answer as he inspects Naomi's blood on it. "Where is the first aid kit, London?" he asks, pretending that is what he wants, instead of the deranged revenge I know he's truly after.

I see a drop of Naomi's blood on the snow beside me, and I know I must have gotten her good. I can't help the small smile that forms on my lips. "Funny girl," he sneers and takes that menacing foot and slowly presses it over my hand, causing me to wince, especially since my shoulder is already at such an awkward angle.

He presses in further, and an audible snap shoots up my arm. My scream slices through the forest as every single bone in my hand shatters.

"Where is it, London?" Naomi asks with clenched teeth. "We're not asking again."

I can't respond because the pain in my hand is excruciating. I close my eyes and wait for it, for Nigel to finish me. He grabs the spear and digs it into my side. He presses right into the bit of open skin on my side, piercing my skin and twisting it.

"I don't know," I sob. "Micah hid it."

"We should go get Ezra and let him know we have her," Naomi says, as if sensing Nigel's sinister intentions to kill me right here and now. "I can stay with her."

Nigel takes a step back, and for a second, I'm eternally grateful for Naomi. I wonder if either of them knows what happened to Thomas or if they even care, or how much of a monster Nigel really is. I'm Naomi's enemy, the one who stole Micah from her. That's the narrative she has in her head—the poison they are feeding Maison.

Nigel shifts but doesn't make it far before Micah is in front of him, seemingly coming out of nowhere, and all my tension releases.

The look on Micah's face is nothing short of terrifying as he pushes Nigel relentlessly until he falls over, tripping into the snow. Micah uses a voice I've never heard before, one that makes my insides squirm with delight and fear all wrapped into one.

"Get. The. Fuck. Away. From. Her."

"What the hell, Maison?" Nigel looks up from where he lies on the ground. "Don't act surprised. You knew we were going to question her."

My eyes widen as recognition courses through me at which twin I'm actually looking at. It's not Micah, it's Maison.

CHAPTER TWENTY-THREE

Maison pushes Nigel back even further into the woods and away from me. "If you touch London again, I will break your fingers," he growls at him.

Nigel recovers and lifts the spear he stole from me and points it directly at Maison. His lips twist into an utterly cruel smile, even though his face pales. "Back off, Maison. Don't get distracted by her. She's only here to get food. She already chose Micah over you. Remember who's had your back the last few days. They are attacking us, just like you said they would."

Maison pauses and looks at me, his eyebrows pulled together as if I represent everything that pains him in this life.

Olivia.

I remind him of Olivia.

It breaks my heart how Nigel is using his pain against him.

"He's Olivia's brother," I shriek, and even Naomi eases her relentless grip on me as I finally call out his revenge plot.

It's time to lay it all on the table and end this.

Maison runs his hands through his hair and stares at him, then at me, confusion etched on his face. "What are you talking about?"

"That's why he was doing the story on you," I blurt out. "It wasn't about the newspaper. He wanted to bring you down for killing his sister. That's what this is all really about."

Maison flexes his jaw, like Micah does when he's about to go off on someone. They are identical when they are mad—and I had no clue. I don't think I've ever seen Maison this lit up.

Fresh emotions are displayed in his eyes, as if seeing Nigel for the first time. In a single moment, it clicks for him, as it did for me. I see the resemblance, clear as day from when I saw the picture of Olivia. Same eye color, same hair, complexion, jaw line—everything.

It all makes sense.

"Get the fuck out of here, Nigel." Maison's deep voice makes Nigel stumble back.

Maison, I've decided, is much scarier when pissed off than even Micah is. Much, much scarier... especially as the shadows flicker off his face under his gray hood.

Nigel recovers and puffs out his chest but doesn't make any motions to use the weapon in his hand. He's not that stupid. "I'm getting Ezra. He will side with me on this one, since you destroyed his life, too."

Nigel flees into the forest in a blink, and Maison turns his attention to Naomi, who's examining us carefully, although her knee is still pressed into me.

His eyes flash. "Get out of here, Naomi."

She releases my arm, and I blow out a breath. All the tension in my body disappears, but I still can't bear to lift my head from the snow. "She's lying, Maison," she says. "If Nigel were related to Olivia, we would have known. London's desperate right now because she got caught. She'll say anything to you right now to side with her."

I give him a pleading, teary look, which he seems to be immune to, as he works through what this all means. I've said the truth, and Maison now has to come to terms with it.

He stomps toward Naomi; he doesn't put his hands on her, but his body language causes Naomi to flinch, barely recovering enough not to fall over. "Hurting London was never part of the plan," he spits at her. "So get out of here."

Her lips form into a snarl. "Fine, but I'm finding Ezra with Nigel. He needs to know she's here. I'm not giving up our food, Maison. Not for you, not even for Micah. It's ours."

She heaves herself through the snow and out into the woods, leaving me a crumpled mess on the ground. My chest rises and falls with a heavy breath. Every nerve in my body heats when he walks over and stands over me. My hand and hip throbs as I turn in the snow to look up at him.

His face immediately softens as I stare at him, wide-eyed, with blood rushing to my cheeks. He leans down and pulls me up and I fall into him. A shooting pain hits my side and I suck in a breath. My hand is shattered.

He rubs his hands down both arms, touching me as if he doesn't believe I'm really here.

I revel in his touch, his heady scent.

"Are you okay, baby?" he asks. "I missed you so much."

Baby...

I don't think. I just wrap my arms around him, breathing in his deliciousness as tears flow out of my eyes. I let out a shaky breath. "Maison, I—"

I can't formulate a thought. The throbbing in my bones and crushed veins are crippling. I'm with Maison... Maison, and despite the pain, it's only relief I feel. I missed him so much, it hurts. It hurts more than anything Naomi or Nigel could do to me.

His lips find my forehead, but the kiss is short-lived. He pulls away, his eyes drawing down to my hand. "You're hurt." It's not a question.

"It's my hand, and I think Naomi got my side, too, but it's not too bad."

I'm noticing Nigel prefers severing a certain appendage on the human body, twisted as he is. I suppose it's as good of a way as any to cripple someone.

He pulls up my shirt. "You're bleeding, London. We have to get you out of here. Can you walk?"

I swallow and nod. Although I don't think I should move, a twinge hits my hip every time I move.

Then he leans down and kisses me, and I absorb him—his scent, his tongue, his hands, all of him. Our lips grind together, and it reminds me why I fell in love with him to begin with. I close my eyes, thinking how different he feels from Micah. His softness, and warmth, and stubbornness.

Especially his stubbornness.

My mind quickly drifts to Micah, and my heart lurches. He's still out there, and I have no idea if he is okay. I shift toward the direction Naomi disappeared to, the same break in the trees Micah ran through mere minutes earlier, and the directions he gave me to stay in this spot no matter what.

I pull off Maison and whisper, "I... I can't leave."

He wraps his arm around me and leans his head toward my ear. "We have to move, baby. I don't want Nigel coming back for you right now. I need to hide you."

"Micah's coming back here, Maison. We have to wait for him."

He swallows a bob in his throat, his body visibly tensing. "Micah's not coming for you, London. I'm all you have right now."

My heart stills, and I can't bear to look at him. "What do you mean?" I ask him meekly.

"Ezra set a trap for him. If he went anywhere near our food, he's not getting away. He can't try to steal from the group and get away with it. What did he think would happen?"

I smack his chest and my lips quiver. I know my measly punch did little to hurt him, but he winces anyway. "Ezra doesn't know how to trap... You set it, didn't you?"

A silent, painful pause. "Ezra has him, London. We're not going to hurt him; we just want to talk. We will wait till he's level-headed. He's dangerous when he's like this. You can't reason with him."

I now know what Maison means about Micah. The scratches on my back attest to his imperfections, yet... Micah's not as dangerous as the boy in my arms.

He's never killed anyone.

I lean up and get a good look at him. "Maison, he's not your enemy. He's not the person you believe he is. He didn't intend to cause you harm. In fact, he gave up everything to keep you safe."

Maison's dark eyes flare as he takes in my words. "There are things you don't know about him, baby. When I told you he's sick, I really meant it. He gets paranoid and violent. He used to take meds for it, but stopped right before Olivia died. He's smart, but he's sick. Look what he's making you do. He's making you attack people, London. This isn't you, baby. He's changing you... just like he changed her."

I shake my head, a tightness forming in my gut. "No. You're so wrong about him. He's not making me do anything."

He presses his lips together. "London, he has PTSD, which causes his episodes. I know he hurt Olivia before she died, then he crashed the car to cover it up. I just hope he didn't hurt you. Tell me he didn't fuck with you. That's all he does with girls. He's incapable of feeling anything. He did it with Olivia and Naomi; you watched him do it with Naomi."

I'm a terrible liar. Micah's mind games are nothing short of agonizing, but still, he's wrong—Micah feels something for me. He hasn't said as much, but I know it.

"Thomas lost his hand." The words pour out of me like a leaky faucet.

He flinches and moves a piece of loose hair out of my eyes. "What?"

"That's why we came back the other night, to get the first aid kit to save his life. We were too late, though. His palm turned all black; Micah had to cut off his entire hand to save him, and I helped him. We. Cut. Off. His. Hand, Maison."

He takes a deep breath. "Fuck. London, I didn't know."

"Micah's not paranoid about anything. Every decision he makes is about helping people. He's doing what he thinks is the right thing. He crashed the car because Olivia died in his arms, and he didn't know why she died, or what caused it, and he didn't know what to do. He was scared… but he didn't kill her. You did, when you gave her those drugs. She overdosed, Maison, that was her cause of death."

His eyes become clouded—thinking, remembering everything he did back on that night. That dark look returns, and I know what it means now.

I softly run my hand over his cheek. "You know what I'm talking about Maison… you know what you did. That's how she died. That's what the coroner's report said, and the only reason your father did what he did to Ezra's family. He sacrificed everything for you; your brother was about to go to prison for life. He saved your life, and Thomas's, too."

His lip quivers, his body hunches over, and a few painful seconds go by. I keep my shaking hand on him. "I loved her, London…" His voice breaks. "I didn't want her to die. I didn't do it to kill her."

I hitch a breath. "I know you loved her, Maison. I can see it; I can feel it."

I feel her, like she's been with us the whole time. He's never gotten over her, never dealt with her death.

"It was an accident," he says, shaking his head, the admission finally escaping him, all that pent-up tension from what he must have known the whole time. "I thought she just needed to relax. She broke up with me because of him… She left before the drugs kicked in, and I could stop her."

She left and drank a stupid amount of alcohol, not realizing she was already messed up. I lean on him, partly because my knees wobble, but also so he knows I'm here for him at this moment.

"Fuck!" he cries out. "Why did he hide this from me? Why didn't he think I could handle it?"

I tighten my hold on him. "Because he loves you, Maison, but that love has a cost that was in the millions, and it cost Micah a piece of himself. You would have gone to jail for the rest of your life; they would have made an example of you."

"Well, I fucking deserve it, don't I?" He shakes his head.

No... no. It was manslaughter. He didn't intend to kill her.

"Is that what really happened to Ezra's family?" he asks. "I thought Ezra's dad was just shitty at investing."

I can't help but laugh at that, even though it's inappropriate.

We stand silent, my arms still wrapped around him, while the sun sets to it's fullest. The dark shadows tease the surrounding trees, the air now deathly cold. "Come back with us, Maison. We need you," I breathe, and I can once again see my breath coil through the air.

He pulls me into him as frosty winds cut through the trees. We need to move—we won't last much longer with the sun now fully set, even if the stars twinkle brightly in the sky.

"Does Ezra know this?" he asks. "How do you know that about Nigel? Olivia never mentioned him... not even once."

I lean my head toward him. "Nigel admitted it to me a couple of nights ago. They are half siblings. He mentioned her to Jade once, and that's how she made the connection. I'm going to assume Ezra knows, too. Nigel and Ezra hate you and Micah, and they have a valid reason to. It's not safe with them out here, especially when hunger drives their vengeance and every decision they make."

He presses his forehead to mine. "I'm sorry, baby. I didn't mean for you to get caught up in this. I hated Micah when you left. I thought he was stealing you, and he was losing his mind. I lost my mind, too."

I hood my eyes. "I only followed him because he was alone. He had no one, and he wasn't wrong to defend Thomas when no one else did."

Even I don't believe the lies spewing out of me.

He lets out a sigh. "Were you with him again? Do you love him?"

I suck in a breath. "Maison, that's not what this is about."

He reaches his fingers to my face, wiping the single tear that escaped down my cheek before it can freeze on my skin. He leans down and presses his lips against mine.

I gasp as his tongue tickles my lips, and heat warms my heart. His fingers softly caressing my lower back. I open my lips and let him in, getting lost in his savoury taste, his soft skin, and the memory of when it was just me and him. The nights I spent cuddling with him, kissing him, making love to him—Maison.

Before everything got screwed up and I fell in love with his brother. A wave of guilt envelops me.

Micah—he's still out there somewhere, and he needs us.

Maison senses my tension and pulls back from the kiss, his eyes softening. "I know you're confused, baby," he whispers, pressing his lips to my forehead. "But I still love you. I need you to know that."

My heart melts and I let out a sob, letting out all my emotions I've been bottling up over the past two days I spent with Micah. They spill out of me—every single one.

Love and hate, fear and danger, even a false sense of hope.

Two days. That's how long I've spent away from Maison. The time it took to realize which brother I'm in love with. And as much as it pains me, and as much as I love Maison, adore him, actually... Micah truly has my heart.

I have to find Micah.

My body suddenly goes limp, my knees buckle, and my hip throbs. Maison lifts me into his arms, and I flinch as the skin at my hip splits open. "Come on, baby," he says, carefully stepping through the thick snow, "let's grab Micah and get you somewhere safe."

I allow Maison to carry me, and in this moment as I lean into his safety, I'm completely sure that although I am deeply in love with Micah, Maison is my closest friend, and no one can ever replace him in my heart.

Maison walks up to the camp, his footfalls barely a whisper on the snow. Micah apparently taught him the art of silence as well, the skill of the quiet hunter as we approach Nigel, Ezra, and Ollie as they surround Micah.

My whimpers are the only noises heard as we make our way through the forest. Even though he carries me as softly as he can, the split in my side is a raw, open wound.

"Okay, baby, time to be quiet now." I have to hold my breath to accomplish that.

A fire roars in front of us—the biggest I've seen since being here—and it lights up the whole site.

They don't notice him because they are sloppy and pathetic. They look wild, resembling zombies in the wilderness. Naomi and Serena sit a few feet away, stress etched on their faces. Naomi's hands grip her sides as she hunches over with a bloody face. Serena sits beside her with her head in her hands as well. Naomi's not well, I realize.

Ezra's really desperate for that first aid kit, because I sliced up his girlfriend. Serena barely looks like she's faring any better.

Should have stayed with James, sweetheart.

I can't help but internally croon at her, although I feel bad for her. She really hasn't done anything to me personally, even if her friends are assholes.

My mouth goes dry as I take in the sight of Micah, hunched over and rigid, with his gray hood over his head and his arms tied behind his back. They don't notice us, but he does. His eyes flick, unyielding as he takes in the sight of me in Maison's arms in the shadow of the trees. He makes no motion, movement, or any sign the two of us are nearby. The other three's senses are not nearly as keen as Micah's, and they don't even notice he's staring right at me.

It makes me almost laugh to think mere hunting wire would stop Micah from getting free. He's biding his time for something. Ezra holds his knife in his hand and the sight of that makes my blood freeze.

Maison places me down beneath a tree well, a small deep spot with no snow. "Stay here, baby. Please," he whispers. "I need to handle this."

My primal instinct is to attack them—to protect the guys I love—but I hold back as the scene unfolds. I curl up, holding my shattered hand, keeping myself hidden, but watching. My eyes are fixed on Micah, whose head is slumped forward and motionless.

Maison makes his presence known, purposely snapping a twig with his foot. He looks otherworldly as smoke circles around him, glimmering off the snow. All six of them stare at him as the fire pops, spooking the girls.

Nigel straightens his bow tie and does not look surprised to see him. "Where is she?" he asks casually.

"Safe."

I bite my lip, nerves shaking, and my stomach clenches at the weapons in everyone's hands. Everyone, except for Maison. But his muscles ripple beneath his tight, fitted sweats and gray hoodie—identical to what Micah's wearing. If I hadn't known in my truest heart it was Maison's arms I was just in, by his rigidity alone, I'd think it was Micah. He stands tall and proud and incredibly handsome.

Nigel waves a dismissive hand. "Are you going to come out, London, so we can end this? The food you want is not here, so you can call off your dog."

"Fuck," I curse under my breath, and Maison presses his lips together in a silent hint he doesn't wish for me to come out. Of course, they weren't going to make this easy on us.

Ezra doesn't take his eyes off Micah, the knife right at Micah's throat. "Yeah, come on, London." He follows Nigel's lead like the sheep he is. "Come out and save your boyfriend." Ezra's straggly hair now falls nearly to his chin. The athlete I saw in the lunchroom is unrecognizable now. He chuckles. "Although, you seem confused who your boyfriend is these days."

"Shut the fuck up, Ezra." Maison takes a step forward and Ezra stiffens. "This has nothing to do with her. Your issue is with me. I caused everything you're mad at him about. Let Micah go." The three of them double down, pressing their weapons into Micah. Ollie looks miserable, but following along with them because, right now, he has no other choice. And he picked his side when he didn't go with James. Micah's head is down and he's still unaffected by the blades sticking into him.

He says nothing.

Nigel snickers. "I don't think so. He's the only one who knows where you hid the first aid kit. That's all we want, that's all this is about, Maison. We just want to stay alive."

The lies and deceit... Sure, he's hungry, but he'd like to see these twins die and use this island as an excuse for committing murder. If we ever get saved, no one would suspect Nigel if they died of starvation.

Ezra turns to look at Maison, but only for a moment. He's not stupid enough to turn his back on Micah for longer than a second. Sweat pours off his forehead from the stress of it. "Your bitch girlfriend hurt Naomi; she stabbed her. That's not okay... So this is what you're going to do. You're going to go back to wherever your douche bag brother hid it, and you're going to get it for us. And if you don't do it, I'm going to have fun slicing Micah up. And it might have been you who killed that silly girlfriend of yours, but it was Micah who put his fucking elbow in my throat. I don't fucking trust him."

Vengeance, hunger, and pride... the worst combination.

Ezra twists the blade dangerously close to Micah's throat one inch, and he's close to slicing his esophagus, causing me to lurch out of my hiding spot.

This is not Micah's day of retribution.

"Stop it," I scream, pulling on any threads of strength I have left as I lift myself out of the tree well. My scream is so loud, it bounces off the snow and echoes back to us three times.

Everyone turns to stare at me, and Micah jumps up, twisting the spear out of Ollie's hand as if he were a toddler. He pushes him down to the ground, while Ezra and everyone else is distracted by my sudden presence. I never noticed when Maison jumped to his brother's side, but during the few seconds of confusion, he stands next to his brother. Both have defaulted to their natural athletic stances.

Ready to pounce.

The brothers exchange a look, pain equally etched in their beautiful chestnut eyes. Anger seeps out of them both, sliding over every tense nerve. Both look god-like... and about to take back their control.

"Back the fuck off, Ezra," one of them says with a dangerous edge in his voice, and I realize I have no idea who said it. Ezra stands in an equally dangerous position with a much, much sharper spear than the wooden ones in the twins' hands. It must be Micah, since he grabbed the spear out of Ollie's hand.

"For fuck's sake," Nigel sneers. He moves with a swiftness and strength I didn't think possible from him, and he grabs the wrist of my shattered hand. I keel over from the pain as it shoots into my shoulder blade, slicing every vein and blood cell within me. He then sticks a knife right into my cut where they sliced me earlier, keeping a grip on me. His vile breath teases my nostrils as he pulls me in close. "Everything is so violent with you people," Nigel says casually, as if he wasn't the cause of it all. "Can't we just have a discussion? It's really too bad Thomas couldn't join us today for this little reunion, although I hear he's not *hand*ling things very well right now." My body is broken now, utterly broken. A bone juts out of my hand. Nigel grips onto me, knowing I'm his best leverage.

Micah doesn't move from his tense position. Micah and Maison both jerk their head to me, their motions similar, their expressions identical, but it's the retracting fingers of Maison that gives me pause.

That's a Micah tell...

They've turned the twin thing on, I realize, and I'm suddenly not so sure Micah's the one holding the spear anymore. Micah hasn't spoken, just gives a lethal look without blinking. I wonder if Nigel or Ezra realize what they're doing, if that is indeed what they're doing.

"Go get the kit, Micah," Nigel says again. "If you do, I will spare you some food and give you your girlfriend back."

"He's lying," I shout. "He won't give you anything."

Ezra lunges forward with the knife, and neither twin even so much as flinches. "Let's play a game to see if that changes your mind," Ezra says darkly, and spits right into Micah's face. "Which boyfriend do you like better, London?"

Dead—truly, Ezra has a death wish. Nigel's hold on me is the only reason he's still breathing.

Ezra chuckles as both twins remain still, careful as my life hangs in the balance.

"Come on, London, just choose. Which brother do you love more?"

I press my lips together, refusing to engage. I focus on the intensity of both twins as they watch me. One of them subtly shakes his head. Micah... I think, I hope. Because if it is him, he's finally communicating with me.

Ezra waves the knife like he's holding a wand and orchestrating a play.

"Go to hell, Ezra," I spit out, trying to distract him, trying to do anything to give the twins an edge.

He chuckles. "I guess you don't want to play. That's okay. I guess since you came back with Maison, we all know your choice."

He jerks his head to Micah. "See? You're fucking worthless, Micah. Even your girlfriend doesn't want you."

Micah's jaw flexes, but he remains silent, though I can see all the thoughts swirling in his head right now. I wouldn't want to be on the receiving end of whatever he's thinking.

"What, nothing to say?" Ezra steps closer to Micah, lifting the knife. "Not so tough right now, are you? Daddy's not here to save you. No one cares about how rich you are. On this island, you are nothing. Both of you are *nothing*." Ezra stomps his foot at him, making even me jump back. "Fucking say *something!*" he screams in Micah's face.

Micah stands there and takes it, saying and doing nothing.

"I should just fucking kill you, Micah." Ezra's tone shifts, walking back to Naomi and placing his arm around her. "No one would even care that you're gone. The world wouldn't miss you."

This can't be happening.

Micah's voice cuts through the air. "I'm not giving you shit, Ezra. Kill all of us if you need to, but I'll die before I give anything to you."

I shake my head. "Just give it to them, Micah. It's not worth it. It's not worth fighting over."

My heart pounds in my throat as Micah takes a step to the side. He's circling, like a lion would circle its prey.

Testing him, teasing him, drawing him out.

"No. No fucking way," Micah says. "It's the only leverage we have." He casts his eyes to Naomi's gash, where I cut her. "She needs the first aid kit. She will bleed out if she doesn't get it."

Ezra laughs. "Oh, you'd love it if I killed someone, wouldn't you, Micah? Then at least you wouldn't be the only murderer on this island."

My eyes shoot up and I cringe. The look on Micah's face is deadly.

Maison takes a step forward. "That's enough, Ezra. This isn't funny. Thomas already lost a hand from when you cut him. How far are we going to let this go?"

Ezra's eyes flash, and he hesitates for a moment.

He didn't know...

He only grips the knife harder. "I'll go as far as I want to. I'm in charge of this fucking island. I have the knife, the food; I have the power. I am God here, Maison. Micah's reign of terror is over."

Jesus.

I let out a small laugh at the absurdity of it. He's not God, he's a psychopath. A hungry and pathetic one at that.

His eyes narrow. "What are you laughing at, London? You're the stupidest bitch on the island. You have no idea what kind of guys you spread your legs for. You think you matter to them? Because you don't. Olivia bounced between them like a fucking ping-pong ball. You're not special, London. They don't care about you, you're merely one of many." He waves his hand the between twins. "This is what they do. The game they play with girls. They fuck them, then they fight over them. I've watched them do it for years."

I bite my lip and my eyes dart to Micah. His head is down, his jaw set tight. He's planning something, plotting how to end this.

Ezra's just trying to fuck with me. Turn me against them.

"That's enough, Ezra," Maison grits out. "Put the knife down and tell Nigel to let London go."

He lets out a little laugh. "Oh, I don't think so. This is way too much fun."

Micah's eyes shoot up as Ezra draws his attention back to me.

"You have no idea, do you?" he asks me. "What they really did to that girlfriend of theirs? They both belong in prison."

My insides burst.

Nigel grips me and blurts out, "And Micah gets to keep going on with his life as if it never happened, while my sister is rotting in the ground. Daddy just made it all go away. Well, she was a person, with a family and a future. She didn't deserve to die."

I bite my lip, my eyes trying to meet Maison's. He won't look up; he won't give me anything.

"He didn't mean to kill her," I whisper. "Everything was an accident, Nigel."

Nigel lets out a snort. "Then own it. Put the time in for what you did to her, Maison. But it's much easier to keep your scholarships if you don't have murder on your record, isn't it?"

Ezra's body tenses and he screams, "You took *everything* from me. All my life, the two of you were the stars of the team, and everyone looked at me like I was nothing. But none of that mattered, because I knew one day, I would get away from you, go off to another college, and leave our fucking town for good."

"Then go fucking do that," Maison yells. "What's stopping you?"

Ezra's eyes grow wild. "I can't. Your dad bankrupted us. *We. Have. Nothing.* I had no idea why your dad did that to mine, but now it makes sense. Covering up a murder is expensive."

Nigel leans forward, pressing the knife to my neck. "This isn't getting us anywhere, and I'm getting bored and tired. Get the first aid kit, Micah, or I will kill London. Is that black and white enough for you?"

I let out a whimper because that's all I can manage, the cold steel pressing into my neck, and Nigel's thumb curling into the slice on my side.

"Fine," Micah says as his dangerous energy swirls around him, like a lightning strike waiting for thunder. "I'll go."

Nigel lessens his hold on me. "Finally, you see the light."

"Now let her go," Maison says, his eyes on my hand and the blood pooling beneath my sweater, dripping on the snow below me. "She's hurt, Nigel, she needs help."

Nigel knows... he's the one who hurt me, then claimed he wasn't violent.

Nigel clicks his tongue. "Well, you better be quick about it, then. Both of you can go, but don't come back until you have it."

Micah steps forward but Ezra's there, waving his knife, stopping him from getting close to me. "If you hurt her, I will fucking kill you," he says to both of them. He turns to walk into the dark, menacing forest.

"Hey, Micah," Nigel yells, releasing his grip on me.

It all happens so fast.

I crumple to the ground as he takes a step forward, grabbing the hunting knife from Ezra's hands. He lunges forward and slices Micah right in his side. And Micah goes down, hard, into the layered snow.

"That," he spits as he stands over him, "is for killing my sister."

For a second, everything goes black. I can't see, hear, or feel anything after watching Nigel stab Micah. Then the cry of agony was loud, piercing the air, reverberating through the trees. The birds we didn't think were there anymore flock and crow from trees that surround us, leaving a plume of snowflakes in their wake.

My eyes snap back into focus, immediately seeing Micah bleeding out on the ground in front of me. I lie cold and alone as Maison and Ezra struggle now that the knife is no longer in Ezra's hand.

I cry out, although I don't think my voice makes the airwaves. My breath chokes my lungs as I try to scream.

Nigel stands like a stone-cold killer—standing over Micah's body, doing nothing to help him. Zero remorse for what he just did. Ezra is frozen, dumbfounded, as if this was all just a joke to him, and no one would actually die today.

Maison tackles Nigel, causing Nigel to drop the knife, then pushes himself to his feet and scuttles off into the forest. Nothing else matters to me right now but Micah. So I crawl over to him, a bloody mess myself.

Maison is no longer in view. I breathe a sigh of relief to know Maison's okay. The knife missed him, but that's because it wasn't intended for him. But Micah is on the ground, blood seeping out of his side—the cut so deep and ugly, it's five times the size of my wound. The surrounding snow is like a ruby-red painting. Blood—so much of it surging out of him like a river.

My world implodes.

"Micah," I finally cry, crawling over to him. His eyes are almost black and he's lying on the ground, his body convulsing.

The reality of the situation smacks me in the face.

It's Maison I'm looking at, not Micah...

I verify it by pressing my hand on his back and feeling his scar, and the sob that escapes me is partial relief and part utter devastation. Relief it's not Micah, and pure guilt for even feeling that way. He took the fall for Micah. He took on his persona, knowing it may be a sacrifice. I grab his hand, oblivious to everyone around me. Oblivious to where the knife is now, or even if I'm still in danger, or where Micah is right now.

I don't care at this moment.

Maison's beautiful eyes find mine, and I let out a sob as I drape my body over his and he stares into my soul. He's seems... at peace, looking at me, almost as if he planned this. I can't swallow the sobs trying to come out of me. "It's okay. You're going to be okay."

He can't die—he can't.

Wiping the stinging tears from my eyes, I look up as Ezra and Micah fight, and Micah's able to push Ezra to the ground. He presses the spear into Ezra's throat.

Micah looks at Ollie, who's stunned by the whole thing.

Micah's eyes flash at him. "Choose a fucking side," he roars at the younger kid. "Right fucking now."

Ollie hesitates for only a minute before he lunges to grab Ezra's arms to help contain him.

Naomi stands. "Maison, stop... don't hurt him," she begs. "It was Nigel who hurt Micah. Ezra's your best friend; don't do this."

His eyes flicker up to Naomi, who still hasn't clued in that it's not Maison, and he cocks his head to her. I hear other voices, and Jade, James, and Nathan come into view.

"What the fuck happened?" James asks, running over to us, seeing Maison lying in a deep pool of his own blood.

Serena rushes over to James, who places his arm around her. "Nigel did it," she whimpers. "He killed Micah."

I stare at the three newcomers, wide-eyed, taking in the pure evil that happened here tonight. James darts his eyes between the real Micah and Ezra, trying to assess what to do.

"It was an accident," Ezra shouts to everyone, his eyes wild and panicked. "I wasn't going to hurt Micah. It was all Nigel. Nigel made me hurt Thomas... You all just saw what he's capable—" His voice cracks. "You all saw it."

I ignore his desperate attempts at feigning innocence and turn my attention back to Maison. I press my hands on his wound.

Blood... so much of it pouring out of him. I can't stop it.

"It's okay. It's okay," I repeat over and over, desperately trying to convince myself that it will be. Jade comes into view and places her hand on my arm. My head turns to see if I can find Micah. It's like he just disappeared. My eyes find hers. My voice is desperate, pleading with whoever will listen. "Go get the first aid kit. Go please, go quick. He's dying."

She nods, wiping tears from her eyes, but she doesn't move. Nobody moves. Why aren't they moving? Why aren't they helping him? And where the hell is Micah?

"Please, somebody… Do something!" I scream, then my voice fades. "He's dying, please… He's *dying*."

A throb hits my side, causing me to place my fingers on my sore hip. Blood spills on my fingertips, and I know this blood is all mine that's slowly seeping out of me from my fight with Naomi. My focus now is only on Maison. Grabbing his hand, letting him know he's not alone.

"It's okay, baby. You have Micah. You won't be alone." His voice is calm, relaxed, and he doesn't move his eyes from mine.

I sob on his chest. Even as he's dying, he still wraps a protective arm around me.

"No. No. No. This isn't happening."

I can't imagine life on this island without Maison.

"I can't lose you," I whisper. "Just stay with me, okay? We'll make it better. Micah will make it better."

Where the fuck is Micah?

A small whimper brings me out of my trance. I whip my head up as Micah holds the massive hunting knife out in front of him a few feet away. His head is down, his hair shadows his face. He grips the knife with shaking hands. I don't recognize the look on his face as he raises his brows.

The whimper, I realize, came from Ezra.

Ezra's eyes grow wide with panic as Micah raises the knife. "Hold him down," he says to James, Nathan, and Ollie. James jerks his head to his two friends, and the three of them spring on Ezra, pushing him to the ground right in front of Micah's feet.

"What are you going to do, Maison?" James asks, leaving Ezra's fate in Micah's hands. They still don't realize it's Micah. How do they not see it yet?

Ezra pisses himself, a dark pool of urine emerging between his legs. Micah stands over him as Ezra hunches over and shakes. Still, no one has clued into what's going on, and who is really holding the knife. I wonder if they'd be so accommodating knowing it was Micah who wields the sword of power.

I'm not saying anything.

Ezra's desperate eyes plead. "Man, bro—it was an accident. It was the only way I could think to gain the upper hand with you. I wasn't going to hurt Micah, I swear. It's me, Maison... I'm your best friend."

Micah stops shaking, his voice calm and clear. "Shut the fuck up, Ezra. Or I will slice out your fucking vocal cords."

This renders Ezra speechless.

Jade rushes to my side and takes over my hands, trying to stop Maison's bleeding. I have to stop Micah—he can't do this. I rise and step toward him. His eyes flit to me for one brief second before turning back to Ezra, who is nothing but a pathetic heap on the ground—a far cry from the confident guy in front of us only moments before.

Everyone is here now, witnessing this, yet no one moves to stop it.

I step forward carefully. "Micah," I whisper, "don't do this. It's not worth it. He's not worth it."

Micah turns to Maison. Tears well up in his eyes—so much emotion behind those dark eyes, behind his steel face and the armor he always has up.

"Please, Micah, you're not this person. You're not a killer."

His eyes tighten and muscles flex as he finally looks at me. His voice is rough and shaky. "He deserves to die."

I swallow. "He does, but we are not the judge and jury. We cannot be the person he is. You're better than that, you are better than him."

He shakes his head and runs his free hand through his hair. "I'm not, though. I am everything he says I am."

I let out a sob as the tears stream out of me. "Then do it for me," I beg. "Please, don't kill him. I need you. Please. I need you. Stay with me, don't lose control, Micah." I stumble toward him, placing my hand on his, wrapping my fingers around his hand with the knife.

He stiffens at my touch, but his eyes draw down to my shattered, bruised hand and the blood seeping out of me. "Micah, please."

He closes his eyes, his lips quivering. He keeps the knife gripped firmly in his control. I let out a sigh of relief.

"Hold him down," Micah spits out. James, Nathan, and Ollie jump to grab Ezra before he can run off.

With Ezra contained and everyone else too stunned to move, Micah steps toward Maison. I move out of the way to give them some space.

He grabs his brother's hand and squeezes it. Maison can barely talk now; he can barely breathe. But somehow, even as he's dying, he manages a small smile. Before he closes his eyes, he says, "Take care of her, brother."

No, no, no.

I run to him and grab his hand. He squeezes it to let me know he's still with me—for now. Micah crouches beside me for a moment, watching his brother as Maison gets dangerously close to taking his last breath.

Micah stands and faces the silent crowd before his eyes focus back on Ezra. "Hold out his hand," Micah demands.

Jesus.

Nathan and James wrestle with a panicked Ezra on the ground.

Ezra's eyes grow wide as he tries to wrestle out of their grip. He convulses in fear and slumps, as if resigning to what's to come. I stand back, completely stunned, watching this all unfold. A sharp ache hits my chest, knowing there is nothing I can do to stop what is about to happen. The pain from my own injuries fade from what's unfolding in front of me.

Micah walks toward Ezra, gripping his knife in one hand. With one slice and zero hesitation, Micah chops off four of Ezra's fingers, leaving only his thumb of his right hand.

Ezra belts out a sickening scream—that damn scream when someone loses a limb. The same scream I told myself

I never wanted to hear again. The same swell of nausea hits me.

More blood... so much of it spilled today.

Everyone is ghostly silent as Micah lifts his hand, gripping Ezra's hair, pulling his face up to meet him. "If I ever see you again, I will fucking kill you." He throws him onto the ground and kicks Ezra in the ribs.

Ezra rolls to the side, his body going completely limp—his cut off fingers resting a mere inch from his face.

Micah takes one last look at Maison, his eyes glisten. "It's over," he grits out, then he disappears into the dark forest. I don't blame him for not wanting to watch his twin die.

His scream pains every ounce of my soul.

I don't follow him.

I can't leave Maison like this, to die alone. Plus, I don't have the strength to move. No one's noticed the amount of blood I am losing, and I don't say anything. Part of me wants to die right here with Maison, to close my eyes and have this all be over. I wrap my body over top of him. I feel his breath and I squeeze him.

Jade's hand rests on my arm.

"Give me a minute with him," I whisper to her. "Please."

I feel her get up and shuffle away. Maison is unconscious now. He's lost too much blood to survive this, and we all know it. My wound pulses as I rise and fall with Maison's last breaths until finally, his chest stops moving and his life seeps out of him.

A piece me dies too before I pass out right on top of him.

CHAPTER TWENTY-FOUR

I can't remember being lifted off the ground, or how long I was there, lying over top of Maison. I woke up briefly to strong arms wrapped around me, carrying me back to our camp, with Micah's heartbeat in my ear. The last sound I heard before passing out entirely.

I peel my eyes open and even the bit of light in the shelter is blinding. My fingers trace down the pulse in my side to find a bandage over my wound. I'm back in our shelter, the warm wolf blanket draped over me. Someone bandaged my wrist, too.

I twist my head and realize I'm alone. Micah is not here. The sun shining through the roof of the shelter indicates mid-day.

How long was I out?

I must have lost a lot of blood because I can barely move. Every muscle is weak, and my bones are brittle from the lack of fat on my body. My lips are dry, and the cut pulses in my hip. I take a deep breath and choke back a breath as everything comes rushing back to me and I look at my tightly wrapped, mangled hand.

Maison is dead—gone. The whole incident comes rushing back like a strong wind. I lay my head down, wishing I can fall back asleep. I'm not yet ready to face the world.

It doesn't take me long before I pass out again.

This time my sleeps not dreamless—I replay the entire time on this island in my head, starting with the plane crash and ending in Maison's death.

When I wake up again, the fire is crackling beside me; it looks like someone just placed a piece of wood on it. A water bottle is by my head. I have no idea how long I was out for again, but it must have been a while as twilight is settling in.

My new bed is comfortable—someone took great care to make it. I never had nearly this many blankets before. It's so soft, my body feels like it's floating on clouds.

I find enough strength to grab the water and drink most of it down. I force myself up and take careful steps to meet whoever is outside. I can barely walk, so I stumble forward instead before steadying myself.

The number of people around the fire pit in the meadow makes me blink. A new pit... one that wasn't there before.

Six of them. Jade, Thomas, James, Nathan, Ollie, and Serena all huddle around the flames. A soft mist hangs above the stream, although the frigid temperatures have only increased slightly. Canned food is added to the existing stockpile.

I don't dare to think of where Nigel, Naomi, and Ezra are, but I hope they are suffering.

Thomas is upright and mobile, and my heart sings at the sight of it, quickly replaced by guttural rage, like I truly believe Maison took his place in death. The enormity of my vicious thoughts surprise me, and acid fills my throat.

I've lost Maison... and Micah, too. I can't see how Micah and I can move forward after this. Nothing will ever be the same between us... not that it was ever really normal to begin with. The pain we're both feeling right now is too much. I'll be a living reminder of his loss for the rest of his life.

Rage guts my insides, watching them hang out by the fire like they belong here. They are not supposed to be here. This is Micah's home.

Where is Micah?

And why am I asking the same damn question to my-self, over and over? I scan the crowd and see Jade sitting with Thomas. Her head tilts up as she notices me, and she immediately rushes over.

"Take it easy. You lost a lot of blood," she says as she wraps her arms around me, helping my feeble attempts to walk. I lean into her to ease the tension on my legs. She helps me back into the shelter because my body is too weak to move. Those few steps took all my strength.

"Come on, let's get you back to bed. I'll bring you some food."

I blow out a deep breath as I lay my head down. "How long was I out for?"

"Two days."

Two days?

"Where's Micah?"

She presses her lips together, but I don't miss the twitch in her eye. "He went out to hunt."

I narrow my eyes and fall back into the bed's comfort. "Alone?"

She nods carefully, as if seeing the darkness now residing in my soul as I do my best to suppress it. All I can think about is killing Nigel, stabbing him with that knife and ending his pathetic, feeble life. The regret I feel for not letting Micah end Ezra's life.

If I had killed Nigel when I had the chance, Maison would still be alive.

"Yes, he went alone today. He says he hunts better that way. He's trying to prepare for winter. Now that it's freez-ing temperatures, we can stockpile and save food. He'll be back, though."

He's avoiding me.

She pauses at the entrance and looks in on me. "He'll want to know you're awake. He told me to find him if you woke up. I'll send Nathan or Ollie out to let him know."

I swallow a razer-sharp pit in my throat. "How is he doing?"

She moves in to grab my healthy hand and squeezes. She seems strong, her hair bouncier, and her dimples accentu-ated on her slender, pretty face. Probably because Thomas looks like he will make a full recovery from his ordeal. "I don't know," she admits. "He doesn't say much to anyone. He's either over here, watching over you, or in the woods. He's worried about you, London."

I shake my head and look around; his absence is noticeable. "Clearly, he's super worried about me," I say dryly.

She sits beside me and her eyes soften. "London, in my whole life, I don't think I've ever seen anyone love someone the way he loves you. The way he looks at you. You have no idea, but I do. I've seen it from the beginning. He carried you the whole way back, refusing help from anyone. And since we've been here, the only person he lets near you is me. He barely left your side for the two days while you were out, but he had to go hunt. He has to keep you alive, and we need more food."

I want to believe her. With my whole heart, I wish what she was saying was true. I just don't think Micah is capable of love—of loving me. How do you love someone when you don't even like yourself? I'm hating myself more and more. I think I understand him better now, especially why he's incapable of the emotion.

I shake my head. "Leave him be, don't call for him. He needs this time." He knew I was going to wake up, and he left before I did. He can't face me.

She sits on the end of the bed, a worry line forming on her forehead. "I'm sorry, London. About Maison, about everything... It's all so wrong."

I let out a sob. My emotions are raw and real, and they bubble close to the surface. Hearing her say it out loud validates that it wasn't just a horrible nightmare. I lost my best friend, and I will miss him with every ounce of my heart, forever.

She places her hand over mine, and her eyes gloss over. "We buried him, London. I can show you where."

I breathe through a wave of nausea that storms my insides as the others' voices travel over the meadow. "Why is everyone even here? Why are they not back at the other camp?"

She sucks in a deep breath. "Everyone came with us right when it happened. We all know what Nigel and Ezra did.

James and the others want nothing to do with it. They are going to set up a new camp for themselves close to us."

I close my eyes as pure exhaustion consumes me. "And what about Naomi and Ezra?" I can't bring myself to say Nigel's name out loud. "Do they get a fair share of supplies? What happened to them?"

Last I saw, Ezra lost four fingers. If he's not dead, then that means they wasted critical supplies on him. I also noted Serena's presence next to James, clinging to him now that Maison's dead.

Jade senses the tightness in my body, my leading questions, my pure animalistic rage.

"Did you help them?" I finally muster up the courage to ask. I hardly recognize the voice that comes out of me. "Did you help Ezra? Is Micah okay with this?"

She runs her hand through her hair, suddenly seeming very uncomfortable, and looking at me as if I'm not a cripple, but someone capable of hurting her. "No one wanted this to happen, London," she says. "But the rest of us aren't here to condemn and kill people. We'll leave that for the authorities when we are rescued. We cleaned Ezra up and gave them their fair share of supplies on this island. It's a call we made as a group. Micah didn't have a say in it."

"Maison is *dead*," I remind her in a putrid, hateful voice. "And we aren't *getting* rescued. You gave them food that we need, and it could have kept us alive for one more week out here."

A bob slides down her throat. "We did what we thought was best. Micah doesn't think they'll survive winter, but none of us need their deaths on our conscious."

I lay my head back down. "So just Maison's, then. Don't worry about it. They will get what's coming to them."

I will make sure of it... even if I do it alone.

"Micah is our leader," she continues. "Everyone agrees, but we didn't trust him to make the right call on this one."

I'm not surprised they still defer to him. He never stopped being in charge. No one else realized it, but he was always in control.

"He told us we only have one rule to follow."

I smile despite myself. "Oh yeah? And what is that?"

"That we all have to stay alive." She squeezes my hand. "Get some rest. You'll feel better tomorrow. And I know you'll feel better when Micah gets back. Everything is always better when Micah is around."

The thought of Micah makes my stomach twist. But the grief I'm feeling must be a thousand times worse for him. How could he ever look at me the same?

What if everything between us is broken? What if I don't love him anymore?

My love for Maison is strong, real, and it will never go away. I close my eyes, rocking my body back and forth. Jade was right; everything is always better when Micah is around.

So where is he, then?

A couple of days go by, and Micah doesn't come to see me, but I know he's around. He comes at night and drops off dead animals. He must know I'm awake. I get he's not ready to face anyone, but I wish he would at least check on me. Talk to me. A big part of me needs to grieve with him, and all he ever seems to do is hide from me.

My strength gradually returns over the two days since I woke up. Due to exhaustion, I spend most of the day in bed, reading and avoiding everyone else. I think I've read *The Great Gatsby* six times since I've been on this island. I then go to bed, only to stay up all night crying, and the vicious cycle starts over again.

Grief is overpowering, and even food doesn't bring joy. I barely eat, and what I do eat I usually end up throwing back up, anyway. I finally mustered up enough courage to visit the shallow grave they buried Maison in. He's downstream, away from camp. Sometimes I talk to him as if he's right beside me. It's my favorite place—it's our place, and I'm glad he's close.

I let out an icy breath and stoke the fire before bed. The nights are freezing now, sub-temperatures right through the night. I've completely lost track of what day it is, but I would guess we are now in mid-November.

And still, Micah has not come to see me, as if he's living elsewhere.

I wrap myself up in a blanket and curl up. Nightmares will haunt my broken sleep as they have every night since Maison died.

I'm not sure how long I'm out, but a twig cracks and it jolts me awake. It's dark—middle of the night, dark, but the moon casts a glow through the roof of the shelter. Micah's hunched down just outside, staring at me through what's left of the embers glowing in the fire. I bite my lip as my heart races.

He looks wild. His eyes glazed over, his hair long and dishevelled. He looks sexy—as sexy as I've ever seen him—and I know in this instant that my feelings for him are unchanged. I search for every emotion swelling through me over the last couple of days.

Anger for pushing us to have that confrontation to begin with, intense sadness for him, and heartbreak. Love... bone-crushing love.

And a need for the primitive destruction for those who have wronged me.

It would be easier to hate him, to block him out, but I can't. My heart is so desperate for him. I want him now more than ever. I blink at him as he takes in the sight of me. He stokes the fire, then turns back to me.

"Hi," I say through the crackling flames and flickering firelight.

He narrows his eyes and crawls over to me, his hands immediately tracing down to my wound. He shifts his body, so his head is near my waist. I part my legs to give him better access.

He pulls at the drawstring of my pants and slips my sweats down. His fingers are careful—soft, like he's touching glass. After unwrapping the injury, he applies lotion and bandages it back up.

"It's healing. I'm feeling better," I tell him.

His eyes flick up to mine, but he keeps his lips pressed together. I reach down and move the hair out of his eyes as he just stares at me, his eyes blazing.

A moment passes, then another.

"I hate them, Micah," I finally say. "I want them to die. I should have let you kill Ezra." Saying the words out loud feels right; it's my truth in this moment.

The emotion is all-consuming.

"Say something, Micah." My voice is pleading.

He closes his eyes and lays his forehead on my bandage. He parts his lips and presses a kiss on my belly, making my entire body shiver. I crave more of it, more of his touch. I missed it.

"I know, London..." His voice is deep and soft. "I hate them, too."

He moves his lips down to my pubic bone, then places gentle kisses between each of my thighs, causing my body to tremble beneath him. His kisses are soft, softer than what I'm used to with him. After each one, I feel myself become more alive, like his lips alone can reinvigorate my dead soul.

I let out a heavy breath and arch my back, enjoying every moment, hoping he doesn't stop. Wetness pools between my thighs as I reach down and tug on his hair, pulling my fingers through it.

"Micah, you can't leave me again," I whisper.

He looks at me beneath his dark lashes, then moves his body up so it's flush with mine. His lips find mine and I'm desperate for his mouth, so I lean in and deepen the kiss.

I slip my tongue inside his lip, dragging my teeth along them. I moan as his hand slides down my body, and I arch my chest into him. He moves his kisses from my lips to my neck and pulls off my shirt. My hair is now long, long enough to cover my breasts, and I even manage a little smile.

He looks at each of them, then back up at my face. "You're so fucking beautiful, London, and strong and brave," he whispers, leaning in and nibbling on my ear. "I want you more than anything right now. You're so perfect."

"Micah, I…"

He presses his fingers to my lips. "I promise I'll never leave you again. Never again. I'm done with games; I'm done hurting you. I'll be everything you need me to be."

I close my eyes, wishing that were true. Hoping he's doing this not out of pity or a sense of duty, but because he wants me and loves me. His hand slides down my stomach and my body lights up as he slips his finger between my legs.

I tense slightly, causing him to stop and pull away.

"Micah," I breathe out his name as my chest rises and falls. I relax and grab his hand, placing it back down between my legs. He needs this, and so do I. I want him all over me, inside me. Maison would want this for us. I know he would.

But I can't let him have me, not yet. I need to say something.

"Micah, I love you. I chose you. I was going to choose you. Even if you don't feel the same way, I want you to know it was always you. But I'm not Olivia; I can never be what she was to you."

Whatever that was.

He pulls his finger out and starts kissing me between my legs. My clit throbs under his tongue. I arch my back as he moves his kisses up my stomach.

I love how he's taking his time, like it's the first time he's ever looked at me.

His eyes find mine. "If you knew how much I fucking love you, London, it would scare the living shit out of you. It would tear you to shreds. I know I don't deserve you, but you're mine now. No one else matters but you."

My chest tightens at his words. Because I love him, too. And I'll love him forever if he'd let me—even if forever is short-lived.

I close my eyes as an overwhelming sense of fear takes over. "I don't want to die out here, Micah. We're all going to die, aren't we? Maison was just the first."

Wrapping his arm around me, he pulls me in closer. My head nestles in the crux of his arms and his body heat instantly warms me.

He pauses, and when he finally speaks, his voice breaks. "You're not going to die because I'm not going to let you. Promise me right now, you won't fucking die."

I swallow, but don't answer him. How can I promise him that? He's already lost so much, but I can't give him that reassurance.

Truth be told, I'm scared shitless.

My voice breaks. "I'm sorry you lost him, Micah. For a moment I thought it was you, and I wanted to die, too."

I've now experienced what it is like losing both of them, and I'll gladly end someone else's life, never to have to feel that loss again.

He doesn't respond, but I don't expect him to. He draws circles over my stomach with his fingers, then he runs his hands up my face and down my arm, over my bandaged wrist.

We lay in silence for a few moments as I cling to him, then I say, "They will come for us, won't they? This isn't over." My body trembles at the thought.

He stiffens. "Probably. If Ezra survives the winter, he will come for me. He won't rest for long, not after what I did to him. Nigel already tried to kill me once."

I grab his hair and move it away from his eyes and grind my teeth together. "The others helped them, and now they expect us to be okay with it."

He strokes his knuckles against my cheek. "I know... Once you're stronger, I'm taking you away from here. The rest of the group will have to fend for themselves. I'm taking our food and we're leaving. I found somewhere else for us to go."

I shoot my head up. "What? Where?"

"It's a hunting shack. I found it a couple of days ago. It looks abandoned, but it's intact, and I set it up for us."

So that's where he's been hiding.

"What about the others?"

"They will be fine. I've taught them everything I can. And this way, I can just focus on you and making sure you live to see the spring. It will be you and me against the world, London."

Just me and Micah against the world.

Me and Micah.

I press my lips to his cheek and lay my head down on his muscled arm. "Okay. But what if they come for us?"

I know in my heart, it's not a matter of if, but when.

His eyes grow dark, and he slips his hand on my chin as a frosty wind shutters through the shelter. The hate in Micah's eyes matches my own and brings heat to my core. "Then we will kill them, baby," he murmurs in my ear, nibbling the edge. "And next time, we'll do it together."

To be continued....

About the Author

Rhea Ryan is a spicy writer of romance on the edge of dark and twisty. Her stories are a masterful exploration of the human heart, skillfully navigating the complex and often grey terrain of our inner lives. After writing in the corporate world for over a decade, she realized she had a desire and compulsion to write creatively. She lives in Western Canada with her husband, two young children and a fur baby.

Pretty Little Island is her debut novel.

Follow her on Social Media

Instagram: https://www.instagram.com/rhearyanwrites/
Website: www.rhearyan.com
Goodreads: www.goodreads.com/rhearyan
Facebook Group: Rhea's Dark Hearts | Facebook
Newsletter: bit.ly/Rheasnewsletter
Email: rhearyanwrites@gmail.com

OTHER WORKS BY RHEA RYAN

The Bone Love Duet

Twice Love Burned (A Prequel Story)

Twice Love Burned

This isn't a regular love story, and it doesn't have a happy ending.

My bond with my twin was impenetrable, until a blonde femme fatale walked into the party, capturing our attention and burying her way into our hearts.

As Olivia took control of our lives, the three of us forged an unconventional relationship that fooled everyone—including ourselves.

But it wasn't meant to last.

One moment, one mistake, one bad decision, and my world shattered to pieces.

Olivia was never meant to be mine, and she never was, even though I was the last person to see her alive.

Sea Queen Reborn

A Dark Fairy Tale Retelling

Sea Queen Reborn
To discover the truth of my sister's demise, I must infiltrate the legendary Pearl Castle. The home of ancient magic and ruthless Atlantean Kings. Fueled by a thirst for revenge, my path is paved with bloodshed.

As I get swept away by the castle's irresistible charms, treachery threatens to expose my true identity and I undergo a transformation that will shape my destiny. Now faced with imminent danger, will love and power be enough to save me from destruction?

A Message to My Readers

What really happened between Maison, Micah, and Olivia? Find out through the eyes of Micah.

Twice Love Burned is a bonus prequel novella as part of The Bone Love Duet. Although the events of Twice Love Burned happen before Pretty Little Island, this story is meant to be read after.

I promise you I am furiously writing the sequel to Pretty Little Island, so you can enjoy the conclusion of this story. Estimated publication date for the sequel is Fall 2024 and you can preorder now.

Enjoy!

ACKNOWLEDGEMENTS

I had no inkling of the adventure that lay ahead when I began this book in November 2022. I thought of this baffling plot line while in my kitchen having pizza and wine while on a "break" from a completely different manuscript, and I thought to myself, I'm going to write this story. Pretty Little Island was born.

This book wouldn't be what it is without the army of people that helped me. So where do I start?

Deepest thanks and all my love to my husband and children for giving me the space to follow my dream. Dealing with my early morning wake ups, my wandering mind as I get lost in the details of my story, and the stress of what it takes to put a quality book on the market. You are the true backbone of this book.

I can't describe the impact my beta readers had on my writing and on my confidence in doing this. To my sister Sarah, mom, and friend Jen for your unwavering support and friendship. Growing up, my sister and I shared an obsession with high school shows, especially those featuring "that guy" (inside reference). Abigail Hunter, I have no words for how much you helped me from the very beginning. You were my first author friend and I am so grateful to have met you. Melissa Smith, your cheerleading means the world to me, and I love how much you love my characters. Roxy Leigh, for helping to bring this book to life through your beautiful design. Shelbie, I am so glad you asked to read it early! And finally, to all my friends in the baby romance author group (you know who you are), you inspire me every day.

Special thanks to my editors, Editing for Humans, and Sylvia's Reading Corner, for your wonderful and professional guidance to make my manuscript shine.

To my readers, ultimately, I wrote this for you. Thank you for taking a chance on my story.

www.ingramcontent.com/pod-product-compliance
Lightning Source LLC
Chambersburg PA
CBHW021232190726
48289CB00005B/1291